SILVER
ROAD

ALSO BY JAMES MAXWELL

THE SHIFTING TIDES

Golden Age

EVERMEN SAGA

Enchantress
The Hidden Relic
The Path of the Storm
The Lore of the Evermen
Seven Words of Power

SILVER ROAD

THE SHIFTING TIDES BOOK II

JAMES MAXWELL

47NORTH

Text copyright © 2016 by James Maxwell

Published by 47North, Seattle

www.apub.com

ISBN-13: 9781503938236
ISBN-10: 1503938239

Cover illustration by Alan Lynch
Cover design by Ryan Young

Printed in the United States of America

For my wife, Alicia, with all my love

1

Palemon crossed the frozen wasteland, every step taking him farther from the city of the dead. He took long strides, boots crunching into the packed snow, not hurrying but walking with purpose, aware that he had distance to cover and there was always the chance a sudden blizzard could take him by surprise. The frigid air made his eyes water and stung his cheeks, but these were sensations he'd experienced his entire life and he was used to them.

In another man this monthly habit would have been called a ritual, even a pilgrimage, but Palemon's people knew him as a practical ruler, never superstitious. He believed in the things he could see with his own eyes, not the future that some said they could read in the stars or the entrails of birds.

But as he walked, squinting ahead to where the pale sun glared above the white horizon, frowning and tugging on the braids of his gray beard, he still felt unsettled. Palemon was the thirteenth successive king to carry his name. He longed to unshackle himself from the ill-omened number. Despite the fact that the lost nation of Aleuthea was slowly, inexorably dying, he was determined to show his people that his reign would not be the last. Like his ancestor, the first King Palemon, he would save them from their plight.

As he focused on a tiny dark speck that grew larger with every step, he was reminded by the expanse of emptiness around him that both he and the object of his interest didn't belong in this place. They belonged in the world of men, rather than a domain where the true ruler was nature. Palemon and his people were destined for greater achievements than mere survival. This land was not home.

He wondered what his forebears would have made of their descendants' present state. Though this was the only life Palemon and his people had ever known, they had information on the old Aleutheans in abundance; the magi could describe their way of life in detail. They'd clothed themselves in togas and tunics, thin clothing worn mainly for modesty and to ward off the worst of the sun's rays. They had grown crops and herded animals. There had been time to develop culture, metal weapons, and the might to enthrall an empire.

Today, Palemon wore the finest clothing his people and their nusu slaves could make: a thick black cloak with a hem of soft fur, a leather vest the shade of smoke, black woolen trousers fashioned from the fur of the musk ox, and high boots. His head was crowned only by his hair, which was long, thick, and streaked with gray. He looked like a barbarian, and compared to the ancient Aleutheans, he was.

But on his back he carried a broadsword, long enough that the hilt stood higher than his right shoulder. It was a symbol of his kingship as much as any crown. One day, if the gods smiled on him, Palemon could restore his people's greatness.

Setting his jaw, he fixed his gaze ahead. The ancient relic he now approached contrasted with the monotonous white of the terrain. It was made of weathered timber, black as coal. Though it appeared completely abandoned, half buried in the ice, unloved and ignored, it was valuable beyond belief.

It was a ship.

Palemon's vision never left it as he drew closer. It was larger than the house he lived in, and he was the king. A long bowsprit jutted from the front where the sweeping lines of the rails met. The black vessel's sides at the bow were high, rising even higher at the stern, where a mighty wooden castle comprised the ship's topmost deck. Three masts stood proudly erect, with the central mainmast dwarfing the other two in size. Diagonal crossbeams were at odd angles to the vertical masts.

The weather had erased the footprints from Palemon's last visit. It had also long eroded any evidence of the other ships that once rested here. The most recent left this place a hundred years ago and never returned. This ship, of a type called a galleon, was the last of its kind.

Approaching the vessel until he stood just a few feet from the hull, Palemon now commenced his monthly routine. He circled the ship slowly, one hand on the smooth, hard timber. Though the hull was preserved by the dryness of the air and the severity of the cold, he checked every plank for signs of wear, reaching high and crouching low. Circling the front and passing under the bowsprit, he didn't move on until he was completely satisfied that each section of wood was whole and undamaged. He passed to the galleon's other side, taking his time, meticulous in his attention. Rounding the stern, he was just able to reach up to wipe the accumulation of frost from the letters of the ship's name, untarnished due to the fact that each letter was solid gold. The vessel's name was now clear, written proudly across the stern: *Solaris*.

After completing a full circle, he stood back and appraised the galleon once more. The solid timber keel was buried in the ice, otherwise the *Solaris* would have been leaning to the side. Though the magi said that this was best for the ship, Palemon insisted that once a year they dig deep and examine what they couldn't see. Despite the lack of sails and men scurrying on the decks, it looked like it was poised, ready to sail on a sea of ice. He nodded, satisfied with the state of the vessel's hull. It was time to complete his inspection.

Palemon wasn't a young man but he was in the peak of physical condition. There were only two castes in the society of exiles that had evolved over the last three hundred years: warriors and magi. The magi he left to their own devices, but he demanded that his warriors be as hard as stone, hunters beyond compare, as proficient with bow and harpoon as it was possible for men to be, and as their warrior king he led by example. Constant fighting with the kona, a tribe of nomads, much more warlike than the docile nusu, kept his men's weapons sharp and their skills even sharper. His were a hard people, and he wouldn't have it any other way.

His muscles bunched as he took hold of the rope ladder and began to climb. He was pleased to note that he wasn't even breathing heavily when he reached the rail and pulled himself over.

Soon he was pacing the main deck, eyes roving over the vessel from one end to the other.

Every surface was bare of ropes and sailcloth; it was all stored in the hold, away from the elements. He strode to the bow and examined the vessel's timbers, scanning and crouching, touching and scraping, making his way slowly back toward the rear. Just behind the mainmast he opened the central hatch and descended to view the interior.

Skipping the crew's quarters, less crucial to the vessel's ability to sail, he made his way to the hold, which at sea would be below the waterline. He checked over every rib of the galleon's entire length, crouched low in the cramped conditions, muttering to himself and occasionally tugging on his beard. Finally his frown relaxed and he climbed back to the main deck until he was once again in the open air.

He glanced up at the sky but the weather was still fine, with not a cloud in sight. He didn't have to worry about darkness, for the sun would never set in this place, not in summer. His work nearly complete, nothing requiring attention, he would soon head back to the settlement. There was just one last part of his ritual remaining. If there was one element of his routine that was more ceremonial than practical, this was it.

Walking to the rear of the *Solaris* and climbing a set of steps, Palemon headed to a wooden door set into the wall of the castle at the stern. As always, the door made a faint creak when he turned the handle and pulled. Leaving it open, he waited for his eyes to adjust and then he was looking into the personal quarters of the man he had been named after. He entered a paneled room filled with unadorned wooden furniture, all fixed to the floor. The bed, clothing chest, recliner, chair, and desk had all once been utilized by King Palemon the First.

He closed his eyes and drew in a deep breath through his nose, exhaling slowly. Though it was far too cold for him to smell anything, he imagined the scent of salt and wood. He pretended to hear the creaking of the ship as it leaned against the wind and to feel the rocking from side to side that the stories said was ever present at sea. Opening his eyes, he then walked to the desk, where a book of vellum stood open, the large pages ready to be read. He took a seat at the desk and then looked down. The vellum was perfectly preserved, but the book's spine had broken long ago. He had to be extremely careful when he turned each page, or it would snap.

When he finished, he wouldn't return to this place for another month. Even though he knew every word, he leaned over the book and began to read.

Before I leave the *Solaris* high on the ice, I have decided to write this last entry. Now that it's clear we are truly lost, that to combat

5

this frozen wasteland we are going to have to build shelters and develop relations with the local tribes, it is plain to me that we will settle here for a time at least. At some point, perhaps when summer comes, we will send out scout ships to navigate a path to the open ocean. But the *Solaris* will stay here until the end, until all of us are truly heading home.

When that day comes, I hope that I shall be the one to command, but the gods often have their own plans. And so I write this for posterity, that it should never be forgotten.

For my final entry, I will tell the full tale of the fall of Aleuthea. Cast your mind back and remember, or imagine, if so much time has passed that the memories are gone.

Under my rule, the Aleuthean civilization brought almost every chieftain in every barbaric land into our dominion. From our island homeland first the region surrounding the Aleuthean Sea, then the Maltherean Sea, and finally the Ilean Sea came into the fold. We levied our armies from across the known world. We fought with the eldren and won.

After the defeat of my great enemy, King Marrix, peace finally came to the Realm of the Three Seas, but not without a price. The eldren homeland changed. Sindara became a place of swamp and ash. Wildren roamed, cursed to wander restlessly throughout the place they once called home.

Even so, there were no more bitter wars, and I was content. I thought our supremacy would remain unchallenged until the sun set on the last day of existence.

But I was wrong. I was arrogant, and I was complacent.

Marrix fled, but had not, as we presumed, turned wild along with many others of his kind. The eldren king had lost everything. He was plotting his revenge.

We must now assume that he was exploring the watery depths, learning about the seams and plates in the planet's crust. Eldren have always had a harmony with the world beyond our race. The most powerful of his people, who made the world shake when he changed, would stop at nothing to have his vengeance.

The fall of Aleuthea began at night.

The golden rays of the Lighthouse swept the seas. As I often did, I stood high on an upper balcony of my palace, looking past the glittering city below and out at the dark waters of the Aleuthean Sea.

Then, without warning, the sweep of the Lighthouse caught a great serpent circling the island. Silver scales reflected from an undulating body the width of my palace, as long as the broad avenue that ran the length of the city. At first I thought my eyes were deceiving me, and then I assumed it was a wildran, although it was rare for them to come so close to populated areas. It was only when I saw the glaring red eyes that I knew for certain, and the creature's size confirmed it. For the first time since the destruction of the eldren homeland many years earlier, I was looking at their king.

The copper bell on the summit of the Lighthouse pealed, sounding the alarm. The magi took their iron-tipped staffs and ran out to the balustrade circling the city. They lifted their weapons and balls of fire shot from the metal claws. Archers on the towers fired arrows at Marrix's body but the range was too great. The great serpent circled the island at a distance, caught with every sweep of the Lighthouse's rays. He completed a full rotation and then, before the fleet could be assembled, he disappeared under the sea.

The city remained on high alert. Like everyone, I wondered what the purpose of the visit was. The horn that won us the war was safely in the golden ark, under the watch of the magi. Marrix's ability to summon his wild kin was harnessed in the magical relic; he could never reclaim it. Surely there was nothing to his visit at all. Perhaps he was wild, and his motives were as unknowable as the fish he shared the sea with.

Such speculation was soon given clarity.

The ground began to shake. The upheaval was like nothing I'd ever felt before, and I know I will never be able to describe what it was like to have the ground drop away from under me in a heartbeat.

As buildings started to fall across Aleuthea, I ran back inside the palace, descending the wind tunnel to exit the shuddering structure. I saw the archmagus Nisos standing at the balustrade that girded the city's edge and staggered to join him. The sorcerer was staring down at the sea.

Even as the shaking grew worse, the waters of the Aleuthean Sea were climbing the stone wall with impossible speed. But, despite what I was seeing, I knew it wasn't the ocean that was rising; even Marrix couldn't do such a thing.

Aleuthea was sinking.

Everything ponderously tilted, and the archmagus and I began to run. We swiftly gathered some men to secure the golden ark from the house of the magi. The upper floors of my proud palace slid off those below and crashed into the rising sea as enough soldiers finally arrived to lift the ark on stout poles. We then sped to the docks. We had to flee. The water was rushing through the streets.

We reached the harbor where ships were being loaded, desperate citizens climbing aboard. The archmagus beckoned to the men charged with the ark, who struggled under its weight as he hounded them up to one of the closest ships.

My commanders said we would be vulnerable to Marrix on the water. But we had no other choice. So we loaded up all the people and supplies we could. Finally I climbed aboard the *Solaris* and saw Archmagus Nisos on the next ship in line, together with the ark and several of his order. The *Solaris* was the last to push off from the dock. Waves tossed us to and fro, as we began to drift.

Fear was now on every man's face. The ocean wasn't our element. We were vulnerable. We needed to flee before Marrix returned from the sea bottom and slaughtered us all.

While dozens of ships tried to find cohesion, I witnessed the death throes of my beloved homeland. The sea boiled like a cauldron as Aleuthea sank beneath the waters forever. Some had been saved, but I knew that even if every ship was full, nine out of every ten Aleutheans had just met their end, and we had perils yet to face.

The rays of the descending Lighthouse continued to sweep the sea, forty feet below the surface, deeper with every passing moment. Then I saw something revealed in its watery glow that made me cry out with rage. A huge reptilian body, silver scaled and monstrous, weaved around the plummeting structure and sped up for the surface. Eyes blazed as red as fiery coals. Marrix had returned, and he would destroy this fleet with ease.

I turned and saw the half-dozen magi aboard the *Solaris* transfixed with shock. I called on their courage but what could they do? Balls of fire were little use against an enemy underwater. Light would blind us more than him. Sound would be difficult to direct. Wind could not touch this enemy.

Wind. As soon as I thought of it, I knew what we had to do.

I grabbed a sorcerer with a resonance staff in his hand and pointed at Archmagus Nisos. The sorcerer used his talents to convey my words to the archmagus, who relayed them across our drifting fleet.

Moments later – even as Marrix smashed into the first galleon, dissolving it into splinters in an instant – across the fleet, silver cones on the tips of staffs began to glow. Marrix shattered a second ship, and then two more detonated in swift succession, his sweeping tail breaking them into halves. Summoning their magic, the desperate magi cried out as one.

The wind was sudden and out of control. The sorcerers unleashed chaos.

Nothing could have prepared me for it. With no time to coordinate their magic the sorcerers each chose a different direction for the wind. The only commonality was that the wind's summoners wanted to be taken away from the sinking island and away from Marrix. Uncontrollable wind and waves did just that, thrusting the fleet out to sea.

I heard a mighty crack. Turning, I saw the archmagus's ship heel as a gust struck from the side and the mast snapped, crippling the vessel. Then the towering waves hid the ship from sight, and I never saw the golden ark again.

The storm the magi created sent the fleet away from danger, but it also swept us far from the lands we knew. Out in the open ocean, the magical winds merged and collided with other winds, and a hurricane struck the fleet, driving it north.

Later, much later, when the weather finally calmed, we were surrounded by ice floes. We tried to navigate through, but the wind continued to push us onwards. At some point our navigators ceased to know where we were. We were so far north that every other direction was south. Then a ship became stuck, and when we tried to free it the ice trapped another. The floes crowded closer together. The fleet became lodged.

But one day, despite Aleuthea being gone forever, one day, we will return to reclaim our dominion. One day we will return to the Realm of the Three Seas.

———

The account of the fall of Aleuthea finished there.

Palemon lifted his gaze, thinking about the events that had befallen the Aleutheans since that fatal night. Of the forty ships that made it to this land of cold, most had been destroyed when they were trapped by the ice, with only a handful still serviceable. The exiles salvaged everything they could; all wood and metal would henceforth be prized.

The greatest problem was that they were lost. Over the years the exiles sent the surviving ships out one by one. They never returned. With no guide, no working compass, and no sun that rose in the east and set in the west, they could never find their way home.

Now this galleon, the *Solaris*, was their last ship. And with the herds of musk ox and reindeer being thinned too quickly to sustain themselves, in a year, perhaps two, Palemon's people would be starving. The nusu natives who had lived in these lands far longer than the Aleutheans had taught them to hunt whales and fish, but the taller, stronger Aleutheans had become victims of their own success. The numbers of nusu had declined as the Aleutheans took over the natives' traditional hunting grounds. Now even the once-plentiful ocean life was scarce. It had been several weeks since a whale had been butchered. Soon it wouldn't be just the savages who were starving.

Palemon frowned as he clasped his palms and rested his elbows on the desk. Before long they were going to have to send this last ship out, perhaps even this summer, while the ice had retreated. The *Solaris* would sail again. But likely, as with the other vessels, it would never return.

He started as a crack of wood against wood broke his reverie. The sound sent a shock through him. He was alone, on a ship, in the middle of a snowy plain. He shot to his feet.

2

The two nusu boys hurriedly climbed out of the hatch in the center of the main deck and sped for the ladder. The boy in front was slightly older, with wild hair and ruddy skin, while the other, jabbering and moaning as he urged his companion on, still had the round cheeks of a child.

Palemon's long strides took him over to the boys in a heartbeat. The youngest saw him approaching and quailed with fear. Wide-eyed and terrified, he fell to the ground and raised an arm over his head.

Ignoring him, Palemon drew his broadsword in one swift movement and pressed the point to the older boy's throat, halting his rush for the ladder. The two boys' faces were similar, and Palemon decided they were brothers. He might have seen them before; they might even know him well. He rarely paid attention to the savages.

Swallowing, the older boy froze, suddenly as still as a corpse left out overnight. Showing the whites of his eyes, he ran his gaze from the shining steel to the gloved hand of the man holding the hilt, until he met Palemon's cold stare.

Even Palemon was surprised at the rage that bubbled to the surface. The curiosity of the young had no place here. This ship was the only thing that remained as an example of his people's former glory. It was their last link to the world they'd left behind. With it they had hope. Without it they would all share the same graves as the nusu savages they held in such contempt.

Soon first one boy, then another, made a cry of pain as Palemon threw them off the precious vessel, sending them tumbling to the frozen ground beside the galleon. He jumped down a moment later, landing easily on booted feet, sword still in hand. He then made the boys kneel side by side as he considered, resting on his sword, point pressed into the ice.

Palemon judged their ages. The youngest was perhaps ten and his older brother two years his senior. They were old enough to know right from wrong.

'Your people are forbidden to come near this ship,' Palemon stated, his intonation low. 'You know the rules, yet you broke them willingly. You know what we are. We are cold bloods. We have no warmth in our hearts. We are as strong as iron, as hard as ice.'

He looked from child to child. Both knelt with heads tilted back, staring up at him. The younger boy's expression showed utter terror, but there was defiance in the older one's face.

'As king, I pronounce your punishment thusly. One of you must die. The other will watch, in order to bear witness and warning to the rest. I now must decide. Which of you dies?'

He pondered, shifting his gaze from face to face. The nusu were kept in line by fear. Nothing was more powerful than fear: not greed, not lust, and not envy. He made his decision.

'I choose you for life.' Palemon pointed his sword at the younger boy. His terror would be contagious. His story would prevent the necessity of doing this again. 'And you'—he leveled his weapon at the defiant youth—'I choose for death.'

Palemon moved to stand beside the older boy and lifted his sword above his head. 'Watch,' he instructed the boy he'd spared, who now had tears streaking down his cheeks. 'This ship is more important than your people know. But how could you know? You are our slaves. All you have to do is stay away.'

Arms held high, he tensed as he prepared the blow that would end the boy's life, promising himself he would make it clean. But then a voice called out, making him lower the sword and frown.

Palemon turned and saw a man in furs stumping toward him, walking with a strangely stooped gait. The newcomer's back was bent at a sharp angle, just below his neck, and his arms were outsized, so thick and muscled that they should have belonged to a much larger man. He had deep-set eyes and thick black eyebrows.

'Sire,' the hunchback called again as he approached.

'Kyphos,' Palemon said, ignoring the two boys as he once again rested on the point of his sword. 'What brings you here?'

'The witch, Zara, requests your presence.'

Palemon shook his head. 'I hope you don't call her witch to her face. She is a sorceress, and a powerful one. Why not come herself?'

'She didn't say, but she was anxious that you come immediately.'

'Bah,' Palemon growled. Only Zara had the nerve to send for her king as if he were a common house slave. He glanced at the pair of nusu. 'Sort out these boys. Kill this one.' He pointed to the older of the two. 'And send the other one home.'

King Palemon knew that Kyphos would carry out his orders; he would take no pleasure in it, for unlike some others in the city of the dead he didn't have a cruel streak, but he was utterly loyal.

'Of course,' Kyphos said. He rested a hand on the axe hanging from his belt. 'What did they do?'

Palemon didn't hear him; he was already striding away, wondering what Zara thought was so urgent.

Two mighty ridges of black and white rock traveled at angles to each other until they met and became one. The settlement nestled in the apex of the fork they formed, sheltered from the cruel winds, huddled in the lee like a cub nuzzling closer to its mother's body.

It was more a large village than a town, a collection of crude conical huts covered in furs, erected on frames with streams of smoke trickling from the tops. The settlement's inhabitants burned human and animal dung for warmth, and the vast majority of their furnishings, clothing, and diet came from beasts. Whales gave them bone for the ribs of the huts and oil for their few lamps. Furs made their clothing. Water was stored in reindeer stomachs. Fish bones were crushed and eaten along with the flesh. Bear and wolf were both predator and prey.

As he walked, Palemon passed one of the few houses in the settlement constructed from wood, and reflected on the fact that, like his people, he had never seen a tree. With planks of dark timber and strangely warped curves, these larger dwellings were built from the ships of the fleet that originally fled the fall of Aleuthea, those that were too crushed by the ice to ever sail again.

The hunters were away and the women and children were all indoors, and so Palemon strode along the avenue that ran from one end of the settlement to the other alone.

The area was completely deserted. Necropolis, city of the dead, was a fitting name.

Yet the settlement's founders hadn't chosen the name because of the eerie emptiness or the ghostly mists. It was called Necropolis because the ancient Aleutheans wanted to impress upon anyone who lived here that this was a temporary home only. The city was dead from the moment of its establishment. Their true home was far away. Despite the fact that the island of Aleuthea was sunk beneath the waves, gone forever, the entire Realm of the Three Seas had always been their dominion, and would provide a home again.

A wind came up, blowing tiny crystals of ice from above, and Palemon scowled as he brushed flecks from his eyebrows, lips, and beard. He looked up at the sky and saw that the blue overhead was dissolving into white. The snowflakes were descending in flurries by the time he came to the house of the sorceress.

Zara's single-storied wooden hut was half buried in snow, the entrance dug out a good three feet lower than the surrounds. The door was plain, its panels pockmarked by exposure to the sea. Palemon raised a hand to knock and then hesitated.

His lips thinned and instead of knocking he pulled the door open, struggling with its bulk as it scraped over the icy ground.

The comparative warmth within caressed his face. Golden light revealed an interior furnished with low stools and animal-skin rugs. Shelves had been fashioned from precious timber and then filled with priceless books. A pile of dung cakes glowed in a hearth at one end, the smoke funneled upwards into a chimney. Besides this main room, there were two other chambers at the back. It was a small house, but only Palemon's was bigger.

'Close the door,' a soft, feminine voice hissed. 'Now!'

Palemon stepped inside and hauled the door closed behind him, stamping his feet and feeling the strange sensation of chill that always came when one was well and truly out of the cold. Facing the center of the room, he regarded the owner of the voice.

Zara wore a long-sleeved navy dress of thick dark wool, somehow managing to make the garment appear supple and rich as it clung to her lithe frame. The sorceress was beautiful but ice cold, her face carved like marble, with high cheekbones and parted lips that were chill blue rather than ruby red. Her hair was long and straight, as black as night, and she had brilliant blue eyes that glittered, eyes that were focused on something else entirely than the man who had just entered.

Palemon cleared his throat, but she still didn't even look at him.

The sorceress had her sun staff in her hand. She stood in the middle of the room, every element of her posture and facial expression indicating complete concentration. Her legs were apart and she clutched the wrist-thick staff with her right hand, close to the hoop of solid gold at the top. Her left hand circled slowly around the hoop, which was the size of a man's hand and etched with arcane symbols.

Zara was obviously exercising her power, but Palemon couldn't even hazard a guess as to what she was doing.

It was clearly related to the sun staff, he could see that much. The interior of the house was bright not because of the meager fire in the hearth but because the gold circle was glowing fiercely, so radiant that it almost hurt to look upon it.

The sorceress grunted and a darting flame suddenly flickered into existence inside the hoop. She shot out a breath, making a sound similar to the cry of a warrior striking an enemy with a sword, and the flame lengthened and grew brighter. Like an extending finger it left the circle and wavered before seeming to pick a direction as the flame prodded the empty air.

Zara gasped and the flame vanished. She shuddered and her shoulders slumped. The fierce light shining from the gold hoop at the summit of the staff began to fade, and then went dark altogether.

Now there was only the faint red light cast by the fire to see by. Zara turned to Palemon and he tilted his head in puzzlement. She looked exhausted, which didn't surprise him after the display of power she'd just given, but she also appeared strangely triumphant.

'I am sorry, sire, to have spoken to you in that way when you entered, but the wind interferes. Wind is silver, and I am working with gold.'

Palemon frowned. 'You sent Kyphos for me. I was busy.'

She smiled softly. 'Busy examining the ship for the thousandth time, sire?'

'It is our last chance, our only chance,' he growled. 'And I found some nusu hiding aboard.' She raised her eyebrows. 'It's fine.' He waved a hand. 'I left Kyphos to deal with them. They'll remember their place. So, magus, why am I here?'

'You saw it, didn't you?' Her gaze flickered to the golden circle. 'Tell me you didn't miss it.'

'I saw light and flame.'

'Look,' Zara said. 'Come closer. Watch.'

Palemon came to stand beside her as she closed her eyes. Her breathing slowed as her chest rose and fell. Finally the sorceress's breath stilled altogether and, despite himself, Palemon held his breath along with her. Time stretched out, and he wondered when she would resume breathing.

She opened her eyes, clutched the top of the staff in a white-knuckled grip, and let out an explosive cry.

The gold flared up brightly. With eyes narrowed in concentration, Zara began to pant, lines creasing in her forehead as she drew the magic into herself and channeled it into the pure metal at the top of her staff. She grunted once more and again Palemon saw the flame appear inside the circle.

As the sorceress harnessed strange forces, the flame lengthened, and then it darted out of the hoop and projected itself in a direction outwards and to the side. It was angled, like a string was trying to tug on the golden light, pulling it, drawing it somewhere specific.

The sorceress finally sighed, releasing the magic's grip on her senses. Palemon frowned but he didn't speak, giving her time to regain her composure. Instead he stared at the fading gold circle and imagined all his people could accomplish if they also had quantities of silver, copper, and iron.

But gold was the only materia left. The other metals had tarnished long ago, used in too many emergencies. As the magic of the materia was utilized, the metal corroded and eventually became unresponsive, even to a magus with Zara's skill.

Only gold never tarnished.

Finally Zara turned her weary but excited eyes on him. 'Please,' she said. 'Don't make me show you again.'

'I saw it,' he said. 'But what does it mean?'

'It has taken me time to learn to control it to this extent,' she said. 'And I had to be sure before I told you, but the light is seeking a kindred spirit. It is being called to something.'

'I don't understand.'

'I think I do.' She smiled. 'I believe I know what it is. A magical source of gold has been drawing energy. Something built by our people. Something we left behind.'

Palemon gasped. 'The ark?'

Zara nodded. 'It has to be.'

'What are you saying? The horn has been uncovered? After all this time?'

'Sire, all I can say is that I believe the ark was opened. A burst of the magic containing the horn was released. The horn may be in the hands of our old enemy, the eldren, or a curious barbarian may have opened the golden chest to see what is inside. Speculation aside, there is only one way to discover what has transpired in the Realm of the Three Seas since the fall of Aleuthea. And that is to go there.'

Palemon, the thirteenth king to carry the name, swallowed. 'You . . . You're saying?'

'The sun here does not rise in the east and set in the west. A compass travels only in circles. Every direction is south. But yes, King Palemon. I believe I can use the magic of the ark to find our way home.'

Hope surged through him. This was the only world he had ever known, but every night stories were told of the Realm of the Three

Seas. It was warm. The sun shone brightly, even in winter. Food was plentiful. People lived in grand buildings.

And there was metal. Zara and her magi would be able to harness the power of gold, silver, copper, and iron. They would be able to find a new home, perhaps a place already established, a place they could nominate to be a new Aleuthea.

New Aleuthea. King Palemon nodded to himself.

He would push his people. The magic of the ark would guide them. The magic of gold, and light, and power.

The *Solaris* was ready. Palemon would gather a select group of his strongest warriors; he'd already decided to lead them himself. It was summer and the ice was clear.

Three hundred years had passed. But the last ship to survive the fall of Aleuthea would soon depart.

3

Chloe and her father Aristocles, first consul of Phalesia, climbed the winding series of steps cut into the cliff. The midday sun beat down from high in the sky as a fresh sea breeze blew her dark hair around her face and made her yellow chiton cling to her slender frame. She felt her heart race, and not only from the giddy height and the exertion of the ascent. Leaning against the rock wall for support, she couldn't help relive when she'd last come this way.

Chloe had descended from the Temple of Aldus after the death of Solon, ruler of the Ilean Empire. She had stumbled down, almost falling more than once, wide-eyed and shaking.

She fought to control her breathing. She was facing her fears by returning. The visions of blood and death were in the past.

The wind gusted as first Aristocles and then Chloe ascended the final step, and now they were on the small plateau that was home to the temple. Suddenly the memories were driven home with force.

She saw the circle of wide marble columns, framing the paved center, each holding up nothing but the sky. Earth-shattering force had smashed one of the columns into two pieces; the top half lay thirty paces from its base. She again saw the two dragons fighting, rolling and biting, wings snapping like sails in the wind, skittering across the ground and cleaving the column as they struck. One of the dragons was powerful and silver-scaled, one-eyed, and vicious. Its opponent was black as night and fought with equal savagery to defend Chloe from certain death as she tried to prevent Solon from opening the ark. The black dragon was Dion.

Aristocles turned when he noticed that Chloe had stopped in her tracks. 'Daughter? Are you well?' His high forehead, framed by wisps of white hair at his temples, creased with concern. He shook his head. 'I shouldn't have brought you here.'

Chloe drew in a deep breath. 'I am fine, Father,' she said, walking forward to join him. 'I was just . . . remembering.'

In the center of the plateau was the eternal flame, a captive fire on a stepped pedestal, bright and fierce even in the daylight. Half a dozen paces in front of the flame's pedestal stood the ark itself, a chest of solid gold the size of a large table. Ornate and artfully decorated, it had a flat lid that was small compared to the chest. Strange, sharply angled symbols were arranged along the front, underneath lines of cursive text in a language no one could read.

But it wasn't the ark that drew Chloe's attention. It was the splotch of red blood nearby. She had plunged her sword into Solon's body and ended his life, as well as Triton the eldran king's chance of seizing the horn of Marrix. Zachary said that the horn would enable Triton to control the wildren, and that the one-eyed eldran had only one aim: to destroy all of humanity.

'Daughter?' Aristocles said again.

'I'm fine,' Chloe repeated, tearing her eyes away from the crimson stain.

As her gaze lifted she saw that between each pair of the perimeter columns stood a Phalesian soldier in leather breastplate, skirt of leather strips, and short blue cloak. Every soldier faced outward and had a bow in his hand and quiver of arrows on his shoulder. The circle of guards scanned the sky and scoured the sea.

'Then come,' her father murmured. He planted a smile on his face and walked toward the temple's center, and the man waiting for them near the ark.

Nikolas, king of Xanthos, looked strange out of armor. His warrior physique filled his white tunic, leaving one muscled shoulder bare, making the garment appear too small for his body. Though his skin was like leather, Chloe could still see white scars on his arms and hands, and if his face hadn't been covered by a thick black beard she was sure she would have seen scars there too. He was tall, but his thick torso made him anything but rangy, and curly hair coated the visible skin of his chest like an animal's pelt. His eyes were dark and haunted: before Nikolas had seized victory at the Battle of Phalesia, the Ileans had taken everything: his beautiful wife, strong young son, and beloved father.

He did, however, have another close family member still living. And despite all he'd lost, it had been his choice to exile his only brother, Dion.

Glancing at her father, Chloe contrasted him with the king of Xanthos. Aristocles had a bald crown with thinning white hair at the sides of his scalp and a skinny frame. Nikolas stood proudly, impatiently, while the first consul of Phalesia was anxious and friendly, both at the same time.

The balance of power between the two neighboring city-states had changed. Phalesia had lost her entire navy. Most of the dead at the battle had been soldiers in cloaks of blue. Nikolas had saved the city, but by arriving late he'd ensured that the blood of Phalesia's young men had been spilled in volume. He'd come in time, but he had also come too late for Phalesia's strength to survive intact.

Chloe tried to bury her resentment. It had happened swiftly, while she was still stunned with the knowledge that she'd just killed Solon, and was struggling with Dion's true nature, but she was now betrothed. The king of Xanthos and her father had already announced the engagement to their peoples. Chloe's dark hair was piled high on her head and fastened with several pins, the style of a maiden who had been claimed by a man. Nikolas was going to be her husband.

Long ago, when Chloe's mother was alive, she'd smiled and told Chloe that she'd always known she and Aristocles would be married. If Chloe was lucky, she'd said, she would have a husband as kind, a man who would also be a gentle and generous father to her children.

The fates had been cruel. Chloe had prayed to the gods to release her, but she was trapped.

The Oracle at Athos had prophesied the exact year of Solon's death. The Seer gave Chloe three prophecies of her own, two of which had already come true. The final prophecy was that Chloe would marry a man she didn't love.

The Seer's predictions always came true.

Rather than greet her or the first consul, Nikolas frowned at Chloe and then directed his words to her father. 'I asked that you come alone, First Consul.'

'I am an old man,' Aristocles said with a disarming smile. 'My daughter was assisting me up the stairs.'

It was untrue; he hadn't needed any help. Chloe had wanted to be here, and it was rare that her father refused her.

Nikolas addressed her directly, dark eyes narrowed. 'Go home, Chloe.'

Chloe opened her mouth but bit down on a retort. She instead clutched the copper medallion she wore around her neck and slowly inhaled, praying for Aeris to give her serenity. Aristocles and Nikolas also had medallions hanging from chains around their necks, but in Chloe's father's case the symbol in the circle of gold depicted the scales of Aldus, god of justice, whereas Nikolas had the bull of Balal, god of war, hanging from a circle of iron links.

Aristocles lifted his chin. 'I'm certain that it is custom in Xanthos, as well as Phalesia, that the father is the custodian of the bride until the wedding day. Until then, Chloe is under my protection, and I would like her to stay.'

'If that is your wish, then so be it,' Nikolas said stiffly.

It was clear that he wasn't a man who liked to be thwarted. But turning his attention to the task at hand, Nikolas now faced the golden ark. Chloe and her father did the same, and they gazed at it as they spoke.

'We are here to discuss the Ark of Revelation,' Nikolas said. He snorted. 'I'm sure you've both noticed that the priests have stopped calling it that. They now say that the true location of the tablets on which Aldus inscribed the laws of man is unknown.'

'It's irrelevant whether they exist at all,' Aristocles said. 'They were never intended for us to look upon. The ten laws of man were always for us to discover for ourselves.'

'That is a matter for the magi,' said Nikolas with a shrug. 'But your words give me hope, for it seems we are in agreement. This chest is not sacred. It is merely a container, made of pure metal, intended to confine the power of the horn of Marrix. Eldren cannot willingly touch pure metal, which is why Triton enlisted the sun king's help to retrieve the horn.' He glanced at the first consul. 'The question now becomes, what do we do with the ark?'

Aristocles frowned. 'I would have thought it to be: what do we do with the horn of Marrix?'

'Easily solved.' Nikolas waved a hand. 'Any container of pure metal will serve the same function, whether gold, silver, copper, or iron.'

'How can you be sure?' Chloe asked.

Nikolas's lips thinned, but he answered her question. 'I consult with my magi, just as your father does.'

'The ark is Phalesian,' Aristocles said. 'What we do with it is our decision—'

'Is it truly?' Nikolas asked. 'We thought it came from the gods, but now we know otherwise.' He pointed. 'Is that writing Phalesian script? Are those symbols made by Phalesian hands? Do you know when it was made and by whom?' He cut the air with his hand. 'The Aleutheans, led by King Palemon, stole the horn of Marrix, that is what the legends say. We now know that they built this chest and placed the horn inside. How it ended up here is anyone's guess—'

'It is Phalesian,' Aristocles said through gritted teeth. 'You and I can decide together what we do with the horn, but as for—'

'If we're going to stand against Ilea,' Nikolas said. 'We need gold.'

'The fates put the ark here, where we have protected it and cared for it,' Aristocles said. 'It certainly isn't Xanthian.'

'Then why haven't you done anything with it, besides place a few of your poorly trained soldiers as guards?' Nikolas demanded. 'You say the ark is yours to deal with, so do so! The secret is out. Triton knows where the horn is. Meanwhile your fleet is destroyed and you have a relic of pure gold here that will draw enemies like moths to a flame.'

Despite Nikolas's manner, Chloe had to admit the truth of what he was saying. The Ileans had been humiliated at the Battle of Phalesia: they would return. Triton knew exactly where the horn was, and was desperate to claim the kingship of all eldren, with only Zachary and the eldren in the Wilds standing in his way.

Aristocles was silent for a time. Usually diplomatic, he'd uncharacteristically allowed his wounded pride to show. 'So how would you have it?'

'The warships we captured are being repaired, but the work is costly, and building more takes time. I suggest you move the horn to an iron box and then melt down the ark. Aristocles, I will grant you that the gold is yours. But you must use it to rebuild your strength.'

Aristocles drew in a slow breath before he reluctantly nodded. 'I will consult with the Assembly of Consuls.' Chloe realized how hard this must be for him: he was a deeply religious man, and had prayed to the ark fervently over the years.

'No.' Nikolas shook his head. 'I need a promise.'

'Wait,' Chloe said. Both men looked at her as if they'd forgotten she was present. 'There's something we're forgetting. Why is the horn kept in a chest of gold, rather than another metal? Perhaps there's a good reason. We aren't certain that there won't be consequences for moving it.'

Nikolas's eyes narrowed.

'I have an idea,' she continued. 'We consult with Zachary and find out if the horn will be safe in an iron container. Then, Father, if Zachary says it's safe, perhaps there'll be no need to convene the Assembly. King Nikolas is rightly concerned. It's only fair that we do our part, and if the ark can help us rebuild, we can thank the gods for the gift of the gold.'

Aristocles pondered. 'I can agree to that,' he said finally, looking at Nikolas and waiting for his reaction.

'Agreed,' Nikolas said. He scanned the perimeter of the temple. 'In the meantime, I will order an equal number of my king's guard to stand here with your men.' Aristocles opened his mouth, and Chloe knew he was going to protest about Xanthian soldiers on Phalesian soil, but Nikolas forestalled him, speaking firmly. 'I hope you appreciate this gesture of cooperation.'

Chloe's father closed his mouth, and then nodded. 'Agreed.'

'Now,' Nikolas said. 'One last thing. I want to look at the horn.'

'Do you think that's wise?' Aristocles asked.

Nikolas barked a laugh and indicated the empty sky. Aristocles scowled and beckoned one of the nearby soldiers to come forward. Meanwhile Nikolas slowly approached the ark. He crouched in front of it and spoke to the Phalesian soldier.

'Lift the lid carefully. Close it again on my command.'

Chloe stayed with her father, but she suddenly longed to know what Nikolas would see. The soldier grunted as he heaved at the handle of the golden lid. Rainbow light welled from underneath, bathing Nikolas's broad face in rippling colors as he gazed inside.

———⁀———

For hour after hour, King Palemon stood at the galleon's stern, wind whipping his hair, hands on the rail as he looked back at the departing shore. It was high summer; there was no better time to depart, and though the occasional ice floe drifted past, the sea was mostly clear. He watched the white landmass of his birth as it grew distant, until the crowd of forlorn watchers left behind became little specks, and then couldn't be seen at all.

The *Solaris* could accommodate just a small proportion of the city of the dead's population, which meant that he'd taken only the strongest with him: the fiercest of the male warriors and the most powerful of the magi. He vowed to himself that he would find the warm lands he'd heard stories about his whole life and claim a new dominion for his people. He would return with a fleet large enough to accommodate them all. He would come back for them before starvation and cold claimed their lives.

'Sire!' He heard a female voice cry.

Palemon turned and saw Zara standing nearby, sun staff in hand. Despite the chill air she still wore nothing but her long-sleeved dress. Her curved lips were blue, but magic warmed her blood.

The golden hoop glowed as the pull of the ark guided them. She cried out and a spear of yellow flame darted through the hoop, the longest and brightest flame Palemon had yet seen. With wide eyes he went to stand beside her, mesmerized by the dance of the flame that led the way.

Her startlingly blue eyes met his. 'It is the ark,' she said. 'I am certain of it. Right now. At this very instant. It is drawing on the gold to contain the horn's power.'

———⌣———

'Close it!' Aristocles said. Chloe could see that the soldier was struggling to hold the golden lid high as Nikolas peered in. 'We don't understand it!'

Nikolas was blocking her view of the ark's interior, but when the soldier lowered the lid and she heard the heavy clunk she knew she had missed her opportunity.

'Thank you,' Aristocles said to the Phalesian soldier. 'You may return to your duties.'

The soldier bowed and departed. Nikolas took a deep breath and then returned to the first consul and Chloe.

'It's a conch shell,' Nikolas said. Even he appeared awed by what he'd seen. 'Like the stories say. It's . . . I find it hard to describe. It is powerful. I don't need to be a magus to know.'

'I do take the danger seriously, King Nikolas. I assure you. As my daughter has suggested, we will discuss this with Zachary, and if he gives his blessing we'll move the horn somewhere safe. Perhaps we can also speak with Queen Zanthe of Tanus about sending a combined force into the Waste. The eldren there were always too far away to be a threat, but now . . .'

Nikolas nodded. 'I was going to wait, but being here, seeing the horn with my own eyes . . . The Ileans will be back. Triton will do what he can to seize the horn.' He gazed directly into Aristocles' eyes. 'First Consul, I intend to reform the Galean League.'

'The Galean League?' Chloe asked with a frown. 'Wasn't that a response to the barbarian invasion a hundred years ago?'

'The horde was unstoppable,' Nikolas said. 'Yet with Tanus, Phalesia, Xanthos, and Sarsica working together, we held them off.'

'Before the league fell apart in a decade-long war,' Aristocles said.

Nikolas reddened. 'I can see that this isn't the time. We'll discuss the league another day. As I said, I will accept that the gold is yours, if you use it to promptly rebuild your strength and contribute fairly to the new fleet that defends us both.'

'Provided the horn will be safe contained by iron,' Chloe said.

'Yes, yes,' Nikolas said impatiently.

Aristocles spoke. 'And the fleet will be under our joint command, rather than that woman from across the sea—'

'Roxana knows her business.'

'She is a foreigner.'

'She serves me well.'

'That is the problem,' Aristocles said. 'She serves only you.'

'Enough!' Chloe glared at them both. 'We've agreed to go to the Wilds to speak with Zachary. Other decisions can wait. I'll depart—'

'Wait.' Nikolas's eyes narrowed. 'You? I never agreed to you going. No.' He shook his head. 'I forbid you to go.'

'King Nikolas, it does make sense,' Aristocles said. 'Chloe knows Zachary—'

'I don't care who it is,' Nikolas said. 'But,' he scowled at Chloe, 'it won't be her.'

The king of Xanthos stormed away.

Chloe and Aristocles exchanged glances and she could see the unspoken regret in her father's eyes. In the aftermath of the battle for Phalesia, he'd thought to bind the two neighboring nations closer together. But that had been before he'd realized the terrible impact that the murder of his family had made on Nikolas.

'It's fine, father,' Chloe said. She reached out and squeezed his hand.

'I am sorry,' he said softly.

———————

It was only a few hours later that Chloe left the Phalesian agora and followed the stepped marble paths down to the lower city. Glancing over her shoulder, she saw that the soldier of Nikolas's king's guard – noticeable by his bronze breastplate and the helm that hid his face with cheek and nose guards – was still following her.

She scowled. Nikolas would simply tell her father that his men were keeping his future wife safe. There was nothing she could do to complain.

Traveling the broad avenue, she was careful to walk in the middle of the street, away from the sickening stench of the refuse that filled the gutters on both sides. She passed city folk of all descriptions: dusty laborers in smocks, colorfully dressed women with young children in tow, farmers leading burdened donkeys by the reins, and market vendors calling out from wooden stalls. Turning into an alley, she lifted the hem of her chiton so it didn't drag until she reached a wider street. Another turn took her between two rows of mud-brick houses, and then she stopped in the middle of yet another avenue.

She glanced over her shoulder. The helmeted soldier was still following, not even trying to stay hidden.

Her destination lay just ahead, and she walked along the avenue until she arrived at a single-storied house made of pale stone. She came to this place often; as a healer she bought her supplies from the apothecary who lived and worked here.

The eyes of the soldier followed her as she entered.

Shelves crowded the front room from floor to ceiling, arranged against every wall. A bewildering array of gourds, skins, jars, jugs, and bowls of all shapes and sizes filled the shelves. Sour and spicy aromas made her nose wrinkle. Bushels of dried plants sat beside mortars and pestles. Bright powders formed piles on round plates.

'Balion?' Chloe called out. She hoped he came quickly.

The apothecary appeared a moment later, entering through the arched opening at the back that divided his shop front and the workroom where he mixed his powders and potions from the quarters where he lived with his wife and two children. A curly-haired older man with smile lines around his eyes, his gait was more of a waddle than a walk: he had a heavy paunch. Chloe had known Balion and his family since she'd first started studying the healing arts; his wife made the best honey cakes she'd ever tasted.

'Princess,' he said, beckoning her forward. 'Come. Everything is ready. This way.'

She followed the apothecary through the archway, continuing past the cooking and eating area until she came to the room where he and his family slept. Balion pulled aside a curtain to reveal another exit, this one leading to the house's rear, and a moment later she was once more in the open air. Rows of herbs and vegetable plants made up a small garden. Each house in the row backed onto the same area, with a rough wall separating it from the street.

Chloe breathed a sigh of relief when she saw Balion head directly toward a horse tethered to a gnarled olive tree, saddlebags packed.

'He'll do well by you,' Balion said, patting the horse's flank affectionately. He pointed. 'Head that way and you'll be back onto the street.'

'Thank you,' Chloe said sincerely.

'Anytime you need me,' he said, handing her the reins. 'You sure you're not in trouble?'

'More of an annoyance.' She squeezed his shoulder. 'If he asks about me just tell him the truth, say I left out the back.'

Chloe led her horse between the rows of houses until she was back out on the street. Pulling herself up onto her mount's back, she leaned forward and dug in her heels. She headed directly for the city's main gate, taking a route for the open road.

4

Dion blinked sweat out of his eyes. He ran wildly through a region of tall trees and thick undergrowth. Leaping over a wall of brush, he heard a beastly roar fill the forest, making his blood run cold. There was no way he could run any faster; he was already sprinting as fast as he could.

He looked over his shoulder, almost tripping in the process, and caught a flash of shaggy brown fur. The sight of his pursuer spurred him on. Thick branches behind him snapped like twigs, not slowing it down in the least.

Racing after him was the largest bear he'd ever seen. When he'd first seen it he'd been frozen into place, awed by its size: the massive creature stood easily twelve feet tall when it rose on its hind legs and challenged the trespassers in its territory. As the long snout parted it had revealed rows of sharp teeth, head tilted and jaws open wide as it emitted a groaning cry so loud it reverberated around the surrounding hills. The bear had then lowered its head and begun to run directly at the pale-faced young man who had been foolish enough to enter its domain.

And the bear wasn't just quick. Its lumbering run was faster than Dion thought possible. This was its place, and it knew the terrain.

As Dion sprinted, another bellow made a shiver of fear travel up and down his spine. Forced to head left and then immediately right to get around a thicket of impenetrable trees, he tried not to think about a meaty paw raking down his back, shredding his skin with razor slices. He ducked under a horizontal branch and then tripped over a rock, stumbling forward until he righted himself. A moment later his heart went into his mouth; he was at the edge of a cliff, partly obscured by the foliage. He looked around, wondering which way to go.

Hearing the swish of branches, Dion tensed as he prepared for the huge brown beast to emerge from the trees, but instead he let out a gasp of relief when he saw Zachary. Both men were bare-chested, wearing nothing but deerskin leggings, but the similarities ended there, for Dion resembled any Galean man, with a lean, athletic build, flaxen hair, and brown eyes. Zachary, in comparison, had silver, shoulder-length hair, with thin eyebrows arched over brown eyes flecked with gold. His face was narrow and his features were sharp, almost gaunt, with a crescent-shaped scar on his left cheek.

'This way!' Zachary cried.

The bear crashed through the undergrowth a moment later, lunging at the eldran, who narrowly missed the gnashing teeth. Bellowing again, the bear caught sight of Dion. It lowered its head and charged. Zachary dodged around the monster and grabbed Dion's arm, hauling him out of the animal's path. The bear crashed into a thicket as Zachary pointed to light between the trees. Once again they started running, heading for open ground.

Taller by far than a human but also lithe as a sapling, Zachary was panting lightly as he glanced at Dion, whose breath was running ragged.

'This is madness!' Dion gasped. Struggling to keep up the pace, he looked over his shoulder but saw only forest. The undergrowth in this part of the Wilds was thick; the bear could be on them in moments.

'We are trying to feel as the bear does,' Zachary called out. 'We must forget for a time that we stand and talk. This is about feeling wild. Can you feel it? The desire to be an animal. To be strong. To roar. To devour.'

'I feel fear.'

'That is a start, but you must let yourself go.'

The trees finally thinned and gave way to rolling hillside, descending into the base of a wide valley. Crags loomed on both sides and white boulders littered the landscape. The air was warm and fresh; it had rained recently and the wet smell was still in the air. Freed of the forest, the two men ran now with a loping gait rather than a mad sprint and, glancing once more over his shoulder, Dion couldn't see any sign of pursuit.

'Wait.' He coughed, slowing his run to a jog, and then stopping altogether. A searing pain clutched at his chest as he placed his hands on his hips, bending forward. Finally he swallowed and then coughed again, before he felt able to speak. 'I think we've lost it.'

'I know where the bear is,' Zachary said, 'and the direction of its travel.' His gold-flecked eyes swept the valley, his vision taking in not just the forest they'd emerged from, but also the cliffs and distant groves of evergreens, before finally alighting on the gorge at the valley's base. He then turned back to Dion. 'I can feel it. Can you?'

Dion closed his eyes and tried to focus his mind on the bear.

'I have told you, young Dion, closing your eyes does nothing,' Zachary said; the tone of his voice was amused.

Dion opened his eyes again and tried to sense the bear, but he didn't know exactly what it was he was supposed to be feeling. He reminded himself of the lessons he'd already received from Zachary, thinking about hunger and warmth and territorial pride. He was the bear, the bear was him. He had chased off the invaders and would now . . .

'I think I can feel it,' Dion said. 'It's heading . . .' He pointed to the winding gorge. 'There.'

'It has given up the pursuit and now returns to its lair.' Zachary nodded. 'Go. Find it. I will wait here.'

'But . . .' Dion faltered. 'What do I do when I find it?'

'You will awaken the beast inside you,' Zachary said.

'And if I don't?'

'If you don't, the bear will perhaps leave you alone. Or he will attack you and you will die.' Zachary smiled. 'Now go.'

Dion walked alone, heading farther down the valley as he descended toward the gorge that followed its base, carved long ago by the patient action of water. He tried again to sense the bear but he wasn't sure that he'd even sensed it the last time. Perhaps he'd simply used logic – definitely a trait valued by his human heritage – to determine what the bear would do next and where a likely place for its lair might be. He had hunted with his father and older brother, back when he'd had a family and a home. Perhaps rather than employing the magical ability of an eldran to sense life beyond sight, he was simply using forest lore.

As he approached the gorge he could see that it forked multiple times and then rejoined, before opening up in a part deeper and wider than the rest. He saw caves, and then in the distance a gentle slope rose and climbed to the area of the forest. The river that flowed along the gorge's bottom had dried up long ago, leaving a bed of smooth round stones. Scanning the area, he saw a place where the cliff was broken and provided a steep slope of rubble all the way to the base. He knew he would need to be careful not to become muddled in the maze-like canyon.

He headed to the slope and began to inch his way down.

It took some time, but he reached the old riverbed and started to walk with caution. The first time the canyon split, he realized he was going to have to pick a direction, and then not long after he chose the left path it diverged again.

Forest lore was no use in navigating a maze. He wondered if Zachary had chosen this task in order to truly test his ability to sense the animal. Despite what the eldran had said, Dion closed his eyes at the next fork. He tried to become the bear in every way.

Left. He should head left.

He'd now been walking for long enough that he knew he should soon be coming to the section of caves. Wearing just deerskin leggings, with no bow or spear and Zachary far away, he approached warily. His heart hammered in his chest as he kicked a stone, the sound bouncing around the canyon. If the bear was ahead, it would hear him.

The cliffs on both sides now pressed together, close enough at some places that he had to turn his body to the side to shuffle through. The rays of the sun were blocked, darkening the area in shadow. He felt like an intruder in another's domain, his heart pounding faster and faster, fearful at every turn, worried about what was around the next bend.

Zachary had said he should be able to sense the bear, but Zachary had never known a half-breed like Dion before. What if Zachary was wrong?

He came to another fork.

Dion didn't dare close his eyes. He stood and waited, thinking of the two options. Should he go left or right?

He tensed when he heard a sound. Poised, ready for flight, he looked at the path that headed left. He could definitely hear panting, the hoarse breathing of a beast. Each inhalation was a long exercise, rumbling and throaty. Each exhale was a groan. Something big and bulky moved.

He swallowed.

The only safe route was back the way he'd come. But he had promised himself that he would follow Zachary's guidance. He'd been cast out of the life he'd known and welcomed into Zachary's fold: he had no other place to go. If this was a test of his bravery, he would not fail it.

He took two steps forward, and then three. The thin gully curved, and he followed the curve as the panting and groaning grew louder and louder. More stones kicked from his feet and bounced off the walls, making him wince.

Then he heard a rasping roar. It was different in nature to the bear's roar in the forest. He bent down and picked up a stone the size of his fist. Summoning his courage, he continued along the path.

He rounded a knob, and saw that the passage came to an end. The gully terminated in a cul-de-sac, and Zachary stood waiting for him. He was in his normal form, but Dion knew that a moment ago he had been changed.

The eldran saw the rock in Dion's hand and shook his head. 'You were not listening to your abilities. You were too focused on your human senses. In the other direction the bear was waiting. You heard me, rather than sensing the bear. Couldn't you feel it?'

Dion dropped the rock. 'The truth is I can't feel anything.'

'You knew where to find the beast's lair.'

'I didn't feel that, Zachary. I deduced it. I didn't sense anything at all.'

Zachary shook his head. 'Even now?' His eyes drifted past Dion's shoulder. 'You can't sense it now?'

Dion whirled.

The brown bear was a blur, bellowing as it lunged at him. Dion knew what he was supposed to do. He willed himself to become a giant. A mighty, strong, indomitable giant. Three times the height of a man, with arms the thickness of a man's waist. Legs the size of tree trunks . . .

Nothing happened. Dion waited for the bear to knock him down, its jaws to close over his face.

A huge hand swatted him to the side as a tall giant with a crescent scar on its cheek loomed over the bear and roared, every element of posture threatening to the creature that was tiny in comparison. The bear quailed like a child cowering under his father's fist. With a strange yelp it turned on its tail and ran.

Mist clouded the giant, shimmering and then clearing to reveal Zachary once again in his normal form.

The eldran sighed. 'It will come. I thought the bear's attack might prompt it, but it will come.'

Dion's voice was bitter. 'No. It won't.'

'It will. You changed before. You can change again. Remember, Dion. The magic of an eldran is in the mist. The mist claims us, clothing and all. Fears and all. We must become wild to become something more, and then we must fight becoming wild with everything we have.'

'I don't sense anything, and I don't feel the things you're saying I should.' Dion looked down at his bare chest and deerskin leggings; the clothing still didn't feel right on him. 'I appreciate what you're trying to do, but maybe my place isn't in the Village. The others aren't as accepting as you are.'

'You just need to embrace who you are, rather than fight it. You changed before. You felt another's need and you brought out the ability in yourself.'

'But I've never changed again.' Dion was staring at the ground as he spoke. He felt lost. In the land of the humans, in Xanthos, the city of his birth, he'd been rejected for changing his form. In the Wilds, living with a strange race, he was different because he couldn't repeat the feat.

'You will,' Zachary said. 'You just need to understand yourself, to embrace who you are. You need to love yourself, as much as you love her.'

40

Dion's head shot up. 'What did you just say?'

'I speak of Chloe, of course. For you to sense her need so strongly, to change your very shape to save her life, your love for her must be strong. It is like this between Aella and me. The bonds of love are felt more keenly by eldren than by humans, at least in my experience. Perhaps that is the wrong way to say it,' Zachary mused.

Dion's eyes narrowed. 'Zachary. Listen to me. Chloe is marrying Nikolas. Where I come from you can't say these things.'

Zachary shrugged. 'She does not love your brother.'

'Listen to me!' Dion drew in a deep breath. It still hurt to think of his older brother marrying Chloe. Something had grown between them when they'd traveled together from Lamara, but he knew he now needed to forget they'd ever met. 'I don't need to be spoken to like one of the younglings in the Village. I am a man. I use arrows with iron heads. I grew up in a palace made of stone. I don't have feelings for another man's betrothed.'

Zachary's ancient face curled in puzzlement. 'I think I understand,' he said. 'It is true, I am not familiar with human ways. I apologize for any offense.'

'There's no need to apologize,' Dion said wearily. 'I just don't want to hear any more about Chloe.'

Zachary nodded. 'I think we have done all we can today. There are matters I must attend to in the Village. It will be well, young Dion. You will see.'

5

Feeling a sudden lifting of her spirits at the sensation of being in the Wilds, far from the bustling city that was her home, Chloe dismounted and tied her horse at the bottom of a thin trail. Inhaling, breathing in deep lungfuls of the fragrant air, she followed the trail as it entered sparse woodlands. The sounds and sights of the region filled her senses: distant waterfalls gurgled; bright butterflies fluttered among the swaying evergreens.

She continued along the path as it wound over hills and entered thick forest before the trees began to thin. Finally exiting the forest, emerging onto a grassy knoll, she paused to get her bearings.

The woodland trail had been easy to follow but there were few travelers between the Wilds and the Galean nations, which meant that the field of lush grass ahead didn't show any worn patches at all. A distant river curled back and forth like an endless snake, girded by green banks on both sides. The hill on which Chloe stood undulated like bunched carpet, descending slowly as it rippled, before finally dropping all the way to the water.

She nodded to herself. It had been a while since she'd last visited, but the Village was somewhere ahead, farther upstream on the river's other side. No doubt an eldran would challenge her when she neared.

Resuming her journey, she descended the grassy hill, reaching the flowing water, and began to follow the bank. As she walked, the bank grew higher and the water slower and deeper, and then, as she glanced ahead and to her right, she saw an island in the middle of the river.

The grassy island, a hundred paces long, was only accessible across a fallen log that stretched from the crumbling riverbank, forming a kind of bridge. Closer to Chloe, the island had a steep, graveled bank, while at the far end the water lapped against the gentle shore near a large, solitary tree.

As she approached, Chloe suddenly stopped in her tracks.

A sandy-haired, bare-chested man in deerskin leggings stood near the center of the island, holding a bow. She might have noticed him before, but he was quite still and wore little in the way of clothing, a creature to match the Wilds. Despite the fact that he had his back to her, she recognized him in an instant. She felt her heart rate increase.

Dion was shooting arrows. He stood facing the broad tree, taking careful aim and then releasing. Chloe watched him at practice, feeling a mixture of emotions ranging from trepidation to tenderness. She could see half of his back and his face in profile. He was frowning in concentration, his posture somehow angry. He was shooting arrows in the same way that a man kicks a dog, throws furniture to the ground, or drinks jug after jug of wine. He was upset.

Chloe saw that he wasn't just shooting at the wide trunk, he was aiming for a black discoloration in the pale wood the size of her palm. He bent down, picked up an arrow from the cluster at his feet, nocked the shaft to the string of his bow, then in one smooth movement drew the string to his cheek. The muscles in his arm bunched as he held the position for the briefest instant, sighting along the arrow shaft. He fired, and yet another arrow sank into the tree trunk, joining a circle of other shafts embedded in the dark area. He immediately crouched to fetch one more, making no sound of pleasure or acknowledgement at the fact that he had struck an impossible target at more than sixty paces.

He was lost in concentration, so rather than calling out from across the river, she decided to use the fallen log to cross to the island. Hoisting herself up, she stepped gracefully along the log until in just a few moments she was halfway across. The riverbank was taller than the island, so with every step she was losing height. She glanced at the water below; it was slow-moving, deep enough that she couldn't see the bottom.

Chloe kept her eyes on Dion as she drew nearer. She had seen bare-chested men before, but she'd never been so fascinated by the play of muscles on a man's back. He was tanned and lean, clean-shaven and square-jawed. He was opposite to his brother, the man she was destined to marry, in every way.

So suddenly that it shocked her, Dion whirled.

He roared a challenge, his arrow suddenly pointed directly at her. His expression was murderous. The bow creaked. Deadly power was about to be unleashed.

Chloe's arms waved at the air, searching for something to grab hold of. She slipped.

———

This was Dion's special place, his alone. He came here when he wanted to be away from the Village, and away from the eldren who lived there. When he was hot he would swim, and when he was frustrated he would shoot arrows.

His old life was gone, yet this new life felt wrong in every way. All the talk of wildness made him feel even more out of control. This focusing of his concentration and release of sudden energy calmed him.

He even perversely liked the fact that the sharp arrow points were made of iron. The eldren didn't like him to keep them in the Village – even being close to metal made them uncomfortable – so when he wasn't hunting he kept his bow and arrows in a sheltered hollow in the base of the tree. Humans felt an innate passion for metal; it invoked completely opposite sensations in eldren. Dion had always struggled with steel swords and shields, but he sometimes sat and sharpened an iron arrowhead with a stone. There was no pain when he did, no sense of distaste. He couldn't do all a human could, and he couldn't harness all the abilities of an eldran, but he could do some things in both worlds.

Picking up yet another arrow, nocking and drawing, he sighted along the shaft and tried to find an empty space in the cluster of its kin where he could make his strike. Despite Zachary's teaching, he didn't want to lose his skill with a bow, and if anything he was better now than he'd ever been. Dion was worried that if the eldren under Zachary ever came into conflict again with Triton, he would be useless, unable to help in any way. The Village had guardians – like Eiric, Zachary's son, and Jonas, a powerful warrior – but every member of the group was expected to do his part.

Thinking of forthcoming conflict, Dion spied movement out of the corner of his eye. A figure, dressed in yellow or perhaps the tan color of deerskin, was creeping across the log that led to the island.

Already tensed, mentally prepared for battle, he whirled.

He roared a shout of challenge. But with stunned surprise he realized he was aiming his bow at Chloe, dressed in a pale yellow chiton, not creeping across but so shocked by his cry that she was suddenly struggling to keep her footing. Her brown eyes went wide.

Chloe's hands waved vainly against empty air. Staggering as if he'd actually struck her, she slipped. Her body tumbled and then she hit the surface of the river with an ungainly splash.

'Chloe!'

Shaking himself into action, filled with panic, Dion dropped his bow and began to run. Images flashed through his mind as he remembered their time together, fleeing Lamara, sailing across the Maltherean Sea, fighting storms and bailing water, leaving the *Calypso* behind at Cinder Fen, and the savagery of the battle to save Phalesia and the golden ark. He plunged into the shallows, searching the river in desperation. He hadn't seen her swim . . . But surely a Phalesian princess could swim?

Moving swiftly, he clambered over a flat rock to reach the deeper water. He prepared to dive in when Chloe's head popped to the surface and she opened her mouth to gasp in a lungful of air. He instead crouched on the rock and leaned out, holding out a hand. She reached up and gripped tightly, her face filled with terror.

In an instant her expression shifted to narrowed focus and fierce determination. She yanked hard, pulling with surprising strength. Dion tried to resist but, caught off-balance, he toppled into the river head first.

For a moment everything was cool water and darkness. Feeling gravel under his feet, he kicked to bring his head back to the surface. But he felt strong hands take hold of his shoulders and press down. He spluttered and fought, kicking at the riverbed again.

Finally, she let him rise to the surface.

After drawing in a breath he met her eyes, too taken aback to know what to say. Her legs kicked as she trod water; Dion's feet could just touch the bottom but it was too deep for her, so she still had her hands on his shoulders.

Chloe's face was just inches from his, and although her eyes were still narrowed, their brown color was soft, and they were large eyes. Her arched, upturned nose still gave her an imperious, proud air. Her wide mouth pursed as her red lips parted.

'Cold, isn't it?' she said, scowling.

Dion steadied his legs so that he was supporting them both. He took her hands and pried them away from their dangerous proximity to his throat.

'What are you doing here?' he asked. 'I almost shot you.'

The contact between Dion's hands and hers was electric. For an instant he didn't know where he was, only that he was holding the hands of a beautiful woman. Chloe was panting, her chest rising and falling with every breath. Dion knew that just below the surface there was only a thin, sodden garment, wrapped loosely around her body, separating the two of them.

'Yes, you did,' she replied. '*You* almost shot *me*. And now look at us.'

'Are you . . . Did you come here to see me?'

'What makes you think I would come to see you? I've known Zachary since I was a child. You don't think I might have my own reasons for visiting?'

Despite his conversation with Zachary, he was surprised at how disappointed he felt. 'Fair enough.' He still held her hands. Seeing her glare, he was vaguely worried that she planned to strike him. He frowned. 'Does Nikolas know you're here?'

'What does it matter?' Chloe lifted her chin. Her voice shook with suppressed emotion. 'Is he all you care about? After what he did to you?'

'You know I care about you.' The words were out of his mouth before he knew what he was saying. But rather than turn her nose up at him, Chloe's face softened.

'Dion . . .' She said his name slowly. 'Since I last saw you . . .' She faltered and then tried again. 'I don't care what you are,' she murmured, so low that if her face hadn't been inches from his he wouldn't have heard her. 'The Oracle said I would fear you, and I did, but I don't anymore.'

Dion's face moved forward. He felt like he could hardly breathe. In a haze he released her hands, but only to pull her closer. Her legs curled around him; he was now supporting her entire weight. One of his arms traveled down her back, curling around her narrow waist, while the other supported the back of her head. His hand on her waist felt the curve of her hip and then traveled along her leg, feeling the bare skin of her thigh. Her arms went around his neck.

Before he knew what was happening, Dion's lips were on hers. If the contact before had been electric, the kiss was the most intense sensation he'd ever felt. He lost track of where he was and even who he was. He only knew that what he was doing was right. Time stretched out; every thought vanished into oblivion.

After an eternity they broke the kiss, smiling, lowering eyes and then lifting them, bodies pressed tightly in the water, each looking into the other's face. He knew he would never tire of examining her features. Her dark hair was piled high on her head, wet through but styled and pinned in a fashion he'd never seen on her before.

Dion's smile slowly faded.

Remembrance thrust itself forcefully into his consciousness. With a sudden sense of horror, he realized why her hair was arranged the way it was. She no longer wore it free, cascading down her back. She was a woman betrothed to another man. And that man was someone he had known his entire life.

'No!' Dion gasped. He shook his head violently. 'You're marrying my brother!'

She swallowed, wet material floating around her as he disentangled her arms, pushing her away and turning his back, not trusting himself to look at her. Soon he heard sounds of swimming and then the rush of water as she left the river and climbed up onto the bank.

Turning, he saw that she was standing with her back to him in her wet chiton, in the middle of the grassy area where he'd been firing arrows. He made his own exit and came up to stand behind her.

He realized she was crying.

'Come back with me,' she said. 'You don't have to go to Xanthos. Come to Phalesia.'

He drew in a deep breath; even now he wanted to take hold of her. 'I can't go back with you. This is the way things have to be. It's better if we forget each other.'

'Your brother rejects you. I know what he did. I know he sent a messenger here, telling you not to return.'

'That is his choice. He is the king.'

'Why do you support him? What about your choice?' Her voice firmed; she spoke bitterly. 'Or my choice, for that matter. My life is cursed.' Her shoulders shook. 'For now, I still have my father and my sister. I still have my home. But when I . . . When I marry him, I will lose everything.'

Dion spoke softly; he wished he wasn't speaking to her back. 'Why are you here? What is the situation in Phalesia? Are you safe?'

She gathered the folds of her garment, checking them before turning around to face him once more. Her eyes were slightly red, but her strength had returned.

'I need to see Zachary. That's why I came here. I have to talk to him about the ark. Nikolas wants to move the horn to an iron box and melt the gold, using the money for the navy.'

'I suppose that makes sense.'

'But why put it in gold if it doesn't need to be? Why did the Aleutheans place it in such a valuable container?'

'I can't answer you,' Dion said. 'You're right, you need to speak to Zachary. They say Aleuthea sank beneath the waves. So why didn't the ark sink with it? It's likely something Zachary can't answer. But something tells me we need to know.'

'Will you come with me? Just as far as the Village?'

'Chloe . . .' Dion hesitated. His heart was still pounding in his chest. She was his brother's betrothed, he had to keep reminding himself. His mind was in turmoil, thoughts conflicting. A moment ago he'd been worried that his place wasn't with the eldren, and now her arrival had made him even more confused. 'I think I should stay here.' Then a rustle of leaves made him look up. Despite himself, he smiled. 'But I might know someone who can guide you.'

As he fixed his sights on a thicket at the top of the riverbank, he heard Chloe exclaim when she also saw the young eldran woman's face, merged with the brush so she was difficult to make out.

Dion called, 'I can see you, Liana.'

The eldran's face became startled and she looked like she might flee, but she left her hiding place and walked out into the open. She was slight, short for her race but pretty, with a heart-shaped face and shoulder-length silver hair that fell in front of her eyes.

'Come with me.' Dion took Chloe by the hand.

6

As she often did, Liana had been watching Dion. She found him fascinating. It wasn't that he was handsome, like Zachary's son Eiric, or imposing, like the warrior Jonas. Dion was like her: he couldn't change.

Maybe if he learned, he could tell her how to change. Perhaps he could show her how not to be so afraid.

She thought she'd been silent, as only an eldran could be, but she knew she'd been caught when he called out her name and looked directly at her. She left the bush she'd been peeking through and sheepishly showed herself, but neither Dion nor the young human woman with him seemed angry. Following the high bank, Liana approached the end of the fallen log as Dion assisted the dark-haired woman across.

Liana heard Dion murmur something to his companion. 'Be gentle with her, she's an orphan. Both her parents were lost to wildness in the battle. Zachary and Aella care for her now.' He then smiled warmly when he neared. 'Liana,' he said. 'This is Chloe.'

'It's a pleasure to meet you, Liana,' Chloe said with a gentle smile.

Liana had thought that Chloe's wide mouth and upturned nose made her look a little haughty, but when she smiled it transformed her face. Liana said the first thing that came into her head.

'You are very beautiful when you smile.'

Chloe's smile broadened. 'That's kind of you to say. How old are you, Liana?'

'I am no longer a youngling.' Liana scowled.

'Chloe,' Dion said. 'Eldren are long-lived and don't commonly discuss the age of adults.'

'Oh,' Chloe said. 'I apologize.'

He grinned. 'Liana is young, though, so you can be forgiven. Not too long ago she was a youngling, and every birthday was celebrated with a feast.'

'When winter comes I will have nineteen years,' Liana said, lifting her chin.

Chloe made a sound of surprise. 'We're close to the same age, then.'

Liana was also surprised. Chloe carried herself in a way that made her think she was much older than she was.

A shadow suddenly crossed Dion's face. 'How long were you watching us?'

Color came to Chloe's cheeks.

'Not long,' Liana said.

They both looked relieved. Dion spoke again. 'Liana, Chloe needs to find Zachary. Can you help her?'

Liana tilted her head and then nodded. 'Yes.'

Chloe then went to say something to Dion, but he forestalled her, holding up a hand. His next words made the human woman's face fall.

'Chloe,' he said softly but firmly. 'This is the last time we will meet.'

'The last . . . ?'

'We live in different worlds now. The next time your father wants to speak with Zachary, tell him to send someone else. I think it best we don't see each other again.'

After leading Chloe back to her horse to get fresh clothing, Liana took her to the Village. They traveled through the woodlands and the region of grassy hills where the river snaked back and forth, Liana setting a swift pace as she and Chloe asked each other questions.

'Do you know Dion well?' Liana asked.

Chloe pushed a branch out of the way; she was lumbering through the forest like a bear, although Liana decided against saying anything.

'I . . . I suppose I do.' Chloe looked sad. 'Perhaps I know him better than anyone.'

'How did he manage to live among so many humans?'

Chloe took some time to answer, making Liana look at her with open curiosity. What was so difficult about the question?

'He didn't find it difficult at all. He said he found it difficult to carry and use steel weapons, and at the time he didn't know why. But there is a lot of variation in the way we live, and what we do. He found his place as a sailor and trader. He could use his bow to hunt and fight in battle.'

'That weapon frightens me.' Liana shuddered. 'I am glad he keeps it outside the Village.'

'You don't have bows?' Chloe asked, surprised. 'Arrows don't have to have iron heads.'

'Why would we?' Liana shrugged. 'As ogres and giants sometimes spears and clubs are used, but a bow is too fragile, too complex, for a giant.'

'So you rely on changing, even to eat?'

'Yes,' Liana said bitterly.

They crossed the river at a ford, where the water only reached their ankles and they were able to hop from stone to stone. Traveling uphill again now, Liana glanced at Chloe when the human woman spoke again.

'Dion said you lost your parents, in the fight to save my city. I'm sorry, Liana. I'm sorry for your loss.'

'It wasn't your fault,' Liana said. 'They didn't change back in time.'

'It's a dangerous thing, changing.'

Liana suddenly rounded on Chloe. 'Yes, he told you, but that doesn't mean I want to talk about it. It is certainly nothing you can help me with.'

Chloe's brow furrowed. 'I don't understand.'

'I can't change. I try, but I am too afraid.'

'I didn't know,' Chloe said softly. 'You're right, I don't understand. There are a lot of differences between your people and mine. But perhaps by talking, we can learn a little more, and bridge the differences.'

'Enough,' Liana said, turning away. 'We're nearly there. I don't want to talk anymore.'

———

It had no other name than the Village, and it had never needed one. More than sixty houses framed both sides of the dirt thoroughfare and bisecting lanes, filling the low ground between two hills where there was an immense clearing with a floor of brown soil and dried leaves. The surrounding trees were ancient and tall, but also spaced far apart, giving the eldren enough space for their settlement to grow. With no stone used in its construction, it looked like part of the surrounding forest, and in the vast region of the Wilds the Village was impossible to find if one was unfamiliar with the way.

Each house took years to form, but eldren were a patient people, with close family ties, and as younglings became adults there was never a rush to get children settled in new homes of their own. When a man and woman married, the community came together to plant a cluster of willow trees in a circle. As the saplings grew, their thin trunks and branches were bent forward over a period of time. Tied together in the center of the circle, the growing trees now formed a roof. A gap in the initial planting made for an entrance. Thin green branches soon threaded in and out of the walls horizontally. Everything became thick with foliage.

At this juncture Zachary and Aella, as village leaders, bored holes in the trunks of the trees planted years before. They drained the sap to kill the willows, for if they kept growing the house would become misshapen. The green trees, branches, and leaves became dry. The structure, now twelve feet tall at the apex, was complete.

Weddings were celebrated, but when a house dried out and the excited couple moved into their finished home, the entire village feasted for a week. Every part of the couple's new life was a joyous occasion, from the first sharing of a blanket at night, to the first morning's waking to the sound of birds and insects.

'Have you been here before?' Liana asked, glancing at Chloe as they approached.

'Yes,' Chloe said. 'A few times.' She smiled ruefully. 'It rained, the last time.'

Liana gave her own ghost of a smile. 'They say you humans like to keep out all moisture, and you don't like dirt in your homes.'

Chloe's eyes sparkled with mirth. 'Correct in every way.'

'Our legends say that in Sindara we didn't have houses at all. As one people we slept on the grass and when it rained we became wet and when it was sunny we moved to the shade.'

The trail took them between the first two houses, and then they were in the Village. The entrances to the houses were wide open; there were no doors and, looking back at Chloe, Liana saw her glancing inside at the wooden stools and beds of animal skin slung on timber frames. Fires burned at some of the intersections, smoke trickling up in wriggling streams. Silver-haired men and women sat around the fires, attending to one task or another: skinning rabbits, stitching clothing, cooking, and weaving. At the settlement's far end half a dozen eldren were working on a new house.

'And it's all done without metal,' Chloe murmured. 'Still, it must be difficult for Dion, living here with your people.'

'His people,' Liana said sharply. Regretting it immediately, she softened her tone. 'Zachary tells us we must do everything we can to make him feel like one of us.'

'But he isn't. He's half human, raised by humans. You can't make him be something he's not.' Liana saw Chloe gazing around the Village as if seeing it with new eyes. 'Does he share a house with you?'

'No,' Liana said. 'He prefers to live alone. We lost many of our number in the battle. There was no issue giving him an empty house.'

'You see? He's struggling—'

Liana scowled. 'What else would you have Zachary do? He is a good man, and he was close to Dion's mother. Dion lost everything. He almost turned wild.'

Chloe's eyes widened as she stared at Liana.

'Perhaps I should not have told you, but it is the truth. He was close to turning, on the very edge, about to become a vicious wildran, a black dragon roaming the skies, eating livestock and destroying human lives. Devouring even children.' Liana shuddered. 'Your distrust of our people drove him to us. And we are all he has.'

'I didn't drive him away—'

Liana pointed out a nearby house, close to the middle of the Village but no different from any of the others. 'We are here. Zachary is inside.'

Zachary came to the entrance as they approached. He stepped forward and smiled, crouching slightly, opening his arms. Chloe came forward, closing her eyes and entering his embrace. He held her for a long time, stroking her hair and saying nothing.

Liana felt a flash of jealousy; after the loss of her parents, Zachary had taken her in, and he was now the closest thing she had to a father.

'And you, little one.' Zachary turned to her, his smile broadening.

'I am no youngling,' Liana said. 'I don't need a hug.'

'We all need hugs sometimes.'

Liana shook her head, crossing her arms in front of her chest. Zachary gave a small sigh and turned back to the interior of the house. 'Aella,' he called. 'Look who it is.'

An older eldran woman exited the structure, coming to stand so near to Zachary that it was obvious how close they were. Willowy and graceful, with glossy silver-white hair and eyes of gold and emerald, Aella smiled at Chloe, causing crinkles to form at the edges of her eyes.

'Welcome, Chloe of Phalesia. I am making mint tea. Would you like some?' As Chloe vanished inside, their voices drifted away.

Liana was about to leave but then she had a sudden thought. She wanted to learn more about the humans, about Chloe but particularly about Dion. Zachary might sense her nearby, but he would be distracted.

She scanned the area and decided that no one was looking at her.

Moving quickly, she circled around to the back of the house and crouched down near the wall of branches, head cocked as she listened.

'. . . talk to you about the ark.'

'The ark?' Liana recognized Aella's soft voice. 'Is there danger?'

'Nothing immediate,' Chloe said. 'But we don't understand it, and although we know it wasn't made by your people – far from it – we think you might know more about it than we do.'

'What is it you wish to know?' Zachary asked.

'The fact that it's made of gold brings trouble,' Chloe said. 'Humans . . . We value gold above all other metals.'

'We know this,' Aella said wryly.

'The new king of Xanthos believes that we still have many dangers to face. Triton wants what's inside the ark, and although we have our walls, an attack could come in many forms.'

'That is regrettably true,' Zachary said.

'There's also the risk of the Ileans returning. With their king dead they might have bigger concerns than vengeance, but at some point they will want to show the world they are still the strongest nation on the Maltherean Sea.'

'I understand,' said Zachary. 'But I am not certain if there is much we can do here. We helped you the last time, but we have no wish to be drawn into years of fighting and turmoil. We just want to be left alone.'

'I'm not asking for you to fight again. I only came for knowledge, the answer to a specific question. King Nikolas says—'

'He is to be your husband, is he not?' Aella asked.

Liana put a hand to her mouth as her eyes went wide. She had seen enough, when she had been watching Dion and Chloe. Enough to know the truth.

'Yes, he is . . .' Chloe murmured, her voice trailing off. There was a moment of quiet before she spoke again, her voice strengthening. 'King Nikolas says that we need to prepare for these dangers, and that to do so we need gold.'

'Ahh,' Zachary said. 'He wants the ark.'

'I've come to ask: is that safe? Surely there's a reason that the horn is kept inside gold, rather than another metal? Would it be dangerous to move it to a different chest, perhaps one made of iron? Eldren also can't touch iron. It should be safe, shouldn't it?'

There was a pause, and Liana pictured Chloe and Aella, both watching Zachary and waiting for him to speak. Zachary was pensive for a long time. Finally his voice broke the silence.

'Many have forgotten this, but long ago, magic was much more prevalent in the world than it is today. We eldren have always possessed the ability to change our form, but you humans also had your own power, linked to the four metals, iron, copper, silver, and gold. During the war between Aleuthea and Sindara, magic was used on both sides, with devastating effect.'

'Humans had magic?' Chloe sounded surprised.

'Yes, my dear,' Zachary replied. 'The knowledge was lost, along with Aleuthea.' His voice became reflective. 'I suppose it is possible that some descendants of Aleuthea remain.' Liana could picture him shrugging. 'But no matter, in these lands, even your magi don't remember, although the metals are so often seen in your ceremonies and in the necklaces you wear around your necks. And of the four metals, one in particular is the most durable, able to outlast any other, and survive even submersion in the sea.'

'Gold,' Chloe said.

'Yes, gold. The ark is the work of the sorcerers of Aleuthea, and they chose to make it from gold. But if the purpose is to prevent an eldran from coming near, then any other of the three metals will suffice.'

'So . . .'

'Tell Nikolas and your father they need not concern themselves,' Zachary said. 'Provided they move the horn to a container of pure iron, there is no danger.'

Chloe let out a breath. 'You're certain?'

'Have you ever known him to lie?' Aella asked.

'No,' Chloe replied. 'This is good. I will tell my father. Thank you, Zachary. And you too, Aella.'

'We did nothing, Chloe of Phalesia. And know that you are always welcome here,' Aella said. 'How is he, your father?'

'Well enough,' Chloe said, in a way that told Liana there were things she didn't want to go into. 'He still wants to give you a gift, something, anything, to show his appreciation—'

'We fought for ourselves,' Zachary said. 'We have no wish to be subservient to one such as Triton.'

'And may I ask about the preparations for your wedding?' Aella asked. 'Are you at least excited for the day?'

Another silence grew; this one was uncomfortable. 'I must do what I must do,' Chloe said.

'Seeing your heartache makes me sad,' Aella said. 'If I could wish anything on you, it would be the love I share with my husband. Please, stay longer. At least spend some time with Dion.'

'No . . . I can't.' Chloe sounded downcast. 'I . . . I need to tell my father what you've said. I must go.'

Chloe said her farewells and then left the house. Liana started to rise from her crouched position but then she heard Aella speak again, this time saying something that shocked her to the core.

'You lied to her.'

'I had to.' Zachary's voice was filled with regret.

'Zachary, why?'

'You heard her. Humans desire gold with a hunger that we will never comprehend. It did not matter what I said, the ark would still be melted, and the horn would still be moved.'

'Then what will happen when they move it to iron?'

'The humans have forgotten the magic of Aleuthea, but I still remember the things my father told me, knowledge he obtained first hand in the relentless fighting. The four materia all have different properties . . . different powers. Drawing on those powers causes the metal to tarnish, eventually corroding and becoming dust. But of the four, gold is unique. Gold does not tarnish. The horn is powerful, and containing its power saps the energy of its container. The ancient Aleutheans built a golden ark for a reason.'

Liana tilted her head, brow furrowing. She heard Aella gasp.

'Then what do we do?'

'They were willing to leave the ark alone for as long as they thought it was sacred to their gods. But now that they know the truth, nothing will prevent them from claiming the gold it is made of.' Zachary sighed. 'We have no other choice. We will have to take the horn.'

'But if it is contained in a chest of iron . . .'

'The iron will rust.'

Aella made a sound of realization. 'So we have to take it before Triton does.'

'Exactly.'

'And what do we do with it? Will you . . . Do you want to be king?'

Zachary barked a laugh. 'Not at all. Even if I did, I do not have the blood of Marrix and the horn would never respond to me. I prefer a simple life. This life. The life we share together.'

'You know that our son . . .'

'Yes, I do.'

'We would have to hide it.'

'From everyone.'

'This plan frightens me,' Aella whispered.

'We stay out of trouble,' Zachary said firmly. 'That is what we do.'

'We aren't prepared for war . . .'

'Don't worry about Triton, my love. Our home is hidden. Our warriors protect us.'

'Jonas . . . Have you found him?'

'No. Not yet. I will continue my search tomorrow. Until then, we have another to discuss.'

'Husband, I know you worry, but Liana is one eldran you should not concern yourself with. Let her be. Give her time. What she needs is to forget about changing and fighting.'

Hearing herself discussed, Liana listened as hard as she could, eager to catch every word.

'But changing is a part of us . . .'

'Yes, but not the whole. I've made a decision. I am going to teach her the healing arts. She is wiser than you give her credit for, and the Village could use her help.'

The smile was evident in Zachary's voice. 'A healer?'

Liana felt a thrill course through her. Aella was the most skilled healer in the Village, and Liana was immediately excited at the idea of spending so much time with her. Together they would explore the forest for herbs, barks, and mosses, and eventually Liana would be useful to the others without taking part in the fierce hunting.

But then Liana jumped when a male voice spoke from directly behind her.

'What are you doing?'

Whirling, she saw Eiric, Zachary's son, frowning and looking down at her. As tall as Zachary but with broader shoulders, he would never be able to pass himself off as human, for his skin was so white it was nearly translucent, and his irises were solid gold, the color of honey. He had close-cropped silver hair crowning a narrow face, with a hawk-like nose and a jaw like a knife. Undeniably handsome, his head was tilted, a puzzled expression on his face as he regarded her.

Liana rose from her crouch, guilt written across her face. Eiric would know exactly what she'd been doing.

He hadn't spoken loudly, however, and Liana's main priority was that Zachary wouldn't hear.

'Shh,' Liana hissed. She took hold of Eiric's upper arm and dragged him away from the house, heading into the trees until they were far enough from the Village that she could speak freely.

'Well?' Eiric asked.

'I was . . . I was . . . listening.'

'Why?'

Liana said the first thing that came into her head, which was her initial reason for eavesdropping. 'The princess, Chloe, visited Zachary. I wanted to learn more about the humans.'

'To what end?'

'Because I was worried that if I ever had to leave here, there's no other place I could go.' Flustered, the words were out before Liana could take them back. She put a hand over her mouth, looking down and then glancing at Eiric, waiting for his reaction.

'Liana,' Eiric said. He sighed as he put his hands on her shoulders and turned her around. 'Do you see that house down there? The one you were hiding behind? That is your home too. You don't need to hide to hear what people are saying. You could have joined the conversation with Chloe. Father would have welcomed your presence. You can come and go as you please. You understand that, don't you?'

Liana hung her head. 'I have no one.'

'You have Zachary and Aella. You have me.'

'You don't have to worry about me.'

'We all worry for the ones we care about,' Eiric said with a smile. Crouching, for he was much taller than her, he turned her to face him. He brought up his hand and opened his palm. 'Here, I made this for you. I've been looking for you. I thought you might like to wear it at the next feast.'

Liana saw a leather thong in his hand, with a circle of polished amber threaded through.

'Take it,' Eiric said.

Glancing up at him and then down at the necklace again, Liana picked it up and examined the amber. 'It's beautiful.' She shook her head. 'But I don't deserve this. And I don't want to go to the feast.'

'But you have to,' Eiric protested.

'Why?'

'Because I'm expecting you to dance with me.'

Liana laughed out loud, and realized that it was the first time since she'd lost her parents.

7

The stockade was an ugly structure, a square fort crowning a crumbling rust-red hill. Straddling the high ground for miles in every direction, it had been built in this place rather than another for two reasons. The first was that the summit of the hill was approachable from only one side; in every other direction an approaching force would face steep cliffs. The second reason was that just half a mile away there was a trickling river, which provided a source of drinking water. Water was essential, out in the Waste.

A tall palisade built of stout sharpened logs surrounded the interior on all sides. There was a second wall inside, forming a square within a square, but this interior wall was made of mud brick. The gap between the two walls was a killing ground.

Within the inner wall, misshapen houses leaned against each other haphazardly: eldren were not skilled builders. The houses dissolved when it rained, but fortunately it rained rarely and the occupants cared little for appearances. The fort wasn't built for comfort, or beauty, or even to provide refuge from the baking heat of the constant sun.

The stockade was built for defense. And it had proven itself, time and time again.

Just half a dozen years earlier, when Solon, the ruler of Ilea, who styled himself the sun king, conquered the thriving port city of Koulis, he had pressed on farther north. Trying to find a route to the Galean continent, his path took him into the Waste.

There, Solon and his army found the eldren. And like the Galeans across the sea, the Ileans possessed memories of the great war fought between the two races.

All wildren were once eldren, and so all eldren should be butchered without remorse.

The Ileans laid siege to the stockade, as humans tended to do, and sent wave after wave of soldiers swarming up the sole approach to the solid fence of spikes. But Solon had never fought eldren before, and it was simple for Triton to lead his warriors out as furies and dragons to descend on the yellow-cloaked soldiers. The eldren could fly away to fetch meat and to drink. Their structure was under siege, but they could come and go as they pleased.

'So why build it at all?' Jonas asked.

Triton looked away from the stockade and fixed his one good eye on the man next to him. Jonas wasn't a small eldran, and he was both experienced and magically strong – Zachary had nominated him to be a guardian of his village for a reason – but compared to Triton all eldren were slight.

They were both standing by the edge of the thin stream, and Jonas's gaze was drawn to the stockade, beyond which a dusty, blood-red plain spread in all directions. Scrubby trees scratched an existence among the lizards and scrawny birds. In the distance, the edge of the dark mountain range surrounding Cinder Fen was hazy against the red horizon. It was an inhospitable place, but Triton knew that it kept his eldren strong. Zachary and those with him were weak, and Jonas, supposedly one of his finest warriors, was proof of that weakness.

Jonas had spiky silver hair, gray eyes flecked with gold, and an incongruously low voice. His eyes were shadowed, the look of a man bearing terrible grief, and he was uncertain of himself, agitated.

He was also hot, wearing deerskin completely unsuited to the climate. Triton was instead bare-chested and wore trousers made of hide. His muscled chest was as tanned as his bald head, where his angular features made the ridges of skull prominent, giving him an intimidating cast he relished.

As time dragged on and Triton's remorseless attention had an effect on his new companion, Jonas broke his gaze and stared down at the ground.

'Why build it?' Triton looked up at the stockade. 'Its purpose is to break our enemies. Humans like to conquer and destroy things. Cities, fortresses, palaces, temples . . . By building it, and holding it, we give them something to attack. They must know that if the fort is about to fall, we can simply leave, flying high in the sky and never returning. Yet they attack nonetheless. They think that losing half their army is the price they must pay . . . that it is worth it to drive us off and to occupy something we took the time to build in the first place. We let them think that. And in the end, when Solon led his army here, it was we who were victorious. So many men died trying to conquer this structure that he was forced to retreat. In truth, seizing a place like this means nothing, nothing at all. Humans don't have wings. They never will.'

'Then how did Solon take you hostage?'

Triton's one good eye flashed. 'That, my friend, is a story for another day.'

Jonas took a breath, perhaps realizing he'd gone too far. 'I shouldn't be here. I should go.'

Triton pointed his finger at Jonas's chest. 'Tell me something, Jonas of the Wilds. What is it you want most?'

'I told you. I want my family back.'

'And you have my promise. They will return to you.'

Triton could see that he almost had him, but Jonas was still dubious. 'And when you sound the horn, what happens then?'

'The wildren will approach, summoned by the horn of Marrix. Your son will be with them, and your wife.'

'But they won't know who I am.'

'No, they won't,' Triton said. 'But I will remind them.'

Jonas wiped at his eyes. 'I want to believe. But Zachary always said that once we are gone, we can never come back to who we were.'

Triton spoke firmly. 'The horn changes that. Zachary is weak. He wants to lead a village of cowering eldren, subservient to the humans in Xanthos and Phalesia, fearful of attack at all times. That is not how I rule. My people are strong. Humans do not dare confront us. It is we who hunt them. Zachary doesn't want the horn because he is afraid. He does not have the blood of Marrix, and so if the horn is recovered, he loses his position.' Triton's voice became low and full of import. 'He is happy to let you suffer.'

Jonas nodded. Triton felt a thrill of victory course through him.

'I will get the horn, and I will sound it,' Triton pronounced. 'Your family will return, and I will bring them back.'

'How can I trust you?'

'Believe my actions. Soon we will depart this place, permanently. Now that the horn has been rediscovered, I am leading my people to Cinder Fen in order to prepare for the reclaiming of our homeland.'

'But how can you be so sure you will get the horn?'

'The gold,' said Triton. 'They won't be able to resist it. They will move the horn. All we need to do is wait until they do, and then, when it is no longer shielded, it will be a simple matter to seize it.'

'What if they don't move the horn?'

'My friend, the difficult part was discovering where it is. Yes, we cannot open a metal container, but there are many possibilities.' He shrugged. 'I find some human couple. I torture the wife while the husband watches. I force the husband and others like him to bring me the horn in return for their women. Don't you see? The horn was lost to us. Now that it has been found, it is just a matter of time.'

'And all you want is the location of the Village?'

'Yes,' Triton said. 'The one who reclaims Sindara must unite all eldren behind him, not just those here in the Waste, but also those in Zachary's thrall. Tell me where I can find the Village, and I promise you, you will see your wife and son once more.'

Jonas slowly nodded.

8

Aristocles walked down a long, winding tunnel. The sloping floor told him he was heading deep into the earth, and the walls of smooth rock glistening with trickling moisture told him he was in a cave.

He frowned. He had no memory of how he'd ended up in this place.

Following the tunnel, footsteps making no sound on the smooth floor, he rounded bend after bend, somehow drawn ever onward. The ceiling was so low his bald crown nearly brushed against it, making him feel the oppressive weight of solid rock, and then, as he pressed on, it was high enough that he moved more freely. He had no sense of the air at all, whether it was dry or moist, redolent of mold or crisp as fresh snow. He felt neither hot nor cold.

Lifting his hand in front of his face, his eyes widened. He could see through his palm; checking the rest of his limbs confirmed it: his body was ethereal, transparent. His sandaled feet appeared ghostly on the floor.

But strangely, the realization wasn't concerning. Instead, the sensation of pulling became stronger. He felt like water being drained from a bath, sliding inexorably down.

He continued to walk along the tunnel, peering around each corner, surprised that he could even see. But rather than becoming darker, a strong light welled from somewhere far ahead. Pushing on, ever on, he turned a final corner and stopped, dazzled by whiteness.

The sudden light was startling, brightest in the center of the broad cavern the tunnel opened onto. It came from a white fire blazing on the stone, burning without embers or fuel. The flames were as high as the hunched figure who sat facing the fire with her back to him.

Aristocles suddenly felt terrified.

The woman had pure white hair cascading down her back, stretching all the way to the ground. She wore a black robe with long sleeves that covered every part of her skin. Staring into the fire, she spoke without turning around.

'Aristocles.' Her sibilant voice hissed, filling the cavern. 'You have prayed for guidance for many hours. Your prayers have brought you here.'

'Where . . . Where am I?' Aristocles stammered. He stood motionless behind the woman, his feet frozen into place.

'That is not the question that is in your heart. We do not have much time. You will not remain here for long, and so I will answer what it is you truly wish to know.'

She paused, drawing in a long, slow breath of air, before speaking as if with great effort.

'My prophecy is thus. If the ark that was built by the ancient Aleutheans is destroyed, the horn will sound.'

She whirled to stare at him, and her face was a grinning skull without flesh.

———

Aristocles' eyes burst open. Scanning wildly, he saw that he was in his villa, lying on his bed, staring up at the wide beams of his bedchamber's ceiling. He had been dreaming, but it was like no other dream he'd ever experienced, for he could remember every detail.

He fought to control his racing heart and gasping breath.

9

A soldier of Nikolas's king's guard, complete with face-hiding helmet and crimson cloak, was waiting for Chloe as soon as she rode through the city gate. Accepting the inevitable, she reined in and dismounted. As he stormed toward her, dark eyes glaring, she couldn't even tell if he was the same man she'd eluded when she left.

Ignoring his approach, Chloe held her horse by the reins, scanning the crowd of hawkers and street urchins thronging the area near the gate, always a hive of activity from the constant comings and goings of traders, farmers, and city folk. She felt relief when she finally saw a youth she knew and called out his name.

The youth saw her and came over. 'Princess?'

'Would you take this horse to Balion? Tell him I'm grateful for all his help.'

He nodded and she handed him the reins. The Xanthian soldier ignored the youth's departure; closing the distance, he gripped Chloe painfully by the arm.

'I am to take you to the king.' He spoke in a low growl.

Chloe opened her mouth but realized there was no purpose in argument. Not long ago, if any man, king or not, had seized her in this way, there would have been a furor. But she was betrothed to Nikolas and he had a claim on her, body and soul. All Chloe could look forward to was the day that Nikolas's duties called him back to Xanthos and the return of her liberty before the wedding itself. Perhaps when Nikolas heard the news that it was safe to move the horn of Marrix, and saw Aristocles making preparations for the golden ark, he would be satisfied and leave.

'Fine,' Chloe said. 'Take me to him.'

The guardsman didn't relinquish his tight grip, forcing Chloe to skip to keep up with him. Seeing a shocked expression on one of the wine merchants manning a stall, a man she knew well, she tried to hide the fact that she was being half dragged across the city. Leading her to the upper quarter, the soldier evidently knew where he would find Nikolas, for he took her directly to the agora.

Soon they were crossing the expansive rectangle and weaving through the crowds as the summer sun shone brightly overhead; the agora was always busy at midday. The temples thronged with worshippers and children played games, hopping from one rose-colored paving stone to another, avoiding the gray stones between. Chloe's stomach rumbled as the sea breeze carried cooking scents from the food stalls.

Nikolas was deep in discussion with Nilus, one of Phalesia's senior consuls and a colleague of Chloe's father. A plump, round-faced man, he had a short crop of neatly trimmed gray hair on his crown and wore a white tunic and belt that matched his gold necklace. Of all the consuls, Nilus had been spending the most time with Nikolas during his visit, becoming a bridge between the king of Xanthos and Phalesia's first consul.

As Chloe and her escort approached the two men standing on the wide marble steps at the side of the agora, away from the bustling crowds in the market, she saw black-bearded Nikolas scowl at something Nilus said. Suddenly imagining herself sharing a bed with him, she forced down a shudder.

She tried to think about him positively, to bring to mind his admirable traits. He was passionate about defending his kingdom, and by association the neighboring nation his future wife belonged to. He was a strong warrior; the soldiers said that not a man among them could best him in combat. The savage deaths of his wife and son had affected him deeply; he wasn't without a heart. He lived in a palace that was far grander than the villa where Chloe lived with her father and sister.

Yet every thought also carried a darker side. He was passionate about his kingdom, but he disdained the proud tradition of Phalesia's democracy. Bringing to mind his skill in battle only made Chloe remember the way he had been at the Battle of Phalesia, covered in blood and gore, howling for the sun king's head. Reminding herself of the love he'd borne his wife and child only made her more aware that he felt nothing for her; theirs was a marriage of duty. Picturing herself in the Royal Palace at Xanthos, she could only think about how far she would be from her family and her home.

Nikolas was saying something to Nilus when he saw Chloe. His scowl deepened. 'I thought I forbade you to go to the Wilds.'

'And I thought my father made it clear that I am under his protection until the wedding.' Chloe glanced pointedly at her escort. 'Not yours.'

Consul Nilus's mouth dropped open. He looked like he wanted to be anywhere else.

Nikolas shook his head. 'Woman, you know we are to be married. We will share a bed and more. Why risk my wrath?'

Chloe folded her arms over her chest. 'Sire,' she said with emphasis, 'would you like to hear what I learned?'

Nikolas hesitated, and then nodded. 'Did you . . .' He scratched at his thick beard, suddenly unsure of himself. 'Did you see my brother?'

'I saw him.'

'Is he well?'

'Well enough. But despite what you know about him, he's no eldran.'

Nikolas shook his head. 'If he were a commoner, I could allow him to live in Xanthos, provided he wore a necklace and hid who he was, but he is a noble. It isn't right that his loyalties are divided.'

'Loyalties?' Chloe felt her blood rise. 'How are his loyalties divided? Speak the truth. You don't want him because he's different. You're worried about how he might reflect on you.'

'And if I am? If I'm worried that the brother of the king of Xanthos can change his shape, and that one day I might return from some distant conflict to discover my brother became a monster while I was gone? That he killed my citizens before they were able to put him down? It's no light concern, lady. I think it best that he remain with the eldren.'

'He doesn't know how to do the things they do.'

'He obviously does. All you're telling me is that he cannot control himself, which makes him more of a danger than any of them. I would allow any eldran to live in my city before I would consider my brother, and that is my final word on the subject.'

Nikolas calmed himself with an effort. Nilus was wringing his hands, obviously wanting to extricate himself from the group. The guardsman was impassive as always.

'Now, please tell me you learned something of value. The ark. Can the horn be moved?'

'Yes,' Chloe said stiffly. 'Zachary said it is safe to move it to an iron container.'

'Have you told your father?' Nilus asked, the first time he'd said a word.

'I've only just returned. But I'm sure he'll do what needs to be done.'

'I hope you speak the truth,' Nikolas said. He nodded to himself. 'I have matters to attend to. Consul Nilus, we'll speak again soon.

And Chloe?' He met her eyes. 'Think about the kind of marriage you want to have.'

Nikolas left with the helmeted soldier walking briskly at his side.

Nilus spoke softly to Chloe. 'He is under a lot of strain.'

'As is my father,' she said.

'I know, I know.' Nilus opened his mouth and then rubbed his jowly chin. 'Chloe . . . Speak with your father. Convince him to side with Nikolas, rather than against him. Nikolas doesn't always have a soft touch, but he's determined to face down the might of Ilea. He needs our united support. Your father has to understand that Nikolas feels he's the only leader with military experience, the only man able to defend us all.'

———

Nighttime in Phalesia made the city more beautiful than it could ever be by daylight, with the refuse in the gutters hidden from sight and costly lamps and torches situated only near sights people wanted to see: the statues and gardens, temples and grand houses. Waves crashed onto the pebbles of the harbor shore. Every ship rested next to a fellow, its work done for the day. A silver moon hung over the horizon and stars peeked through night's curtain in countless multitudes.

At Aristocles' villa, flickering candles and scented oil lamps filled the interior with light, the warm glow reflecting from the shining white marble of the walls, highlighting the statues and decorated ceramics. The heat had finally gone out of the day, and a cool breeze now wafted through the curtained windows of the reception.

Chloe and her younger sister, Sophia, sat at the high table with their father. Just turned twelve, Sophia was a younger version of Chloe, down to the long dark hair, wide mouth, and oval face, although Sophia's eyes were blue and Chloe's brown, and Sophia had an impish cast to her expression and dimples on her cheeks.

Aristocles was looking out the window; his mind was far away. He had a cup in front of him and a jug just a few inches away. Chloe had been watching; he'd refilled his cup at least three times.

'Father,' Chloe said delicately. 'You haven't said what you're going to do about the ark.'

Aristocles frowned. 'Not with your sister here.'

Sophia looked from face to face, unsure if she should leave.

'She should hear. She is also a princess, and one day she might be in the same position that I am.'

Aristocles let out a breath. 'Fine.'

'Nikolas is growing frustrated. Nilus is concerned.'

'Nikolas may be frustrated, but he's a foreign ruler, and the ark is ours to preserve or destroy. My dear'—Aristocles tried to give a reassuring smile—'he may seem fearsome, but it's all bluster.'

'But you made an agreement,' Chloe persisted. 'You promised that if Zachary said it was safe, you would move the horn and make plans for the gold.'

'I know what I said . . .' Aristocles hesitated, looking down into his wine cup. 'I simply no longer believe it a wise course of action.'

For a moment Chloe was speechless. 'You're going back on your word?'

Aristocles glanced at Sophia, who was silent but watching with rapt attention. 'I've spoken with my allies. We agree that destroying the ark – the ark that has resided at our holiest temple for hundreds of years – is not a decision I can make alone. We are an assembly. There should be a vote.'

Chloe blanched. 'I'm not sure if that's a good idea.'

'Well that's what's going to happen,' he snapped.

'Father . . .' Chloe said, hurt. It was uncharacteristic of him to speak to his children with anything but kindness.

There was silence for a time, before he reached out and clasped her hand. 'I am sorry,' he said. He opened his mouth and then closed it, obviously struggling with something. 'Chloe . . . I've . . . had a vision. From the gods.'

Chloe frowned. 'What vision? Were you at the temple? Did the priests see it also?'

'The Oracle of Athos spoke to me in a dream—'

'A dream?' She was unable to prevent her voice rising.

'Yes, a dream. It was unlike any dream I've had before. The Oracle gave me a prophecy. If the ark is destroyed the horn will sound.'

'But Zachary said—'

'I know what Zachary said! Nikolas pressured me into promising something I should never have promised. We are an assembly. As always, there must be a vote.'

'And which way will you vote?'

'That's never been your concern.'

'It is this time. If you campaign against what you agreed, Nikolas will find out. He will be vengeful, dream or no dream.'

'I should never have mentioned it,' Aristocles muttered. 'All you need to know is that my allies are with me, and there are enough of us to decide the vote. It isn't for Nikolas to say what happens to Phalesia's relics, nor our finances.'

Chloe shook her head. 'You made an agreement, at the Temple of Aldus, in sight of the gods, and you need to keep to it. Think of your actions, Father. What will Nikolas do?'

'There is nothing he can do.'

'Don't be naive, Father. Nikolas has power.'

'Power lies with the people,' Aristocles said firmly.

Chloe was frustrated. Her capture, journey to Lamara, and time in the sun king's palace had taught her the value of power, real power.

The power of strong soldiers and of men who ruled by decree.

10

Creeping forward, hidden by the undergrowth, Dion tracked the doe along the shaft of his arrow. Aiming for the heart, above and behind the foreleg, he continued his silent approach, quiet as a mouse.

The deer was in the open grassland. Dion was in a nearby stand of trees. It was going to be a clean kill.

The muscles in his arms tensed as he straightened and drew the bowstring tightly to his cheek. He breathed slowly and evenly. Craning her neck, the doe nibbled at the lush foliage sprouting from a young sapling. At the point when he was ready to release, Dion held his breath.

He paused. He suddenly sensed something . . . a closeness . . . the existence of another mind nearby.

I have you, little doe.

The sound of snapping wings crackled like a horsewhip as a monstrous silver-scaled dragon plummeted from above. The size of a large boat, with angular ridges behind its wedge-shaped head, rippling leathery skin, and clawed limbs, the dragon's veinous wings were pulled tightly into its body, giving it incredible speed. Startled, the doe tensed and then shot into a sprint even as Dion loosed his arrow. The shot went wild as the deer bounced left and right, weaving like a rabbit to escape the terrifying predator descending from above.

The dragon's claws were outstretched, jaws parted wide as it grasped at its intended prey. The doe leaped to the side, narrowly evading the clutch of the reptilian limbs. Wings fluttered as the dragon gained height and then sped forward; now it was a race, with the deer at full sprint and the dragon gaining on it as it dived. Again the winged creature descended and the jaws opened wide. Teeth the size of daggers gnashed onto the doe's shoulder and threw the animal to the side before the dragon rose into the air again. The deer crumpled, legs kicking at the air before it shuddered and became suddenly still. In an instant it was fresh meat surrounded by valuable skin, rather than the living, breathing animal it had been.

The dragon glanced back at Dion, revealing almond-shaped golden eyes and an expression somehow gleeful. It wheeled tightly, wings drawing in as it landed near the fallen doe and arched its spine. It roared in triumph, wings folding along its back. It was a strong creature, youthful and glossy, with white teeth and rippling muscles, not quite as big as Zachary but that could change: Zachary had said an eldran's power waxed and waned over time.

Gray mist billowed, enveloping the winged creature, thickening and elongating, cloaking the entire silver body. The mist shimmered, and then cleared. A pale-skinned, hawk-nosed eldran now stood in the dragon's place, wearing deerskin leggings and a brown tunic.

Dion left his concealment, looking for his lost arrow and shaking his head, finally finding the shaft embedded in the soft grassland. By the time he'd reached his friend, Eiric had already dragged the doe to a nearby oak and was kneeling at its side.

'You stole my kill,' Dion said.

With an expert slice from the obsidian knife he wore at his belt, the eldran cut the deer's throat. Blood welled from the gash, spilling out onto the surrounding grass.

'You had your chance,' Eiric said. He grinned up at him. 'Don't worry, you'll learn one day.'

'Learn?' Dion's eyes narrowed. 'I would have killed it quickly. You made it run, the meat's going to be as tough as leather. You've got no finesse. Who taught you how to hunt?'

Eiric laughed. 'You're just jealous. Pass me your rope. We'll hang it up overnight to drain the blood.' He glanced up at the oak's lofty branches. 'We'll need it high to keep the wolves away.'

Dion slipped a coiled rope off his shoulder and tossed it to Zachary's son. He watched his friend work for a time, his irritation finally melting away; to the eldren the only animal that could be claimed was a dead one. A thought occurred to him as he suddenly remembered the strange voice he'd heard inside his head. 'I think I sensed you, just before you struck. I think I felt something.'

'Really?' Eiric looked up from tying the rope around the deer's hindquarters. His eyes widened in mock surprise as he stopped what he was doing. 'You do feel something. I can tell.' He chuckled and resumed his work. 'Shame. I've killed six deer to your four in the last week. And please, remind me of the week before?'

'I mean it,' Dion said seriously. 'I thought you'd gone farther afield. But then when you came just now . . .'

Eiric finished tying the rope around the deer and straightened. 'I told you, given time among us, you'll learn.'

He passed the rope to Dion, who deftly looped the end over an overhead branch while Eiric wiped his hands on the grass. Grunting as he pulled, Dion soon had the doe in the air, her blank eyes staring at the ground far below.

'So where have you been all day?' Dion asked.

Eiric's golden eyes were grave now as he watched Dion tie the rope around the trunk to finish it all off. 'Looking for Jonas. After he lost his family . . . Father's worried that he's turned wild. We have a saying: grief brings out the beast inside.' The eldran's

82

expression darkened. 'If he doesn't turn up soon, we may have to search Cinder Fen.'

Seeing Dion's puzzled expression, he continued. 'If Jonas is still himself he should have come home long ago. It's hard to say how the wildren think, or if they do at all, but there is no doubt they're drawn to Cinder Fen.' The tone of his voice lowered. 'We must know.'

Dion knew Jonas from the Village, but he didn't know him well. He clasped his friend's shoulder. 'There are many reasons to be missing,' he said. 'Often the answer is simple. He could just be grieving.'

'I know.' Eiric nodded.

'I wish I could help . . .'

'You can.' Eiric met his eyes. 'Change your shape and fly with me.'

'I can't . . .'

'You can. You only need to let go.'

'That's what your father keeps telling me.' Dion tried to keep the exasperation out of his voice. 'You'd both be as out of place in a human city as I am in the Village.'

Eiric smiled. 'Out of place? I'd be more than that. Despite what you think, I do understand.' He gave Dion a sympathetic look. 'But have you ever asked yourself what you want? Did you choose to join us, or did you have no other choice? I consider you a friend, and I am glad to have you with us, we all are. But finding your place in the world is something only you can do.'

'So everyone keeps telling me,' Dion said.

Eiric gestured up at the sky. 'If you can't change yourself, why not try flying with me? You will be able to feel what it is like to be high in the sky, free as a bird. Father said you have flown on his back before.' He smiled. 'We can continue our hunt. Perhaps together we will have a good combination of my power and what did you call it . . . your . . . finesse?'

Strong wings pushed at the air underneath, forcing the dragon's lean body to lift, leaving the landscape of undulating grassland and forested hills far below. Dion felt the sensation of his stomach climbing into his mouth and then dropping back down again with every beat. Tightly gripping the protuberances behind Eiric's angular head, he leaned forward and clutched with his knees as he prayed to every one of the gods that he wouldn't fall off.

The dragon increased speed, soaring through the air until the howling wind rushed past Dion's ears and he found himself constantly blinking to clear the tears. The scaled body tilted, gradually at first, and then more and more as it executed a rotation, turning on the tip of a veined wing.

Dion felt himself slipping.

The dragon that was Eiric was turning so tightly that the wings were nearly lined up vertically. Dion knew his senses must be deceiving him, but then his eyes went wide with shock; suddenly he was sliding. He tried to clutch tighter onto the ridges with his hands, to squeeze on the leathery flanks with his knees, but he was at such a sharp angle that gravity was stronger than his ability to hold fast. At any moment he would fall. He wondered fleetingly if Eiric planned to make him tumble off, scrabbling at the sky, screaming as his legs and arms kicked, until he transformed out of sheer terror and became a dragon himself.

Holding his breath, Dion resisted the urge to shut his eyes. The feeling was terrifying and exhilarating. He tried to focus on the thrill, to let happen what may. To drive away the terror he cried out, and then the dragon began to complete its turn, slowly tilting back to the horizontal. Dion's fear of slipping subsided. He finally understood what Eiric was doing.

Eiric was showing him the joy of changing. An eldran's ability to alter form wasn't all about fighting, hunting, and the risk of turning wild. Nor was it about the ability to sense one another or to communicate without speech. Eldren could become serpents, and explore the ocean depths, encountering whales, sharks, and turtles. They could become giants, more powerful than the biggest bear, able to roam other beasts' terrain with impunity. They could become winged creatures, viewing the world from a lofty height, wheeling and swooping, soaring and simply watching.

Dion's fear melted away. He was with his friend, his only friend, a man who happened to be an eldran. He was with one of his people.

The dragon was now flying straight ahead, wings sweeping up and down with long, leisurely movements. The outstretched wings then became still for a time, effortlessly coasting. As the soaring flight took Dion high above the occasional clouds, he finally had the courage to look down and gain an appreciation for how swiftly he'd come to entirely new surroundings.

Far below he could see the valley leading to the maze-like canyon where he'd encountered the bear. The trees of the forest looked like blades of grass, despite the fact that they were the same huge trees that surrounded the Village. Taking in the vista, Dion was surprised to feel disappointment when the dragon began to lose height. He guessed that Eiric needed to rest after being changed for so long.

The ground now approached at speed, Eiric choosing to land on a flat region of smooth rock, halfway up the valley slope. Dion braced himself but the sweeping wings beat down at the ground at the last minute, slowing the rate of descent so that the clawed feet touched down with the slightest jolt. Knowing the eldran would be anxious to shift back to his normal shape, Dion slipped off swiftly while mist clouded the dragon's body. The mist shimmered. A moment later Eiric stood in its place, smiling at Dion and panting.

'Well?'

'I can see the attraction,' Dion said, returning the smile.

'You need to experience it first hand.' Eric glanced at the nearby forest. 'Another day though. We're only an hour's walk from the

Village. I shouldn't risk changing more today . . .' He trailed off as his eyes became unfocused. He cocked his head to the side. 'Wait.'

The hawk-nosed eldran suddenly looked up, scanning the skies, craning his neck as he swept his gaze across the surrounding peaks. Searching with him, Dion grew worried but then he heard his friend laugh.

'Jonas,' Eiric said, grinning with relief. 'I sense him.' He lifted his arm and indicated the distant mountains. 'Over there.'

The rising terrain and peaks that grew higher and higher in rows were lit by the afternoon sun, but even so it took Dion a long time to see what Eiric was pointing at. Finally he spied what looked to be a large bird, wheeling in the sky as it flew in a direct line for them. With every passing instant it grew larger, and then it was unmistakably a dragon, longer and leaner than Eiric had been, with a wide wingspan to match.

Dion had never seen Jonas in changed form and without Eiric's pronouncement he would not have known who it was. The silver dragon descended, scales shining in the sunlight, but landed a surprising distance away, shifting shape a stone's throw from where Dion and Eiric waited on the rocky hillside. Now a tall and wiry middle-aged eldran with short spiky hair, there was something to Jonas's manner that made Dion uneasy. The shadow in his gray eyes was still present, but there was a feverish cast to his expression that hadn't been there before. He didn't approach, remaining far enough away that when Eiric spoke he had to raise his voice to call out.

'Jonas! We've been searching for you. Where have you been?'

Jonas still didn't approach, and Eiric frowned, puzzled, starting to move forward. When Dion caught movement in the sky, he grabbed hold of Eiric's upper arm. 'Eiric, stop.'

Eiric shook his arm free, turning to glare at him. 'Dion, what—?'

Ignoring him, Dion slid his bow off his shoulder. He reached back to take an arrow from the quiver and nocked the arrow, swiftly pulling the string to his cheek. He sighted along the shaft at Jonas's chest. It was a difficult shot, but not impossible.

'Dion,' Eiric hissed. 'What are you doing? You know Jonas.'

Dion called out a challenge, brow furrowed as he held the arrow at the point of release. 'Why are there others following you? Who are they?'

As Eiric scanned the sky, Jonas spoke in a low, deep voice. 'Triton will sound the horn of Marrix, and he is going to bring my wife and son back to me.'

Eiric gasped. His gaze shot back to the eldran in front of him.

'Even I know that once someone is gone, they're gone,' Dion said.

'You know it?' Jonas asked scornfully. 'You know nothing, half-breed. You know what Zachary tells you and no more.' He nodded at Eiric. 'I can say the same for all of you.'

'Jonas,' Eiric said slowly. 'What have you done?'

'Your father lied. He does not have the blood of kings, and so he tells us there is no purpose in reclaiming the horn of Marrix and with it our homeland. But if we do, our loved ones will return.'

Dion murmured to Eiric. 'Above the twin peaks, on the left.'

Dozens of specks now filled the sky, and like Jonas a moment before, it was clear that they were far larger than birds. Dion glanced at Eiric, seeing his face filled with horror.

'You need to leave,' Dion said. 'Go as fast as you can. Warn the others.'

Jonas's eyes were on the iron point on Dion's arrow.

'What about—?' Eiric stammered.

'Go!' Dion cried.

When urgent need was on them, eldren could shift between forms as quickly as a man could draw a breath. Elongated smoke covered Eiric's body and then the silver dragon burst from the center, propelled upward by wings beating furiously as it shot away, heading directly for the forest and the Village beyond.

At the same instant, Jonas began to shift form and Dion released his arrow. The string hummed and as the mist cleared he fumbled over his shoulder for another. The dragon rising from the cloud roared in pain. Dion saw a gash scored in its soft underbelly. For a moment he thought it would attack, but then it flew higher into the air.

The cluster of furies and dragons was now close enough for one shape to be distinguished from another. An immense monster was in the lead, a one-eyed dragon bigger than any of the creatures following. Jonas flew high, his flight erratic; he was waiting for Triton to join him.

As a united group, they then flew in the direction of the Village, leaving the insignificant half-breed far behind.

Dion started to run.

11

Dion sprinted through the forest, leaping over a fallen tree and picking a path down a steep slope, leaving the trail to take the shortest route to the settlement. Slipping and sliding down the hillside, his legs threatened to give way underneath him as he struggled to maintain his footing while gravel skittered around him. The slope ended at the bank of the river and without pausing he jumped over the divide, nearly falling as he hit the opposite bank, but stumbling and continuing on.

The Village wasn't much farther: one more hill and he would be in view of the clearing in the ancient trees. His calves burned as he climbed and his pounding heart caused blood to roar in his ears. Louder still, he began to hear grunts, roars, and bellows. Fear clutched hold of his stomach when he smelled the sharp stench of char.

Finally, he reached the hill's summit and saw the Village.

Clouds of gray smoke filled the air in all directions, rising up to disperse in the treetops. Already breathless, he found himself choking and coughing. He drew up near one of the ancient trees, assessing the scene in the clearing, trying to understand the struggle that was well under way.

There were giants and ogres everywhere, circling each other, wrestling and grappling, wielding sticks, stones, and even burning brands as eldran fought eldran. Dion watched a red-faced giant throw a flaming log onto a wooden house. A conflagration soon enveloped the structure that had taken years to grow and was the treasured center of a family's life.

At least half the houses in the Village were already blazing. The smoke made the scene fragmented and unreal, arms and legs and monstrous heads flashing as if disembodied. Some of the creatures were male, some female, but all had silver hair of varying lengths, with faces stretched and misshapen, like too much skin had been pulled over their skulls. Jaws were enlarged, ears flattened, teeth protruding, growls bestial. They snarled and roared. They cried out in pain and made the ground shake when they fell.

Dion didn't know which in their changed form were friends or foes, and although he tried to open his senses, his thoughts were filled with confusion. As he stood on the hillside, looking down into the Village, he nocked an arrow, but didn't know who to aim for.

Then he again saw the red-faced giant that had tossed the fiery log at the house, facing off to an older and slightly larger opponent. They snarled at each other in the center of the Village, surrounded by burning houses and billowing smoke. When Dion saw the crescent scar on the older giant's face and recognized Zachary, he began to run.

Now close enough to chance a shot, he was forced to wait his opportunity as the red-faced giant swiped a clenched fist at Zachary's head. Baring his teeth and stepping to the side, Zachary evaded the blow but was prevented from countering by a second attack as an ogre lunged at him with a pointed stick used like a spear. When Zachary leaped out of the way, finally Dion drew the string to his cheek. He released his arrow and heard it whistle through the air before plunging into the red-faced giant's side.

The giant roared in pain and whirled but it was far from incapacitated. The spear-wielding ogre turned and caught sight of Dion already fitting a second arrow. Dropping its spear, the ogre ran forward to grab its larger, wounded companion. The two fled, disappearing into the billowing smoke.

Zachary saw another ogre throwing burning logs onto a house and lumbered over, crashing into it from the side and becoming embroiled in a match of strength. Seeing Zachary gain the upper hand, Dion left him behind, peering through the smoke as he reached the Village's center, trying to discern friend from foe.

He heard a high-pitched scream.

Whirling, his eyes widened when he saw a young eldran woman fleeing an ogre, and immediately recognized Liana. The monster was snarling and chasing her with a length of flaming wood; they were heading away from the direction of the fiercest fighting, toward the Village's outskirts. Without changing her form, compared to her pursuer, she was as weak as a newborn babe.

Dion dashed after them, coughing in the smoke as he ran. He lifted his bow and drew, firing an arrow at the ogre, but missed. The two shapes became distant and clouded by haze as he put down his head and ran.

Liana was heading for a cluster of a dozen houses at the Village's far end, the only place still untouched by the enemy. A puff of wind cleared the air for a brief instant and Dion saw the young eldran woman take refuge in the closest house. The ogre stopped, uncertain, head turning as it searched for her. It lumbered over to another structure and touched its fiery brand to the dry tinder wall.

Something smashed into Dion's back.

The force picked him up and threw him forward. He felt the breath knocked out of him and found himself face down on the hard ground. Lifting his head, gazing at the place where he'd last seen Liana, he saw a dragon plunging from overhead, outstretched claws aimed directly at the ogre setting houses aflame.

Dion rolled over. A one-eyed giant loomed over him.

A hairless head, ridged and bony, sat squarely on the broad shoulders. It was the biggest giant he'd ever seen, dwarfing all others. Filled with menace, it carried no weapon, instead flexing fingers and curling them into fists.

I know you, the voice spoke inside Dion's head. *Why do you not change your form, black dragon?*

Desperately Dion tried to remember everything Zachary had taught him. He imagined himself in another shape, a gigantic creature of strong limbs and indomitable strength.

Nothing happened.

Reaching forward, the one-eyed giant crouched and Dion felt fingers clasping around his neck. He choked as the hand tightened on his throat and then he was being lifted. The monster picked him and held him in the air as his feet scrabbled uselessly at nothing.

With a grunt, the one-eyed giant threw Dion like a man throwing a spear. He saw the approach of a wide tree trunk.

Then his head struck with force, and darkness filled his vision.

———

Dion's eyelids fluttered. Pain burst inside his head, diminishing only slowly. He felt hands on his shoulders, shaking him, and opened his eyes.

He was lying on his back and a young silver-haired eldran was hunched over him, his brow furrowed. 'He is alive,' the eldran called to someone behind him. 'Can you stand?' he asked.

When Dion nodded, the eldran gripped his hand and helped him to climb to his feet before leaving to aid others. Weaving slightly, Dion touched a hand to the top of his head. It was tender, but he couldn't feel any blood.

He breathed slowly in and out, wondering how he was still alive. His senses dulled by pain and fatigue, he only slowly managed to take stock of his situation, turning away from the broad oak that had broken his fall.

Smoke still filled the area, which told him that he hadn't been out for long. Silver-haired eldren ran in all directions while others stood staring disconsolately at the burned husks that had been their homes. Triton and those with him were gone. The Village was razed in its entirety.

He heard a sudden cry and looked up.

The eldran who had assisted him to his feet suddenly sprinted past, gold-flecked eyes opened wide as he ran. More cries and shouts filled the air in a growing chorus. An older eldran ran in the same direction, and then more villagers, until it seemed that everyone able to do so was all rushing to the same place. Dion wondered dimly where they were going.

Then he remembered. As the cobwebs cleared from his mind the visions came flooding back.

Liana. She had taken shelter in a wooden house, hiding from the conflict. An ogre had been burning every house in the area. A dragon had plunged down from overhead . . .

Dion turned and commenced a staggering run, joining the throng of eldren, all heading toward the Village's outskirts. As he passed the last of the blackened circles that had once been a proud house, he saw a growing crowd of villagers surrounding a commotion in the middle.

He pushed his way forward. Looking between the shoulders of two tall eldren, he gasped.

Eiric was facing his father sternly, gripping both his shoulders as Zachary struggled to push past the obstruction that was his son.

Zachary's expression was wretched, curled up in anguish. Eiric was strong but even he was struggling to impede his father's progress.

Dion continued to shoulder his way through the crowd. Finally he could make out what was in the center of the circle.

A snarling dragon, tail lashing the ground, whirled to face any eldran who came near. With mottled scales, pale scratches on its belly, and yellowed teeth the size of Dion's fingers, this was clearly an older, more powerful eldran. The shuddering wings folded and unfolded as the almond-shaped eyes darted from face to face, man to woman to child, daring anyone to approach. While Eiric held his father away, another eldran stepped slowly forward, arms outstretched to show he meant no harm, but the jaws parted and the dragon lunged. The eldran jumped back as the sharp teeth gnashed together.

Dion suddenly realized that Zachary was screaming, over and over.

'Aella!'

The dragon was Zachary's wife. But she was also a wildran, a monster that could kill any of them in an instant. If she hadn't been so staunchly defending her ground, blood might have already been spilled. He wondered what she was trying so hard to protect.

Then he saw a pale limb as the dragon spun again, teeth snapping at another brave villager who tried to approach and he realized. The dragon wasn't defending an empty patch of dirt. Aella's final thought before turning wild had been to continue her last task.

She was defending Liana.

Terrified beyond belief, the orphan girl had her arms wrapped around her knees. Tears leaked down her cheeks and her eyes were pleading as people from the community tried to get close enough to seize her and get her free.

For now the dragon was consumed with protecting Liana from any threat. But perhaps soon, as madness overcame any other thought, the creature would think only of clawing and tearing, of threat and food. Liana was in terrible danger, and there was nothing they could do.

The crowd cried out as Zachary finally tore free of his son and rushed forward. As the dragon that was Aella whirled to face him, he slowed and took a deep breath. Spreading his arms, lowering them at the ground, he began to speak in a tone that was both soothing and ragged, the plaintive voice of a man who was desperate not to lose the love of his life.

Zachary was murmuring so that Dion could only just hear him. '. . . my love, remember who you are. You are Aella. You are my heart. You are everything. Without you I am lost. This form is not your true one. Please, come back to me.'

A crash of falling wood came from the distant wreckage of a house. The dragon roared and the wings fluttered. Liana wailed in fear, and the creature faced her, neck craning, snout touching Liana's face. The jaws parted and the roar lowered in volume, becoming a throaty rumble.

'No!' Zachary cried, stepping forward. But the dragon's interest in Liana continued. 'Aella, this is not who you are.'

Eiric ran forward and pulled on his father's arm. 'Father. She is too far gone!'

Zachary again shook him free. Eldren came to take hold of Eiric, calling out to Zachary, telling him that Aella was lost.

'She'll kill the girl!' someone cried.

Yet even when the dragon rounded on Zachary and roared in his face he wouldn't relent. He reached out and stroked the dragon's head, heedless of the danger he was in. For an instant, the barest moment, the wildness in the glaring eyes cleared.

Then the wings stretched out. With an ear-splitting cry that sounded like a screech of pain, or perhaps farewell, the creature rose into the air. With each fluttering of the huge wings the silver body became more distant as the wildran left its home behind.

Pushing through the crowd, Dion ran forward to crouch beside Liana. He checked her over and lifted her head, seeing soot on her face, streaked by the passage of tears, but she was unharmed.

'Father!'

Eiric cried out but Zachary was already in the process of changing his form. Before his son could reach him a second dragon was roaring, bursting out of a cloud of mist, a huge and ancient creature with a crescent scar on its cheek. Wings beat down at the ground and in moments Zachary was gone.

'Eiric,' an older eldran called. 'You must let him go.'

Eiric stood frozen with indecision, fists clenched at his sides. Slowly, he turned to face Liana, still seated on the ground with Dion crouched beside her.

Dion had never seen him look so angry.

Liana looked up at Eiric as he strode over and bent down. He took hold of a leather thong around her slender neck, gripping it by the glossy circle of amber that hung from the simple necklace.

He yanked, pulling at the necklace hard enough to break it. While Liana looked on, Eiric strode to the nearest house and tossed it into the smoking remains.

Liana climbed to her feet, pushing Dion away, staring at Eiric as he deliberately turned his back on her. She then ran into the forest.

'Let her go,' Eiric said.

12

Nikolas stood at the summit of the sloped defensive bastion that guarded Phalesia's small harbor, gazing out to sea and wondering at the different forms of power a man could possess.

He had a reason for his pondering, for he wanted to be a strong king, but he also planned to have the scales of life tilt in his favor when he was judged at the gates of paradise. He desired to keep his people safe and to maintain order, but not to be needlessly ruthless or cruel.

There was a time, as a younger man, when he had thought he would never raise his sword against a man who didn't threaten him physically. Many of his soldiers still lived by this code, the warrior's code, and even in the heat of battle would never slay a surrendered opponent or kill innocent townsfolk.

But Nikolas was a king, and he had to live by a different code. There were various forms of power, and the magi and philosophers posed many questions that the warrior's code found difficult to provide a solution for. A true warrior would never kill an unarmed man. But if a villain robbed a family of food, causing starvation and death, the fact that he didn't carry a sword shouldn't grant him immunity from the executioner. If a nobleman gave orders to slay women and children, killing the unarmed nobleman rather than his followers would result in fewer deaths and greater justice.

To wield power – the power of life and death – meant to play a dangerous game, and any man who played dangerous games should suffer the consequences when the game turned against his favor.

'A man who orders soldiers is a soldier himself,' Nikolas muttered. This was what his code of kings told him.

It was evening and the sun had just set, finally taking the heat out of the day. The waves below came in and out with every breath of Silex, god of the sea, making a hissing noise as the water struck the pale stones of the shore. Nikolas wore a white tunic with a black corded belt that matched the iron bull he wore around his neck.

'Balal, god of war,' he said, clasping the medallion. 'Be with me tonight.'

Flanking him on both sides, two soldiers of his king's guard stood a short distance away to give him privacy. They were veteran warriors clad in strong and well-made armor, with bronze breastplates on their chests and skirts of overlapping leather strips around their waists. Fastened to their necks were short crimson cloaks. A wide-bladed sword the length of a man's forearm hung at their sides. Black-crested helmets with long nose and cheek guards hid their faces.

Hearing a voice, Nikolas's gaze left the darkening sea, sweeping back to the Phalesian agora and the surrounding temples. He saw round-faced Nilus approaching, his hasty walk hampered by his small steps.

'Consul Nilus,' Nikolas said. 'At last.'

'You wanted to see me, King?' Nilus asked.

'This vote that the first consul is planning. I hear that the consuls' positions are often decided before the actual vote.'

'That is true,' Nilus puffed.

'Aristocles still pushes for the horn to stay in the ark?'

Nilus hesitated. 'I've spoken with him at length. He understands, truly, that the gold is needed. He wants to rebuild our navy and army as much as you do.'

Nikolas scratched his thick black beard. 'Then why does he say that the consuls should vote against moving the horn?'

'He says that he has prayed to the gods and been given a warning. The Aleutheans made an ark of gold for a reason. He is afraid that if we move the horn we will be at increased danger.'

'Bah.' Nikolas scowled. 'His own daughter said there is no risk.'

'Nonetheless, he truly is concerned.'

'And his allies?'

'They will follow where he leads. He reminds them that the ark is still a mysterious relic, and brings up the fact that no Phalesian consul should be pressured by a foreign ruler.'

'And you, Consul Nilus, where do you stand on this?'

'Aristocles and I have been allies on many things,' Nilus said delicately. 'But, on this, I confess that I do not agree with him. There are times to show independence and strength, and times to work with our friends and allies.' He looked up to meet Nikolas's eyes. 'I believe that Aristocles and his supporters are perhaps suffering from an indignant loss of pride, and are looking to make up for it.'

'So the future of both our nations rests on a group of old men who long for the days when Phalesia's navy was second to none?' Nikolas shook his head.

'I've seen it before at the Assembly,' Nilus said, spreading his hands. 'The more a swift agreement is needed, the more the consuls divide into factions. And the voting men . . . They don't know the true state of our finances, but nor do they want to know. They want to belong to a proud, strong nation, and that is all they care about. The ark was sacred, and now we say it isn't, but it's still sitting there, high in the Temple of Aldus, with an eternal flame shining on it night and day. Some consuls say that their opponents – and you

– simply want to take away a beloved public monument, and use the gold to enrich your personal coffers. When Aristocles reminds them that the ancient Aleutheans were victorious against Marrix only because they sealed the horn inside that very golden ark, he makes a convincing argument.'

Nikolas nodded. Nilus wasn't telling him anything new, but it was useful to know where he stood. 'So where a king would simply do what's best and damn the people, Aristocles is weak enough to listen to weak voices, and weak enough to need weak allies in order to stay in power.'

Nilus protested. 'Our system of governance is different, King, but it has its strengths. Phalesia's great culture and prosperity is in many ways due to the fact every voice is heard at the lyceum. Our—'

'Enough,' Nikolas interrupted. 'You're a canny man, Nilus. You know who plans to vote with the first consul?'

'He has his supporters. I know them all.'

'And which way will the vote go?'

'It will be close, but Aristocles is persuasive, and he is speaking words that his listeners want to hear. Phalesia is a proud nation. He will win the vote.'

'And what then will be Phalesia's contribution to our collective defense? The Ileans will be back.'

Nilus pondered. 'I would suppose that Aristocles is already seeking alternative ways to fund the rebuilding of our forces. A proposal for income generation through taxation and trade tariffs will be debated, most likely in tandem with a loan from Sarsica. In time, another vote will ensue, this one with an outcome much closer to your heart, King Nikolas.' He smiled. 'Remember, democracy is directing a theatre of unwilling participants, not leading an army of loyal followers.'

'And how long might that take?'

'Well . . . It's difficult to say.'

Nikolas nodded. 'I want you to do something for me. I'd like to speak, in person, with those who will support Aristocles in the coming vote. I wish to have my say. Consul Nilus, please give me a list of their names and where I can find them.'

Nilus frowned. 'I'm not sure if . . .'

'If you're not up to the task, I'm sure there are others who can give me the same names . . .' Nikolas's voice lowered. 'Other consuls I can work with.'

Nilus was a long time in answering. He opened his mouth and then closed it, brow furrowing as he considered his position. 'I can do it. Rather than give you a list, though, I'll take you to each consul myself. I might need a few hours . . .'

Nikolas waved a hand at one of his nearby guardsmen. 'This is Nestor. He has a perfect memory. Names and where I can find them. Begin.'

Nilus took a deep breath.

———

Aristocles was working late in his villa. Though he was speaking earnestly to his guest, Carolas, a young and ambitious consul charged with procuring supplies for the army, another part of him wondered where his two daughters were. Chloe and Sophia had left to make some purchases in the agora but that was some time ago now.

Concentrating on the task at hand, he paused in his speech as Aglea, a matronly servant, poured the wine, then with a nod of thanks he resumed.

'So, my friend, we must choose our moment carefully. I need you to prepare the cost of recruiting, training, and equipping an army to match the size of the force Nikolas can field. Don't hide what you are doing, obtain quotations from everyone you need, make the tanners fight over each other to give you a price for leather and the dyers argue about the qualities of their indigo. Word will get around, firstly that we need a vast quantity of silver to match our forces to the Xanthians, and secondly that the wealth will spread its way throughout the city. In a few weeks they'll be begging for a motion for funding to cross the floor.'

Carolas slowly nodded. 'I can do that, First Consul.'

'Excellent,' Aristocles said. 'I'll send Nikolas to see you in the coming days. I want him to see how serious you are about invigorating our army. He is a military man—'

Consul Nilus burst into the villa's reception, startling the two seated men. His eyes widening with surprise, Aristocles saw that Amos, the veteran captain of the city guard, was with him.

Nilus's round face was red; he looked like he'd run all the way to the villa. Amos was barely out of breath but his craggy face was filled with concern. Aside from his expression he looked the same as ever, an athletic man rarely out of armor, with short curly hair, a scar on his forehead, and stubble on his strong chin.

'Nilus, what—?'

'Get out of here!' Nilus uncharacteristically barked at Carolas. 'Now!'

Aristocles opened and closed his mouth, frowning as his puzzled guest looked to him for orders. He nodded, and the perplexed young man rose from his seat, glancing from face to face as he moved past the two newcomers and exited the villa.

'Amos, what's this about?'

Amos's voice was grim. 'Consul Nilus grabbed me just a moment ago. You need to hear what he has to say.'

Nilus held up his hand. He waited until Aristocles' guest was long gone before speaking rapidly. 'Aristocles, you have to get out of here. Now.'

'What are you talking about?'

'Listen to me. Nikolas is planning something. For tonight. We're only fortunate he has no experience of politics. He thinks he's hiding his plans but they're plain to see. He's asked me for a list, the names of all the consuls who are your closest supporters.'

'And you simply gave him this list?'

'You know as well as I do that if I hadn't given him the names another would have. You have enemies in the Assembly, all of whom would happily see your allies get a rude visit from the king of Xanthos. Of itself the request seems innocent enough.'

'I don't understand. What is he planning?' Aristocles asked.

'What do you think?' Nilus looked at him like he was a fool. 'He's going to kill them.'

Aristocles stood up so quickly that his stool fell backward. 'He wouldn't dare!'

'He didn't want the names himself, he's giving them to his personal king's guard. Have you noticed how many Xanthian soldiers are out tonight?'

Now it was Amos who spoke. 'First Consul, pull your head out of the sand. This is happening.'

'If he plans on killing your allies in the Assembly, what do you think he intends for you?'

Aristocles felt light-headed.

'Listen, Aristocles, you know I believe in the Assembly. If I am not the ally I've convinced Nikolas I am, he will only find another. Then where will we be? You would be dead, and so would I.'

'But he's engaged to my daughter.'

'And when he marries Chloe he'll have a claim on Phalesia. He may intend to dissolve the Assembly of Consuls. He may even intend to become king of Phalesia, as well as Xanthos. He has a plan.'

Events were moving too quickly. Aristocles was a meticulous thinker. He worked in longer timescales than this. 'Can't Amos summon his men?' He turned to the captain. 'Can't you do something, Amos?'

Amos shook his head. 'You heard Consul Nilus, Nikolas's king's guard is out in numbers.' His face mirrored the way Aristocles himself felt; it was the look of a leader caught unawares. 'I could gather my men . . .' He scratched the stubble on his chin. 'He's been planning this for some time.'

Nilus spoke. 'Or he may have been holding this option in reserve. First Consul, do you really want confrontation between the soldiers of Xanthos and Phalesia? Xanthos would win. What would happen to the Assembly, then?'

Aristocles drew in a shaky breath. 'By the gods,' he whispered.

Amos cocked his head to listen, then ran out to the terrace. A moment later he re-entered, his face drained of color. 'There's fighting in the agora. I can see Xanthian soldiers heading this way.'

Nilus cursed. 'I thought we'd have more time than this.'

'Who will warn the others?' Aristocles asked.

Nilus shook his head. 'It's too late for them.' He glanced at Amos. 'And Amos . . . Nikolas has remarked on your loyalty to the first consul more than once.'

Amos clenched and unclenched his fists. 'First Consul, tell me what to do.'

Aristocles looked at Nilus. 'Nikolas will find out that you've warned me.'

'Or he'll find out that when the fighting started I immediately sought out the captain here to tell him to stand down and avoid bloodshed. I found him here with you.'

Realization dawned; there was no other option. Aristocles had to flee.

Nilus turned to Amos. 'Amos, I think you know what has to happen.' He pointed to the side of his head. 'Make sure to draw blood.' He nodded at Aristocles. 'Take care of him. I'll do what I can from here.'

Aristocles cast pleading eyes on Nilus. 'My daughters?'

'I'll look after them, you have my word.'

'Nilus, you can't let Chloe marry him.'

'One thing at a time. First we get you to safety. Then we can make plans.'

'I want to see them.'

Amos shook his head. 'It's too risky.'

'We'll head for Tanus,' Aristocles said, his voice shaking. 'Queen Zanthe is a friend. When things settle here, I'll make my return.'

'You have gold?' Nilus asked.

Aristocles nodded. 'Yes.'

'Take all of it.'

Aristocles lifted his chin. 'I am the rightful leader of the Assembly of Consuls. I will return.'

Amos drew his sword, and the sound sent a shiver down Aristocles' spine. With a sharp jab, he smashed the hilt across Nilus's head.

13

'Chloe!'

Someone said her name, anxiously tapping her on the arm.

Busy in the agora, browsing the bustling night market with her younger sister, Chloe turned in surprise. She recognized the blue-trimmed robe and copper medallion of a priestess of Aeris, but it was rare for the soft-spoken healers to be so bold.

'Sophia,' Chloe called to her sister.

Sophia turned in surprise and saw Chloe with the priestess. Leaving behind the jewelry she'd been inspecting, the girl tucked a lock of hair behind her ear as she came over to join them.

'Alexis,' Sophia said when she saw the priestess, who was young, just a few years older than she was.

Chloe nodded, recognizing the name. Sophia had recently started training at the temple, just as Chloe had at the same age. It was a common rite of passage for daughters of the nobility, their studies commencing soon after becoming a woman. Though Sophia was only twelve, her manner had changed since she'd started spending so much time with so many girls older than herself, making Chloe wonder if she'd ever been as confident at the same age.

'I'm sorry to disturb you,' the priestess said, 'but there's . . . an injured boy at the temple. We need additional help.' The priestess's manner was strange; she seemed particularly worried. 'Could you . . . Could you come with me?'

'Of course,' Chloe said. 'Should my sister come also?'

'Yes.' Alexis nodded. 'Both of you. Come. Please follow me.'

Chloe took Sophia by the hand but the girl glared at her older sister and shook her hand free. Together they followed the priestess away from the market and crossed the expanse of multicolored paving stones before climbing the broad marble steps at the agora's edge. The path leveled off before it split and they took the fork leading to the grand colonnaded temple with its peaked roof, nearly as familiar to Chloe as the villa where she lived with her father.

Hearing a commotion back in the direction of the market, she glanced over her shoulder and saw movement in the crowd. A gap opened up and she saw several soldiers of Nikolas's king's guard fighting with a pair of Phalesian soldiers with blue cloaks. She heard shouting before the crowd swallowed them again.

Chloe shook her head. It was never a good idea for soldiers from different nations to be housed in the same city.

'Please.' The priestess grabbed her arm, steering her until she'd once more started walking to the temple. 'Come.'

'What are the boy's injuries?' Chloe asked as they entered.

Though it was nighttime, braziers filled with crimson coals framed both sides of the stepped entrance and every marble column had a flaming torch on a pole resting against it. The Temple of Aeris was often full at odd hours – sickness tended to strike more often during the night – so Chloe wasn't surprised to see dozens of people inside. Rugs, cushions, and bed pallets littered the floor. A groaning man clutched his belly while a priestess the same age as Alexis tried to get him to swallow a potion. More priestesses knelt by prone figures, administering medicines, discussing treatments, soothing family members and bandaging wounds. The scent of incense dominated the interior. The aroma was cloying, despite the fact that with only the columns for walls there was nothing to block the gusts of wind that came in from the sea.

Chloe was surprised to see two soldiers of Nikolas's king's guard standing at the edge of the colonnade, close to the open air. They were watching the agora below and had hands on the hilts of their swords.

She and her younger sister were following the priestess along a cleared pathway near the edge of the columns, away from the busy healers. Seeing that they were approaching the pair of Xanthian soldiers, she called out to the priestess. 'Where are you taking us? Where is the injured boy?'

'Please.' Alexis turned, and her eyes were pleading. 'Follow.'

Her suspicions now raised by the presence of so many Xanthian soldiers, even in the Temple of Aeris, Chloe stopped. She folded her arms over her chest. 'What is the extent of his injuries? You still haven't said, Priestess.'

Chloe heard a scream and her gaze shot out to the agora.

She saw something she'd never expected to see.

A Xanthian soldier of the king's guard pulled his sword out of a bearded consul's chest, in the middle of the square, just a stone's throw from where Chloe and her sister were standing. Liquid gushed out of the white-clad consul's mouth; red stained his robe. Staggering, he lurched and then fell down, toppling to the side, before sprawling out on the paving stones.

Chloe gasped. She knew his name, Consul Charon. He was a gifted storyteller and was particularly fond of Sophia. He was one of her father's closest allies.

Horrified by the sight of a harmless old man she knew well murdered in front of her, she grabbed her sister, pulling her close.

She had always felt safe in the temple of her goddess; it was her refuge when she needed to escape the cares of the world. Now she turned to the pair of helmeted soldiers and realized they were both looking directly at her.

'Chloe?' Sophia was close to wailing. 'What's happening? Why did they do that?'

Nikolas had soldiers in the agora, and a pair watching Chloe ahead. She turned back the way she'd come and saw yet another pair of king's guardsmen approaching from the other side. There was no escape.

Chloe prayed to the gods that whatever was happening, her father was safe. Perhaps he'd requested Nikolas's help in suppressing a rebellion. Perhaps Nikolas had discovered that some of the consuls were traitors, working for masters in Ilea.

But she knew the truth in her heart. Nikolas had run out of patience with the endless deliberations, constant bickering, and pandering to factions in the Assembly. He'd taken matters into his own hands. By silencing the opposition, he would secure the vote in favor of the swift outcome he needed.

Chloe bent down and hugged her sister, her eyes never leaving the two watching soldiers. She wondered how much Sophia understood about what was happening.

'Is Father going to die too?' Sophia asked in a broken voice.

Chloe felt tears on her cheeks and shook her head, but she couldn't answer. Inwardly cursing Nikolas, hating him with every fiber of her being, she felt powerless. What would happen to her father?

And if Nikolas was bold enough to do this, what would happen to her?

She heard a throat clear behind her.

Whirling, Chloe saw Nikolas himself, standing with a wrinkled and pale-skinned old man in a black robe that covered him from

109

head to toe. She recognized a priest of Balal by his robe and the flame on the plate-sized iron medallion hanging from his neck. But why was Nikolas here, and why bring a Xanthian priest to the Temple of Aeris?

She thrust her sister behind her as she defiantly met Nikolas's gaze. He looked weary, but he was also dressed in the finest tunic she'd ever seen him wear, a gold-trimmed garment of silk.

'Where is my father?' Chloe was proud when her voice didn't shake.

'For the time being he is alive,' Nikolas said softly. His eyes narrowed. 'But what happens next depends on you.'

'On me? I don't—'

The priest stepped forward. His cold fingers took hold of Chloe's hand, and she felt dread sink into her chest when he spoke.

'Chloe daughter of Aristocles, tonight, in the sight of the gods, you are to be married . . .'

14

Liana bent over the circular stone basin and gazed at her reflection in the water. A young human woman with wide, frightened eyes stared back at her.

The young woman in the reflection wore a dirty brown tunic – stolen from a farm the previous day – and had shoulder-length hair the color of fire, dyed with henna. Her heart-shaped face was covered in streaks of mud but displayed what the humans might call a fragile beauty.

Liana was short for an eldran and her grass-green eyes were captivating rather than alien. Staring at her own face, she told herself to be brave. She could do this.

Trying to ignore the city folk scurrying about the square – there were so many of them! – Liana bent further over the pool and washed the mud from her face. She then straightened and set her jaw with determination as she scanned the area.

She wasn't far from Phalesia's main entry gate, and had headed directly for the basin as soon as she'd seen it so that she could check her appearance. So far no one had pointed at her and screamed. She was managing to blend in. There was just one piece of her disguise left, the most critical part of all.

She had been considering this idea ever since the loss of her parents. Eldren were close, but she wasn't one of them. She couldn't change. She was more like the humans.

There had been a brief moment, when Zachary and Aella had taken her in, showing her love and warmth, giving her a home for as long as she wanted it, when she'd believed she might be accepted. Dion had been kind to her, and shown her that she wasn't the only one struggling to embrace the beast within. Eiric had seemed to like her.

But then came the attack.

Aella was now lost, turned while defending Liana, who because of her own fear of changing wouldn't defend herself. Racked by grief, Zachary had vanished after his wife, although it was clear that the only choice he had was to end her life. Eiric had torn away the necklace he'd given her, a gift that had made her happier than he could know. He'd turned his back on her.

She now had no choice but to find a new path. Life among humans would be difficult, but unlike eldren they valued privacy and individual destiny. Zachary always said that of all the Galean peoples, Phalesians were the friendliest toward eldren, which was why she'd chosen this city over Xanthos. Eventually, she would find her place.

With her thoughts on the final element of her disguise, Liana left the square, following a narrow street that opened onto the avenue that was the lower city's main thoroughfare. She kept to the edge of the street, which was clearer than the center because of the filth and garbage in the gutter. Trying to emulate the city folk around her she walked briskly, with purpose, even though she only vaguely knew where she would find what it was she needed.

Her eyes alighted on a strip of market stalls ahead, and she slowed as she approached. The vendors all called out for her to inspect their wares: ceramics for her table, powders for her skin, blankets for her bed. Liana saw that the other women scanning the stalls were ignoring the cries of the vendors, so she did the same.

At the fourth stall she stopped.

The old man with a wispy white beard was selling trinkets: bracelets and earrings, rings and decorated cups, along with small statues of gods and goddesses. Liana scanned the array but couldn't find what she was looking for. She was about to leave when the old vendor finished a conversation with a woman his own age and smiled down at her.

'If you tell me what you're looking for, young lady, I might be able to help you.'

Liana took a deep breath as she turned to face him. When she spoke, her voice initially quavered, but grew in resolve as she went on. She could do this.

'I'm . . . I'm looking . . .' She cleared her throat. 'I'm looking for a necklace.'

She touched her bare throat, as if to feel for something, only to discover it now missing.

His eyes creased with sympathy. 'Lose it, did you? Get it stolen?'

'Yes,' she said.

Sympathy became mirth. 'Well? Which is it?'

'I lost it.' Liana looked down.

'Let me guess . . .' He made a show of pondering. 'Copper?'

She nodded.

He grinned. 'I'm a man of iron, myself.' He indicated his chain of black metal links supporting a medallion imprinted with a hammer. 'It's no wonder I'm still working at my age.' He let it fall and shrugged. 'Silver and I'd have wealth and fortune. Iron says I know how to make things, but it doesn't mean I'm good with the money I make.' He barked a laugh.

'Can . . . Can you help me?'

'I can't, but my brother can. Unlike me he's a true artist, a man of copper. He'll be able to help you.'

'Where can I find him?'

Liana had to get a necklace or suspicion would fall upon her. Everyone knew that eldren didn't like pure metal, and couldn't willingly touch it, and the wise men at the temples – magi, she remembered they were called – were likely aware that an eldran couldn't change shape when confined by metal. Perhaps the practice was a legacy of the war between the Aleutheans and the eldren long ago. At any rate, it made it difficult for an eldran to hide among them.

With a necklace, despite her reddish hair and lithe frame, she would be accepted as human.

'Just head further along the avenue, in the direction of the upper city. Before the steps, turn left, and his house is the third along. Has an oversized iron chain out the front, you can't miss it. His name is Ambrose.'

'Thank you,' Liana said.

'Good luck.'

She left the vendor behind, thinking that the exchange had turned out better than she'd hoped it would. If all the city folk were as amiable, she might like it in Phalesia. Perhaps, like the late queen of Xanthos, she would find a human husband one day and have children . . .

Following the directions, she turned off the avenue and soon found the house with the iron chain out the front. Steeling herself, she boldly approached the open door and called out.

'What is it?' A fat man with a moustache and beard covering his mouth eventually came to the doorway. He had deep-set eyes, a curl to his lip, and a bald head. A leather apron covered his wide belly and he held a little hammer that was like a child's toy in his massive hand.

He looked Liana up and down, sizing her up immediately. 'I'm not sure if I can help you.'

'Please.' Liana swallowed. He wasn't as friendly as the old man at the market stall. 'Are you Ambrose?'

He frowned. 'I am.'

'I need a necklace.'

'Silver? Copper?' He scratched at his neck. 'I'm guessing copper.'

'I don't want it to be pure,' Liana said. 'A mixture of metals.'

His scowl deepened. 'The priests say the metal should be pure.' He sighed when he saw Liana's set jaw. 'Bronze, then. Copper and tin alloy. I have one ready-made, but there's a flaw. And you won't have the medallion to go with it, not unless you'll take copper.'

'Just the necklace will do,' Liana said.

He gave a gruff nod. 'Come in, then.'

It was a strange moment for Liana as she crossed the threshold and for the first time entered a human dwelling. Eldren talked, of course, and some had visited Phalesia several times. But following the jeweler, as she passed through the furnished room at the front, traveled down a hall, and headed to the side chamber that was evidently a workshop, Liana felt nervous. She had a ceiling over her head. There were stone walls on all sides, formed of blocks that had been cut and fashioned with metal tools. She could smell the vague aromas of human food and already the presence of metal was making her skin itch.

Ambrose glanced behind to make sure she was keeping up. 'Are you all right?'

'I'm fine,' she said. 'But perhaps I can stay here, rather than follow you to the workshop?'

He made a non-committal sound and rounded the corner, leaving Liana in the communal cooking and eating room. She heard sounds of him rummaging around inside and then he returned a moment later.

'Here you go,' he said, holding up a necklace formed of delicate bronze hoops. He ran the chain through his fingers until he came to a link that was misshapen. 'There's the flaw. I tried fixing it but the metal's too weak. It'll hold, provided you don't pull too hard. It's more about the appearance, but'—he ran his eyes over her, taking in the grubby tunic and uncombed hair—'I'm guessing in your case the lower price will help. Let's see if it fits.'

Ambrose leaned in close to her and she smelled his sweat as he fastened the chain around her neck. He then stood back and nodded.

'Not bad,' he said. 'Let's talk about payment.'

Liana looked up to meet his eyes. 'I don't have any money.'

His nostrils flared and he gritted his jaw as his body tensed. As he drew in a breath, she saw a vein in his neck sticking out and thought for a moment he might strike her, but instead he let out the breath and spoke in a voice like rolling gravel. 'Give me the necklace'—he held out his hand—'and get out. Right now, and don't come back.'

'Please, there must be a way,' she pleaded. 'I need it. Let me work for you. I'll do anything.'

The jeweler paused for a minute and glanced from side to side. He tilted his head, considering. Stroking his moustache and beard, he reached around and slowly untied the leather apron covering his girth. He kept his eyes on Liana, as if waiting for her to balk, but she merely frowned, puzzled.

He tossed the apron to the side and stretched. 'How old are you?' he asked.

'Nearly . . . Nearly nineteen.'

'You sure you want to do this?'

Liana nodded.

He now reached out and rested his meaty fingers on her chin. Lifting her head, he leaned forward, and before she knew what he was doing, his lips were on hers and he was kissing her.

Liana didn't know what to do. It was the last thing she expected to happen. She froze, unresisting, wide-eyed and terrified.

Ambrose broke the kiss and met her eyes, gauging her reaction.

As Liana looked up at him, a terrible sound split the silence.

The snarl was utterly strange even to her. It was the bestial cry of a cornered animal, trapped but willing to fight back. The jeweler's eyes shot wide open and he suddenly looked afraid.

'What . . . What are you?'

A rumble now came from deep within Liana's chest. Eyes narrowed, she stared into the man's face as he began to slowly back away. 'Go,' he said. 'Get out of here.' His voice rose to a shrill scream. 'Go!'

Townsfolk in a bewildering array of costumes passed the striking red-haired young woman with the shining necklace. A radiant sun shone down from overhead and with no shade in the street the heat bounced back, reflected by the pale stones underfoot. Liana walked in a daze, her task accomplished, but wondering at the wild beast that lurked inside her.

She also had no plan for what she should do next.

She'd heard that humans had occupations, but that most of them required years of training and were performed by men. She had seen the priestesses though, in their smart uniforms, given respect wherever they traveled. Aella had thought she would make a good healer, and she'd heard that it was the priests and priestesses who learned the healing arts. Perhaps she could become a priestess? Other women sat on stools beside the avenue and worked with needle and thread. Liana had sewn clothing back in the Village, but she was worried that the women's patterns and stitches looked complicated, and she wouldn't be able to work with iron needles.

Peering into the open doorway of a house as she passed she saw an old weaver with a loom, passing a thread horizontally through a rainbow of strands and then clamping it all down before beginning on the next row. She knew what it was from the stories, and guessed the weaver was making a mat or a carpet, but it looked far too difficult for her. She supposed it was another trade that required a large amount of skill. Would the woman teach her? Even as she thought of it, the weaver looked up and noticed Liana's attention, directing a fierce scowl at her that sent her walking hurriedly away.

Reaching the end of the avenue, Liana climbed steps that felt like they would never end. The houses on both sides were grander, with more white stone used in their construction and fewer of the mud bricks she'd seen in the lower city.

Finally cresting the end of the steps, her mouth dropped open when she saw she was in another square, similar to the one with the water-filled basin, but containing a huge stone statue of an old man. His face was noble and wise and he held two tablets to his chest while his free arm pointed into the distance.

None of the other city folk making their way between the upper and lower city paid it any attention at all. With an effort she tore her attention away from the statue and kept moving.

Another avenue beckoned, and she once again tried to copy the pace of the Phalesians. She knew enough not to stare, but surreptitiously she tried to guess their occupations as they went about their business.

The consuls were easy; they were the men in white tunics and were generally old, with gray or white hair and lines of concern written across their foreheads. They mostly walked in groups of two or more and at all times appeared to be deep in discussion, making points with hand gestures. Mothers with children in tow were even easier, as were fishermen and soldiers, priests and beggars. But there were many others whose role she couldn't begin to hazard a guess at. They were dressed in finery or poor clothing, sometimes carrying metal tools or baskets of goods. She wondered if she'd ever feel at home in this strange place.

The street she was following was smaller than the broad avenue she'd left behind, connecting the city gates and the endless stairs, but it was even more filled with people, like an endless stream of ants crossing a stick from one leaf to another. Hoping that at some point inspiration would strike, and she would think of an occupation that might suit her, she reached the street's end, heading toward the upper city, but couldn't see what was to come through the press of people.

Trying not to feel overwhelmed by the sheer number of humans bustling to and fro, she at least began to relax about being spotted. With so many people around, and such incredible variety of physical appearance and clothing, there was little chance that she would be singled out as different.

Then she saw that the path dropped away in a series of glistening marble steps, broad and wide. Despite the press of people against her back, she stopped and stared, and this time she was so consumed by what she was seeing that her awareness of the crowd melted away.

An immense rectangular area opened up ahead, occupying a large portion of the city's available space. It was big enough that even the volume of people entering was accommodated easily, perhaps helped along by the fact that for every dozen people who descended the steps another dozen ascended in the opposite direction, creating a constant flow in and out of the plaza. The stones of the floor were paved in alternating rose and tan colors, creating a decorative pattern. A market containing dozens of rows of stalls filled the end closest to the harbor, and as she lifted her gaze further still she could see deep blue water and fishing boats.

There were wide steps in front of her and along the rectangle's entire left side, and now the huge temples drew her attention. City folk climbed the steps and followed pathways that forked as they led to the shining structures with wide circular columns and triangular roofs. The largest of them all was a long building with a stone statue outside that also held two stone tablets but made the statue she'd seen earlier look tiny.

On the right she could see high cliffs and a plateau on the summit of a broken peak. A cluster of people appeared to be gathering at the base of the cliff, near the stairway cut into the stone. Turning further she saw a region of houses and hills, almost out of view.

She had heard stories of this place, but she had never believed it was as big as they'd said it was.

'The agora,' she whispered.

15

At that moment Liana felt a bump from behind as the press of the crowd knocked her forward. Stumbling into the stair in front, she almost fell, but arrested her motion and was faced with no choice but continuing on with the mob. Carried along by their numbers, she felt adrift, like a leaf floating on the river. But rather than disperse, as she'd expected, the throng continued past the agora. She realized that the voices she was hearing were excited. Some people sounded angry, others curious, but everyone was heading in the same direction, and they were eager to reach their destination quickly.

Skirting the market, the stream of people continued all the way to the steep cliff at the right-hand edge of the embankment. They joined the crowd already there and Liana now realized that everyone had come to watch something happening at the top of the cliff, where an array of stone columns was the only thing she could make out from her position.

Suddenly the crowd began to shift and move, as some force shuffled the onlookers. Liana felt pressure and turned, seeing a column of more than twenty soldiers crying out for people to stand clear as they pushed through. Along with the people around her, she backed away, pressing herself against the woman behind her to give the menacing men as much space as possible. Finally the soldiers were through, and their officer then formed them up in a line in front of the steps.

'Back!' he cried. 'Everybody back!'

Occasionally glancing up at the summit high above, the officer wasn't satisfied until the crowd had cleared a wide space from the steep rocky slope. He then left a dozen soldiers to keep order and led the remainder up the steps cut into the cliff. Soon everyone present was watching them climb.

Liana noticed that some of the men carried stout wooden poles, leaned against their shoulders like spears. She wondered what they were doing. One soldier hefted a heavy iron box, carrying it with both arms all the way to the summit.

Then the soldiers had made it to the top, and the crowd grew restless. The time trickled past and still Liana couldn't understand what had made the people so curious, and why some of them were so angry.

'Look out!' a strong voice cried. 'Stand back!'

Along with everyone around her, Liana held her breath.

And then it happened.

An extremely heavy golden object, a chest, rolled and prodded by sweating and grunting soldiers, approached the edge of the plateau. It reached the precipice and wavered, leaning out and back in, with hundreds of eyes on it, tensed, everybody holding their breath.

It slowly leaned far enough that its weight was pulling it forward.

Ponderously, inexorably, the chest of gold fell.

The shining box tumbled down the cliff face, bouncing and rolling, so heavy that any human caught in its path would have been killed. It fell in slow motion, tearing at the rocks it encountered, knocking them free and bringing them along for the journey.

When it struck the ground Liana felt the earth tremble. The crowd around her tried to press forward and the soldiers cried out, spears held horizontally, forcing the onlookers to stand back.

Liana put a hand to her mouth.

She knew suddenly what the golden chest was, and she knew now what she had just witnessed. She remembered overhearing Zachary's conversation with Aella. They were both gone now, and only Liana could bear witness to what they'd discussed.

The horn is powerful, and containing its power saps the energy of its container. The ancient Aleutheans built a golden ark for a reason.

The crowd surged forward, every man and woman desperate to see the ark up close.

They were willing to leave the ark alone for as long as they thought it was sacred to their gods. But now that they know the truth, nothing will prevent them from claiming the gold it is made of.

Liana struggled to maintain her footing. With the golden ark now resting at the foot of the cliff, the dozen soldiers suddenly weren't enough to contain the onlookers.

Zachary's final statement rang in her mind like a bell. *We will have to take the horn.*

The crowd rushed the soldiers, knocking them aside with sheer pressure. As she felt herself carried forward by the mob, streaming toward the golden relic, Liana gasped as a pain clutched hold of her chest. She recognized the feeling, it was the same sensation she had felt when approaching the jeweler's workshop, only magnified a thousand times. She was in the presence of so much pure metal that she felt physically ill. She had to get away from it, immediately.

Liana tried to break free, but her frantic movements were in vain. She was being carried along with the crowd.

She screamed.

The cliff loomed overhead, the wall of black rock becoming closer with every passing moment. In front of her eyes were the backs of men and women's heads; at her left and right people jostled and pushed, hands out to steady themselves. Behind her two strong hands clasped down on her shoulders, nearly pushing her down to her knees with the sudden weight, but when she cried out and glanced over her shoulder the middle-aged man who'd fallen mouthed an apology and let go a moment later.

The pain in her chest grew sharper and tighter. Liana felt blinded, dazed, unable to see clearly through a haze of yellow light. Blinking through it she could now see the ark, a huge golden chest lying prone on its side. Soon she could make out the cavity in its center where the horn had recently resided.

As the growing agony made her gasp, she fought and wriggled, twisting her body and flailing with her arms. She tried to push obliquely through the crowd, even as the onlookers tried to get closer to the ark.

The pressure eased. People threw angry looks her way, but they moved. As she put distance between herself and the source of the pain, relief flooded her as the prickling sensation faded and her vision cleared. Head down, jaw set, she developed a forward and back motion with her shoulders that enabled her to fight her way through.

She didn't stop until she was heading toward the open air at the edge of the embankment. Coming to a halt, breath ragged, she stopped at the summit of the high wall that sloped down to the shore. She realized she was near the steps that the soldiers had climbed earlier, when they'd headed up to the temple.

Liana finally regained enough of her wits to look around her. The crowd clustered at the site of the fallen ark. Soon it would thin as each man or woman took a last look inside a piece of history, now open to the world, and gave way for the next person to have his or her turn.

She tilted her head back to follow the steps as they climbed the cliff, winding back and forth. Armored men were moving. The soldiers were returning.

Their attention on the ark, most of the people at the base of the cliff paid the descending soldiers no heed. But Liana swallowed and didn't take her eyes off them.

The first two men were young soldiers, empty-handed. But the third white-haired man wore the black robe of a priest and was careful with his footing as he descended, taking each step one at a time.

In his arms he held the iron chest that she'd seen earlier.

From the way he was straining it was obviously heavy, but the priest was strong and able to carry it alone without pausing. It was a simple square box, unadorned and much smaller than the ark, perhaps twelve inches on each side.

The two soldiers in front glanced back to check on the priest's progress at regular intervals. Behind him more soldiers descended the steps in single file. Some scanned the skies, others searched the agora for possible threats.

The first soldier reached the base of the cliff and drew his sword. The next followed suit, and then the white-haired man with the box was down. An escort of swordsmen and archers soon surrounded the priest, who nodded, and they began to move as a column.

Their path took them past Liana. Soldiers scowled at her, but their eyes were dismissive: the frail young woman with the wild hair and copper necklace posed no threat. She knew she was staring at the chest, but her interest wasn't unusual, for it was clear that the soldiers escorting the priest and his burden were protecting something of great importance.

They moved past her, heading back into the city, but in the instant when the priest passed close by she squinted intently at the chest. She swallowed.

It wouldn't be noticed, but there was a tiny patch of rust on the iron box. The faint discoloration was like red powder flicked at the side of the chest with fingertips. The Phalesians would think nothing of it; iron would always tarnish so close to the sea.

But as she watched, the patch grew, ever so slightly.

At that moment Liana knew. The chest contained the horn of Marrix. When it tarnished completely, the proscription about eldren touching pure metal would no longer apply. Liana could open the box, and take what was inside.

Triton could open it.

Zachary's plan had been to take the horn, for it was no longer safe; the humans couldn't be trusted to protect it. Liana didn't know what he had intended to do with it then. Zachary had admitted that he didn't have the blood of Marrix, and could never reclaim Sindara, and kingship of all eldren. But she knew what he would want her to do.

She followed the column of soldiers as they left the agora behind and headed back the way she'd come, in the direction of the lower city.

———

Liana crouched in the middle of the street, glancing frequently at the arched stone entrance nearby. It was guarded by a tough-looking soldier with a scar that started on his cheek and swept diagonally across his lip. She patted the ground, pretending to be searching for something, which gave her an excuse to circle the area and peer through to the other side of the archway from different angles.

She'd heard one of the soldiers say that this place was called the barracks. It appeared to be the place where the soldiers operated from; perhaps they lived here also. Thinking about what she needed to do, she supposed that it was one of the safest places they could take the iron chest.

The arched entrance opened up directly onto the training ground, with a sandy floor providing room for a great number of men to spar and learn maneuvers. Rows of buildings at the back framed the arena. The horn would be guarded night and day.

But it was a place unprotected from the sky. And with every passing day the iron would tarnish.

Liana had to get inside.

Taking a deep breath, she ceased scanning the road for her imagined lost item and straightened. Walking with purpose, she approached the guard, whose eyes narrowed as she approached.

'Excuse me.' Liana spoke softly. She cleared her throat. 'Excuse me,' she said more firmly. 'Do you—?'

'No,' he interrupted. 'I haven't seen whatever it is you're looking for. Now clear off.'

'I think . . .' Liana hung her head. 'I think the silver's gone. The captain's going to kill me.'

'Captain?' He frowned. 'Which captain?'

'Are you sure you won't help me find it?'

The guard looked toward the middle of the street, scratching his chin. As she held her breath, Liana saw him take three steps away from his post, his eyes on the ground as he searched for the imagined silver.

'What exactly happened—?'

He turned at just the wrong moment and saw that Liana was looking inside the barracks rather than helping him scan the ground. Without realizing, she'd been inching forward to get a better look.

The guard's eyes narrowed.

Liana quailed as he stormed toward her and then pushed her away from the entrance so hard she fell down. She struck hard stone, barely bracing her fall with the palms of her hands. She cried out.

'Trick me, will you?' he spat.

Liana heard a new voice, and as she winced and looked up from her position on the ground, she saw an older woman crossing the sandy arena, heading toward the archway. She was the fattest woman Liana had ever seen, but she had kind eyes and dimples on her cheeks and chin. She wore her curly dark hair tied at the back of her head with a girlish tassel that made Liana think she was younger than her first estimate. A dirty apron was stretched tightly around her paunch, and she had her elbow hooked around a basket, evidently on her way to market.

'What's happening here?' The woman frowned.

'She tried to trick me to get inside, cook.' The guard glared. 'She's a thief, no doubt.'

The cook crouched down at Liana's side. 'What's your name?'

'Liana.'

'Where are you from?'

Liana shook her head.

'Come on, Liana.' The cook helped Liana back to her feet. 'Hungry, are you?'

'She's trouble,' the scar-faced guard said.

'She's also stick thin.' The cook indicated for him to make way, and with a shake of his head, he finally moved.

'She'll steal from you the first chance she gets.'

'What's to steal?' the cook asked. 'A sword she can hardly lift? A helmet? She's after food. And after she sweeps floors and cleans out the mess, I intend to give her some.'

'Thank you,' Liana murmured.

Leaving the guard behind, the cook gave Liana a smile. 'These men take a lot of cleaning up after. I'll give you a meal and you can tell me your story.'

Liana bit her lip. 'No.'

'No? You don't want to tell me your story? Fair enough. You will or you won't.'

Her mind on the horn, Liana allowed herself to be led inside the barracks.

16

The black galleon rode the monstrous waves, a creature born to the sea, lifted up on each towering crest before plummeting down the far side. Wave after wave rolled remorselessly from one side of the open ocean to the other, to be met head on in a shower of spray. Hundreds of years old but preserved by cold, dry air, the *Solaris* was proving to be dependable and true, everything Palemon could have wanted the ship to be.

The same couldn't be said for the crew.

'We must go back,' Vorn said, lifting his chin and meeting Palemon's gaze.

The proud warrior, a stocky swordsman with high cheekbones and deep-set eyes, held onto a spar as the vessel leaned from one side to the next, sending chill water sluicing across the deck. Behind him stood a group of grumbling men, ranging in age from forty to more than sixty. They staggered with each lurch of the ship, grim-faced and clutching onto the nearest support with white knuckles. Still wearing the furs and skins they'd been clad in when they set off, their garments were now sodden and bedraggled. Hands patted swords, axes, and hammers at their waists; the weapons were solid, reassuring.

Palemon's lips thinned. 'There is no turning back. You know that.'

They'd made it free of the drifting floes and icebergs, forced to learn how to handle the ship with frantic haste. They'd survived their first storm, more of a blizzard than a gale, but nonetheless it had been an experience Palemon never wanted to repeat. The frozen wasteland that the lost Aleutheans had called home for over three hundred years was now far behind them. They were committed to their quest. Out on the open ocean, still too far north for the sun's passage across the sky to lead the way, they had to find the Realm of the Three Seas and then return to Necropolis for their women, old men, and children. Rather than a single ship, they would have to come back with a fleet.

Facing this small knot of resistance among his crew, Palemon stood with legs apart, riding the rolling of the ship, keeping his footing despite the constant motion. His black cloak kept him dry, although the constant drizzle plastered his graying hair to his scalp and dripped from the braids of his beard. The sky above was perfectly white, with just a faint glow somewhere astern telling him where the sun was. The air was frigid and salty.

'I understand that we must help those we left behind at Necropolis, which is why we must turn back,' Vorn persisted. 'When there was a chance that we would find the lands we left behind long ago'—he indicated the men with him—'we were proud to do what we could to help. But the witch no longer knows the way. Now that chance is gone.'

Palemon nodded, keeping his face like stone. If he was going to stamp this out completely, he had to allow their fears to be voiced. Vorn had faced down orcas from a tiny boat and hunted white bears. Until now, Palemon had considered him to be a true cold blood. If he was afraid, then others were too. Palemon swiftly assessed the scene; only half a dozen warriors faced him now, but scores more watched from the rigging and would report back to the men below decks. A cluster of magi taking shelter beneath a square of canvas could also hear every word.

'And we ask ourselves,' Vorn said, emboldened. 'What if not only the island of Aleuthea, but the entire world of the three seas sank beneath the waves? What if the ice realm is the last land left? What if there never was an Aleuthea, and it is all just a myth?'

The grizzled veteran at Vorn's side, Longbeard, looked past Palemon's shoulder. Following Longbeard's stare, Palemon saw Zara coming down from her cabin in the stern castle, where she'd been practicing her magic night and day, to no avail. Slim and supple as always in her long-sleeved navy dress, her body was bowed down by fatigue and despair, and she leaned heavily on her ever-present sun staff. When he cast her an inquiring gaze, her brilliant blue eyes met his and she shook her head.

'Either way, the witch no longer knows the way.' Longbeard made as if to spit on the deck, but then blanched and halted mid-motion as he realized that his king was standing in front of him.

Glancing back at Zara, Palemon realized she'd heard. He saw her brow crease before he turned back to face the group of men.

'I know you realize it, sire,' Vorn said. 'We are adrift on the open sea. If we don't turn back now, our chances of finding our way back to Necropolis will be slim to none.'

Vorn spoke the truth, which was why Palemon needed to let him speak, to air his grievances in this public space. None of them were experienced sea travelers. They didn't know how to use the stars. They'd come to rely on Zara so much that they now couldn't say for certain that they were traveling in a straight line.

'We are your warriors,' Longbeard said. Zara came forward to stand beside Palemon but the grizzled warrior pressed on, scowling at her. 'You must no longer listen to the witch.'

Foolish, Palemon thought.

'You must listen to us, sire. Your men,' Longbeard said. 'We tried but failed. It's time to go back.'

'Tell it to us plain,' Vorn challenged the sorceress. 'Will the power of the ark guide the way once more?'

'No,' Zara said softly, but in a voice that told Palemon to always be careful about angering the most skilled of his magi. 'The magic is simply . . . gone. It is as if the ark has been destroyed.'

'Then it is clear—' Vorn began.

'Wait.' Palemon held up his hand and spoke the single word, and in a heartbeat all eyes were on him.

He hadn't needed to raise his voice; these half-dozen warriors were some of his proudest, but Palemon led by example as well as by right. He'd hunted whales, wolves, and bears alongside them, and fought in bouts against all of them. Of all his people, he was the strongest, despite his age, and they knew it.

'Listen to me,' he said, lowering his hand. 'I could tell you that our people need to leave Necropolis, that there is no future for us there.' He stared into the eyes of each of the warriors in front of him. 'I could tell you that any land is better than that frozen hell . . . that death by blade is far more desirable than watching our children starve before hunger forces us to eat their remains.' He swept his gaze over the rigging, his voice clear enough for them all to hear and growing in volume. 'I could tell you that you are part of a trusted crew, and that every man among you volunteered to see this journey through.'

He paused to let his words sink in. 'But I won't.'

He stepped forward to meet Vorn's gaze. Palemon was the taller man, and his shoulders were broader. He pulled the dagger out of the scabbard at his waist, raised it, and kissed it.

Then in one swift movement he plunged the dagger up to the hilt into Vorn's eye. Teeth gritted, he held the warrior up by the blade as his legs twitched, before withdrawing the dagger as quickly as he'd stabbed.

Too shocked to react, the other warriors watched in horror as Vorn's body collapsed to the listing deck.

'I won't reason with you.' Palemon's gaze encompassed the entire ship. 'Any of you! I am your king. You do as I command.'

He crouched and worked again with the blood-drenched dagger. A moment later Palemon rose and held up the warrior's head, gripping it by the hair and displaying it to all present.

'And Vorn here just called my ancestor, the first Palemon, who led us to victory against the eldren, a liar. For that I could never forgive him.' He threw the head over the side of the ship and then turned back to the mutineers. 'All of our warriors carry steel weapons made in Aleuthea. There is no iron in Necropolis; we have no forges. Tell me'—he directed his gaze at Longbeard—'if not our ancient homeland, then where were your swords, axes, and hammers made? Who built this ship? Who wrote in the ship's log and left us the tale of the fall of Aleuthea, imploring us one day to return? Who among you hasn't heard me vow to return to Necropolis for our people, and to give them a future that leads to something more than certain death?'

Those arrayed behind Longbeard nodded. The men in the rigging met their king's determined glare with steady expressions of their own.

'We continue!' Palemon called. 'Our people are depending on us. We will search, and we will find the warm lands. I never want to hear about turning back again.'

The group of warriors swapped expressions as they backed away.

'Not you,' Palemon said, pointing his dagger at Longbeard.

The grizzled old warrior paled, but he clasped his palms and faced his king. He drew in a long, shaking breath, and finally nodded. 'Please, sire,' he said. 'Make it quick.'

Palemon glanced at Zara. 'There is one you insulted more than I.'

'No.' Longbeard shook his head. 'No!' His pleading became a growl. 'Not the witch.'

Palemon drew back as Zara advanced and lifted her staff. Longbeard grabbed his axe from the loop at his waist, shifting to fighting stance as he raised the weapon. Zara smiled as the golden hoop flared up, so bright for an instant that Palemon could see only white. He blinked and his vision slowly returned.

Longbeard roared. He put a hand to his eyes while he swiped the air with his axe. 'I can't see!'

Zara took her time, easily evading his stumbling blows, stepping around him as he staggered. The sorceress then lifted her staff high, revealing the spike at its base. With a grunt she plunged the point into the old warrior's foot. He screamed and fell down, his axe skittering across the deck. She then stepped forward until she was directly above him as he quailed on hands and knees. She hovered the sharpened point of the staff between his shoulder blades.

With a grunt, she brought it down. Palemon hid a wince.

Longbeard twitched, limbs scrabbling at the deck, until he finally went still.

'Throw the bodies to the sharks,' Palemon said.

Palemon found Kyphos the hunchback riding the bowsprit, at the very front of the ship, staring into the waves with grim determination. The motion of the sea here was stronger than anywhere else, a sickening up and down that made the stomach lift up to the throat before dropping down through the guts. The muscles in Kyphos's outsized arms were bunched tightly as he gripped the rail at both sides.

'I noticed you stayed clear,' Palemon said.

Kyphos shrugged, thick black eyebrows coming down over his eyes as he regarded his king. 'You didn't want help. They needed to see a strong king. You showed it to them.'

'Soon we won't be able to turn back regardless,' Palemon said.

'So that's the plan, then?' Kyphos grunted. 'We keep searching until the end?'

'We do.'

'And Zara doesn't know why the ark no longer shows the way?'

'She concludes it has been destroyed.'

'Destroyed?' Kyphos lifted an eyebrow. 'Something is afoot in the Realm.'

Palemon nodded. 'First the ark's power is drawn on. Then it flares up again. Then it disappears altogether.'

'At any rate, it means nothing if we don't find the warm lands.'

'Given time, we'll find them. We must have faith. For now, my friend, keep an eye and an ear out,' Palemon said. 'If you identify any troublemakers, you have my permission to take care of them.'

'Visibly?'

'We need to keep an iron grip on our men. Skin the next man who complains, even if it's about seasickness.'

Kyphos's lips thinned but he nodded. 'I'll see it done.'

17

After days of searching, Dion and Eiric finally found Aella. She'd died in the form of a dragon. The moment she'd turned wild, her usual form was gone forever.

Dion laid a hand on Eiric's shoulder. 'There are the scales of another dragon,' he said softly. 'Zachary?'

Eiric nodded but didn't turn around. He stood on the edge of the forest clearing, facing the rustling trees, keeping his face hidden. Dion had lost his parents and knew something about how his friend was feeling. But the manner of Aella's death was something he could never have prepared himself for, having grown up in Xanthos, far from the ways of the eldren.

He gave Eiric's shoulder a squeeze, then turned away, leaving him to grieve. Crossing the clearing, he reached the thick brush and broken saplings on the other side. Pushing through, he forced himself to look once again at Aella's body.

The long, lean creature straddled the bushes and saplings that had cradled her fall. Wings were at awkward angles; her angular, wedge-shaped head rested on the ground. She had fallen hard, shedding swathes of mottled scales when she struck the trees, but the gashes on her sinuous neck and pale underbelly were obviously made by tooth and claw. Her jaws were parted in death, displaying yellowed teeth.

Her fall had left an imprint large enough to flatten an entire cluster of trees. Once Dion had spied it from above he'd immediately known what he was looking at and called out to Eiric. She had obviously died fighting, plummeting like a stone. Her gnarled claws held onto a few last shreds of the dragon that had killed her. These larger scales, a darker shade of silver, belonged to an equally ancient creature.

Eiric had kissed her forehead and closed the huge eyelids over her staring, almond-shaped eyes, but to Dion it felt strange, seeing him bid farewell to a winged reptilian creature rather than a willowy woman with a kind smile.

Dion turned away from the dragon's silver-scaled corpse. Once again he approached Eiric, who remained with his back to him, facing a stand of swaying poplars.

'I'm sorry,' Dion said.

Eiric didn't turn around. 'You found her, and for that I'm grateful. We will return tomorrow and burn her.'

'Eiric . . . I . . .'

'There's nothing you can say,' Eiric said, his voice shaking. 'My father was strong. I only hope that I can be as strong if I find him and he is no longer himself.'

'You are strong,' Dion said. 'I know you are. We will find Zachary, but for now, your people need a leader. If your father returns—'

Eiric whirled. 'He will return!'

Dion nearly recoiled at the expression on his friend's face. Eiric's golden irises shone with inner fire and the whites surrounding them were reddened, ravaged by pain. He was panting, struggling to keep hold of himself. With his close-cropped silver hair, hawk-like nose and sharp jaw, his white skin and towering height, the eldran was suddenly intimidating.

'He was forced to kill his own wife,' Eiric said hoarsely. 'He hasn't turned. He's gone because he is grieving.'

'I know this is hard,' Dion said. 'I lost my parents too, and all I wanted to do was be alone. But someone came to me and gave me hope. He helped me to fight against those who were to blame. He helped me to keep going. Eiric, it was your father who did that. We all leaned on him but now he's gone. So it remains for you to decide your people's path. They have lost their homes. They are afraid.'

'What can I tell them?' Eiric said flatly. 'Where can we go?'

Dion had an answer ready. 'Phalesia. The Phalesians saw your people defend their city from the sun king's forces. You would be welcome.'

Eiric began to shake his head, but then pondered for a time. 'Phalesia . . .' He frowned. 'We would be safe within stone walls, although perhaps not as welcome as you say.' He sighed and nodded. 'Seth can lead them. He's the oldest of our number.'

'You won't lead them yourself?'

'No. My mother . . .' Eiric's voice broke. 'Her death wasn't recent. Father should have returned.'

'Your people need you.'

'I can't give up on him. I have to know if he is dead or alive, sane or wild.' He took a deep breath. 'If he is lost to madness, there is one place I might find him.' Eiric's voice firmed. 'I'm going to Cinder Fen. Help the others find safety in Phalesia. That is your world.'

'They'll be looked after without me. You can trust Aristocles to take care of them when they arrive.'

Eiric's voice became bitter. 'And what then? The Village is gone. We can rebuild, but as long as Triton is alive we'll live in fear.'

Glancing at his friend, Dion saw darkness in Eiric's eyes, the same darkness that took Nikolas after the murder of his family. He wondered if seeking out his father was the only task Eiric had in mind.

'As for you, my friend,' Eiric said, 'you took a turn at becoming an eldran. But I have been listening, and even now you refer to our group as separate from yourself. Perhaps my father was wrong. Perhaps you don't belong in our world.'

Dion met his friend's gaze. 'It was your father who persuaded me to try, but now? You might be right.' He reflected. After the loss of the Village, he'd been thinking hard about his place in the world. 'My future might not be with your people, but if there's one thing I've learned it's that the world is endless. Perhaps there is a place out there, somewhere, where the people won't care about my blood. I've also realized something. I miss the sea. I miss sailing with the wind and arriving in a new port. I miss being alone on the water, with nothing but the sun and sea creatures for company.' Now Eiric was looking at Dion with interest, and it was Dion's eyes that were unfocused. 'There is a boat I once sailed in, a beautiful, lean vessel. Perfect for exploring the Maltherean. Just right for traveling and trading, and searching for a place where I won't have to hide who I am.'

'I have never heard you speak like this,' Eiric murmured. 'Where is this boat?'

'I had to leave it behind. But most likely it's still where I saw it last. And with the right materials, repairs will be simple.'

'Where is it?' Eiric pressed.

Dion gave a shadow of a smile. 'Cinder Fen. It appears our paths are aligned.'

18

Chloe walked to the doorway that opened onto the villa's terrace, desperate to get some sunshine on her skin and fresh air in her lungs. As always happened, the soldier, one of Nikolas's king's guard, came forward and shook his head. He blocked the doorway with his wide body, his expression impossible to make out, hidden as his face was by his helmet.

'I need some air,' Chloe explained. She winced. 'I don't feel well.'

'Your king and husband prefers that you stay indoors.'

Chloe tried to get past him but he blocked her way again. 'Fine.' She placed a hand on her hip and made a sound of pain. 'Then you'll have to go to the Temple of Aeris for me. I need peppermint.'

He scowled and shook his head. 'Send one of the servants.'

'They're all out for the day.' Chloe knew they wouldn't be back for hours; she'd made sure of it.

'Then you'll have to wait.'

Chloe hadn't expected him to leave his post, but she now hoped he would at least value her well-being enough for her to get Sophia out of danger. She gasped, clutching her hips with both hands now. 'I need a healer from the temple,' she said, grimacing. 'If you won't go, send my sister.'

'Not without an escort,' he grunted. 'You're going to have to wait for the servants.'

Scowling, Chloe turned back inside. Glancing around the reception, she pulled up a seat and sat at the high table, before placing her head in her hands and groaning. She heard movement as the guard left the doorway, and lifted her chin as she pondered.

Chloe was now married, the Oracle's prophecy fulfilled, although she'd barely seen Nikolas since. Nonetheless, she knew that she was a critical part of his plans. Whether or not he wanted to become king of Phalesia, his marriage to Chloe would bolster his status, making it difficult for Aristocles to later denounce him. His advisers would be pressing him to sire an heir. Any child would have a potential claim on both nations.

Her thoughts turned to her father.

More than at any other time, he needed her.

Soldiers talked, and with Chloe considered safely under guard, confined in her own home, she'd heard them discussing where they might next be deployed. Aristocles had fled, but Nikolas wouldn't allow the former first consul to regroup and whip up opposition to his growing influence. If Aristocles reached Tanus and enlisted the support of Queen Zanthe, the outcome could be war.

Nikolas had sent out men to pursue Aristocles but Amos was a skilled warrior and success wasn't assured. Chloe's guards had heard their king give orders. Nikolas was going to lead the army to Tanus.

And Aristocles wouldn't know they were coming until it was too late.

Still seated at the high table, Chloe looked up when she heard her sister's voice. 'I heard,' Sophia whispered. 'Are we . . . ?'

Despite knowing that what she was going to attempt was dangerous, Chloe nodded. She motioned for Sophia to come closer and gave her a swift hug. 'You know why this is important?'

'I understand.'

'And you can be brave? Just this once?'

Sophia nodded.

'Stay here,' Chloe said.

Taking a deep breath, she rose from the table and crept to the open doorway. Poking her head around the edge of the frame, she saw the guard just a short distance away, pacing and keeping watch on both the streets below and Aristocles' villa. His head moved and Chloe ducked inside before she was seen.

'He's alone. Are you ready?'

When her sister gave another frightened nod, Chloe felt her own fear rising. Before her courage failed her, she collapsed, sprawling out onto the hard stone.

'Please, come quickly!' Sophia ran to the doorway.

Chloe stared up at the ceiling, eyes wide with pain, and made her breath run in short gasps, remembering the lessons she'd received from Tomarys, her assigned bodyguard when she'd been the sun king's prisoner in Lamara. Tomarys had taught her that the seeds of victory are sown before the fight begins, that to achieve victory means not only to be prepared, but also to play with expectations. She was a woman, and so the more skilled and powerful a warrior was, the more he would think she posed no threat. Now she wasn't just a woman, she was a sick woman.

The guard's hurried footsteps accompanied his heavy breathing as he entered and stood for a moment over Chloe's prone form, wondering what he should do. All the servants were away. Chloe knew that there was only one course available to him. He would send Sophia for a healer, but rather than go to the temple, Sophia would go to their pre-arranged hiding place, and with her sister safely out of the picture, Chloe would pretend to become gravely ill. Then, when the right moment came, she would make her own escape.

'Girl,' he said to Sophia in a rasping voice. 'What's wrong with her?'

'I . . . I don't know,' Sophia stammered.

'When do your servants return?'

'Not until the end of the day.'

He grunted. 'Then the three of us are going to stay here until then.'

Chloe couldn't believe what she was hearing. She knew the guard was cold-hearted – she'd seen him kill Consul Charon – but the one thing she hadn't expected was for him to risk her life.

Sophia's voice became shrill. 'But she needs help!'

'I am sure she does,' he said. 'But I'm to keep the both of you under guard at all times.'

Chloe's eyes moved; she saw that the guard was standing with his arms crossed, legs apart like an immovable statue. His attention was on her sister, rather than her.

Suddenly she sat up, putting a hand over her heart and taking in a sharp, choking breath. She'd been around sick people at the temple enough to know what it looked like when someone was struggling to breathe; now she had to trust in her own ability to act the part.

While the guard frowned down at her, Chloe pointed at her chest, beckoning him closer. Finally he bent at the waist, ignoring her flailing hands. She wheezed and continued to wave. Scowling, he leaned farther in. She reached up and her hand closed around the hilt of his sword.

She drew it in a heartbeat, sliding the blade free from the scabbard, and without hesitating she stabbed upwards. The point penetrated his throat, the only place where his armor didn't protect him, opening a gash that grew wider as she pressed the broad blade deeper. Blood gushed out of his mouth and Chloe was forced to roll to the side, keeping hold of her weapon as he toppled forwards. He made a sickening gurgle as she climbed to her feet, seeing him face down with a growing pool of red liquid spreading around his body.

'He's dead,' Chloe said matter-of-factly. 'You did well.'

Her sister couldn't take her eyes off the dead guard.

'Sophia,' Chloe said. 'Look at me. Remember. He killed Consul Charon.'

'What do we do now?'

'We need to leave.'

Chloe placed the sword in the dead man's grip, leaving whoever discovered him to wonder who had battled the guard and freed the two captives. Hurriedly she took her sister's hand, leading her out to the terrace, where a stairway bordered by flowering shrubs descended to the streets below. Taking the steps two at a time, Chloe and Sophia ran as swiftly as they could. They were still in danger; if someone came upon them as they descended the steps there would be nowhere to run.

But the gods were with them, and Chloe had been formulating this plan for days. She and her sister both knew the city well, and soon they were running through the alleys that skirted the agora and would lead them via dirtier streets to the lower city. Chloe had no choice but to take them directly across the broad avenue that connected the two districts, but she dashed quickly and her sister managed to keep up. Finally as she rounded a corner she slowed to a walk. They were close to their destination, and she decided she could risk a moment to speak with her younger sister.

'You understand why you have to hide, don't you? It's not that I want to leave you.'

'It's because of Nikolas,' Sophia said.

'You have to stay hidden until I find Father. I need to warn him that Nikolas is coming with an army. Tanus isn't safe. Father and I will put a plan together. I'll come back for you. I promise.'

Sophia's eyes welled but she nodded. Chloe squeezed her sister's hand as she led her to a tight alleyway, with barely enough space between opposing walls for them both to fit. Approaching the rear of the single-storied stone house, she passed the vegetable garden and washing area until she reached the back entrance to the house itself.

Her heart almost stopped when a bulky shadow approached, but when she saw the anxious apothecary waving to her urgently, she breathed a sigh of relief.

'Come, come,' Balion said. 'Quickly, before you're seen.'

Sophia was hesitant as she followed Chloe and the sweating apothecary inside. But as soon as they had passed through the arched opening to the quarters where he lived with his wife and two children, the round-faced man turned and now he was smiling as he sank to one knee and faced her.

'You must be Sophia,' he said. 'I'm Balion. Your sister's asked me to take care of you until she returns. She tells me you're a promising healer.'

'Is that what you do?' Sophia asked seriously.

'I'm an apothecary,' Balion said. 'I make medicines. They can be made out of berries, roots, nuts, bark, herbs . . . even powdered stones. Would you like me to teach you?'

'Can I help you find the ingredients?' Sophia asked.

'We'll need to give you some new clothing, the same as my children wear, but then yes, once things settle down, I think you can.'

'Balion is very wise,' Chloe said. 'I've been coming to him for years.'

The apothecary returned to his feet and went to a corner of the room, taking a satchel and returning to Chloe. 'Your supplies,' he said. 'You gave me too much silver. The rest is in a pouch inside. Are you sure you don't need a horse?'

'No,' Chloe said. 'I'll attract less attention on foot. Once I've left the city, I'll pick up a horse in one of the villages.'

He harrumphed. 'Be careful then. I wish you weren't traveling alone.'

'It's not far to Tanus. I'll be safe.'

'At least—'

'I've traveled the Phalesian Way before,' Chloe said firmly. She recalled her mad dash with Dion as they'd sped home to give warning of the sun king's attack. She wished Dion was with her now.

'There's a veil in there also. You might want to wear it.'

'Thank you,' she said. 'I can't thank you enough.'

Chloe gave Sophia a final embrace. Her heart aching, she felt her sister's sorrowful eyes on her as she left the house behind.

19

Chloe's heartbeat quickened as she approached the city gates. Exiting or entering was generally a simple matter, and with her veil she should be safe. Surely no one could have discovered the dead guard yet?

Suddenly she heard shouts coming from behind her. A growing commotion made her skin crawl. Men's voices were calling out to one another; she hadn't heard such a din since the Battle of Phalesia.

She tensed, desperate to either turn around or start running. But she knew that if she sprinted through the gates she would only draw attention to herself. If pursuit had started this quickly, she had little chance of getting safely away.

Chloe whirled.

She wasn't alone in turning around. Most of the farmers, herders, and other folk heading out of the city turned also, curious to see what the commotion was. Her heart racing, she saw that the furor came from the direction of the barracks. The avenue was broad and straight, and she could see that soldiers were out in numbers. The entire barracks was emptying out like a beehive struck with a stick.

All over the lower city people stopped what they were doing to watch wide-eyed as officers bawled orders and the soldiers split into smaller groups. Immediately they scattered in all directions, some climbing the stairs to the upper city and others systematically spreading throughout the area.

Chloe frowned; the disturbance didn't appear to have anything to do with her. She even took a step forward, knowing that when she saw her father and Amos they would want to know what had caused the commotion.

Then she saw the last person she'd expected to see.

A slight young woman pushed her way through the crowd, heading toward Chloe, her heart-shaped face flushed and apprehensive. The onlookers, all staring the other way, barely noticed her. She was walking quickly but not running, a young woman with somewhere to be, worried she wouldn't get there in time. She was heading directly for the city gates.

The young woman was Liana.

She had changed, so much that Chloe almost didn't recognize her. Where her shoulder-length hair had been silver before, it was now red, the burnt color of hair dyed with henna, often seen on priestesses of Edra with their age starting to tell. She wore a clean white tunic, well-worn but mended. She carried a satchel over one shoulder and her delicate feet were bare. But, most surprising of all, she wore a copper-colored necklace. Liana was pretending to be human.

Chloe glanced up, past Liana to the commotion in the street. Liana appeared as innocuous as a person could, the very image of weak and defenseless – even her face showed an expression without guile – but Chloe's intuition told her that whatever the soldiers were so perturbed about, it had something to do with her.

Chloe raised her veil. Despite her own need to be free from the city, she called out. 'Liana!'

Hearing her name, Liana's eyes widened and she froze. She saw Chloe and her gaze darted left and right like a cornered animal.

She began to run.

With Chloe between her and the city gates and soldiers behind her, she headed for a side street. Chloe cursed and chased after her, putting on her own burst of speed. Liana glanced over her shoulder and saw Chloe gaining on her, but when she faced forward again she almost ran full tilt into a butcher's cart.

'Liana, stop!'

Panicked, the girl continued into the alley, knocking aside a washerwoman carrying a basket. Clothing scattered over the ground and the washerwoman screamed after Liana, who ignored her and continued to sprint, looking back at Chloe with every stride, heedless of the cries she left in her wake.

Chloe began to follow, but then slowed, finally coming to a halt. She felt the blood drain from her face.

Half a dozen soldiers had their backs to Liana but they were blocking the narrow street. At any instant they would hear the shouts of the angry washerwoman and turn. Caught on both sides, Liana stopped.

Chloe approached, realizing she had only a brief moment to talk to the eldran. 'Liana, listen to me. I don't know what you're doing here, but I'm fleeing the city,' she said. 'If you want to come with me, we have to go now.'

Liana's chest heaved. Her wild eyes turned on Chloe; she pondered for the shortest instant.

Then she nodded.

⌣

Sunset found the two new companions, one eldran, one human, passing through the farmland that surrounded the city, climbing hills, following the wide, rocky road that eventually became the Phalesian Way. Olive trees spread gnarled arms on both sides of the trail. The sun's slanted rays bathed the surrounding peaks in a crimson glow. Now that they were away from the stench of the city, the air smelled fresh and fragrant, carrying scents of lavender and rosemary. Both Chloe and Liana were traveling on foot and burdened by satchels, but they were young and strong.

Now Chloe listened to Liana's story, shocked to hear that the eldren in the Wilds had suffered their own tragedy. Phalesia wasn't the only place to have changed.

'. . . and Zachary went after her,' Liana said. Her voice was hollow. 'It's my fault.'

'How could it be your fault?'

'Aella was protecting me. I couldn't change . . . I couldn't defend myself.'

'But that doesn't make it your fault. Triton attacked the Village. If anyone is to blame, it's him.'

'Eiric blames me.'

'He was upset. Is that why you went to Phalesia?'

Liana nodded. 'I wanted a chance to start again. To make a new life. Others have done it before.'

'So what happened? Why were there so many soldiers looking for you?'

'A . . . A woman gave me a job, working in the barracks.' Liana glanced at her. 'You know, cleaning and scrubbing.'

Realization dawned. 'Let me guess,' Chloe said. 'You were found out.'

Clutching her satchel tightly, Liana answered quickly. 'Yes. That's what happened. I thought I could fit in. But living in a city full of humans is not easy.'

Chloe shook her head. 'There is a lot about our culture your people aren't aware of, the way we interact with each other and work together.'

'I know. I've learned that now.'

'The assault on the Village,' Chloe said. 'Dion . . . He wasn't hurt?'

'He took a blow to the head, but he was well enough last I saw him. And you, why are you fleeing the city?'

'My father needs me,' Chloe said. 'Something went wrong between him and the king of Xanthos. He was forced to flee to Tanus. Now Nikolas is trying to outmaneuver him by leading the army to Tanus. Father is in more danger than he knows.'

'Chloe,' Liana suddenly said. 'Can I ask you something?'

'Of course.'

'Who is the wisest person you know? Someone you trust more than any other. If you had a burden to bear, who would you choose to share it with?'

'My father,' Chloe said with certainty. 'He is wise and kind.'

'Do you think . . . Will you take me to him?'

Chloe glanced up at the sky, seeing that it would be dark soon. Fortunately it was summer, and it wouldn't be cold beneath the stars.

'I'm going now to find him. But, Liana, it's going to be dangerous.' Chloe glanced at Liana's satchel. 'Do you have supplies?'

'No.'

'Then what's in there?'

'Something precious to me,' Liana said defensively.

Chloe decided to let her have her secret. 'I have some silver, and we can pick up supplies on the way, but there won't be enough left for horses. That means we'll have to travel hard, from sunup to sundown.'

'I don't mind. Please, let me come with you.'

Seeing Liana's anxious expression, Chloe reached over and gave her hand a squeeze. 'Come on,' she said. 'Let's find a camp for the night.'

20

The dawn sky dripped with the colors of the sun god Helios's paintbrush, early light sparkling on the curling waves and the placid waters farther from shore. There was little wind, and though the day promised to be burning hot, the morning was still and tranquil, giving Nikolas some much needed time to think.

He stood on the beach of white pebbles, legs astride and head tilted back as he watched a distant rowing galley draw inexorably closer. Oars swept back and forward in unison as the vessel fought the outgoing tide. Behind Nikolas the defensive bastion loomed, casting a wide shadow over the area. His king's guard would be standing on the embankment, eyes on him at all times. The sense of solitude was pretense, but it was calming.

Gazing out at the blue water, watching the approaching galley, Nikolas thought about how small the Maltherean Sea had become since the Ileans' attack. At any moment his enemy could come again, striking Xanthos, Phalesia, or both. The secret route through the Shards was secret no more. He was working to repair the biremes captured after the battle and to build new warships until he had a large fleet. But building ships took time, and time didn't work in his favor.

His commanders told him that Balal would give them the strength to prevail, but Nikolas knew that achieving victory over a mightier foe would require more than trust in prayer. He had to take the battle to his enemy's heartland.

'King Nikolas.' A hesitant voice spoke behind him, interrupting his thoughts.

Nikolas turned and saw Nilus, looking ill at ease despite his fine embroidered tunic and the new gold medallion dedicated to the god of justice hanging from the chain around his neck.

'Nilus,' Nikolas said, turning his attention back to the approaching galley. 'Come to welcome the newcomers to your city?'

Nilus came to stand beside him and wrung his hands. 'No, not exactly.'

'Well?' Nikolas asked, still staring out to sea. 'What is it?'

'I take it you haven't heard?'

'I spent the last night in the Temple of Balal,' Nikolas said. 'Seeking answers to important questions.'

'If you'd left word, we could have found you . . .'

Nikolas frowned. 'Since when should I notify you of my comings and goings, First Consul?'

'The horn of Marrix is missing,' Nilus said the words in a rush.

Nikolas felt his heart beat out of time. He rounded on Nilus and lifted a finger, speaking in a low tone. 'You told me soldiers would be surrounding it at all times.'

'Someone got past them. The . . . The iron chest is rusted through. I don't understand it, but it appears that Aristocles was right. It needed a container of gold.'

'Rusted? So an eldran could have taken it?'

'It is possible. Yes.'

'So any day we could be facing an army of wildren, if sounding the horn truly allows them to be controlled?'

'I honestly don't know. We're doing all we can. I have men out in numbers . . .'

Nikolas took a slow, steadying breath as he thought. 'Stay quiet about this. Keep it among the men. The last thing we need is a panic. And if Triton wasn't the culprit, it's better for us all if he believes we still have it.'

Nilus nodded. 'I concur. Leave it to me, King. We'll find it.'

Nikolas turned his attention back to the galley but his mood had been shattered by the news. His teeth were clenched tightly. Either Chloe had lied about what Zachary had said, or Zachary had lied to her.

The large rowing vessel left the deeper water and passed into the light blue shallows. Nikolas could now make out the occupants: a dozen crew, led by a stocky woman with close-cropped blond hair. She stood with her hand on the mast, barking orders and shielding her eyes. Seated at the bow was a well-dressed rangy man with short gray hair and a neat beard. Nikolas began to walk forward to greet them as they disembarked.

'Wait,' Nilus called after him. 'There is something else.'

'What is it this time?' Nikolas turned to face the portly consul.

'Aristocles' daughters are missing.'

Nikolas felt a surge of rage, bringing heat to his face. His mouth worked soundlessly, before his face finally curled in a scowl. 'My wife is missing and you're only telling me now?'

Nilus's eyes narrowed. 'As I said, we've been looking for you. You picked a poor time to sequester yourself in the temple. It was only now when I thought you might be here . . .'

'Enough.' Nikolas cut the air with his hand. 'Tell me what happened.'

'Someone freed the two girls. Stabbed their guard in the throat.'

'Amos?'

'It's possible, but unlikely. I would expect Aristocles to be halfway to Tanus by now. Perhaps someone else, a friend? There may be a connection to the horn's disappearance. Chloe is close to the eldren as you know. Perhaps even your brother . . .'

Nikolas's scowl deepened. 'I see the connection.'

'With no heir of your own, your death would make him king.' Nilus glanced back at the helmeted guardsmen watching their king from the embankment. 'You are wise to keep your guards close.'

Nikolas shook his head. 'He wouldn't harm me directly. We were once close, as close as brothers can be. No, it is the threat from across the sea that keeps me awake at night.' His lips thinned as he muttered. 'First she defies me and travels to the Wilds, now this. I'll find her, Nilus, as the gods bear witness. She'll learn her place.'

'We've initiated a search.'

'She'll be on her way to join her father. Likely where I find one, I'll also find the other.' He looked down at the galley as the crewmen pulled the vessel up on the beach. 'Come, First Consul.'

The stocky woman and rangy man were already climbing the shore, and Nikolas couldn't help contrasting them. Roxana was as rough-voiced and thick-skinned as any sailor, at ease on the sea, and even now her coarse trousers were wet through from jumping out early to help her crew with the ship. She was originally from Efu, in Haria, a place Nikolas knew nothing about, where she'd performed much the same role she performed for Nikolas now, but she had been enslaved after Solon conquered her city and taken to Lamara.

Seeing her value, Kargan, overlord of the sun king's fleet, had given her a ship and crew, as well as appointing her to supervise much of the work in the naval yards, but she had kept her status as slave. Nikolas had made her a free woman after the Battle of Phalesia, and was the third successive ruler she'd built ships for. Many of her crewmen and workers were Ileans she'd demanded he free also. Nikolas had given Roxana the villa she'd demanded and tasked her with making Xanthos into a naval power.

The lean man who walked beside her, Glaukos, had weathered skin, a trimmed beard, and tidy gray hair. He was a farmer through and through, a typical Xanthian who disliked the sea and any form of restless roaming as much as he felt pride in a well-ordered homestead and a freshly plowed field. He was the owner of an immense farming estate inland, the largest in Xanthos. He hated being an administrator, which was one of the reasons he made such a good one.

'Uncle Glaukos,' Nikolas said warmly, opening his arms and gripping him in a strong embrace. He was the younger brother of Nikolas's father, the late King Markos, and had been a part of Nikolas's life for as long as he could remember. He'd always been fond of Dion, Nikolas remembered. He squashed the thought down. 'How goes the kingdom?'

'Well enough,' Glaukos said wearily. 'When will you be coming home?'

'And Captain Roxana,' Nikolas said, ignoring the question. 'How goes the fleet?'

'You know as well as I do,' she growled. 'The work moves forward in fits and starts. I can't perform magic. Where is the silver you promised me?'

'Coming,' Nikolas said. 'When you return to Xanthos, you'll be heading back with as much as you can carry.' He made way for Nilus. 'This is Phalesia's new first consul.'

Nilus greeted them both, still a little flustered after his conversation with Nikolas.

'What happened to your predecessor?' Glaukos asked Nilus. 'I thought he'd be first consul until the day he died.'

'Forgive my uncle,' Nikolas explained with a smile. 'He's always been plainspoken.' He turned to Glaukos. 'There was a conspiracy and he fled the city.'

Glaukos shook his head. 'I will never understand Phalesian ways. Give me a strong king and a brace of healthy sons any day.' He raised an eyebrow at Nikolas. 'Speaking of sons, your message took me by surprise – my congratulations on your marriage. As hasty as it was, I understand the need. Do you have a day in mind for the wedding feast? Xanthos is ready to welcome a queen.'

'Yes, well.' Nikolas glanced at Nilus. 'You'll have to wait a little longer for my return to Xanthos. I'm afraid your visit will be a short one. I need both of you back home, doing what you do best.'

'There are two things I do best,' Roxana said, arms crossed in front of her chest. 'Building ships and sailing them. I'm going to need you to choose what it is you want me doing, King.'

Nikolas's brow furrowed. 'Go on.'

'We're sending more merchant ships out to sea, which brings more trade, but also means more contact with pirates. At the moment you're keeping our warships close to home, so the merchants are out there defenseless. Fair enough, that's your choice, you're worried about the Ileans. But lately things have become worse. One pirate in particular, Jax, is all I hear about. Has everyone scared witless. Calls himself the king of the Free Men.'

'Hunt him down,' Nikolas said flatly.

'No. You have to choose. I can hunt pirates or build warships. I can't do both.'

'Can't someone else hunt pirates?' Nilus ventured.

Glaukos snorted and rolled his eyes. 'Here we go,' he muttered.

'No,' Roxana said, prodding a finger into Nilus's chest. She spoke slowly, as if speaking to a child or an idiot. 'No one else can hunt pirates. The Xanthian captains would be eaten alive.'

'Let the pirates be,' Nikolas said. 'Build me more warships.'

'Fine,' Roxana said. 'But we're going to have to protect our trade at some point.'

Nikolas turned his attention to Glaukos. 'Uncle, I have a duty for you also. I'm going to need you to manage the kingdom for a time longer. I'm officially naming you my regent.'

Glaukos groaned. 'And here I was expecting you to ask me to step down. Hoping, might be another word.'

'I also need you to pass orders to my officers. They're to turn out and join me here in Phalesia. Send word to the Tharassan mercenaries. Recruit as many as you can with the silver I'm sending home with you.' Nikolas's gaze swept over the group. 'I'm taking the army to Tanus.'

Nilus frowned. 'To what end?'

'As Captain Roxana here is so quick to tell me, we can't defend ourselves by sea from another attack, which means we have to take the fight to Ilea on land.'

'It's a long way,' Nilus said.

'I'm aware of that,' Nikolas said with a frown. 'And I'm also aware that the Waste lies between Tanus and Koulis. But I'm not afraid of Triton, and perhaps with the armies of Phalesia, Tanus, and Xanthos at my back, we can finally end the eldren threat for good, before pushing on to Lamara itself.'

'But Tanus and Xanthos—' Nilus began.

'Queen Zanthe's hatred was for my father, not me. I plan to persuade her to forget our past.'

'But your new wife . . .' Glaukos protested.

'I was going to wait for the wedding feast, but it appears my wife has taken an unexpected absence.' Nikolas left unsaid that heading to Tanus might also lead him to Chloe. 'There's no use waiting any longer.'

Nikolas now looked out to sea, but he wasn't seeing the sun shimmer on the water; he was seeing plains and battles, and the sacking of Lamara, the hub of the Ilean Empire, the greatest city in the world.

Kargan was no doubt back in the Ilean capital, licking his wounds, plotting another attack on Nikolas's homeland. A new king, some son of Solon's, would have filled the void that the sun king left behind.

The Ileans had killed Nikolas's family, impaling his beautiful wife and loving father, slitting his young son's throat. He would have his revenge.

'I'm reforming the Galean League,' Nikolas said decisively. 'Zanthe of Tanus will join us or we'll raze her city to the ground.'

21

Kargan of Lamara had fought in more engagements than he could count. He'd crushed armies in the field and destroyed fleets on the open sea, crucified pirates on lonely shores and hunted serpents greater in size than the vessels he commanded.

He was a brave man, loyal and experienced, the son of a minor khan who had wealth and land but a weak bloodline. He'd risen to the top by being stronger than anyone else, but also by knowing when to fight and when to bide his time. His men loved him, for he rarely lost a battle. Even now, after the terrible defeat at Phalesia, he'd managed to withdraw from the fight with most of the fleet intact, leaving just a handful of vessels on the beach. And if it hadn't been for Solon's mad obsession with gold, he would have saved them all.

Yet despite his lifetime of service, and after proving himself time and again, he was worried.

He'd done the right thing, sending word ahead of the defeat, and of the death of the king of kings, the ruler of the Ilean Empire. Solon's great tomb had come to naught; he'd perished on foreign soil, and his body was no doubt burned along with the rest of the Ilean fallen. All the slaves who had died, the wars fought for gold, the chants of the yellow-robed priests, the plans of the engineers, the many years of ceaseless labor . . . It had all come to nothing.

Knowing his position back in Lamara was made precarious by the defeat and the imminent appointment of a new ruler, Kargan had nonetheless fulfilled his moral duty to his men. The homeward journey had taken far longer than the original voyage because he'd shepherded every single ship home, leaving no man behind. Broken vessels had been repaired and broken limbs set. Limping along with the rear, he knew that the fastest ships would have arrived in Lamara long ago, and the palace would have had ample time to prepare for his return. Maneuverings for power would have taken place. The council of lords left in charge might have already crowned a new king. Only time would tell who was now giving the orders in Lamara.

But would he be returning to chains or would he advise the new king, as he had advised Solon? Was his head about to be parted from his shoulders?

He had his men's loyalty and their trust, but these were things that counted for little in court. Frustration coursed through him, combining with his fear and anxiety. Solon's death wasn't Kargan's fault; he'd had his chance to flee. Instead Solon flew on Triton's back to the temple on the plateau. Kargan then saw Triton fight a black dragon in the sky.

At the end, when Triton fled, scratched and bleeding, Solon didn't flee with him. As Kargan's warship the *Nexotardis* drew away he saw soldiers climb up to the temple and a limp body carried down as the men around them cheered. The lanky figure clad in a sun-colored robe was unmistakable.

Kargan clenched and unclenched his fists as he watched the approaching city of Lamara from the bow of the *Nexotardis*. He wondered if he should have forced the faster ships to travel at the ponderous rate of the others, rather than giving his allies and enemies among the nobility so much time to plot and plan. But to do otherwise wouldn't have been right. The empire needed leadership. He couldn't allow it all to crumble.

As the ship navigated the brown river the familiar tall city wall passed by on the left, terminating in a hexagonal tower, and then he could see the structures on the other side. Rolling rows of mud-brick houses descended from the central ziggurat, spreading to fill the area in between the walls, opening in the area of the bazaar and then closing ranks again as the river prevented the myriad of dwellings from multiplying farther. The sprawling palace crowning the city's heart speared the sky with tall spires, yellow pennants snapping in the breeze.

His eyes roved over the temples of basalt and marble statues, sprawling slums and grand villas. It was a hazy city, yellow and dusty, where palm trees clustered around manicured gardens, beggars filled the streets, and produce from every corner of the world could be bought and sold. There was no other city like Lamara. It was home.

The *Nexotardis* now slid along the surface of the river at a walking pace, drum pounding slowly below decks, oars rising and falling with a stately rhythm. Lifting his gaze, Kargan squinted into the dusty horizon, looking for what would give him his first indication about what had transpired in the empire since his absence.

Wind blew fine particles of orange dust into his eyes, making him form them into slits, but still he stared. It was an exceptionally dusky afternoon, and it was longer than usual before he could see it.

But then it appeared, taking shape in the clouded sky like some magical home of the gods. The triangular mountain, formed out of huge stone blocks, with each level slightly smaller than the one below, filled him with the same awe that it always had, despite the fact that he had borne witness to its construction. Rising from behind the city that obscured its base, the pyramid was testament to the power of one man, the king of kings, and his ability to bend an entire empire to his will.

Kargan sighed. Solon had come close to achieving his goal of immortality. But when the Oracle's prophecy had proven true, and he'd died in the thirty-first year of his reign, he hadn't been interred in his completed tomb, to take his place among the gods. It hadn't even been the sickness in his chest that killed him.

Kargan never again wanted to follow a king into such folly.

And evidently someone agreed with him. For now he could see that where before three-quarters of the pyramid's stones had been clad in shining gold, now every surface was uniformly bare. Someone had directed that the gold be stripped, someone with enough power to give that command.

The river opened up ahead. The right-hand bank was home to fishermen and farmers, with passage across made possible only by ferry boat. Fields of hardy crops spread over the flat land, overlooked by olive trees on the higher slopes. The left bank grew larger as the *Nexotardis* neared, curving in the stretch of pale beach that was Lamara's harbor, while above the shore the city teemed with scurrying folk in an array of colorful costumes.

Kargan frowned when he saw merchant vessels beached side by side with dozens of warships; the order that usually existed here was absent. There were no marines drilling and the mess was completely empty.

Nonetheless, he stood tall as he made his return, arms crossed in front of his chest, legs far apart on the deck of his ship. He might be coming home from defeat, but a true captain stayed with his ship, and as commander of them all, he had remained with his fleet until the end.

Then, as the *Nexotardis* slid up on the sandy shore, something happened that caused Kargan to nearly recoil in surprise. A resounding cheer started on the top deck, continuing below decks, until the entire vessel was roaring as one. He heard his name repeated again and again.

But as a commander should, he made no reaction other than to stand sternly and wait for the oarsmen to pour out the sides of the ship and haul her up higher on the beach. The gangway slid out soon after, and Kargan, a striking man, with his barrel chest and powerful frame, mop of black hair and curled beard, descended the ramp, to finally feel his homeland under his feet again.

⌣

Keeping his dainty slippers clear of the fine-grained sand of the harbor, Lord Haviar waited with half a dozen soldiers to escort Kargan to the palace. A short, dark-skinned patrician with a thin nose and even thinner lips, he wore an orange tunic over brown trousers and had a limp he swore was a war wound, though he'd never held a sword in his life.

Kargan kept his face blank as he approached, but the relief he felt was overwhelming. If they were going to make him a scapegoat, they wouldn't have sent a man he could squeeze the life out of with one hand tied behind his back, leading a contingent of common soldiers he knew well, even to the point of remembering some of their names.

'Lord Kargan,' Haviar said. 'Lord Mydas requests your presence.'

'Ahh,' Kargan said as he joined the shorter man. 'So Solon's brother is acting regent.'

'He arrived as soon as he heard the news.' Haviar hesitated. 'It is good to see you well. Despite the reports, we were concerned when you didn't arrive with the first of your ships.'

'I had to take care of my men.'

Kargan glanced at Haviar as they commenced their walk up to the nobles' quarter and the palace, wondering what the man knew, wondering what would happen next. If they weren't going to kill him, all he wanted to do was head to his home and have a slave rub the tension out of his back.

Lamara was just the way he remembered it, the streets and alleys a confusing maze, the soldiers Haviar had brought with him clearing a path through the beggars and citizenry indiscriminately. The spicy scents wafting in the hot air mingled with the ranker smells of the gutters. Step after climbing step made his calves burn; there wasn't much opportunity for exercise aboard ship.

'What of Solon's sons?' Kargan grunted.

'Prince Caran is here, but the other two have yet to arrive.'

'And the coronation?'

'The priests have yet to set a date.'

'Caran is the eldest and Solon's named heir. What's taking them so long?'

'Lord Mydas waits for all, Lord Kargan, yourself included. All must swear fealty to the new king of kings.'

Kargan shook his head. 'I'm worried about the dominions. A strong hand is needed. If Solon's death becomes common knowledge throughout the empire, rebellion will be likely.'

Haviar gave him a sidelong glance. 'I always forget that you have a sharper mind than appearances credit you with. You are correct, of course. Some are stirring.'

Kargan scowled. 'Which is it? Haria? Shadria? Imakale?'

'The Council of Five in Koulis knows. Most likely when Mydas sent word to inform Caran, who was satrap there, of his father's death.'

'And . . . ?'

'Nothing as yet, only a message from the council expressing sympathy and solidarity. Taxes are overdue, though.'

'Koulis will try to assert its independence,' Kargan said. 'The dominions will find out. All of them. There are more spies in the palace than there are rats in the bazaar. It's going to be difficult to hold on to the empire.' His voice turned bitter. 'They'll find out we were defeated by a rabble of Galean barbarians.'

'Lord Mydas says we must ready our forces for a punitive attack. Nothing must survive this time. We must raze their cities to the ground, and kill every man, woman, and child.'

Kargan gave Haviar a shadow of a smile. 'Have you ever killed a child, Lord Haviar?'

The thin-lipped lord opened his mouth, blustering. 'Their soldiers are no match for ours—'

'It wasn't the question I asked, but it's always simpler to answer a different one. Never mind.' Kargan clapped his companion on the shoulder with a meaty palm. 'I'll save my words for Mydas.'

'Lord Kargan, Overlord of the Fleet, Adviser to the—' the steward making the announcement suddenly paused.

'Never mind,' Kargan said, grinning at the steward as he strode forward. 'I'm sure you'll stumble over that one for some time, unless our next ruler decides to call himself sun king also.'

Mydas waited with his hands behind his back, his lips pursed and forehead creased as he watched Kargan approach. Solon's brother was a heavyset man, with dark oily hair in ringlets and emotionless eyes. Gold rings glittered on his fingers and he wore a white silk robe with a golden belt. Glancing briefly at the nobleman's feet, Kargan saw that he even had gold thread woven through his sandals.

Mydas stood on the terrace, where he'd evidently been gazing at the river. He would have watched the *Nexotardis* draw near, and he'd had ample time to decide what approach he wanted to take with his late brother's loyal commander. Kargan wasn't surprised to see him acting as regent: Abbas, where he'd long governed, was Ilea's second-largest city and an important center for commerce, particularly the slave trade. Mydas's wealth flowed from the blood and tears of wretches.

'My brother is dead, and you come at me with a smile,' Mydas said. The grin faded from Kargan's face; he knew he tended to say the wrong thing when he was around men who took themselves seriously, a trait Solon had eventually become accustomed to.

'I wasn't jesting about our ruler's death,' Kargan said flatly. 'I was there when he died. I saw them carry his body down from the cliff, and I knew I would have no chance to retrieve it, not after what he ordered done to the king of Xanthos and his family.'

'You sent word ahead,' Mydas said, staring at Kargan with his dead eyes. 'And I questioned some of your men. Not a single Ilean died defending him at the end.'

'A multitude of Ileans died,' Kargan growled. 'The waters ran red, and piles of corpses spread over the land.'

'But my brother was alone at that temple—'

'He was alone because he left us. The eldran king convinced him to go with him to the temple, and Solon took his chance.' Kargan spread his hands. 'I've had a life full of accomplishments, and I can do many things, but I have yet to learn to fly.'

Mydas nodded slowly. He watched Kargan for a while, pondering, and then spoke again. 'You are aware that I am leading the empire until a new king is crowned?'

'I'm aware, yes,' Kargan said. 'I'll also say this. Your brother led Ilea into a golden age. I don't want to see the empire fall apart. I'll do my best to help Solon's successor.'

'We are in accord then,' Mydas said. 'The empire must remain whole and undivided. We need a show of strength.'

Kargan pounded his fist into his palm. 'Without a doubt. First, the Council of Five in Koulis. We should send a division—'

'I won't countenance sending any soldiers to Koulis,' Mydas interrupted. 'No, not while there is another, more pressing target. A target I would have thought to be close to your own heart.' He looked out from the terrace, gazing north, in the direction of the Maltherean Sea. 'You were humiliated, Lord Kargan.' He turned to meet Kargan's eyes. 'Ilea was humiliated.'

'There was a fire at the harbor,' Kargan said. 'We lost two-thirds of the fleet. Yet your brother wouldn't wait. With repairs and time, we could have embarked with twice the numbers we did.'

'Regardless,' said Mydas, 'our dominions will see only that we were defeated by Galean barbarians. You need to show that you, and by association Ilea, are still a force to be reckoned with. Only then can you be forgiven for your defeat. I will accept you in the role you performed for my brother, and recommend you to the future king, if you agree that our priority must be vengeance.'

'Lord Mydas,' Kargan said carefully. 'I understand what you're saying. But the next time we come they'll be ready. It's not the right moment to commit ourselves to another hasty attack, to war against a land far away in both distance and culture, when we're sure to have problems closer to home. What we need to do is crown the new king quickly. Then we should lead the armies on a tour of the capitals.'

'I thought you were a naval commander?' Mydas murmured.

'I command men.'

'Yes,' Mydas said. 'At the moment you do.'

Kargan frowned. 'Let's simply say we disagree. At any rate, Lord Mydas, the next move is for the king to decide. It is to be Caran, isn't it?'

'He is the eldest and heir,' Mydas said, looking away.

'Then . . .'

'But I am not certain if he's ready.'

Kargan steadied himself with a slow breath, nostrils flaring. 'This is a dangerous time for uncertainty.'

'The empire's finances are solid and our pride must be restored. I'm sure you've noticed the pyramid. I've ordered the gold to be coined.' He gave a wry smile. 'The priests now tell me that the pyramid does not require gold . . . They now say that the specifications Helios gave them were for a pyramid of yellow stone. Lord Kargan, my brother was foolhardy, but I am not. Prepare plans for another assault on Phalesia.'

Kargan shook his head. 'My men just went through hell, and I won't order more of them to throw their lives away. I think I'll wait for the new king.' He gave a brief bow. 'By your leave.'

Mydas scowled, as Kargan turned on his heel.

22

The heavens rumbled, threatening rain; the gods were bickering. A full moon shone brightly overhead, but then became covered by sinuous clouds, speeding across in thick smears, darkening the night. Only a handful of stars clung to the horizon in the one place where the sky was clear.

Shivering, Aristocles leaned forward and held his hands out to the coals, rubbing the palms together and bending forward until he was almost touching the low embers. This campsite was the worst so far. Close to the high road, with mountains on both sides, a cold wind blew constantly. With his back against a log and a blanket covering his raised knees, he glanced up at a second peal of thunder and prayed it wouldn't rain.

He glanced around, but this was a barren region of rock and gravel, with only a few sparse trees that were far too wretched to shelter under. If rain came, he and Amos would get wet; there was nothing they could do about it. He was weary of traveling and tired of living in fear, with days spent on horseback from sunup to sundown and nights lying by a fire that was warm when he went to sleep but cold as the grave when he woke with the dawn.

Groaning as he reached over to the pile, he picked up a stout length of wood and hunched forward to throw it on the dying campfire.

'Don't,' Amos said. Leaning back against his knapsack, his eyes opened, showing slits. 'Keep the fire small.'

Aristocles scowled, but he did as instructed and tossed the wood back where he'd found it. 'I thought you were asleep.'

'I am,' Amos said, closing his eyes again. 'You might want to try it sometime.'

Aristocles contented himself with holding out his palms once more. Though his body was weary to the core, he wasn't used to keeping these hours and still found his mind became active at night. He was accustomed to working late in his villa, hosting and attending symposiums, making plans with powerful men and seeking advice with the magi at the temples. To say he was having difficulty adjusting to the hardships of travel would be an understatement.

But more than the comforts of home, he missed his daughters and worried about them constantly, praying daily to the gods that they were safe. He missed Sophia's nagging questions and Chloe's stern fussing. He promised himself that when he returned to Phalesia he would tell his daughters he loved them every day. Perhaps if the gods were especially kind, Nikolas would die gruesomely in some battle, hacked to pieces by howling Ileans.

Nikolas had made his move because of the ark. No doubt it was gone now, and the prophecy of the Oracle would be fulfilled: the horn of Marrix would sound, plunging the world into yet another war between human and eldran. But crisis was the sire of opportunity. There would come a time when Aristocles could return to his city. All he needed was for Queen Zanthe of Tanus to offer him protection until that day.

Amos suddenly sat bolt upright. Aristocles frowned and opened his mouth to query his companion, but then he heard footsteps crunching on the gravel.

'Hello the campfire!' a voice called out.

A slim man walked out of the darkness. He had neat dark hair and a trimmed beard around his wide mouth. He wore a loose tunic and a sword hung on a scabbard from his waist, a thinner and longer weapon than the one Amos carried.

The newcomer stood for a moment on the opposite side of the fire from Aristocles, looking at the two resting men, and then his weathered face broke out in a smile.

'Friends,' he said, his expression amicable and hands spread. 'Mind if I join your fire? We aren't far from Cinder Fen and you know how it is; everyone says that safety lies in numbers.'

'Of course,' Aristocles said. 'There's warmth for all.'

'I thank you,' the newcomer said. Stepping forward, he crouched at the coals and held out his hands in the same way Aristocles had been doing a moment ago.

Aristocles glanced at Amos, seeing that he was leaning forward, staring at the newcomer intently. The newcomer didn't sit down. Amos's hand inched forward to the bow and arrow placed near his foot.

'You aren't going to sit?' Aristocles asked. 'Where is your pack?'

'I didn't want to bring my things over until I was sure I was welcome,' the slim man said nonchalantly. He gazed directly at Aristocles. 'Who are you, friend?'

'I'm a merchant,' Aristocles said. 'Name of Nikandros.' He nodded at Amos. 'This is Graphos, my bodyguard.'

'Your accent sounds Phalesian,' he said.

Aristocles smiled. 'That's because it is.'

'What goods?'

'No goods as yet,' Aristocles said. 'I'm buying a cargo and hiring a caravan in Tanus.'

'And yourself?' Amos challenged.

The newcomer shrugged. 'I'm from Sarsica. Also a bodyguard.' He grinned at Amos. 'Among other things.'

The smile made Aristocles lean forward. His knees were still bent, covered by the blanket. His right hand began to pat the ground, searching. The next words Amos spoke caused a chill to race along his spine.

'How about your companion?' Amos asked, staring out into the darkness. 'Why is he hiding back there?'

'Look,' the newcomer said, straightening and stretching. Ignoring Aristocles, he addressed his words to Amos. 'There's no need to make this difficult. We'll share the bounty with you. Divide it in thirds. You can keep your horses and your silver. You don't have to die. Just your white-haired friend.' He rested his hand on the hilt of his sword. 'I'm the best swordsman in Sarsica. Fought in the arena for three years. I've killed sixty-seven skilled swordsmen in combat. And'—he cocked his head—'as you've realized, my friend has a bow trained on you.'

'Gastraphetes,' Amos said.

The swordsman frowned, puzzled. 'What—?'

Amos rolled to the side as an arrow skewered the knapsack he'd been leaning against. Picking up his bow and arrow from the ground nearby, he aimed and fired, then discarded the bow and drew his sword, running out into the night.

As the slim man immediately unsheathed his sword, Aristocles threw aside the blanket covering his knees. Fumbling on the ground, he picked up the loaded crossbow and pressed the stock tight against his shoulder in the way Amos had shown him. The swordsman's face and chest were reddened by the low embers of the fire, outlined against the darkness, just a few paces away.

Squeezing the lever, Aristocles fired. The string made a snapping sound and thrummed like a harp as the sharpened arrow shot out along the channel and flew through the air.

The swordsman looked down at his chest. He coughed. The sword fell out of his fingers.

The arrow sprouted from the center of his torso, just below his sternum and rib cage, unimpeded by armor or bone. Showing the whites of his eyes, his gaze met that of Aristocles.

'This,' Aristocles said, his back making a cracking sound as he climbed to his feet, 'is a gastraphetes.' He held up the complex weapon. 'It's extremely expensive, but I think you'll agree that it's worth its weight in gold.'

'You . . .' The swordsman coughed again, and this time red liquid sputtered from his lips. With every breath his lungs made a hoarse whining sound. 'You've killed me.'

The swordsman sank to his knees and then toppled forward. Amos appeared a moment later, glancing at the dead man and then at Aristocles, a bloody sword in his hand. 'We have to go. I'll ready the horses. Retrieve your arrow.'

Aristocles grimaced. All this traveling and soldiering really didn't agree with him.

Aristocles shielded his eyes with one hand as he stood tall in the saddle, reins held loosely in his other hand.

'There,' he said, pointing. 'See it in the distance?'

The Phalesian Way continued to climb ahead, sinuous as a snake, passing between sharp peaks and under rocky overhangs. In every direction were unsurpassed views of wild valleys encircled by tall mountains. The ranges grew dark and forbidding in the south: in that direction lay Cinder Fen, where wildren roamed, a place Aristocles had no desire to visit in his lifetime. The northern lands were just as dangerous, home to a bewildering array of barbaric tribesmen. Aristocles was pointing west.

'Those tiers . . . Is that farmland?' Amos asked.

'Look higher up,' Aristocles instructed. 'See the plateau? You can make out the city walls. That's where we're heading.'

Amos whistled. 'Now that's what I call defensible.'

'It would have to be, out here. Tanus still fends off wildren attacks regularly enough to have an evening curfew. And then there are the northmen to contend with.' He sat back down in the saddle. 'Still, they've found their place. They mine iron and copper, and grow wheat and barley.' He smiled at his companion. 'I hope you like goat.'

'How far?'

'It's closer than it looks.'

Amos turned in the saddle to glance behind them. 'Good,' he said. He raised his voice. 'We've got company!'

Amos kicked his horse forward and Aristocles followed suit, glancing behind even as his mount picked up pace. He saw them immediately, six warriors on horseback, far down the winding road but already galloping. Then he was forced to face front and lean forward in the saddle as he felt the smooth motion of a canter shift pace when Amos's gelding moved into a gallop and Aristocles' mare followed suit. Gripping on for dear life, he tried to steer his horse around the rocks and other obstacles that littered the road. The right-hand side suddenly dropped away in a sheer precipice and the two riders now galloped in single file, with Amos in the lead and Aristocles following close behind.

A rocky hillside rose along the left, a slope that spilled gravel over the road. Aristocles winced as Amos charged straight into the rubble, his larger horse's hooves skittering over the loose stones before reaching the other side of the spill. Aristocles' mare ran into the treacherous patch a moment later and at any moment he expected her to trip, her leg breaking underneath him. The horse whinnied and slipped. Aristocles gripped on for dear life, glancing in terror at the plummet to his right-hand side.

Then they were through and the road widened once more. Now it was Amos's mount who was flagging, burdened by his armor and heavier frame, and Aristocles drew alongside. Amos's face was grim, his jaw set as he spurred his galloping horse forward.

Aristocles glanced over his shoulder. He drew in a sharp breath.

The six riders were just a few hundred paces behind. Nikolas had played his hand but left a loose end; the assassins had come to finish what he'd started.

Cold wind howled and stung Aristocles' eyes. The pursuers reached the section of loose gravel and charged through. At Aristocles' right hand the precipice revealed farmland, steps of irrigated fields one on top of the other. Even though he tried to face forward and focus on the uncertain terrain, he found himself looking back over his shoulder at the assassins. The distance had narrowed to a hundred paces.

'Look!' Amos cried.

Ahead a wall of black stone stretched across the road to fill the space between two mountains. The road reached two broad gates of dark wood, banded with metal, standing wide open. Continuing their mad dash, Aristocles and Amos galloped directly for the gates.

At the last, Aristocles heard a shout and turned back to see the six riders draw up while still far from the wide entrance. The assassins watched in silence as he and Amos entered the city of Tanus.

23

Dion backed away slowly, reluctant to take his eyes away from the giant even for the briefest instant. The wildran moved inexorably toward him, clenching and unclenching fists, lank silver hair greasy on its scalp, bare chest covered in scars, teeth gnashing.

The sand near the water was firm underfoot, but he knew that if he turned and began to run the giant would run also, and having seen the creatures' speed in the past he knew he would never outdistance it. He also had to be careful that he wasn't pinned against the sea. He wasn't sure if a giant could swim, but he had no desire to find out.

His fumbling fingers reached over his shoulder, finally clasping on an arrow, and without taking his eyes off the looming giant he slid the arrow out of the quiver and nocked it to the string of his composite bow. He took a deep breath and prepared to draw, aim, and fire.

The giant suddenly roared at him. Arms outstretched, ready to grab and tear him limb from limb, the wildran lunged forward. Dion leaped back out of its reach, still trying to face it head on and resist the temptation to flee, but the movement caused his busy hands to drop the arrow. He cursed silently as he continued to back away. The giant's foot crunched down on the arrow a moment later, snapping it like a twig.

He felt over his shoulder for the next arrow and his heart went into his mouth when his fingers grasped at emptiness. Staying alive in Cinder Fen had taken its toll on his supply of arrows. There weren't any left.

He took a deep breath, wondering if he could sprint to a place farther up where the cliff met the water's edge and climb to safety. He prepared to make the mad dash that would most likely end with his death.

When the giant roared again, he put his head down and ran.

The bow was awkward in his hand, so he tossed it to the side, throwing it as far as he could. Completely unarmed, he opened up his stride and bunched his fists, spurring on every bit of speed he could, muscles honed by hunting with the eldren in the Wilds and running with Zachary. He was the fittest he had ever been, yet he also knew that this was no bear chasing him.

It was a wildran, hungering for his flesh.

Heavy footsteps pounded on the beach just behind as the giant picked up speed. Rasping breath came louder than the crash of the surf on the shore. He could feel its panting, hot on his neck. His back itched as he waited for the blow that would knock him from his feet and send him flying through the air to lie in a crumpled heap. The giant would rip off an arm or leg while he was still alive; it was their preferred method of killing and eating. His heart would still be beating when it devoured his limbs. He would die only when his lifeblood drained away.

Huge fingers scraped against Dion's back and he nearly cried out, but used the fear to call greater effort from his body. It was too late now to plunge into the nearby sea. When the water slowed his passage the creature would be on him.

The snap of wings suddenly joined the sound of the giant's heavy footfalls. Looking up, Dion saw a dragon plummet through the sky, claws outstretched and muscles rippling. Veined wings the size of sails rose and fell as the reptilian jaws parted. With incredible speed the silver-scaled dragon swooped directly at Dion, approaching so swiftly that he had no choice but to throw himself forward, diving onto the sand and covering his head with his hands.

The dragon and the giant collided. A heavy thump told Dion that the contact was powerful enough to throw the giant onto its back. Roars and groans accompanied the sounds of struggle, and then a sharp crack ended the fight.

Rolling over, Dion saw the giant lying with its head at an angle, nearly severed from its body. The huge eyes stared sightlessly at him, making him shudder. As the sea was carried in with the tide, the frothing waves washed the crimson blood back and forth.

Closer by, a hawk-nosed eldran was bent in the water, washing his face and hair. Slowly climbing to his feet, Dion drew in a deep breath. He waited for his legs to stop shaking before he approached his friend.

'Giant doesn't taste as good as you might think,' Eiric said, glancing at Dion and scowling. He spat into the sea. 'I'll never get it out of my mouth.'

The eldran looked up to the higher ground, where the beach became rocky and dotted with wizened trees and shrubs, eventually climbing in cliffs that loomed over the shoreline. The long escarpment guarded the interior but could be climbed, something Dion knew from the last time he'd traveled in this land with Chloe. Black clouds hung over the long range of mountain peaks, even though it was a bright day and the rest of the sky was clear.

The eldran's eyes finally settled on the distant cavern Dion had been working in, a deep depression at the base of the cliff. 'How are your repairs going?'

'Almost done,' Dion wheezed, hands on his hips as he recovered.

'Good. As much as I've enjoyed keeping you safe while you polish your vessel's timbers, I came here to look for my father.

Instead I'm spending all my time watching your back.' Eiric shook his head. 'One day there's going to be too many for me.'

'I understand,' Dion said. He coughed. 'And thank you. Trust me, I don't plan to spend a moment longer here than I need to. Let me show you.' He motioned for Eiric to follow.

They climbed the shore together, and soon they were leaping from rock to rock and passing under the gnarled trees that grew in this place. Dion led Eiric to the cave, and then he forgot all about the giant as his eyes roved over the *Calypso*.

Though the vessel was small, she was sleek and well proportioned, able to be sailed in the strongest seas. Horizontal blue and yellow stripes decorated her exterior, curving with her body, but her interior was more beautiful still, unpainted and displaying the grain of the wood for all to see. The mast was lowered, resting on the floor of the cave, which made her appear unfinished, like a statue of a shapely woman missing a limb.

'I can see you are in love,' Eiric said, lifting an eyebrow. 'But don't expect me to have the interest you do.'

Dion grinned. 'You're not the first. I understand.'

'So what's left to do?'

'Nothing.'

'Nothing? I thought you said you were almost done.'

'I am. We just need to carry it down to the shore. I was checking the tide a moment ago when . . .'

Realization dawned in Eiric's eyes. 'You're leaving? Look,' he said. 'I didn't mean . . .'

'No, it's time for me to go. Cinder Fen wasn't meant for humans.'

'For humans,' Eiric repeated. 'You're turning your back on us, then?'

'Not turning away,' Dion said. 'Finding a new path, and hopefully a new place to call home. I thought I sensed you, back in the Wilds, but just now when you saved me, again I felt nothing. I couldn't change my form to save my own life. This bond you say you feel with this place.' He shrugged. 'I feel nothing.'

'That's because you've focused again on your human heritage.' Eiric's eyes flickered to the vessel and back. 'I can feel you growing distant.'

'Whatever it is, it feels right.'

'Where will you go?'

'Sarsica,' Dion said. 'It's as good a place as any to make a start, and I'll need supplies if I plan on traveling for a while.'

'And then?'

'I want to find out what I can about the Aleutheans. If their civilization sank beneath the waves, how did the ark end up in Phalesia? What happened to them?'

'My father always told me that for humans, everything comes at a price, even information,' Eiric said. 'Put out your hand.' Dion frowned as Eiric untied a leather pouch from his waist. The tall eldran placed the pouch in his open palm and then spoke again. 'Open it.'

Untying the string, Dion poured the contents into his hand and gasped when he saw a pile of shimmering gemstones ranging from the size of a tooth to as big as a knucklebone. Some were clear but most were fanciful colors: rose and pale green, the light blue of shallow water and the deep blue of the ocean.

'Several are diamonds,' Eiric said. 'The stories your people tell each other are true, you just need to know where to look.' He smiled. 'Enough to help you on your way?'

'Eiric . . .' Dion said, lifting his gaze. 'Thank you.'

'I hope you find your place in the world.'

'Before I go . . . I have to ask.' Dion hoped he wouldn't say the wrong thing; there was still so much he had to learn about the eldran. 'Can you sense your father?'

Eiric's smile faded. 'When I try to sense him, I sense animal urges. But they may simply stem from the feel of this place.'

'And what will you do if he's lost to you?' Dion persisted. 'We're not far from the Waste. Tell me the truth.'

'I won't return to my people until both Jonas and Triton are dead,' Eiric said grimly.

'Be careful,' Dion said, embracing Zachary's son. 'Remember, your people need a leader.'

Eiric nodded, but his eyes were still distant. 'I know.'

24

'Here,' Chloe said, panting as she passed Liana the skin. 'Water.'

The sun blazed overhead, but as the Phalesian Way climbed ever higher, the winds off the looming peaks made the air turn cool. They were still in the region of hills and forests, not even halfway to Tanus, and had a long journey ahead of them. The path would lead up into the mountains and it would grow colder still. Chloe wondered how Liana would hold up; they had blankets, but at nighttime she was shivering already.

'Can we rest again?' Liana asked as they walked, looking hopefully at Chloe.

'Not yet.' Chloe shook her head. 'We have to keep moving if we're going to stay ahead of Nikolas. There's a way station.' She pointed to a distant structure, a stone hut a couple of miles ahead. 'There should be fresh water. We can rest and drink our fill when we get there.'

Liana gave a resigned nod.

The two travelers continued in silence, with Chloe thinking about her father, hoping that she would find him alive and well in Tanus. She thought about Nikolas also. If he caught her, he wouldn't take her flight lightly. Danger was ever present.

They finally reached the way station and Liana seated herself gratefully on the bench of stone under the roof of thatch, shoulders slumped as she recovered her strength. Glancing down at her slight companion, Chloe wondered again what it was that Liana wanted to speak with her father about. The more she'd pressed, the more tight-lipped Liana had become. She was bearing some burden, a secret, something that weighed on her so much that she wouldn't even talk about it.

Chloe went around the back of the way station, where she found a stone basin filled from a natural spring, the cool water trickling in a thin stream from an overhang. She filled the skin and returned to Liana, who was even now still panting.

'I'll fill your skin,' Chloe said sympathetically. But when she bent down and reached for Liana's satchel the girl suddenly lunged forward.

'No!' Liana cried. Her eyes were wide as she grabbed hold of Chloe's wrist. 'Don't touch it!'

'Why not?' Chloe's eyes narrowed.

'Please,' Liana said softly, and now her eyes were pleading. 'I'll fill my own water. Just . . . Just don't touch it.' She released Chloe's hand and, with a frown, finally Chloe relented. 'I don't like people touching my things,' Liana said, staring at the ground.

Chloe straightened and immediately forgave her, instead taking a seat on the bench beside the eldran. Liana had lost her parents and then she'd lost Zachary and Aella. Eiric had spurned her. She didn't have anyone.

'How did you get your necklace?' Chloe asked, changing the subject. 'I thought eldren couldn't touch metal.'

'We can't willingly touch pure metal,' Liana corrected. 'A man . . . He put it on me.' She looked away and darkness crossed her face. 'It's not pure copper but it still hurts.' She met Chloe's eyes. 'I can remove it if I have to, but I'm going to keep it on.'

'That takes strength,' Chloe said. 'To endure suffering in order to belong.'

'Your people do it all the time,' said Liana. 'You make every father spend his days toiling to earn enough money that his son or daughter can wear a necklace like this. Your men pit themselves against each other in contests so that they can prove their worth to the group. Your women spend their lives married to men they don't love because their fathers tell them to, and it is the custom. Everyone does things they don't want to in order to become part of something greater. Sometimes those things are courageous; other times they are wrong.'

Chloe's mouth dropped open. Not for the first time, Liana had surprised her.

'Even you married a man you do not love,' Liana said.

Chloe's lips thinned. 'He said he would kill my father. I had no choice.'

'You didn't?' Liana asked. 'From what I have seen you are a strong woman, and from what I have heard your father loves you dearly, and would not force you. So why did you agree to it in the first place?'

'At one time there was a purpose to it. My father thought it would bring him and Nikolas closer together, and result in a stronger bond between our two nations.'

'I didn't ask why your father wanted it. I asked why you went along with it.'

'I suppose I wanted to make my father happy. I wanted an end to the fighting. Neither nation is strong enough to survive alone. With an alliance—'

'Chloe of Phalesia,' Liana interrupted. 'You are lying.'

Chloe scowled. 'I am not—'

'You are. I was watching you with Dion. I saw what passed between you. You may think he rejected you but when you turned your back on him, I saw the desire in his eyes. And I saw you cry. Are you telling me you gave up your chance of happiness because you wanted to make your father happy? Why didn't you tell your father *no*, from the very beginning? You say he is a wise man. He would have found another way to bring your two nations closer together. Or perhaps'—Liana arched an eyebrow—'it was the marriage that emboldened the king of Xanthos to take action in the first place. Perhaps your father is where he is now because of your refusal to be brave and follow your heart.'

Chloe looked down at the ground. Everything Liana was saying made sense. There was only one piece of the puzzle that the eldran wasn't aware of.

'There was a prophecy,' Chloe said softly. She met Liana's eyes. 'Do you know of the Oracle of Athos?'

'I have heard stories.'

'The Seer's prophecies always come true. She prophesied that the king of Ilea would die in the thirty-first year of his reign and he did.'

'And what did she say to you?'

'She gave me three prophecies. She said I would kill a man I pitied.' Chloe thought of Tomarys, writhing on the stake. 'She said I would fear a man I loved.'

'Dion,' Liana said. 'You fear him?'

'I did,' Chloe said. 'Now?' She looked away.

'He is more human than eldran,' said Liana. She spread her hands. 'Unlike me,' she said in a wry voice, 'he has a good reason for being unable to change.'

'You also have a good reason,' Chloe said. 'You are afraid. I understand why.'

Liana looked away, pensive for a time, but she persisted. 'And what was the third prophecy?'

'The Seer said I would marry a man I do not love.'

Liana tilted her head. She waited for a time and then opened her mouth. 'I am waiting for the rest of it.'

'That is what she said.'

Liana leaned forward, staring at Chloe intently, her head tilted and an expression of shock and surprise on her face. 'There was no prophecy to marry Nikolas, king of Xanthos?'

Chloe frowned. 'No.'

'And you decided that you would interpret this prophecy yourself? That you were destined to follow the path laid out in front of you without deviation?'

'But the Seer's prophecies—'

'Always come true,' Liana said. 'I was listening. But until you and Nikolas were wed, you didn't know what events would come to pass. You should have chosen your own destiny . . . Acted as if there was no prophecy. In future, never accept with resignation a fate that is not set in stone.'

Chloe could now understand how Liana had had the courage to dye her hair, wear a metal necklace, and enter human society.

'You talk about being afraid,' Chloe said, 'and you say that I'm brave. But I think you have it the wrong way around.'

Liana smiled. 'Come on,' she said. 'We should keep moving.'

⌣

Chloe saw that the road ahead bisected a thick forest of evergreens, tall trees that loomed over the very edge of the path and blocked the afternoon light, forming long, tapering shadows. A brook trickled alongside the path, filled with smooth stones and flowing water, enabling the two travelers to fill their skins again before moving on. They were following the floor of a wide valley, with hills on both sides and mountains beyond. The air smelled of pine and dew.

Chloe was anxious. She'd known that on foot they wouldn't make as much time as on horseback, but she hadn't accounted for an eldran's frailty. While in another form they could face down any beast or warrior, but she realized the truth of the maxim that humans were generally stronger.

She glanced at her companion, who looked wistfully into the depths of the forest as she inhaled deeply. 'Perhaps tonight we could rest in the woods—'

Chloe held up a hand and stopped in her tracks. 'What's that sound?'

Liana immediately went silent. Frowning, she tilted her head as she listened, and for a moment there was silence, broken only by the occasional tweet of a bird or chirp of an insect.

Suddenly Liana's eyes widened. She exchanged glances with Chloe. 'It sounds like many footsteps, moving as one.'

Chloe caught the sound again, at the edge of her hearing. The heavy rolling patter of marching men grew louder, until she could easily hear it. The sound grew in volume until it was bouncing around the hills, filling the valley.

'It's an army.' Chloe paled. She frantically wondered what to do. 'It must be Nikolas. They'll have scouts. We're too late!'

A horse whinnied. Hooves clattered on the ground.

Frozen in place, the two travelers looked back the way they'd come as a pair of riders rounded a corner. Chloe recognized the light armor and crimson cloak of a Xanthian mounted scout, and then four more riders joined them. Seeing the two women, the scouts dug in their heels and moved into an immediate gallop.

Chloe clutched hold of Liana's arm. 'This way!' She tried to pull her, but stopped when she felt resistance.

'Not that way,' Liana said. 'That is south, toward Cinder Fen. We must go north.'

Chloe glanced back at the galloping scouts and gave a sharp nod. She and Liana sprinted back across the road, plunging into the trees as the riders gained on them. Men's voices called out, telling them to stop.

It was dark under the shade of the evergreens. Rocks and fallen logs provided obstacles but Chloe knew that the scouts were trained to ride through difficult terrain and to track hiding enemies. Though their mountain ponies were smaller than cavalry horses, they were hardy creatures, and the two women in their pale colors would stand out against the browns and greens. She and Liana had to keep moving until they were far from pursuit.

Chloe's chest heaved as she ran, weaving around the lower shrubs, warding off the clinging branches with her arm, heedless of the scratches to her skin. A horse ran straight across her vision ahead, but the rider plunged back into the trees; he hadn't seen her. She never let go of Liana, even when the girl's gasping breath ran ragged. If questioned, it would soon become apparent she was an eldran, posing as a human. Chloe didn't know what Nikolas would do to her, but she didn't want to find out.

A man's voice shouted something in the distance, and a comrade replied from further away. Heading away from their cries, Chloe and Liana ran until the ground climbed; they were approaching the edge of the valley, where the hills rose to overlook the forest below. Now the ground sloped and Chloe knew it was unlikely that the scouts would pursue this far. She helped Liana climb over the rocky ground, leading the way until they reached a flat place. When she turned around she could see the forest spread below her.

'Stop,' Chloe panted. 'Rest.'

Liana fell to hands and knees as she fought to regain her breath. Chloe looked back and searched for signs of pursuit, hands on her hips as she coughed and wheezed.

As the sound of marching filled the valley with thunderous noise, Chloe decided to climb higher. She hopped from rock to rock, feet scrabbling at the steep slope, bending forward and using her hands as much as her feet as she ascended. Finally she pulled herself onto a ledge, throwing her body up and then standing. From her height she could now see the entire valley. Scanning the break in the forest where the path split it into two equal-sized pieces, she saw the army come into view.

She first saw more mounted scouts, riding ahead of the main force. Next came the cavalry: hundreds of horses in a long file. Officers clustered up front, near a standard bearer carrying a crimson flag bordered with black: Nikolas's personal markings. Most of the other standards were Xanthian, but there were blue cloaks dotted among the red, and even mounted archers on ponies, wild-looking men wearing skins and furs. Nikolas had recruited some northern tribesmen to his cause.

Her attention was drawn to one tribesman in particular, a lean mounted warrior leading a group of his fellows. With a spidery tattoo stretching from his face to his neck and a topknot leaving the rest of his head shaved, his appearance was both striking and sinister. He and his companions would be fighting for plunder as well as Nikolas's gold.

After the horses came the men on foot. Hoplites carrying shield and spear marched resolutely, weighed down by their equipment but strong and fit enough to march for an entire day without pausing. A smaller number of archers followed the hoplites, and then came javelin and sling throwers, followed by a motley collection of farmers with swords and slaves carrying baggage.

It was a long column, and the cavalry had exited the valley long before the baggage train appeared. Chloe's heart sank. She hadn't accounted for Nikolas's decisiveness; he must have left immediately after her. He was heading for Tanus, and he'd evidently taken every able-bodied man with him. By stripping Xanthos and Phalesia of soldiers, he was taking a huge gamble, but Chloe's father had fled to Tanus, and pressing onward would take Nikolas's army to where

Triton led the eldren in the Waste. After the Waste was the city of Koulis, which was founded by Galeans long before the Ileans expanded north.

The pieces lay before Nikolas like stepping stones. Either Tanus would join his cause or he would lay siege to the city. Triton would flee before him or fall. Koulis would be faced with the same choice as Tanus, and then there was a clear path to his true objective: Lamara.

Chloe couldn't stop thinking about her father. She'd come to warn him, but he wouldn't know there was an army approaching until it was too late.

'Chloe.' Liana's voice came from below, filled with urgency.

Looking down the slope to where the nearby forest thinned, Chloe felt her breath quicken as a long line of soldiers exited the trees, approaching with speed. The soldiers started to climb the hillside, fanning out to prevent either of the two women from making a break for the forest.

'Quick!' Chloe scrabbled back down, taking hold of Liana's hand and then pulling her up to her perch. Together they climbed higher still, slipping in their haste, heading for a break between two peaks that might lead to safety. The ground leveled off and Chloe broke into a run, still gripping Liana's hand tightly.

The soldiers were now out of sight but their shouts drifted on the breeze. Sprinting together Chloe and Liana reached lower ground, passing between the two hills. Chloe breathed a sigh of relief when she saw a path out of the valley, opening up in the wild lands of the north.

Chloe exchanged glances with Liana as, helping each other down, they began to descend the hills, following a route that would take them away from pursuit. Together, they ventured into the unknown.

25

'Amos,' Aristocles called. 'Are you ready? We shouldn't make Queen
Zanthe wait.'

He checked his reflection one last time in the bronze mirror,
intensely missing the expensive silver mirror back in his villa, before
he finally nodded and left the house's only bedchamber. Their rented
lodgings were simple: a single-storied stone dwelling in Tanus's
artisan quarter, but he reminded himself that it was only temporary.

Aristocles found Amos in the communal living room,
sharpening his sword as he sat on a stool, making circles with a
stone on the bright steel. His loyal captain looked up and ceased
his work.

'I'm worried about Queen Zanthe. How do you know she'll
stand with us?'

Aristocles' lips thinned. 'This is happening, Amos. Are you
with me?'

Amos met his eyes and nodded. 'Of course, First Consul.'

Like Aristocles, Amos had washed and changed, oiling and
combing his hair. But where Aristocles wore an embroidered silk
toga tied at the waist with a blue rope, Amos wore his leather cuirass
and skirt of leather strips. Aristocles had tried to convince him to

wear a tunic, and even picked one out, but his most convincing arguments fell on deaf ears, with Amos flatly saying that Aristocles should consider himself lucky that he'd taken the time to clean and polish his armor.

'The gifts . . .' Aristocles looked around the room. 'Where are they?'

Standing and sheathing his weapon, Amos indicated the exit. 'Ready and waiting.' He shook his head as he followed Aristocles out the house, and Aristocles heard him muttering. 'Tanusians and their gifts . . .'

Out in the street Aristocles saw six burly bearers wearing sleeveless vests, waiting with arms folded, each standing beside an ornate wooden chest.

'Good, good,' Aristocles said.

'These gifts cost nearly all your gold,' Amos said. 'I hope it's worth it.'

'Queen Zanthe responds well to flattery. Is it all there?'

Amos strode to the first chest and opened the lid, demonstrating the contents. 'Furs,' he said, closing the lid and moving to the next chest. 'Spices.'

Aristocles nodded, pleased. The furs were red fox pelts from the north, soft and luxurious. The spices were in small painted clay pots with tight-fitting lids.

'Wine,' Amos said, tilting back the lid of the third chest. Inside was a thick leather skin bearing the embossed mark of Falio, the best wine merchant in Tanus. 'Six fine swords.' Amos glanced at Aristocles as he showed him half a dozen shining swords with tapering blades.

'Swords?' Aristocles frowned. 'This is no king of Xanthos. We're dealing with a woman here.'

Amos shrugged and closed the chest before moving to the next. 'Incense.' He waited for Aristocles to crouch down and inhale.

'Sandalwood.' Aristocles nodded. 'And finally?'

'Silk.' Amos lifted up a length of pale Salesian silk. 'Undyed. The very best quality.'

'Excellent,' Aristocles said. 'You've done well, my friend.' He glanced up at the sky. 'The hour is almost upon us. Let's go.'

———

The plateau that the city occupied was immense, far larger than the area bounded by the high stone walls. Tanus was laid out in a regular, planned fashion, with three broad avenues and a multitude of streets connecting them at intervals. Temples mingled with markets, granaries, masonries, and potteries; the single-storied houses were crowded close together, filling the spaces in between.

Rather than having an upper city and a lower city, such as in Phalesia, or being split into a palace quarter and residential quarter, as in Xanthos, in Tanus everything was of a single level. Instead, the poorer houses were those on the outskirts or close to the gates, unmistakable by their mud-brick walls and roofs of dried foliage matted with clay. Closer to the center the temples became grander and the houses employed cut and fitted stones in their construction, with those nearest the palace loftiest of all, multi-storied dwellings with commanding views of the mountainous landscape.

As Aristocles, Amos, and the six bearers followed the centermost of the three avenues, the palace loomed ahead. At the end of the city, nestled against the rock, it was high and defensible, affording an additional level of protection for the queen and her court. Four thick columns of basalt held up the peaked roof, which crowned the entire structure, making it difficult to assess how large it truly was. Armored soldiers stood guard at the base of the wide steps leading to the interior, spears held vertically, faces like stone as they watched the group approach.

But rather than feel intimidated, Aristocles kept walking, and the guards made way for the group as they climbed the stairs. He was familiar with kings and queens. Dealing with despots was like dealing with children; they needed to be cajoled and flattered, and they couldn't be allowed to wallow in their ability to make the world dance to their tune. Aristocles was an experienced politician. Any man who had to navigate the waters of the Assembly of Consuls had to exercise a far greater degree of subtlety than a monarch who ruled by decree.

Yet, despite himself, Aristocles remembered what it had been like to raise two daughters. Who had truly determined the way his household functioned? The powerful first consul or the shrieking girls who had decided when he could sleep, when he could leave the villa, and even when he could use the chamber pot?

Reaching the summit of the stairs, Aristocles led the group in between the black columns and entered a cavernous space where the ceiling was so high that he wondered it didn't fall. It was daytime, but the sky outside was clouded and the air chill, and he was grateful for the braziers filled with red coals that framed the hard stone pathway at regular intervals. Walking briskly with Amos at his right hand, he continued onto a section of carpets, with each successive mat more colorful and lustrous than the one before. The six bearers, chests held high, followed close behind.

Flaming torches on poles lit the area at the end of the vaulted corridor; this was an audience chamber far grander than the hall in the Royal Palace at Xanthos. But it was dark and cold; Zanthe was welcome to it. Give him his villa, his work, and his two beautiful daughters and he was content.

A steward with a pole in his hand nodded at them and, knowing the protocol, Aristocles came to a halt.

'Lord Aristocles, first consul of Phalesia,' the steward called out.

A reedy voice spoke. 'Come, Aristocles.'

Aristocles indicated for Amos and the bearers to follow as he stepped forward onto a long crimson carpet. Armored soldiers lined both sides of the passage, four on each side. With Amos near him, and the bearers following, Aristocles approached the throne of black wood and the queen of Tanus, who sat with her elbow on the arm of the chair and her chin in her palm.

Zanthe had aged since Aristocles had last seen her. Her face had always had a drooping quality, but it now sagged in earnest, with bloodshot eyes that appeared permanently sad and cheeks that looked like melting wax. She seemed weary, with the posture of someone who would rather be in bed. But there was still the occasional thread of blond in her long graying hair, and the purple robe and golden chain she wore were finer than anything Aristocles owned himself.

'You arrive at short notice, Aristocles,' Zanthe said. 'Tell me, what brings you here?'

'I am pleased to see you well, Queen Zanthe,' Aristocles said.

She barked a laugh. 'Well? I am alive, as you can see. You look to be holding up well enough. Last I saw you I was a younger woman, and if I remember correctly I drank you under the table. Phalesians never can hold their drink.'

Used to her ways, Aristocles smiled. But rather than speak immediately, he stayed silent. He allowed his smile to fade, and then when he looked up to meet her eyes, he conveyed grave sincerity. 'I am here because dark times are upon us,' he said. 'We, the Galean nations, have always respected each other's borders. We remain united in our independence. But we now face a new threat.'

Zanthe frowned. 'Speak plainly, Aristocles. Are you referring to the Ileans?'

Aristocles blinked. 'No, Queen. I'm referring to Nikolas of Xanthos. He wishes to challenge you, as his father did before him. Xanthos and Tanus fought for control of the Blackwell Mines.

Markos of Xanthos seized them from you and killed your men. His son, Nikolas, now seeks to take still more—'

'The Blackwell Mines,' Zanthe mused. 'If we are bringing up past grievances, First Consul'—she emphasized the title—'where did Phalesia stand in that conflict?'

'We were neutral.' Aristocles frowned.

'You stayed your hand and let the people of Xanthos and Tanus kill each other.'

'It wasn't our conflict,' he protested.

Zanthe leaned forward. 'I despised Markos of Xanthos, as I'm sure you know. But he met his end, and it was a more evil end than even I would have given him. The Ileans shoved him and his wife onto a stake while they were still alive. Nikolas was the one who found them, along with his dead wife and son. I don't think I can blame him for wanting to end the Ilean threat.'

Aristocles' eyes narrowed. 'He seeks to become king of kings, above me and above you. I am the elected leader of my people, and he murdered my allies in the Assembly and tried to have me killed.' He took a deep breath. Tensions were rising. He needed an ally, not an enemy. 'I bring gifts.'

He nodded to Amos, who nodded in turn to the bearers. Each man still held his chest in his arms, stone-faced and motionless, looking like they could hold their positions for an eternity. One after another, they set down the chests with a series of thumps. Amos then went to each lid, tilting it back and calling out the contents to the queen of Tanus.

'Spices.' He moved to the next. 'Furs.' Aristocles glanced at Zanthe, who leaned forward with eyes gleaming, like a girl getting a name-day present from a wealthy uncle. 'Swords,' he called. 'Incense.' Another chest opened. 'Silk.' Amos moved on to the last. 'Wine.'

Aristocles held his breath as he tried to gauge Zanthe's reaction. Far from the Maltherean Sea, Tanus had less trade passing through it than Phalesia, and significantly less than thriving ports like Myana. It had become something of a cultural norm for travelers to bring gifts to Tanus on any visit.

Disappointment crossed Zanthe's face and she sat back in her seat, looking away from the gifts and instead staring disdainfully at Aristocles. The impact of her next words felt like a cold hand gripping hold of his heart.

'He promises gold,' Zanthe said. 'Where you give me cloth and swords. Your timing is poor, Aristocles. His runner arrived last night.'

Aristocles' shoulders slumped. He knew where Nikolas's sudden windfall had come from.

'But also,' she continued, 'he does not seek, as you say, to become the king of kings. He wants my help. The Ilean threat is real, as I'm sure you can attest.' Aristocles felt every word like a blow. 'An army of four thousand approaches this city. Nikolas leads personally, and brings with him an alliance of Phalesia and Xanthos, with soldiers of both nations united in common cause against a greater enemy. And you, spurned by your own Assembly, you ask me to turn him down?'

'I ask that you do what is right.'

'You once told me something. You said that the strongest feature of your system of governance is that when the first consul no longer enjoys the support of his people, he steps down, and a new man takes his place.'

'That isn't what happened here—'

'The fact is,' Zanthe said, 'here in Tanus, as well as in Xanthos, we do not adhere to your rules, and so how can you expect us to care if they are broken? Your Assembly is simply under the control of a man who isn't you.'

Aristocles exchanged glances with Amos. One day earlier and he might have been able to convince her to side with his cause.

Nikolas had moved far more swiftly and decisively in leading the army to Tanus than he'd thought possible.

'Nikolas has made only three requests in return for his gift of gold,' Zanthe said. 'The first is my assistance in clearing the Waste of eldren, something I will give gladly, for it benefits us greatly. He also asks my help in liberating Koulis and attacking Ilea before we are attacked in turn.'

As she spoke, Aristocles realized he had soldiers on both sides of him, four on his left and four on his right, in a file that stretched to the throne. There was no way to escape. If Amos fought eight soldiers, he would die.

'Finally,' she said, in a voice that chilled his blood, 'Nikolas requests that I deliver you, Aristocles, alive or dead.' She lifted an arm. 'Seize him!'

Aristocles' mouth dropped open. The file of soldiers flanking both sides of the long carpet turned as one. Eight soldiers drew their swords.

But then Amos cried out a moment later. 'Protective circle!'

The six bearers dashed to the chest in the center of the array and took a sword each. While Aristocles struggled to make sense of events Amos drew the sword he carried at his side and together they formed a group around Aristocles.

After the clatter of steel and cries of the soldiers, the audience chamber was suddenly silent. Zanthe's guards faced Amos and the six burly men with him. Her bloodshot eyes were wide with shock. The queen's guards looked to her for orders, but her mouth only gaped.

'Back,' Amos hissed. 'Back!'

The circle inched backwards while Zanthe's soldiers stayed with their queen, watching the retreat, unwilling to leave their monarch unprotected to pursue after them.

Finally Amos barked another order. 'Run!'

Turning and moving into an immediate sprint, they sped for the huge entrance, dashing down the steps, and ran full tilt into the pair of spear-carrying soldiers standing at the base of the stairway. Before the nearest could bring his weapon to bear, Amos smashed his forehead into a Tanusian's nose and the soldier went down, blood streaming from his face as he collapsed. Amos then weaved around a thrust from the second soldier before striking with the hilt of his sword into his opponent's sternum, making him cry out and crumple like a rag doll.

Aristocles felt himself whisked between the fallen guards. Soon they were running back down the avenue. City folk leaped away in shock when they saw the group, but Amos seemed to know where he was going, and turned them into a side street and then again into an alley. Houses became crude huts as they turned time and again, keeping to the smaller paths as they came closer to the city wall.

His heart pounding at his chest, silk toga twisting around his ankles and impeding his progress, Aristocles puffed and panted as he ran. Finally Amos called a halt, and he saw that they were at the base of the tall wall of dark stone. Aristocles placed his hands on his hips, bending down to regain his breath.

'You did well,' Amos said to the bearers, handing over a heavy pouch. 'Keep the swords. First Consul? Aristocles!'

Aristocles shook himself; he'd been staring into nothing. He straightened, still wheezing.

'Hurry,' Amos said. 'We don't have much time.'

He waited until the bearers had left and then beckoned for Aristocles to follow. They skirted the boundary until they came to a place where the top of the wall had toppled, leaving a pile of rubble at the base. Amos lifted first one black stone away and then another, finally revealing their two packs. He handed one silently to Aristocles and then they continued to follow the wall until they came to a ladder.

'Our horses are on the other side,' Amos said.

'How did you know?'

Amos gave a wry smile. 'I'm a military man. It pays to be prepared.'

'But . . . Where do we go now?'

'Koulis,' Amos said.

'Koulis?' Aristocles spluttered. 'I don't know anyone there. There's also the Waste between us.'

Amos gave Aristocles a flat stare.

'All right.' Aristocles relented. He placed his hands on the ladder and muttered to himself. 'Koulis it is.'

26

Creeping into the prince's bedchamber, the assassin saw a grand room twice the size of any house in Lamara, complete with an opulent four-poster bed, silk curtains on the windows, and a separate washroom through an opening at the back.

He moved silently, graceful as a dancer despite his size, for he wasn't a small man. Taking a direct line for the huge bed, he stopped beside it and for a moment stared down at the sleeping occupant.

The fat prince lay on his back, snoring blissfully, unaware that he was taking his last breaths. A swarthy noble in his late twenties, he had round cheeks, a square beard on his chin, and a clean-shaven upper lip. It was a warm night and the bedcovers didn't quite cover his broad belly. His inhalations rasped like the scraping of a saw; when he exhaled, his breath whistled.

The assassin slowly drew the slender dagger from the sheath he wore inside his open vest, moving in small increments to minimize the whisper of sliding steel. The bed's occupant snorted as he twitched. Fearful that the prince would wake, the assassin now took action.

Bending down, he clamped his free hand over the fat prince's mouth, at the same time pulling his dagger out completely. Grim-faced and silent, with a strong thrust he plunged the sharp blade into the prince's thick neck. The assassin withdrew as quickly as he could, careful to avoid the splash of blood. He would have preferred to stab for the heart – the throat was a messy place to strike – but his victim's immense girth gave him no choice. The prince gurgled and his eyes shot open.

The assassin grimaced; the sound was far too loud for his liking.

Moving with urgency, he wiped his dagger on the bed linen and returned it to the sheath inside his vest. He then lifted a nearby cushion and shoved it hard over his victim's face, pressing down with all of his weight. The prince's shuddering subsided. The flaccid body stilled.

Tossing the cushion, in the wan light provided by the open window, he now took a moment to gaze down at his victim. The dead man's eyes were wide, staring at the ceiling.

But the night's work was not yet done.

Continuing to move as silently as a shadow, the assassin exited the bedchamber and moved softly down the palace corridor until he came to another doorway barred by thick curtains. A small black mark on the right-hand side of the entrance told him he'd come to the right place. Drawing the curtain aside, he scanned the room's interior.

The bedchamber was much like the last one, but this time the sleeping prince was younger, perhaps in his early twenties. Wearing a loose silk robe, lying on his side, he had his arms around the naked body of a woman ten years his senior, with heavy breasts and a round belly. The assassin cursed inwardly; he'd expected this, but it didn't make his task easier. He drew the dagger again and moved around the bed so that he was facing the young prince's back. Choosing his place with care, he crouched and pointed the tip of the blade between his victim's shoulder blades, taking a deep breath before he made his strike.

He grunted as he thrust. The dagger pierced easily, penetrating the young man's chest from behind, perfectly aimed to strike the heart. The prince shuddered. He died as swiftly as a man could.

The assassin immediately checked on the woman. For a moment he thought she would remain sleeping, but then her eyelids fluttered. Turning her head and seeing the tall man leaning over her, dagger in hand, she opened her mouth.

'Scream and you die,' the assassin whispered.

The first note of a shrill cry hit the back of her throat, stifled when the assassin's strong hand clasped her neck, squeezing tightly enough to choke off her breath.

'Foolish woman,' he muttered.

Her eyes nearly shot out of her head as she moaned, but the sound was quiet enough that the assassin didn't feel the need for another cushion. She took time to go, clawing at the bed sheets and kicking her legs, but then it was done.

He left her behind, along with the cousin who was her lover. Once more the assassin traveled the corridors of the sprawling palace.

One final victim remained.

The last bedchamber was located at the end of a carpeted hallway. As with the others, the assassin peeled the curtain aside and assessed the room. The sleeping form of Caran, eldest son of Solon and heir to the throne, lay silent and peaceful on the bed.

Holding the dagger in front of him, the assassin stepped into the room. He crept toward the bed and then suddenly stopped.

The long bundle on the bed was formed by cushions and linen.

A spike of fear caused his heart to beat out of time. His intuition told him to swerve to the side.

The sword speared the air where he'd been a moment before. Whirling to face the threat, dagger held between him and his enemy, the assassin saw the athletic prince standing bare-chested with a curved sword held out in front of him. His posture was angry rather than fearful. Like his two younger brothers, Caran had been trained from childhood in the use of weapons but, unlike them, he'd thrived under the tutelage of the sword masters.

'Who are you?' Caran panted.

The assassin stayed silent. The prince was whipcord lean and held his sword with accustomed practice, but he was forced to look up to meet the assassin's eyes; few men were as tall.

The prince's eyes narrowed. 'I asked you a question.'

The assassin attacked.

He stepped forward as if making a considered approach and, as expected, Caran shifted to meet him, following the classic moves. But then the assassin did something he knew his opponent wouldn't expect. He lunged with the dagger and the sword came up. He pulled back again as if reconsidering, and the sword point began to drop again.

In the brief spell of time he'd bought himself, the assassin then shifted his grip on his weapon. Taking the point of the blade between thumb and forefinger, he whipped down his hand. He felt the steel glide out of his fingers as they snapped together.

Caran gasped. With the dagger plunged to the hilt in his left shoulder, his knees trembled, but his sword arm was unaffected, and with an effort of will he brought the point up again.

Now without a weapon, the assassin charged. The prince lunged; there was nothing to fault in his technique. But the assassin was the better warrior; he could predict every movement and simply wasn't where his opponent expected him to be. He put his hand on Caran's wrist and applied pressure.

Now face to face, gripping both hands in his own, the assassin met Caran's eyes with a grim stare. The prince tried to escape him, wrestling with his hold, but the assassin was far stronger. The sword tilted until it pointed at the center of the prince's chest. The assassin then pulled the prince in as hard he could, feeling steel meet initial resistance and then slide in easily as the blade entered Caran's chest.

Caran's cry was weak as the assassin let his body fall to the floor. The assassin retrieved his dagger and wiped it on the prince's trousers, replacing it in its sheath. He watched the last of Solon's three sons die before he gave a final nod. He then took a garment of blue fabric from a pocket and draped it over the corpse.

Leaving the bedchamber, the assassin retraced his footsteps. But on his way out his breath caught when he saw a patrolling palace guard blocking the corridor. Their eyes met and the guard blanched.

The palace guard turned his back and moved away, pretending not to see.

———

'Lord Kargan.' The palace guard ushered him through the palace quickly, taking him directly to the audience chamber.

'Eh?' Kargan glared at the soldier. 'What's the rush?'

'Lord Mydas will explain.'

Herded along the corridor, Kargan stopped in surprise as he approached the cavernous throne room from the end.

Facing the harbor, the space was vaulted, with white marble columns holding up the ceiling and tapestries lining the walls. A warm breeze ruffled the curtains of the wide rectangular windows on the right-hand side, bringing in the smells of the city and the faint taste of dust. The last time Kargan had spoken with Mydas on the terrace, the ebony throne he'd passed on the way had been symbolically empty.

The throne now had an occupant.

Mydas sat on the immense black chair. His bulk was big enough to fill the seat but, without Solon's height, Mydas looked out of place, too short to be in proportion to the throne's back. He wore no crown and his oily ringlets cascaded to his shoulders. Kargan found himself staring at the thick gold rings on Mydas's knuckles as he impatiently tapped his fingers on the arm of the chair.

The situation was strange enough to make him stand motionless, wondering how he should react. He glanced at the file of palace guards, framing the long rectangular space in front of the throne. But the man sitting on it wasn't the king; with Solon having three sons, he wasn't even in close succession.

Finally his escort broke his reverie by prodding his back. 'Lord Kargan?' the guard murmured.

Kargan shook himself and strode forward to stand half a dozen paces in front of the throne. 'Lord Mydas,' he said, giving a short bow, as between equals.

'Grave news,' Mydas said, staring at Kargan with his emotionless eyes. 'This last night, a Phalesian assassin penetrated the palace.' His next words made Kargan's mouth drop open with shock. 'The assassin murdered all three of Solon's sons.'

Kargan swallowed; he struggled to think it through. 'Phalesian?' His brow furrowed. 'How do you know?'

'One of the guards saw him before he fled. He was dressed in leather armor and carried a short sword with a wide blade. He was small, with pale skin . . .'

'Still,' Kargan began. 'It could have been any—'

'He left a blue cloak covering Caran's corpse, an obvious message,' Mydas interrupted. 'There can be no doubt as to his origin.'

'Where is this guard?' Kargan looked around. 'I'd like to speak with him.'

'You are too late, I'm afraid. His failure to capture the assassin had to be punished. His body feeds the crocodiles as we speak.'

'I . . .' Kargan thought furiously. He bowed. 'I'm shocked, to say the least.'

'Yes,' Mydas drawled. 'We all are. As the next in the line of succession, I have no choice but to assume the throne, in the name of the empire and in defense of its future. The coronation must be swift, as I know was your wish, for we must now show a strong hand. I have consulted with the priests, tomorrow I will be crowned. In the meantime, I want you to prepare a plan. Vengeance must be had. You have the best knowledge of their defenses. Your men will follow where you lead. We must punish Phalesia for this crime.'

'Lord . . .' Kargan said. 'Great king.' He slowly lowered himself to the floor until he was on his knees. Leaning forward, he touched his forehead to the stone, as Mydas looked on dispassionately. He waited for Mydas to tell him to rise, but when the order didn't come, he climbed back to his feet.

Kargan took a deep breath. 'I'm saddened, but pleased that the empire will be in strong hands.' He tried to phrase his words carefully, cursing his tongue; diplomacy had never been his strong suit. Nonetheless, he had to do what was right for his men, and right for the empire.

'Great King, let me try to sway you again. This isn't the time to be concerning ourselves with military action across the sea. We're in the midst of a crisis. My sources tell me Koulis has declared independence. Shadria will undoubtedly be next. Pirates plague our shipping – I'm sure you have heard of the Free Men. Meanwhile, our navy is in disarray, yet we have entire divisions of soldiers itching to see combat. I'll lead them myself. I'll show the dominions that our forces are as strong as they ever were.'

Mydas's thick fingers continued to tap the arm of the throne with a thrumming rhythm. 'You agree, Lord Kargan, that we were humiliated in that battle? The battle in which you were in command?'

Kargan scowled. 'Yes.'

'Then you must prove yourself against the same foe. When I am crowned king of kings, will you swear fealty? Will you follow my strategy?'

'Yes,' he said hurriedly. 'Of course.'

'Then prepare a plan as I've asked. Thank you,' Mydas said drily. 'That will be all.' He waved a finger, and soldiers came to escort Kargan out of the palace.

27

It was another night of killing.

The assassin climbed the wall of stone, gripping the tough vines, pulling himself up and over the balcony. Stopping for a moment, he cocked his head and listened. He could hear heavy breathing; the sound of a big man sleeping. He nodded in satisfaction.

Treading lightly, parting the thick curtains, he entered the bedchamber and saw the swarthy barrel-chested man asleep, lying on his back. Nostrils flared with every breath; air whistled out of his nose; a rumbling snore filled the room. The assassin crept to the bedside and slowly withdrew his dagger from the hidden sheath. Taking note of the mop of black hair and the curled beard, he made a decision on where to strike. The big man was tall and broad-shouldered, but his girth was the burly mass of muscle rather than fat.

He stabbed into his victim's chest.

Missing the heart on the first strike and instead piercing the lungs, he stabbed a second time.

Blood erupted from his victim's mouth. With a choking scream the barrel-chested man sat up before falling back down again. He coughed and more blood sputtered from his lips. Crimson liquid welled from the deep wounds in his torso. The assassin hung back, watching and waiting.

Then something happened that made the assassin realize he had made a mistake. It was going to be a costly mistake, the most costly he'd ever made. It was an error that would no doubt lead to his death.

The assassin felt a razor-sharp sword blade touch the soft skin under his chin.

A gravelly voice spoke. 'Don't move. Turn and face me. Hands where I can see them.'

The assassin complied, slowly turning to see the large frame of his intended victim step forward out of the shadowed corner of the room.

He sighed.

———— ⌣ ————

'Move closer to the light. Let me get a look at you.'

The assassin did as instructed, and Kargan kept the point of the blade firmly on the man's throat as he inspected him.

Tall enough to stand out in any crowd, the assassin had a wide mouth, thick lips, and fierce, dark eyes. He wore an open vest and loose trousers, and his bristly black hair was tied behind his head with a thong.

The assassin's eyes flickered to the dead man in the bed. 'Who is he?'

'A slave I bought in the market today,' Kargan said. He glanced at the body for a moment before looking at the assassin once more. 'I don't remember his name.'

'You made me kill an innocent.' The huge man's eyes blazed.

Kargan barked a laugh. 'What would you have me do? You're the assassin. If you hadn't come he'd still be alive.'

'Well?' the assassin asked, lifting his chin. 'What are you waiting for? Kill me.'

'I want to speak with you first,' Kargan said. He gave a slight smile. 'Are you in a hurry?'

The assassin stepped forward, forcing Kargan to step back in order to keep his sword point on his throat. 'I don't care what you want.'

'You killed Solon's three sons?' Kargan asked.

'Yes.'

'And it was Mydas who paid you?'

The assassin shook his head. 'No. I received no payment.'

Kargan frowned. 'You're the kind who enjoys killing for pleasure?'

As the assassin scowled, lifting his chin, Kargan decided that he was a man whose honor was easily insulted. 'Mydas wanted them dead, but he did not pay me. I was working in the stables when he came to me. He knew of me from my time fighting in the arena. He offered me a chance at vengeance.'

Kargan raised an eyebrow. 'Go on.'

'Solon killed my brother. He whipped him, cut him, and impaled him.' The assassin's voice broke at the end. 'But Solon died, killed by some Phalesian I would give much to thank.'

Appraising the tall warrior, Kargan began to put the pieces together. 'I think I understand. What is your name?'

'Javid.'

Kargan met his eyes. 'Your brother's name . . . I believe it was Tomarys?'

Javid nodded.

'Javid, my guess is that Mydas told you I was involved with your brother's death.' Kargan spoke clearly. 'I wasn't. I heard the tale secondhand, that he was tortured and the Phalesian girl ended his suffering.' He shrugged. 'I was at the harbor at the time. I can take you to any number of my men who will confirm it.'

Javid tilted his head. 'You were not involved?'

Kargan spoke flatly. 'No.'

Javid looked away, considering. 'So Mydas is a liar.'

Kargan snorted. 'He's a lot more than that. And now he's the king of Ilea.'

'When he came to me, I said I would gladly end the line of the man who killed my brother. I asked only one thing. That Mydas would rule with honesty, justice, and law. That he would not be the king that Solon was.'

'And what did he say?'

'He gave me his word. I ended the line of Solon. I have no regrets. I hope Solon's soul screamed from the lowest level of hell when I killed his sons.'

Kargan shook his head. 'Javid, I'm glad you had your revenge. Solon was cruel. He did terrible things. And the sons were the worst parts of their father. But I also have to tell you that Mydas is as bad, if not worse.'

Javid's shoulders slumped. Kargan relaxed the pressure of his sword on the assassin's throat.

It was a deception.

The warrior suddenly whirled, moving around the sword. He placed a hand on Kargan's wrist. Pain flared in the joint and despite every desire to keep a grip on the hilt Kargan's fingers went numb.

When it was over, Kargan stepped back, hands held high, and Javid now held the sword, with the point weaving between them like a deadly snake preparing to strike.

'You are all liars,' Javid said. 'I will kill you, and then I will kill Mydas also.'

Kargan swallowed. 'Wait, Javid. Think before you act. Has Mydas asked you to kill anyone besides me?'

'No . . .'

'Then you're a dead man. They'll scour Lamara until they find you. And don't think you'll ever get close to Mydas. As soon as you come anywhere near the palace your fate will make that of your brother look merciful. Solon was cruel, but his younger brother is far more creative. His wealth comes from the slave trade, and he's had plenty of opportunity to experiment.'

As Javid pondered, Kargan seized his opportunity.

'Javid, listen to me. Lamara is not safe, not for either of us. There is only one thing we can both do. Leave. Right now. Together.'

Javid's broad face curled up into a frown. 'You want me to leave with you?'

'Mydas wants me dead. I could use a bodyguard, and your future is looking about as bright as mine. You obviously know your way around a sword.'

'Where do you plan to go?'

'Koulis,' Kargan said. 'The city's declared independence but there's a sizeable Ilean population. I can be useful to the council. Have you ever been to Koulis?'

'No.'

'It's ruled by a council. No king.' Kargan smiled. 'You'd like it.'

Javid spoke with determination, still holding the blade leveled at Kargan. 'If I serve you, I want you to know that I expect you to be truthful at all times, as the god Helios says all men must be.'

'Serve me, and help me survive the coming days, and I'll always be fair with you.'

Javid lowered the sword. 'We have an agreement.'

28

Vendors shrieked at passers-by, each man or woman trying to outdo the others with the volume and pitch of their calls. The hawkers were like flocks of birds, descending en masse to engulf everyone who entered the market. The Sarsicans ignored them, pushing through and making it clear there was nothing they could be tempted into purchasing, while the strangers to the city apologized for their rudeness and made empty promises to return later.

Dion grimaced. The noise stunned his senses, and the smells were stronger still, forcing him to breathe through his mouth as he walked. For a time he could concentrate on nothing except making his way through the crowd, eyes carefully straight ahead, ignoring the brightly colored spices and lengths of cloth as he focused on reaching the less popular parts of the market where the crowd began to thin. He clutched his satchel; within it was the gemstone-filled pouch Eiric had given him at Cinder Fen. His dark expression told thieves to beware.

He was navigating the Myana Silver River Market, reputed to be the largest market in all of Galea. Some said it was named because it was a place where silver flowed like water, others pointed out that, less romantically, the market lined both banks of the Silver

River, the Sarsican capital's main watercourse. From what Dion had seen earlier, even the river's name was poorly given; the water was more brown than silver, and rather than being bright or shining it was filled with a floating array of refuse.

The market was long rather than wide, snaking along with the river, lining both banks. Decrepit wooden bridges enabled people to cross from one side to the other, rickety structures that threatened to tumble into the dirty water with every footstep. It was busiest close to the harbor city's port, where the river emptied into the sea, and Dion had left the *Calypso* there, tied up to the quay, not far from the section of fishmongers and chandlers.

Finally away from the crowds, he paused to breathe freely and regain his bearings. He'd visited the Silver River Market before, but it was large enough that every visit was a repeat of the first, with a confusion of stalls selling a bewildering array of items. Perhaps a Sarsican could find his way around, but to Dion there was no order to it at all.

He was now standing between two long files of cloth tents, places where people could trade and discuss business in privacy, away from the scorching sun. He had a purpose for coming to the rambling market's far end where the lanes were quieter.

The gemstones in the leather pouch, sold wisely, would provide him with enough money to travel on for months. For the first time in his life he would make his own way in the world, alone. The thought was both liberating and filled him with anxiety. He didn't know what fate the gods held in store for him but he had a boat and soon he would have a pouch of silver coins, provided, of course, he met the right merchant.

But Dion didn't know where to go, and so he planned to visit a soothsayer.

He had never been to a Sarsican soothsayer before, but Cob, his old sailing master, had told him that, although they often spoke in riddles, every member of their order had sworn an oath to never lie. Unlike the magi, they were a group consisting entirely of women and were consulted for knowledge rather than prophecy, imparting wisdom in addition to paying well for valuable information. Their fees for consultation could be exorbitant, but as a stranger in these parts Dion decided it would be worth the cost to learn the name of a merchant he could trust to sell his gems to.

Scanning each tent as he passed, he wondered which of them might house a soothsayer. There were markings on the woven mats at each covered doorway and he recognized the patterns that designated the sellers of olive oil, foodstuffs, ceramics, and weapons. But there were too many patterns he didn't know. When he'd represented Xanthos on trading missions he'd always had Cob with him to help. He still had a lot to learn if he was going to make his way in the world.

He remembered Anoush, the orphan guide who had helped him survive the streets of Lamara. Passing a street urchin, a curly-haired youth in a ragged tunic roughly the same age, Dion called out.

'Lad,' he said. 'Where can I find a soothsayer?'

The youth tilted his head back to look up at him. His sunken cheeks and thin arms made Dion wonder when he'd last eaten. 'You're in the wrong place.'

Dion frowned. He was sure Cob once said that the soothsayers were on the left bank of the river, toward the back of the market. He made a decision. He didn't have any money now, but he would. 'Will you guide me? I'll buy you dinner when I'm done.'

The skinny youth's eyes lit up. 'You mean that?'

'Lead the way.'

The street urchin took him between two of the tents, crossing another row, weaving confidently through the crowds, heading straight for the murky river. They arrived at a decrepit bridge where a dozen people waited their turn to cross: laborers in dirty smocks, richly dressed merchants in colorful tunics, and women with baskets held in the crooks of their elbows. Each waited impatiently as the next in line, a burly mason clutching a hammer and chisel, stepped onto the precarious planking. The mason grimaced and made silent prayers for the structure to hold.

An old crone tried to push her way on next but a washerwoman grabbed her arm. 'There's a line!' she growled.

Finally it was Dion's turn. He followed the youth across, feeling every shake of the bridge until he'd crossed to the Silver River's far side. The youth beckoned him forward to where the rocky bank climbed to even more clusters of tents, but these were haphazard and the people passing by poorly dressed. Weaving through another file of stalls, Dion followed his guide to a ragged tent of sunbleached cloth.

The youth stopped outside the tent. 'Someone for the soothsayer!' he called.

Hearing a rustling sound from within, Dion thought about the questions he would ask. It wasn't just help with the gemstones he wanted; he would take the opportunity to learn what he could about the ancient Aleutheans and their golden ark. Sarsica bordered the Aleuthean Sea and was once close to their island civilization. Sailing along Sarsica's southern coast, Dion had once passed a crumbling ruin where there were dozens of obelisks so tall that they towered as high as the sun king's pyramid in Lamara.

'Enter!' a woman's reedy voice called.

The youth nodded, and Dion parted the cloth to step inside.

The ceiling was low and he was forced to stoop as the cloth flaps fell back behind him, plunging the interior into darkness. He saw cushions and a low table, revealed by the cracks of light in the walls. A veiled woman covered in a shawl from head to toe sat at the back of the tent facing him. Only a slit at her eyes enabled him to gather any sense of her appearance.

'Sit,' she said, moving her body to motion, so covered by cloth that he only caught a flash of pale skin at her hand.

Dion made himself comfortable among the cushions. He met her stare, reminding himself that a soothsayer could never lie. 'Can I trust you?' he asked.

Her voice was distinctive, thin and high-pitched, with an odd lilt. 'I am a soothsayer. In the names of all the gods, I swear to you I cannot lie. Of course I can be trusted. But first'—she waved her arm at the table—'we must discuss payment for my services.'

Dion reached into his satchel and felt for the leather pouch. He withdrew a single gem, a wine-red stone the size of a pea, and placed it on the table. 'Will this do?'

He saw another glimpse of white skin as the soothsayer picked up the gem and held it up to her eye with long, slender fingers. A moment later the gem disappeared inside her voluminous clothing.

'Oh yes,' she said, moving her head up and down. Her voice broke and she coughed. 'Tell me, traveler, what knowledge do you seek?'

'I want to ask about the ancient Aleutheans,' Dion said.

'And what is it you wish to know?'

'The golden ark is older than Phalesia itself. It was built by King Palemon to contain the horn of Marrix. My first question is: how did the ark make its way to its final home?'

The soothsayer paused for a moment, as if gathering her thoughts. 'The story is known, here in Sarsica as well as in places far from here. When Marrix, vengeful king of the eldren, caused the Aleuthean island to sink beneath the waves, leaving behind nothing more than the field of jagged rocks known as the Lost Souls, not all Aleutheans died in that one moment.'

Dion frowned. 'Go on.'

'They fled on their mighty ships, the like of which we have never seen again. But Marrix had planned for this, and began to destroy the survivors, for the sea was his element. So the Aleutheans used their magic to scatter their ships. One ship in particular carried something purported to be a magical relic. You already know what this item was.'

'The golden ark,' he said.

'Yes,' the soothsayer said. 'The golden ark. The ship that carried the relic became separated from the rest of the fleet. Driven by the storm, it struck shore and broke up, in what we now call Galean lands. The survivors were attacked by local tribesmen. Some died, some fled, and we must assume that the tribesmen captured the ark. These people, the first Phalesians, rose to prominence and conquered the other tribes. Their priests became custodians of the ark and said it must never be opened. Declaring it to be a sacred vessel of the god Aldus, they placed it on the hill.'

Dion had speculated, but it was comforting hearing the words spoken by someone who had sworn to never lie. 'What of the other Aleutheans? The people on the ships?'

'They were never seen again,' the soothsayer said. 'Legend says that one day they may return.' Her thin voice became wry. 'Or they may not.'

Dion nodded. For people who spoke in riddles, this particular soothsayer was being quite forthright. 'Finally,' he said. 'Who should I trust to sell these to?'

He took out the pouch of gems and spilled them into his palm. When he looked up again at the hunched woman, he saw a captivated gleam in her eyes.

The soothsayer cleared her throat. 'You can trust Gilgud the jeweler,' she said. 'He will give you a fair price.'

'How can I find him?'

'In the city, there is a wide avenue that leads to the Temple of Silex.'

'I know it.'

'Halfway along the street is a marble statue of the sea god standing in a pool of water. Facing the statue, look to your left, and there is a narrow street. Follow this to the end, and you will come to a house with an iron chain hanging on a post. Here you will find Gilgud.'

'Thank you,' Dion said. He poured the gemstones back into the pouch and stood. As he exited the tent, the soothsayer was once again holding the wine-colored jewel up to her eye.

Dion swiftly found the statue of the god Silex, scowling and holding his trident. He turned, immediately seeing the narrow street. He was pleased, feeling confident in the soothsayer's directions: he was in a wealthy part of the city, a place where the houses were grand and city folk well dressed, and had already passed three jewelers on his way.

He entered the lane and with tall structures on both sides he felt immediate relief from the bright sunlight – Myana was even hotter than Xanthos and the summer was proving to be one of the driest in memory. A straight length of cobbled stones led him past a row of two-storied houses and he saw children in clean white tunics playing in the street, rolling stones and chasing after them as they called out to each other in high-pitched shrieks. A matronly woman beat a mat with a stick, sending clouds of dust into the air.

Nodding at the woman, he continued along the street, realizing it was longer than he'd thought it would be. Leaving behind the children and the proud houses, he saw that the character of the area was changing, with more mud-brick dwellings and then no houses at all, just high walls on both sides. He passed an intersecting alley and glanced left and right. The area was empty, devoid of people. He glanced over his shoulder and wondered if he'd missed the house with the iron chain at its gate. Perhaps he should turn back . . .

As he walked back and stood at the intersection, he glanced down every street. The soothsayer's directions hadn't mentioned any turns. Rubbing his chin, he decided to head back to where he'd seen the children playing.

Suddenly a rush of heavy footsteps clattered, the sound bouncing off the walls, making it difficult to know where the noise was coming from.

Dion whirled, looking into all four possible directions. His heart hammered in his chest. He couldn't see the source of the sound anywhere.

It was definitely time to leave.

Taking a deep breath, scanning in front and behind as he walked, he hurried now, eager to be away from the area. He slipped his bow off his shoulder and fumbled for the arrows in his quiver even as he increased speed.

A man-sized shape peeled from the wall behind him.

Fear gripping his chest, he whirled to face the cloaked and hooded figure. There was movement on his other side.

Something hard cracked into the back of his skull with the strength of a horse's kick.

Pain burst inside his head. He sank into unconsciousness.

29

Agonizing starbursts exploded inside Dion's skull. He groaned and opened his eyes but could see only darkness. Groggy, incapacitated, he was being moved, manhandled like an animal being prepared for slaughter.

The pain radiating from the back of his head made it difficult to think. His stomach churned; he thought he was going to be sick.

He was thrown heavily against a curved floor of hard wood and with the nauseating motion he felt himself sinking into unconsciousness once more. Fighting the sensation, feeling the pain slowly ebb, he tried to focus on his sight and hearing, to gain some appreciation of what was happening to him. Enough awareness returned that he realized he was blindfolded, and it must be nighttime, for he couldn't see the faintest glimmer of light. Feeling an up-and-down movement and smelling the fresh salty scent of the sea, he heard a scraping sound of wood against wood, and had enough experience on the water to know he was in a rowing boat. His captors had tossed him into the bottom like a sack of grain; his arms were pinned under his body and already numb; his wrists were tied tightly together.

He groaned again.

'Enough of that,' a curt voice muttered. 'No one's going to hear you.'

The rolling of the sea under the boat grew stronger and suddenly the boat went up a crest and then slammed into the following wave. Dion's head smacked hard into wood, the detonation of pain almost causing him to black out again.

The curt voice spoke again. 'Rocks coming up. Be careful.'

'You act like I've never done this before,' a softer male voice said. 'Woah!'

A wave threw the boat forward and timber scraped along stone.

'It's fine,' the soft voice said. 'We're through.'

The boat's motion calmed and Dion heard the splashing of water against a rocky shore. Soon there was hardly any movement at all, the silence broken only by the smooth slipping of the oar blades in and out of the water. Sand crunched under the hull and there were two successive splashes as the boat's occupants jumped into the water. The pair pulled the vessel up a beach, grunting at each other as the man with the curt voice muttered irritated commands at the owner of the softer voice.

'Right,' the sharp-voiced man barked. 'Let's get him out of the boat.'

One of the captors re-entered the boat to haul Dion up by his armpits, lifting him with an effort and passing him to his companion outside. They struggled with Dion's weight and he fell, blind and numb, relieved when sand, rather than rock, braced his fall.

'Stand up! Yes, that's it. Good. Now walk.'

With a man on both sides, he was hauled up the sandy shore and now there was hard but smooth stone under his feet. The journey was arduous; his arms ached and his legs barely kept his body upright and moving; if his captors hadn't been supporting him he would have fallen a dozen times.

He climbed up some steps, then he was walking on timber planking and the going was easier. Finally he could walk on his own, with a slender man, the owner of the softer voice, helping to keep him upright while his companion went ahead. Despite Dion's situation his helper's movements were gentle.

His legs kicked into something and he stopped.

'It's a stool.' The slender man spoke, his light and airy voice somehow familiar. 'I'm going to move it so you can sit. You got it? Slowly now. There she goes.' He now called out to his companion. 'Reece? Where are you going?'

'I'm getting Jax.'

The slender man left Dion and began humming a tune as he busied himself nearby. Bound, blindfolded, seated on his stool, Dion tried to imagine where he was. He'd been taken out to sea for a time, before he was landed somewhere near a rocky shore. Not far from the shore he'd encountered well-made timber flooring underfoot, and then the echo of voices had changed enough to tell him that at the present he was most likely surrounded by walls.

Suddenly Dion froze. He felt a sharp blade pressed against his neck, so hard and tight that he was afraid to breathe or swallow.

'Listen.' The curt voice belonged to Reece, the bigger of the two men. 'We've tracked down your pretty little boat. That's ours now. Your gems are ours too, and if you don't answer our questions we'll take your more valuable stones as well.' His voice was low and ominous, the meaning clear. 'Tell us what we want to know or I'll turn you into something like my friend Finn here.'

'Hey,' the owner of the softer voice protested. 'I'm no eunuch.'

'Well, whatever you are, you're not like other men,' Reece retorted.

'But there are other men like me,' Finn said. 'And those men like me.'

Reece made a sound of disgust. 'I've told you not to speak that way in front of me.'

'You started it—'

Dion was only partly aware of the exchange; the knife edge pressed against his neck was forcing him to concentrate on his breathing, to keep his body as still as he possibly could.

'Enough.' A third man spoke, the sound of footsteps growing louder as the newcomer approached. This voice was strong and confident; the owner was as well-spoken as a noble. 'Reece, ease off a bit, look at him, he's afraid to breathe, let alone speak. And Finn . . . Just keep your mouth shut.'

The pressure of the blade on Dion's neck relaxed slightly. The pain in his head was also beginning to ease from a stabbing throb to a dull ache, enabling him to think more clearly.

'Answer truthfully or you're dead,' Reece growled. 'Where did you get the gemstones?'

Finn whistled. 'Jax, look at this one.'

Dion tried to speak but it came out as a croak. 'I found . . .' He cleared his throat and tried again, choosing his words with care. 'I found them at Cinder Fen.'

'Cinder Fen?' Jax made a sound of surprise. 'You found so many and lived? How?'

'By my wits.'

'Can you find more?' Jax asked.

Dion shook his head. He tested his bonds, but these men knew their business, and with his arms tied behind his back and a blindfold over his eyes there was nothing he could do. 'I found a cave. Inside were some long dead bodies and a pouch. The answer is no.'

Reece sighed. 'I told you this was a waste of time.'

'It was worth a try,' Finn said.

'So what now?' Dion spoke up. 'You've robbed me, taken everything I have. Now what, you kill me?' He lifted his chin. 'What will you do with my body? I don't think I'm able to climb.'

'Who says anything about climbing?' Reece snapped. 'We can just kill you here and throw your body in the water.'

'No, you can't.'

Reece's irritation was growing. 'And why is that?'

'Because, if I'm correct, we're at Smuggler's Cove, and the currents would take my body right back to Myana. You don't want that. The harbormaster doesn't care for corpses drifting into his city.'

Finn chuckled. 'He's a quick one.'

Jax was intrigued. 'How do you know where we are?'

'The sound the waves make on the rocks and the way the walls reflect the echoes. My sense of time since you ambushed me. The smell of wooden barrels and smoke. I'm in a hidden cave near the water, somewhere in the vicinity of Myana. I've heard of Smuggler's Cove. I know currents. So what's your plan?'

Finn laughed shrilly, almost girlishly. 'He's good. We should ask him the questions, Jax.'

'Him?' Reece barked. 'He may be simply dressed but you've heard the way he speaks. And with that boat . . . He's a lord or a lord's son. I'd stake my life on it.'

'Come on, Jax,' Finn wheedled. 'Ask him the questions.'

'Hold on,' Jax ordered. 'Let me think.'

There was silence for a time as the leader considered. Time dragged out as Dion turned his head, looking at where he imagined each of his three captors to be.

'All right,' Jax said. 'We'll see what he says.'

'Him—?'

'Enough. I've made my decision.' This time Jax's order met no opposition. 'Friend, what is your name and where are you from?'

Dion's brow furrowed as he thought. His name might be known in Sarsica. He was the brother of the king of Xanthos. He'd rescued Chloe from the clutches of the sun king and helped her to save the golden ark. 'Andion,' he said. 'Andion of Orius.'

He imagined Jax looking down at him. 'So, Andion of Orius. Second question. What is your trade?'

'Sailor,' Dion said. He'd already proven as much. 'Sometime hunter.' He swallowed, still aware of the blade on his skin. 'I might not wear silver but I follow Silex.'

'Explains the bow,' Finn said in a loud whisper.

'Third question,' Jax went on without pausing. 'How satisfied do you feel with your current life?'

Dion was surprised; he couldn't hazard where the queries were leading. 'My parents are dead,' he said, remembering his gentle mother and stern father. 'I'm alone. I came to Sarsica to sell the gemstones.'

'What did they die of?' Finn asked curiously. 'What did your father do?'

'That's not part of the normal questions,' Jax said in exasperation.

'My father was a . . . fisherman,' Dion said. 'They died of fever.'

'With your accent?' Reece asked.

'He owned a fleet.'

'See, Reece?' Finn spoke in a smug voice. 'He's not a noble. You're always so quick to judge.'

'Listen, you peacock—'

'Both of you. Shut your mouths. I'm not finished,' Jax ordered. 'Fourth question. Do you have a bed somewhere with a woman waiting? Little brats screaming and wailing?'

Dion thought about Chloe, perhaps already his brother's wife. 'No,' he said shortly.

'Fifth question,' Jax said. 'Can you fight?'

Dion smiled, knowing they would see it. 'As long as I have a bow in my hand. Yes.'

'Sixth question. Do you believe that all people were created equal, regardless of race or color?'

'And gender,' Finn said. 'What?' he protested. 'Someone has to speak for the women.'

Dion frowned. 'I suppose I do. Yes.'

'Seventh question. Do you believe a man should be able to attain a station in life according to his skills and merits?'

Dion's frown deepened. 'I do,' he said slowly.

'Eighth. Do you believe everyone should be free to follow any god, or love any person, he or she wants?'

Finn spoke in the sinister voice a villain would use at the theatre. 'Think carefully about this one.'

'Yes.' Dion smiled despite himself.

'Ninth question. Do you believe one man should be able to enslave another?'

Jax's tone told Dion he needed to answer this question correctly. His headache grew as he tried to think. There were slaves in Xanthos, Phalesia, Tanus, Sarsica . . . in all the Galean nations. Most were treated well, but not all, and once indentured it could be difficult, even impossible, to buy a way to freedom. He hadn't given much thought to the practice, only to know instinctively that the cruelty he'd seen in Ilea was beyond anything he'd seen elsewhere. 'No.'

'Last question, do you believe a king should have the full support of his men, otherwise he is no king?'

The pieces came together in Dion's mind. 'I do. And I know who you are. You're the Free Men.'

'You've heard of us,' Jax said.

Reece spoke up. 'You asked whether we plan to kill you. That's not how this works. We either let you go merrily on your way, or you join us.' He chuckled. 'But don't ask for your gems or your boat back.'

'So what's it to be?' Jax asked.

Dion heard new voices approaching. A gravelly older voice contrasted with a deep baritone.

Closer by, Finn spoke in a murmur: 'The old man's returned from town.'

'. . . ridiculous what they're charging for soap,' the old man was saying to his companion.

'Then don't use so much,' the deep voice said. 'For a man with such a small surface area, you go through soap the way our resident priest goes through wine. Woah, who is this?'

'He's our newest member,' Finn said. 'Meet Andion of Orius.'

Reece contradicted him. 'He hasn't decided to join yet.'

'By Silex, it couldn't be,' the owner of the gravelly voice breathed. 'Dion?'

Dion sat up straight. He felt like a bucket of cold water had just been thrown over his head. Shock and amazement coursed through him in equal parts. His mouth worked soundlessly. He tried to speak, but no words came out.

'Take off his blindfold!' the old man growled.

'Jax?' Reece inquired.

The newcomer with the deep voice spoke. 'It appears we're witnessing a reunion.'

Jax gave an order. 'Reece, do it.'

Dion felt hands fumbling at the back of his head and blinked as his blindfold was removed, but the light cast by an oil lamp on a nearby table was dim and his eyes swiftly adjusted. His wrists were freed a moment later and he stood, swaying for a moment before finding his feet, seeing that he was in a circle of men, all watching him with open curiosity.

But his eyes were only on the stunted old man with the bald head, rocking on his heels and grinning at him.

Dion finally found his voice. 'Cob?'

⌣

Dion and Cob left the wooden shack at the cavern's rear. Walking along the raised platform, they stopped near the water and talked.

'I thought you were dead,' Dion said. 'I saw you swallowed whole, along with most of our boat.'

'I thought I was too.' Cob looked away as he ran a palm over his wrinkled crown, evidently reliving the horror. 'That leviathan's gullet sucked me down but I cut my axe into the floor of its mouth. Managed to hold fast, swimming round with half the Maltherean Sea and struggling not to drown or get cut up by the monster's teeth.'

The old sailor shuddered.

'Must have hurt it, 'cause it spat me out and I found a few timbers to float on. I drifted awhile before I was picked up by a boat, part of a bigger fleet. The Free Men made me an offer, so I joined.' He turned back to Dion and shrugged. 'I never had much of a life in Xanthos.'

'It's good to see you,' Dion said, gripping the shorter man's shoulders. 'I can't tell you how good.' His smile slowly fell. 'Listen, there are some things—'

'Lad,' Cob interrupted. 'I know.' He waited for his words to sink in. 'News travels, and the story of the half-eldran prince isn't believed everywhere but it's repeated. You're in the right place here. No one judges. Not for anything. Still, if you want to keep your secrets, that's fine with me. Finn said you're Andion of Orius, so that's who you are. I'll just say Dion is my name for you.' He grinned. 'I've known you since you first grew whiskers. It's my right to call you what I want.'

'They asked me ten questions,' Dion said. 'Then they asked me if I want to join.'

Cob nodded. 'I know the process. And?'

Dion drew in a deep breath and then let it out. He met the old man's gaze and came to a decision. 'I think I will.'

'Good.' Cob slapped him on the back. 'Come on. I'll introduce you properly.'

Cob led him back along the walkway, and now that Dion had more time to appreciate his surroundings, he took in the rows of barrels lining the cavern wall and the cold ashes of a campfire down on the beach. Back at the cove's entrance moonlight shimmered on the water, providing just enough light to see. Ahead of him the timber-walled shack was large enough to accommodate several rooms and even had curtain-covered windows, open to let in the breeze, for it was a warm night. Light flickered from the oil lamp within, silhouetting the four men waiting inside.

'Finished catching up?' said a brawny man with arms folded over his chest when Cob entered with Dion beside him. He had the weathered skin of a sailor, a pinched, rat-like face, and eyes that were too close together. His dark, thinning hair was matched by the color of his eyes, which were narrowed as he scowled.

'Andion here has decided to join us,' Cob said. 'So it's time he put faces to your voices.' He nodded to the stocky man, whose identity Dion had already deduced. 'You've already had the pleasure of meeting Reece, our surly but brave lieutenant.' Reece's scowl deepened.

Cob then indicated a slender, long-haired man with fine features, delicate hands and arched eyebrows, slouching in the corner. He had a crimson scarf around his neck and a silver earring in the shape of a fish dangling from one ear. 'And this is Finn, our purser and aspiring thespian.'

Finn gave a bow with a long flourish, before tossing a lock of his hair away from his eyes. He pursed his lips. 'You can trust Gilgud the jeweler,' he said in falsetto. 'He will give you a fair price.'

The other men all chuckled. Dion's eyes widened: the soothsayer wasn't just false; the imposter hadn't even been a woman. He opened his mouth but decided his questions would have to wait.

'This is Gideon.' Cob nodded at a lean, muscular man with glistening skin the color of ebony.

'Pleasure,' Gideon said; his was the deepest voice. The dark-skinned man had a broad face, high cheekbones, and a shaved head. He wore a loose sailor's tunic, and white whip scars were visible on almost every surface of his skin. Seeing Dion's eyes on his scars, Gideon nodded. 'I was a slave and now I am free.' He tapped the side of his head. 'But the mind can be a prison also, something I urge you to remember.'

'Gideon is our quartermaster and unlikely philosopher,' Cob explained with a grin. 'Where Finn counts our silver, Gideon looks after our blankets and weapons, water and flour.'

'And of the two of us I am far the prettier,' Finn said. 'Gideon's last owner saw to that.'

'Gideon was slave to a magus in Koulis,' said Cob, 'but when his master died they sold him on the block. No one thought a so-called savage from Imakale could read and write, nor recite the epic of Sooth from start to finish, so he ended up working stone in the quarries until he escaped.'

Gideon looked away, and Dion guessed that all of the Free Men had similar stories.

'And finally,' Cob said. 'This is Jax.'

The first thing Dion noticed was that he had a scar in a long line that began at his forehead and followed the side of his face, terminating at his chin. Tall, lean, and undoubtedly striking, he had graying hair at his temples, a neat moustache, and wore a rakish cap at an angle on his head and a pale blue tunic. Without the scar he would have been handsome; with it his features were undoubtedly marred. But he had a friendly, open face and a broad smile that combined with his twinkling eyes to give an impression of mischief. When he crossed the room to clasp Dion's hand his movements were smooth and graceful, but his firm grip told Dion there was also strength in his limbs.

'I ran away from a family of farmers at twelve,' he said. 'And here I am.'

Cob shook his head and snorted, glancing at Dion. 'We'll get the truth out of him one day.'

'Now, how do you two know each other?' Jax asked.

'Cob taught me everything I know about sailing,' Dion said.

'We sailed together in Xanthos,' Cob finished. 'Back when I worked for the king.'

Jax smiled. 'Good! Our admiral will have some long-awaited help then.'

'Admiral?' Dion queried, looking at Cob.

Cob barked a laugh. 'I do all the dirty work looking after our ships. Speaking of which . . .'

Jax nodded. 'We sail at dawn. Andion, your bow will be returned when we arrive.'

Dion knew better than to ask about the gemstones, but there was one thing he had to ask. 'And my boat, the *Calypso*?'

'She's a fine boat,' Jax said. 'We'll look after her for a time. Reece will sail her.'

Dion looked at Jax's surly right-hand man, who was now smiling for the first time. 'Where are we going?'

'Fort Liberty,' Finn spoke up. 'That's where you'll give your oath.'

'And where Jax will decide on your new position,' Reece said.

30

Chloe's anxious gaze swept the sunlit plain, interspersed with rows of windswept hills, like tawny waves frozen in time. There was little cover, and if Nikolas's men were still in pursuit she needed to find somewhere they could shelter and rest before they tried to circle back to civilization.

She glanced at Liana, seeing shadows under her friend's eyes and scratches on her limbs. Like herself, Liana was exhausted, thirsty, and half starved.

Liana suddenly looked up. She cocked her head to the side as her eyes became unfocused.

'What is it?' Chloe hissed.

Liana gave her a horrified stare. 'Horses. I can sense horses.'

Chloe turned back the way they'd come, and then she saw them.

Twelve riders crested a long ridge, rising into view in a line. Chloe's heart beat out of time when she saw their bare chests and furs. These weren't Xanthian scouts, they were barbarians, natives of the northern wilds. Spying Chloe and Liana, they spurred their mounts into an immediate gallop, riding their horses in the way only men born to the saddle could do, recklessly racing down the steep hillside. The hunters cried out to one another, high-pitched calls that sent shivers racing along her spine. They dug in their heels and slapped their hands again and again at the flanks of their mounts.

'What do they want with us?' Liana cried.

Frozen with fear, Chloe suddenly recognized the leader, a lean warrior whose face was darkened by a tattoo, with a topknot leaving the rest of his head bare.

'Nikolas sent them. Run!'

Chloe summoned her last reserves of strength. Sprinting, her eyes wide with terror, she looked back over her shoulder. Seeing the tribesmen gaining rapidly, she focused every thought on running as the ground began to climb. Ahead was another hill, taller than the last, a long escarpment with its highest point marked out by a field of boulders.

The rumble of horse hooves on hard ground sounded behind them. The slope climbed and made it still more difficult to keep up the pace. Gravel slipped under Chloe and Liana's feet, skittering downhill. They were heading to the field of boulders at the hill's summit, though when they reached it there would be no salvation, the tribesmen would simply surround the peak, dismount, and approach with weapons ready.

Despite the difficulty of the ascent, Chloe again glanced behind her. The tribesmen rode side by side, close enough that as the slope took its toll she could see the faces of individual warriors. Their eyes were narrowed, their dark expressions making her wonder what their orders were. Several of the tribesmen had circles of bones around their necks. A hunter lifted his bow, but the leader with the topknot called out and the man lowered his weapon. The leader said something else and they drew up, beginning to dismount.

Spurred by fear, Liana was now ahead, climbing with all four limbs, desperate to reach the false sense of safety at the ridge's highest point. The hill's crown was littered with large rocks, high above the plain. The area would make for a defensible resting place, provided one wasn't already under pursuit: there was an all-encompassing view of the surrounding area, the boulders would screen a fire, and there was no reason to visit other than to make camp.

As Chloe followed Liana in a stumbling run, struggling to suck in lungfuls of air, Liana suddenly cried out.

A solitary man climbed up onto a tall rock ahead. He was shielding his eyes from the rays of the setting sun, waving at Chloe and Liana, urging them on. A round-faced old man in a dirty brown robe, he was unarmed aside from the long staff clutched in his right hand.

Liana tripped over, sprawling on the dirt and gravel. As Chloe helped her up and carried her friend past the newcomer, she gained an impression of a pug nose and white beard. After only a few more steps Liana fell again, and with the stranger now between them and their pursuers, Chloe knew that neither of them could run any farther. Her gaze went back the way they'd come. Silhouetted in the afternoon light, she watched the back of the strange old man as he continued to hold his staff high.

She saw the hunters come into view. Their horses left behind, the cold-faced men of the north climbed remorselessly forward with bows in hand, arrows nocked, moving swiftly. Their eyes were on the old man with the staff, who stood on his rock as if challenging them, and Chloe saw that his hand gripped the staff close to the top, where an odd fork of reddish metal, the size of her hand, crowned the pole. If it was a weapon, it was unlike anything she'd seen before.

The leader with the topknot glanced at his companions. His eyes flickered to Chloe and Liana before returning to the old man. Seeing that the two women weren't going anywhere, he nonchalantly lifted his bow.

Chloe heard a creak as he nocked an arrow and slowly drew the string to his ear.

But the old man stood his ground. Chloe could see only his back, but with his legs astride and staff held high he appeared to be unmindful of the arrow that would soon plunge into his chest. She held her breath. The warrior's eyes narrowed.

Suddenly the old man slammed the base of his staff down onto the rock. At the moment the staff struck, he cried out as if calling on the gods to help him.

A heartbeat later a piercing sound split the air. It was the cry of a thousand shrieking birds, all screeching as one.

Chloe clapped her hands over her eardrums. Liana fell to her knees and put her hands on both sides of her head, her face contorted with pain. But the effect on the tribesmen was greater still.

Their mouths opened in inaudible screams as their hands went over their ears. Weapons fell; the drawn arrow flew harmlessly into the sky as every one of the hunters collapsed to the ground. They began rolling back and forth, writhing and kicking. Chloe continued to watch the leader with the topknot, seeing blood stream from his ears. She could see from his movements that he wasn't dead, but his grimace of torment told her that he wished he was.

The terrible sound projected from the staff lasted for an eternity, a high-pitched warbling that pulsed with a head-splitting rhythm. Chloe crouched down at Liana's side, seeing that her friend was in almost as much pain as the hunters.

Then, as quickly as it had come, the cacophony faded.

The old man turned around, the expression on his face calm and confident. Gathering his robe, he climbed down from the tall rock and approached the two awestruck travelers.

Chloe straightened. She looked from the stranger to the dozen incapacitated hunters, strong men all of them. As she regarded the staff-wielding old man, he returned her look with an appraising look of his own. His deep-set eyes traveled up and down, examining her from head to toe. She saw now that he was plump, with thinning hair and a ragged beard, and that the fingers gripped around his staff were short and thick.

There was something wild about his eyes, but his voice was friendly when he spoke. 'My name is Vikram. Come with me. My home is nearby. Let me take you there.' He gave Chloe an earnest look. 'You will both be safe.'

———

Vikram led them for hours, but the pace he set was an easy one. Chloe gave him their names and told a story somewhat close to the truth, saying they had been heading from Phalesia to Tanus when an army approached. Fearful of the soldiers, they'd hidden in the northern hills but had been discovered by the band of hunters.

'If there's some way I can repay you . . .' she said. 'You saved our lives.'

He waved a hand. 'So you are Phalesian?' he asked, his gaze encompassing them both.

Chloe saw him taking note of her copper medallion and its symbol of Aeris, as well as Liana's unadorned bronze necklace. Liana's tunic was plain whereas Chloe's chiton was thick and well made. Chloe's pale skin and near-black hair, cascading almost to her waist, marked her out as Galean, but Liana's wild red hair, while not exactly rare, was certainly uncommon.

'Both Phalesian,' Chloe said. 'Liana is my maid.' Liana shot Chloe a dark look but Chloe, seeing Vikram's attention diverted, shook her head slightly.

Vikram shrugged. 'I know little about Phalesia other than its name. But it seems to me that two women should not be traveling unaccompanied. Where are your protectors?'

'Our escort . . . They tried to lead off the horsemen. I . . . I don't know where they are now.'

Until she knew more about Vikram, Chloe decided against mentioning more about herself, or even seeing if he would help them get back to the Phalesian Way. They needed food, water, rest, and information.

She also needed to learn about the strange power he'd called upon to defeat the hunters. Zachary had said that some of the magic of Aleuthea might still survive. She glanced at Vikram, who had just saved their lives with nothing but a staff. She wondered if he would share his story.

'Here.' Vikram handed a skin of water to Liana, who drank gratefully before passing it to Chloe. 'So your guards . . . Might they still be looking for you?'

'I hope so,' Chloe said. She drank and then changed the subject. 'You live out here?'

'I do,' he said with a smile. 'I prefer it "out here", as you call it.'

'You don't get lonely?' Chloe asked.

'My wife is long departed but I am known among the local tribes. I have fire at night and music for my soul. And perhaps one day I will find another to share the sun and the wind, the rivers and the valleys.' He swept his arm grandly over the vista, as if claiming the plain and its rows of windswept hills for himself.

'What were you doing when we found you?'

'Contemplating the world. There is a special energy in some places, and I often explore and meditate.' He glanced at Chloe, seeing that she was perplexed. 'To meditate is to delve into the corners of one's mind. I must hone my powers of concentration the way a swordsman does his blade. I am a sorcerer, a true magus.'

Chloe's gaze now went to the metal fork that topped his staff. She was surprised to see a greenish discoloration on the copper.

Recognizing copper tarnish, she frowned. When she'd last seen it, she could have sworn the metal was bright and lustrous.

'A true magus?'

He turned his deep-set eyes on her and something in his glance made Chloe feel that she shouldn't press farther. 'You are both tired.' He smiled, revealing yellowed teeth. 'Explanations can wait.'

The sun set behind them as they traveled; it grew dark and there was still no sign of Vikram's home. But then, as they ascended to the summit of yet another hill, Chloe frowned when she saw a crude village ahead.

It was a small settlement of wooden huts laid haphazardly, black shapes that dotted the low plain near a winding river. She wouldn't have seen it at all if it weren't for the dozens of campfires, yellow lights that dimmed and brightened like stars. Liana cast Chloe a fearful look.

'The village of Pao,' Vikram said. 'Please, Chloe, Liana, you have nothing to fear. Your pursuers were Han. The Pao are gentle folk. And we will not be passing near.' He pointed with his staff. 'Do you see the cliff above the village, on the right-hand side? We'll have to do some climbing I'm afraid, but that is where I have my home.'

Following a winding path, they pressed on in silence, footsteps guided by a rising crescent moon. When they reached the top of the cliff Chloe almost stopped in her tracks when she saw a hulking structure ahead, crowning the high ground like a citadel guarding the village below.

The sprawling villa revealed in the moonlight was once far grander than Chloe's home in Phalesia. Each stone block was fitted perfectly to a companion and decorated with carved impressions of flowers, and it was built in an elaborate style, somehow alien. But it had fallen into disrepair, and while the main body was still in use, the cross section at the far end had crumbled into ruin. Though the columns holding up the ceiling were wide, some leaned at odd angles and dozens of roof tiles were missing.

Trees and rambling gardens enclosed the single-storied structure; once again Chloe gained an impression that the state of the surrounds had once been truly beautiful but had fallen into neglect. A wide stone basin filled with clear water stood outside the main entrance that Vikram led them toward.

'Welcome to my home,' Vikram said. 'You are safe here from the villagers – not only are they primitive folk, foragers rather than hunters, they believe I am a holy man and keep their distance. Please, I want you to feel comfortable here. Stay as long as you wish.'

Vikram led them up a short series of smooth steps and through a wide entrance, framed by tall columns. The inviting glow of oil lamps beckoned to a cavernous interior, with a floor covered by woven mats and items of furniture that wouldn't have looked out of place in Phalesia. Stools and low tables surrounded a central hearth. Urns and ewers rested against the walls. Even the high ceiling was decorated with fluting scrollwork.

'Let me show you where you can bathe. I will serve food in a short while. Rest. Regain your strength, I insist.'

Chloe and Liana both thanked him again, and, looking pleased, with a wave of his hand, the old man in the loose robe led the way.

31

The long, lean dragon looked back over his shoulder. He snarled, racing through the sky, wings sweeping up and down vigorously. The glossy, more youthful dragon pursuing roared in response, his own wings pulled in as he followed his quarry. Far below, the land flashed past in a blur.

The two silver-scaled dragons reached the edge of the mountainous escarpment that encircled Cinder Fen and continued, the foremost putting his every effort into speed, his pursuer unrelenting. Reaching the sandy white beach that surrounded the peninsula, they traveled onward and over the sea, passing turquoise shallows until they were above the deeper water.

Both had angular, wedge-shaped heads with sharp ridges behind the almond-shaped eyes, but where the fleeing creature had protruding teeth that were yellowed with age, the chasing dragon's teeth were glossy and white. They were evenly matched in size, as large as the wooden warships the humans used to wage war across the sea, but the first was sleeker, with outstretched veined wings that matched the length of his body, whereas the second was more muscular, with shorter, more powerful limbs.

They sped over the sea, steadily losing height to skim a stone's throw above the waves of the open ocean. Blue water became darker as the distance from land increased; the Maltherean Sea here was deep. The hunter roared a challenge again at his quarry. The fleeing dragon cast a glance back and shrieked in defiance.

Suddenly the foremost dragon dove for the water. At the same instant he blurred. Mist enveloped him from head to tail as he reached the surface. In a heartbeat he changed from a dragon to a serpent, shrinking in girth, doubling in length. He plunged into the sea, seeking to escape in a new environment, to use his greater age and experience to confound his younger foe.

But, without hesitation, Eiric followed.

Banishing the wild thoughts of flying and command of the open sky, he imagined the sea as his domain, summoning sensations of wetness and a longing to undulate and writhe. He dived down to the circle of ripples left behind by Jonas's descent and at the instant that he struck the water he changed.

Serpent now hunted serpent, with a long paddle-tailed leviathan pursued by a shorter, wider foe. Bubbles burst, confusing vision, and water swirled in eddies left behind by the thrust of each creature's extremity at the sea.

Jonas traveled deep, heading for the safety of darkness, and Eiric knew that if he couldn't increase his speed he would lose him in the depths. Calling on his last reserves of strength, he focused on his rage, using it to feed the wild side within.

The distance between the two serpents narrowed. Even as the breath screamed in Eiric's chest, shrieking at him to return to the surface, still they descended. He opened his mouth and gnashed his teeth together, almost biting down on its quarry's tail.

Eiric . . . Was that his name?

The wildness grew, threatening to burst inside him. The thrill of the chase began to overwhelm all other thoughts. He was an animal born to the sea; he belonged here. When he caught his prey he would bite down and taste blood, before tearing away silver-scaled flesh and devouring chunks of red meat. He reveled in the power of his body. This form was natural; it was who he was.

Eiric! My name is Eiric!

He dug deep to bring to the surface memories of his father, Zachary, and his mother, Aella. He remembered being raised in the Wilds, taught to hunt by his father but also shown how to lead. Zachary had survived the trials of the Battle of Phalesia that took Liana's parents. Even during the darkest times, Eiric had thought nothing could disturb his father's equanimity. But then Jonas betrayed them to Triton. Eiric lost his mother, and he'd also learned what could destroy his father's nature when he'd stood fast against so many trials.

Jonas deserved to pay.

Just as Eiric thought his chest would burst, Jonas finally gave up his mad descent. Twisting in the water, he shot directly for the surface. His body flashed past Eiric's eyes, curling as he changed his trajectory. Eiric's jaws opened wide and he felt his teeth clamp down, but the slippery scales were tough, and his prey escaped his bite.

The two undulating leviathans sped for the lighter water, traveling vertically, with one directly behind the other. Their tails both lashed at the sea with the strength of mountains behind them, pushing hard enough that when they burst to the surface each shot into the air. An instant later Jonas had shifted back to dragon form and was flying. Focusing on thoughts of wings and sky, Eiric faltered, even as his serpentine body launched itself upward, sailing through the sky.

He almost didn't make it. The grip of the sea was nearly too great; he was too attached to the shape.

But with a snarl and a renewed surge of rage he focused on everything his father had taught him. He forced himself to see the ocean as a foreign environment, confining and dangerous, a place where he couldn't breathe. The sky was natural. Wings would propel him forward. He was a dragon.

He felt the familiar sensation of change and then a moment later he was a winged creature once more. Roaring in victory, fighting down the insanity threatening to take him with every beat of his wings, he saw his quarry gaining height and added a burst of speed.

The two dragons now flew back toward Cinder Fen, climbing higher as the looming escarpment approached. They flashed over the strip of crystalline shore and then the jagged range of mountains was below them.

Eiric had never spent so long nor expended such energy in changed form. He couldn't believe Jonas could keep going. As the long dragon dropped, plunging behind the escarpment to become hidden by the heights, Eiric added still more speed to follow, neck craning as he tried to spy his enemy.

Something smashed into him from behind.

As jaws bit down on Eiric's neck he writhed in the air, fighting to get a grip on his opponent. Soon they were both twisting and grappling as they tumbled down to the region of crags and gullies screened by the mountain range.

The ground rose swiftly to meet the descending combatants. Eiric realized that he needed to outwit his opponent in order to defeat him.

He imagined himself as strong, the strongest of all creatures that inhabited Cinder Fen. His arms were as thick as saplings, his legs the size of tree trunks. He brought up thoughts of walking and running. He could grip objects.

The land was his domain.

While still in the air, changing form was the hardest thing he'd ever done, but with a surge of courage he shifted, even as he clutched his opponent.

Gray smoke clouded one of the wrestling dragons and cleared. A giant now roared as it embraced the long reptilian creature in its arms.

With barely time to brace himself, Eiric felt pain shatter his body as he and Jonas struck the rocky ground. But Eiric was on top of his winged foe, and as they rolled over and over, Eiric now had the upper hand. He squeezed even as they tumbled down a steep hillside, hearing a crack as a bone in the dragon's wing broke. Finally they came to a halt. The lean dragon was dazed and shuddering in pain, one wing crushed under his body, the other at an awkward angle. Shaking his head to clear it, Eiric spied a nearby boulder the size of his immense head. He lifted the rock and smashed it into the dragon's skull. He raised the rock again and pounded his enemy twice more in quick succession.

The dragon blurred and changed.

Jonas, now a tall, lean eldran with spiked silver hair, moaned in pain as he lay prone on the ground. The wound on his crown was bloody, but he was alive.

Eiric. My name is Eiric. I am an eldran.

Finally Eiric was gasping, returned to his normal form. He blinked, dazed, almost too far gone to return to who he was.

But his task wasn't over yet.

He leaned down, squeezing both hands around Jonas's neck.

'Why are you here?' Eiric stared down into his enemy's cold eyes. He had been scouting Cinder Fen, looking for signs of his father, when he'd felt the familiar sensation of an eldran he knew somewhere nearby.

Jonas shook his head.

Eiric suddenly sensed eyes on him. Scanning the area, he saw a clutch of furies, wings fluttering from their shoulder blades as they watched with interest. The wildren might not attack, but he knew he couldn't change again. He had to leave the area.

He decided to find a cave. He hadn't found his father but he'd found the next best thing. He'd captured the traitor.

And the traitor could lead him to Triton.

32

Built around the curve of a wide, well-fortified harbor, the port city of Koulis was a center for commerce, where the hilltop homes of the wealthy overlooked the constant activity of vessels coming and going. Towers with catapults guarded the two ends of the harbor's arc and a wall encircled the entire city, which was surrounded by desert on all sides other than the sea.

The buildings were Galean but the geography was Salesian. White marble temples with peaked roofs dedicated to Silex stood surrounded by groves of palm trees; and the city folk more commonly wore Galean togas, tunics, and chitons while they shopped for pungent spices from Ilea. There was a large agora, but there was also a slave market, teeming with activity night and day. Slaves of all description were available, but most popular were young men and women, girls and boys, always a lucrative source of income for the city. Water was scarce, with rights to the usage of wells strictly enforced by the Council of Five.

Kargan and his fledgling bodyguard were at a drinking house not far from the harbor, a well-kept building with a painted orange sign that announced it as an establishment where Ileans were welcome. The clientele, predominantly men, sat on stools in circles around low tables; though it was early evening, most looked like they'd stay there until the place closed.

The drinking house smelled of sweat and stale wine, with an additional whiff of anxiety. It was a difficult time to be an Ilean in Koulis. The Council of Five had declared the city's independence in the wake of Solon's death, but with a large Ilean population to contend with, unrest was likely.

'So,' Kargan said, running his eyes over his dour companion. Unlike Kargan, who wore a crimson tunic belted with a golden cord, Javid had neglected to upgrade his attire – despite Kargan's offer – and still wore the leather vest and tight trousers he'd been wearing when they met. 'From pyramid slave to stable hand, then assassin and finally bodyguard. I'd say you're moving up in the world, my friend. At this rate you'll be emperor in a month.'

Kargan sighed when Javid didn't even crack a smile, merely shaking his head and scanning the room with his dark, brooding eyes.

'Relax,' Kargan said. 'You're the biggest man in the room. We're safe here.'

He meant every word. With Javid's whip scars and dark eyes, not to mention his size, no one was going to start any trouble.

The owner of the drinking house came over to the table, giving the surface a quick wipe with a dirty rag. 'Two cups of wine,' Kargan said in response to his inquiring look.

'I will take tea,' Javid said.

'Fine,' Kargan said. 'A cup of wine and a mug of tea.' He nodded at his companion. 'Can't have my big friend here losing his head.'

The owner left and returned promptly with the drinks. Kargan raised his wooden cup and drained it to the bottom, inclining his head for a refill.

'Why are we here?' Javid asked. 'Is it just so you can drink? I thought you said you had plans.'

'Never fear,' Kargan said, pausing to take a draft when the proprietor refilled his cup. 'I have a good reason. I need to get the mood of the city before I visit the Council of Five. It pays to be prepared.'

'Well?' Javid asked. 'Have you learned anything?'

'These things take time,' Kargan said. 'If I'm going to make myself useful to the Council I have to know what the city's problems are. I'm a better naval commander than I am soldier, but I can put on armor if need be. I might be able to offer—'

'We're being watched,' Javid said softly.

Kargan turned around, scanning the room, bluntly staring at every face. The drinking house's patrons were a motley assortment of laborers and dockworkers, men used to physical work, hauling supplies to and from the vessels that beached at Koulis every day.

Javid was right, he realized. Several of them were speaking in hushed tones as they looked at Kargan repeatedly. Undeterred, Kargan scowled at them.

One of the men rose to his feet.

Seeing a middle-aged laborer, with sloping shoulders and worry lines on his forehead, Kargan relaxed. The stranger hesitantly approached, bowing when he reached the table.

'Lord Kargan,' the stranger said. 'It . . . It is an honor to have you here. May we speak with you? Would you join us?'

Kargan rose to his feet. Not a small man himself, he towered over the stranger. 'Of course,' he said, recognizing the man's accent as Ilean. 'Any Ilean deserves more than a few moments of my time.'

'Your guard.' The stranger nodded. 'He can join us too.'

'Bring the cups,' Kargan ordered Javid, who responded with a glare.

Soon Kargan was drawing up a stool to join the circle of workers, throwing two silver coins onto the table and calling for more wine. They immediately cheered him, raising their mugs to his name. After Kargan drained his third cup of bitter red wine, the careworn laborer who'd first spoken raised his voice again.

'How are you here, lord?'

Kargan slammed his cup back onto the table. 'I had a disagreement with the new king.' He grinned at the group, and chuckles met his words. 'I suppose I'm in exile.'

The same man spoke again; he appeared to be the leader of the group. 'We're all Ileans, living in Koulis. Most of us have been here for years. Since . . .' he hesitated, 'since the city declared independence a few things have happened.'

'Go on,' Kargan rasped, lifting his cup but frowning when he saw it was empty.

The laborer glanced at his friends. 'I take it you haven't heard, then.'

'Heard what?'

'The army garrison managed to escape to Lamara, but it's not so easy for sailors. The Council of Five locked up the entire naval garrison while they decide what to do with them. Lord Kargan, we've friends and family among them. Can you do anything to help?'

Kargan looked from face to face. There were nine men in the circle and he met the eyes of every one. When he spoke, it was with a clear voice. 'I promise you all that I'll free your friends,' he said. 'I'll visit with the Council tomorrow.'

Now the cheers were louder still. The workers thumped their cups on the table. Kargan glanced at Javid and saw the bodyguard's eyes on him, appraising. He remembered Javid extracting a promise from him to be truthful at all times.

Now it remained to be seen if he could keep his word.

The lyceum of Koulis, where the Council of Five met to administer their city, was unlike a palace in every way. Located in the middle of the unpaved agora, it consisted of a grove of trees planted in a circle where inside, hidden from casual view, a walled structure contained five high-backed wooden chairs. A cleared pathway in the trees provided access, guarded by stern soldiers when the council was in session.

Wearing a yellow silk robe over loose white trousers and carrying a jeweled dagger at his waist, Kargan approached the pair of guards blocking the approach. As instructed, Javid walked beside and slightly behind him.

'Lord Kargan, naval commander and fleet admiral, here to see the Council of Five,' Javid announced. Kargan grunted. He'd stumbled through the words, but at least he made it to the end.

The older of the two soldiers spoke. 'You must wait.'

Kargan nodded and folded his arms over his chest, standing stoically. He concealed the hopes and fears that tumbled through his mind, reminding himself that he was a skilled leader, a man who inspired loyalty from his men. The wait dragged out, but then the soldier finally turned his head to look within. He nodded to Kargan. 'You may enter, Lord Kargan.'

'Wait here,' Kargan said to Javid.

The two soldiers parted, and Kargan breathed a sigh of relief when he realized they'd called him by his title. They'd also neglected to take away his jeweled dagger. The signs were subtle, but they told him that he wasn't about to be jailed, executed, or sent back to Mydas.

He walked along the pathway between the trees, heading in a direct line for the pavilion-like structure of stone within. Another pair of guards waited at the end of the approach, raising their barred spears to let him pass.

He climbed the steps.

He didn't know who he would see waiting inside. Koulis didn't practice the strange system of election by votes that Aristocles had described to him when he'd visited the first consul's villa in Phalesia, but instead nominated by an opaque process a group of five noblemen from the city's most powerful families to represent trade, defense, agriculture, water supply, and overall leadership. At any rate, despite the various maneuverings of the city's nobility, Kargan knew there was only one man whose decision mattered most.

And true enough, Lothar, king of Koulis in all but name, sat in a central chair larger than any other. He was famously greedy, a wrinkled old insect of a man, with fingers like claws and silver hair that matched the glossy medallion around his neck. The symbol on the medallion displayed two fish entwined: the guise of Silex as god of fortune. Koulis valued trade above all else, and Lothar epitomized that value.

But Lothar wasn't a king, and so when Kargan entered the center of the lyceum, facing the row of five high-backed chairs, he merely gave each man a small bow, culminating with a slightly larger bow for Lothar.

Lothar didn't even nod in return. He was a practical ruler, and far too busy worrying about money to be concerned with honorifics.

'Kargan of Lamara,' Lothar said without preamble. 'What brings you here?'

'I think I can help you,' Kargan said bluntly.

Lothar's pale lips cracked into a slight smile. 'As plainspoken as ever. In what way?'

'You've declared your independence from Ilea—'

'Not quite true,' Lothar said. 'We simply disagree with the idea of paying taxes to an empire that we don't consider ourselves a part of.'

'You considered yourselves part of it before,' Kargan said wryly. 'I remember Solon counting your taxes.'

Lothar scowled. 'We paid because it served our needs to do so. But now that Phalesia has managed to defeat the forces of the *mighty* Ilean Empire – in the process, killing the only king we have ever given allegiance to – it does not serve us to give tithe to a new king who murdered his way to the throne and who has never set foot in our city. Shadria is in open rebellion. We take a more peaceable approach. We wish to keep trading with Ilea. But if Ilea comes, we will respond with force, and our Galean brothers may even come to our aid.'

'Well said.' Kargan grinned. Surprised, Lothar leaned back in his seat. Kargan glanced around to look at the four other members of the council but they appeared content to watch and wait. 'I'm not here on behalf of Mydas. In fact, I'd be happy to take his head.'

'Ah,' Lothar said, nodding in realization. 'I take it you have had a . . . disagreement.'

'You could say that. He tried to have me killed,' Kargan said. 'I came here for two reasons. One is that you know me, and you know that I command the loyalty of my men. The second is that, as I said, I can help you.'

'Go on.' Lothar motioned with a flick of his fingers.

'You've imprisoned the Ilean naval garrison, men who – until very recently – kept your waters safe. I understand. If you let them take their warships back to Ilea they might return to fight you. If you release them they might cause trouble. If you kill so many men you might have an uprising on your hands.'

'You state the obvious.'

'Here is my proposal. I've commanded the sun king's navy for many years. My men are loyal to me, and their previous ruler is dead. The new king is unloved and unproven. Give me command of the Ilean warships you have here. They're no longer Ilea's, they're yours. Give me a position.' Kargan smiled thinly. 'I'm in need of one. I know this garrison, they've been here for years and most don't intend to leave at any time. I'll keep them in line. You can hold me to their behavior.'

Lothar's brow furrowed as he pondered. Taking advantage of the pause, Kargan pressed on.

'I ask only one thing. When Ilea recognizes your independence, and things calm down, you promise to let the men return home, if that's what they want. In the meantime, we'll protect your waters from pirates.'

'What prevents you from taking the men and ships back to Ilea?'

'I'm the perfect commander.' Kargan spread his hands. 'Mydas wants me dead.'

'What if there's outright war? What if you have to fight to protect us?'

'We won't fight other Ilean ships, but we'll fight anyone else.'

'And if Ilean ships come?' Lothar persisted.

'They won't – your harbor is too well fortified, and we lost too many at Phalesia. If Mydas comes, he'll come by land. But you already know that.'

For the first time, one of the other men in the circle spoke up. 'I don't think . . .'

A newcomer interrupted him by climbing up the steps and pushing past Kargan without a word. Surprised, Kargan stepped back, but then he caught sight of the elegantly dressed man with the gold ring in his hooked nose and knew that he would have been listening for the entire time, showing his face now only because he considered it important.

His name was Mercilles and he was the richest merchant in Koulis. He was wealthier by far than Lothar or even Mydas, but preferred to direct the maneuverings of his city from behind closed doors. Kargan had never spoken with him, but he'd once seen him when he'd visited the palace in Lamara.

Mercilles leaned forward to whisper something in Lothar's ear. Lothar nodded and Mercilles turned away, not even meeting Kargan's eyes as he brushed past again and descended the steps.

'It appears we might have a problem for you to solve,' Lothar said. 'Tell me, Kargan of Lamara, have you heard of the so-called Free Men?'

Kargan smiled. 'I've heard of them. I wouldn't have mentioned pirates if I didn't know you had a problem.'

Lothar's lips thinned. 'We will give you your ships and sailors. But we will keep one in ten men imprisoned as a bond.'

'Fair enough.'

'Your men will be paid as they were before, and you will be paid as their commander. Also, I'm to tell you that if you bring us the head of Jax the pirate, or of one of his lieutenants, you will be paid a bonus.'

'We have an agreement,' Kargan said.

Lothar nodded. 'You may leave.'

Kargan descended the steps and left the grove behind. As Javid rejoined his side, he thought about the task he'd been assigned. He despised pirates, and the Free Men were the worst of all. Their creed was what made them dangerous, for they raided slave markets and targeted the lowest classes, telling them to rise up against oppression, to join their numbers and fight against their former masters.

'Well? What happened?'

'I freed nine in ten,' Kargan said. 'And I have a new position as commander of the Ilean naval garrison. See, my friend? Moving up in the world.'

'It is good that you have such loyalty to your men.'

Kargan clapped Javid on the shoulder, ignoring the huge warrior's frown. He projected confidence, hiding his concern about the delicate game he was playing between masters old and new.

33

The sleek war galley made fair speed with a chasing wind. The vessel's name was the *Gull*, and while it was no match for a bireme, it had a seven-foot-long bronze ram below the waterline, a large square sail, and a crew of sixty men. Barrels and crates filled the hull from one end to the other: the Free Men had been provisioning in Myana and from what Dion could gather the vast quantity of stores was just a small proportion of what they were bringing back.

He'd already met Finn, Gideon, Reece, and Jax, but the journey had given him time to work with an entire vessel full of the Free Men. They were a motley assortment of former soldiers, downtrodden peasants, ex-slaves, and youths seeking wealth and excitement. Wearing an outlandish array of costumes, hailing from every part of the Maltherean Sea, they shared an easy camaraderie even with newer arrivals like Dion. They set to willingly, but most had little experience with seafaring and followed the instructions Jax and Cob gave them.

Dion was surprised to find himself in a teaching role, demonstrating the workings of the helm and the sail to a growing number of interested sailors, pointing out the stars at night and explaining how to sail by their positions. As soon as a crewman became familiar with something new Dion rotated him onto the next thing he was unfamiliar with, and made sure to take part in the less desirable tasks himself: doling out drinking water, bailing, and, most of all, rowing.

Back muscles aching, he now heard Cob call out a change in shift and gratefully left his rowing bench to let a newcomer take his place. Stretching, he glanced at the palms of his hands. The skin was callused after days of pulling at a wooden oar but Cob was a fair master and Dion didn't resent the work at all. He'd already decided that sailing with the Free Men was something he wanted more than anything he'd wanted before. There was nothing for him in Xanthos and even less in the Wilds. The sea was in his blood. He belonged with these people.

Rather than sink to one of the few bare patches of deck like the other weary oarsmen, he saw Finn standing near the vessel's prow and clambered up to join him. The company's purser wore a broad-brimmed hat over his long hair, his features fine and delicate, contrasting with Dion's tanned skin, broad shoulders, and square jaw, as he came to stand by his side.

The sun was shining above and the seas were calm. A wide-beamed merchant vessel lumbered along on one side of the *Gull* while on the other even the sight of the colorful striped paintwork of the *Calypso* – under Reece's command – couldn't dispel Dion's mood.

Finn looked at him and smirked. 'Hmm,' he said, 'being in my company seems to make you happy.'

Dion laughed and shook his head. 'You're in dangerous territory.'

'Speaking of dangerous territory.' Finn pointed at something in the distance. Squinting, Dion saw a tiny island, growing larger with every sweep of the oars. 'Fort Liberty. We're almost there. Is that what you want to speak about?'

'Actually,' Dion said, 'I want to know what happened, back in Myana, at the market. You tricked me.'

'No offence,' Finn replied with a smile, 'but you had it coming.'

'The boy?'

Finn nodded. 'One of us. We're everywhere, not just out here.'

'What were you doing, just sitting in that tent, waiting for someone like me to step inside?'

'Something like that,' Finn said, chuckling. 'I have several costumes.' His voice changed, shifting pitch, becoming sly and wheedling. 'Marbak the wine seller can fetch you the same wine that graces the table of the king of Xanthos.' The tone then lowered. 'Araf the slaver can give you the choice of a dozen virgin maidens, all fresh as flowers.'

'You offer slaves?' Dion's eyebrows went up.

Finn frowned at him. 'We kill child slavers.'

'How does that make you money?'

'It's not all about money,' Finn said. 'Not even for me, and I'm Jax's master of coin.'

Dion was surprised. 'The one thing I've been meaning to ask you, though,' he said. He wondered how to choose his words, but then decided plain speech was best. 'Was it all a lie?'

Finn tilted his head. 'Was what all a lie?'

'The things you told me about the fall of Aleuthea. Was there really a fleet that escaped? Could they truly return one day?'

'Never tell a lie when the truth will suffice,' Finn said. 'I know a lot of people, and I keep my ear to the ground. As far as I know, that's what happened.' He shrugged. 'Although I must say a few hundred years have passed. History can distort with the passage of time.'

The two men were silent as they watched the island, now large enough that Dion could make out steep cliffs and wheeling birds. He'd never heard of the place, but keeping track by the stars, he knew they were somewhere equidistant between the three largest islands of the Maltherean Sea: Orius, Parnos, and Athos. Lifting his head to look up at the top of the cliff, Dion saw houses on the summit. The view would be unparalleled.

'How many people live here?' Dion asked.

'A few hundred.' Finn glanced past Dion's shoulder. 'Ah, here's someone who can answer more of your questions. I need to keep an eye on the silver we made in Myana. You can't trust these rogues with anything.'

Finn departed and Dion saw Gideon come to take his place; for a moment the dark-skinned man stood silently, watching him intently.

'Actually,' Gideon said in his deep baritone, 'it is I who have questions for you, Andion.'

Dion smiled, but Gideon's impassive stare was unrelenting. He waited for his companion to speak, but as the silence continued he finally asked, 'And what is it you would like to know?'

'I would like to know what it is you want most in this world.'

Dion opened his mouth and then closed it. He thrust aside the first thought that came to his mind, instead trying to think of another response.

'A woman,' Gideon said, nodding sagely.

Dion started. 'How did you—?'

'Your face is an open scroll, and I have read many faces and even more texts. What is her name?'

'I don't—'

'Tell me her name.' The words came out as an order, and Gideon's brow creased slightly. With the tall man from Imakale towering over him, Dion found himself answering.

'Chloe,' he said softly.

'A pretty name,' Gideon said. 'A Galean name. So tell me, young Andion, do you intend to leave us at the earliest opportunity to be with her?'

'Is that why you're talking to me? You want to find out if I'm here to stay?'

'I take it upon myself to learn everything there is to know about every member of our group. Well? Why are you not with her now?'

The probing questions were making Dion angry. 'She is betrothed to my brother.'

'Ah . . .' Gideon said the syllable slowly, drawing it out. 'A difficult position indeed. You are close to your brother?'

Dion gazed up at the looming cliff, seeing a multitude of bird's nests in the cracks and ledges. 'We were close once. But I . . . became something he didn't want me to be. He cast me out of my home.'

'An older brother, then. The head of your family, with your parents dead.'

Dion turned back to see Finn issuing instructions as he checked the contents of a barrel. 'They told you that?'

'Of course.'

'You have the story, then. So you can tell Jax I have nothing waiting for me anywhere else.'

'I will,' Gideon said. 'But I have a few questions more, and this time your words can be for me alone. Does Chloe love your brother?'

'I . . .' Dion frowned. 'I don't know. They may have become close, since I left. He is . . . wealthy . . . powerful.'

'No.' Gideon shook his head. 'That is not how the heart of a woman works. Did she ever love you?'

Dion's voice was low now, little more than a whisper. 'I don't know.'

'And does she know how you feel?'

An image came to his mind, a memory of being with Chloe in the water, their faces close together, their bodies closer still. She'd told him she didn't care what he was, that it didn't matter.

And he'd told her to go.

'No. I never told her.'

'Then, my friend, may I offer you some advice? Leave this group. Go back to your home, and find Chloe before she is married to your brother. Tell her how you feel.'

'It's too late,' Dion said, looking away. 'They would be married by now.'

'I am sorry. My advice is now thus. Learn from this mistake, for a mistake it was. You failed. The next time you have an opportunity for happiness, you must take it.'

The fleet of three vessels now approached a headland, the war galley in the lead. Gideon clasped Dion's shoulder, then left him alone at the bow. Cob ordered the oarsmen to slow and the fleet rounded the promontory. Glancing at the two flanking vessels – the *Calypso* and the wide-bellied merchant ship – Dion saw Jax on the deck of the merchantman, giving orders to reef the sails as the *Calypso* hung back to give the larger ships priority.

Dion turned his attention to Fort Liberty as the harbor came into view.

The island was lopsided, with steep cliffs at the rear descending to a crescent cove, half a mile wide. The twin headlands at either end of the strip of white sandy shore jutted out like fingers, and Dion saw catapults at each promontory, guarding the small harbor. Rows of houses with stilts at the front and open balconies leaned back against the hillside. Treetops at the summit told him there was a small forest, mostly hidden from view.

Half a dozen vessels of all shapes and sizes bobbed in the deeper water within range of the catapults. As the war galley's sail dropped and it approached the shore on oars alone, Dion saw two beached vessels at the far end, each significantly bigger than the *Gull*; with a start he realized they were Ilean biremes.

Fort Liberty was small and defensible. The settlement's population was evidently large enough for the pirates to be able to draw on a range of skills from the inhabitants. Though many of the boats were cargo vessels rather than warships, Jax could nonetheless mount a sizeable force.

Dion wondered if he was looking at his new home.

34

'Do you need the articles to be read to you?' Jax asked.

The leader of the Free Men's genuine expression told Dion he wasn't being condescending.

'No, it's fine, I can read,' Dion said. 'I've finished.'

He was in Fort Liberty's sole temple and the only structure to be made of mud brick and stone rather than wood. It was also the closest building to the sandy beach: a general-purpose meeting hall and house of prayer.

Dion was facing the lines of text that had been cut into the interior wall with hammer and chisel. Jax stood on one side of him wearing a loose white tunic, the ever-present cap covering his graying hair. On Dion's other side was Paolus, the settlement's resident priest, although Dion wasn't sure what deity he followed, for he had no chain around his neck and crude paintings of all the gods decorated the walls. A jovial man with a wide belly filling his brown robe, his face was dominated by his huge nose, which was round and florid.

'Read them all?' Paolus asked, and then hiccupped. 'You sure?'

Dion remembered Finn mentioning a priest who drank vast quantities of wine and smiled as he drew the conclusion. 'Definitely,' he said.

There were twenty basic articles of agreement, providing rules for conduct between pirates, disciplinary measures, and division of goods. They also stated the freedoms Jax had spoken about at Smuggler's Cove and even described a system of compensation for men who suffered injuries. Every man had a vote in affairs affecting them all and the right to carry weapons on signing. In return all were expected to follow the commands of their elected leader.

The focus on votes reminded Dion of the system of governance in Phalesia, but strangely, the pirates were far more equitable still. In Phalesia only men could vote for consuls, whereas at Fort Liberty women could sign the articles and fight alongside the men. Dion had already seen several women crewing the *Gull*, shocked at first to see them wearing men's clothing, but soon becoming so accustomed to the sight that he thought nothing of it. Slavery was also mentioned in the articles as a practice not only outlawed on the island but something to be targeted, with slaves freed on all vessels captured and offered a place on the island. Every man or woman could live, love, and worship how he or she pleased.

Jax clasped Dion's shoulder. 'Any questions?'

'None at all,' Dion said with a smile. 'I'm ready.'

'A man of conviction,' Jax said. He returned Dion's smile with a broad grin, dimples merging with the long scar traveling down the side of his face. 'Come, Andion. It's time to make your mark.'

'Which deity?' Paolus inquired.

Dion scanned the walls, resting his gaze on the painted mural of Silex holding his trident. Chiseled marks surrounded the god's depiction, some of them legible as names, others little more than crosses.

'Silex,' he said. The sea god was by far the most popular.

'Would you like to make the mark yourself?' Paolus lifted a hammer and chisel.

'I would.'

Soon Dion stood back from the wall, regarding his name carved just beneath the painting, realizing he'd made his mark not far from Cob's name. Running his eyes over the hundreds of names he also saw the mark of Gideon and most prominent of all, Jax.

'Dion,' Jax said, reading what he'd inscribed. 'That's what the old man calls you, isn't it?' When Dion only smiled he clapped him on the back. 'Welcome to the Free Men.'

As he led Dion to the temple's door Jax stopped, looking into his eyes. The leader of the Free Men was suddenly sober.

'The code you've signed up to is important, something we all have to live by. We are far from simple raiders and thieves.' He paused to gather his thoughts. 'Most merchant vessels travel unprotected, and when they see our approach they find themselves faced with a choice: do they allow us to board or don't they? If they believe we are cruel and barbaric, that we will butcher them out of hand, they will flee at all costs, or fight even against overwhelming odds. But if they have heard of us, and know the trident on our silver flag, most times they will surrender, for they know that the Free Men will seize their cargo and free their slaves, but we will leave them with their ship and, more importantly, with their lives.'

Jax's voice was urgent; his eyes conveyed his passion. 'Do you understand? It is the rulers of Salesia and Galea who say we torture women and burn babes alive. They say this because our values give us power. At all times, we must live up to them.'

'I understand,' Dion said. 'The common people must always know that the Free Men stand for something. The worse the stories are about us, the more we have to be true to our ideals.'

Jax smiled and nodded. 'Good man.'

The pair exited the temple and Dion was surprised to see over a hundred men and women waiting outside. At the threshold, Jax raised Dion's hand, lifting his arm high. 'Our newest member!'

The crowd cheered, and suddenly Dion found himself having his hand shaken and back clapped so many times that he wondered if he'd have bruises in the morning. Cob stumped forward, pushing through a pair of sailors to give Dion a rough embrace. Music started as a youth with a pan pipe played a merry tune, and Jax started filling mugs of wine from a barrel, instantly the center of attention as he greeted each man or woman by name and handed out a brimming cup. The short curve of sandy beach became kicked into a mess by shifting feet. Finn danced a jig while the people around him clapped along. Raucous voices overwhelmed the sound of the small waves crashing on the shore.

Soon, when everyone had a mug in his or her hand, Jax came over to Dion, interrupting Cob, who was busy introducing people to Dion.

'Let him be, they'll all get to know him soon enough. Here,' he said, passing over a wooden cup. 'Drink.'

He and Dion clinked cups together and Dion tipped back his mug to taste warm red wine, tart and sweet.

'Quite a welcome,' Dion said.

'Any excuse for a festival.' Jax grinned. 'To be truthful, they've all been without wine for a while.' He toyed with his small moustache, scanning the crowd. 'Ah, here he is. Finish your mug.'

Gideon came forward and nodded to Jax and Dion. 'Andion, welcome to our number. We have some gifts for you. Come.'

Giving Cob a perplexed look, Dion fell into line behind Gideon as Jax followed. Climbing the hillside, they passed wooden houses with porches on stilts until they reached a locked shed.

Dion remembered Gideon's role of quartermaster as he put a key nearly as big as his hand to the large metal contraption fastened to the door. Frowning and wriggling, muttering under his breath, he finally managed to open the lock, and a moment later he entered the shed and then reappeared with Dion's bow and quiver.

'Take it. It's not a gift. It was always yours,' Jax said. 'Signing the articles gives you the right to carry arms.'

Relieved to have his bow again, Dion slung the quiver over his shoulder and checked the weapon over.

'And this is your share of the booty, as calculated by Finn.' Jax nodded at Gideon, who handed Dion a leather pouch that clinked.

'Booty?'

'Not long ago an intrepid traveler, a man bold enough to venture to Cinder Fen and collect a wealth of gemstones, was also foolish enough to try to sell them in a place where he had no friends.' Jax's eyes creased with mirth. 'That man fell in with a roguish company, a group of pirates, whose leader was generous enough to give him his share of the plunder, even though at the time of its appropriation he was not actually a member of the group.'

Dion hefted the pouch, shaking his head ruefully. As Gideon and Jax both watched to gauge his reaction, he had no choice but to laugh.

'You'll fit right in.' Jax grinned. He glanced down at the beach, where the raucous noise of the music and voices was now loud enough to reach up to the hillside. 'We have one last gift. Most of them will be sleeping on the sand tonight, but not you. This gift isn't ours to give, not really.' He gave Dion a look filled with mischief and then took him by the shoulders and turned him, so that he was looking further up the hillside. 'See that house on the left, near the big white rock?'

Dion squinted and then nodded.

'When you're ready to head in for the night, go there. Her name is Morgana. And because this is your first visit, you don't have to pay.'

35

Bright sunshine poured through the open window that faced onto the small harbor, bringing with it warmth, light, and above all, pain.

As Dion opened his eyes, he immediately closed them again, trying to prevent the searing light from penetrating through to the back of his skull. He groaned and put his hand to his head.

'Sorry, forgot to close the curtain,' a soft voice murmured.

A slim body shifted in the bed, and Dion realized that he was lying on his back and there was a woman pressed against him with her head in the crook of his arm. For a moment he thought he was dreaming, and a young, dark-haired princess of Phalesia was lying beside him. He was in the Royal Palace in Xanthos, his home, and Chloe was with him.

But then, in a series of strong images, the memories returned with sudden force.

He was at Fort Liberty. The previous night he'd drunk far, far too much wine. As the night's revelries came back to him he felt suddenly embarrassed at the things he and Morgana had done. He was almost surprised when he turned his head to look at her and the black-haired woman smiled.

'Good morning,' she said.

Morgana sat up and left the bed, and in an instant he forgot all about the pain in his head, immediately distracted by the sight of her body as she tugged the curtain closed. Despite the fact that she was probably ten years his senior, her olive skin was smooth, glowing in the early light as if she'd been polished. When she turned back to him, brushing curly locks away from her face, he couldn't take his eyes off her.

'We can go again, but I'll need a Phalesian silver eagle, or two Ilean drachmas.' She smiled to take the sting out of her words.

'Andion!' a rough voice called from outside. 'Get up!'

'Ah.' Her smile fell. 'It appears you have business to attend to.'

Dion sighed and swiftly dressed, drinking in the sight of her one last time before he left the small wooden shack that was her home. He found Reece waiting for him outside, pacing impatiently.

'There you are,' the stocky man muttered. 'Hope you enjoyed yourself, I doubt she could say the same. Come on, we've got work to do.'

Dion fell in beside Jax's second-in-command as they headed back down to the beach. 'Listen,' he said. 'We seem to have made a bad start—'

'You're lying,' Reece snapped. 'About who you are. You're no fisherman's son. You might be fooling Jax but you don't fool me, no matter what the old man says. One of your kind hung my pa for theft. My pa didn't steal nothing, but what's a farmer compared to a lord?'

'I'm sorry you lost your father.' Dion's lips thinned. 'But what makes you think I had something to do with it?'

'Bah.' Reece spat on the ground.

Arriving at the harbor, Dion saw that besides the churned-up sand someone had cleaned up and there was little sign of the previous night's festivities. Fishing boats sailed out to make a day's catch, looking like toy boats beside the larger vessels bobbing at anchor in the deeper water. Small figures manned the catapults at the two encircling promontories. Groups of sailors busied themselves around various tasks: mending nets, repairing sails, sparring with practice swords, and rolling a galley on its side to expose the bottom.

Reece led Dion to the area where the two biremes were beached. As they approached, Dion saw that forty or more sailors were working to launch the larger of the two vessels. They struggled with its weight and bulk, working in a disorganized series of grunts that barely enabled the vessel to slide a foot at a time.

'Too few men,' Dion said under his breath.

Jax stood at the side of the activity, exhorting his men to more effort. When he saw Reece and Dion he called out for the work to stop so his sailors could take a break.

'What do you think?' Jax said proudly, indicating the two immense warships. 'We captured them from Mercilles of Koulis, the richest trader on the Maltherean Sea. That one needs repairs.' He pointed to the vessel still high above the tide line. 'But this one is good to go. Provided'—he flashed his broad grin—'we figure out how to sail her.'

The three men paused for a moment to regard the two eighty-feet-long warships, both with long bronze rams, a pair of rowing decks, and rudders at the stern that were as tall as the *Calypso*'s mast.

'It'll take some learning, but once we're operational,' Jax said, 'our new fleet will make us the kings of the silver road.'

Dion frowned. 'Silver road?'

'The Maltherean Sea,' Jax answered with a smile. 'Where tides may rise and fall, but silver always flows.'

'Reece,' Jax said. 'Want to take over getting her into the water?'

Reece nodded, leaving Jax and Dion and summoning the sailors once more, barking orders as they climbed wearily back to their feet and took a place by the vessel's side.

'So, Andion,' Jax said as they watched. 'I've been wondering what position to give you. Cob tells me you're a strong sailor, and he's the best here, so that's high praise indeed.' He glanced sidelong at Dion. 'He also says you're a good leader. Still,'—he rubbed at his little moustache—'I'm not sure what to do with you. Despite what the old man says, I like to judge for myself.'

'Give me a bireme,' Dion said.

Jax barked a laugh, but then his smile faded. 'You're serious? You think you can handle an Ilean warship?' He snorted. 'Go on. Convince me.'

'I once worked under an Ilean captain and shipbuilder in Lamara. She showed me—'

'—did you just say *she*?'

'Her name was Roxana and she was one of the best captains in the sun king's navy. I sailed with her and fought wildren by her side. She let me help her in the shipyards and showed me how the biremes are constructed. I went below decks and learned what the master of oars needs to do. I—'

'Enough.' Jax held up a hand. He shook his head. 'So you really think you have what it takes to command one of these?'

Dion straightened and grinned, hoping he appeared more confident than he felt. 'I do.'

'I'll tell you what,' Jax said. He called out to his second-in-command. 'Reece! Stop what you're doing!' He then turned back to Dion. 'I have a challenge for you, and I don't plan on making it easy. Go and find a crew. If you can launch that ship and circle this island before sunset, I'll give you this bireme to captain.'

⌣

Dion knew he had a difficult task ahead of him. As he considered and made plans he decided that even if he only manned every second oar he would still need more than sixty men in his crew if he was going to be able to handle the heavy ship. It was already midmorning and he guessed that if he didn't set sail soon after noon he wouldn't have time to make it back to shore before sunset.

He needed allies.

It took some time, but he eventually found Cob asleep at the quieter end of the beach, lying on his back with both hands clasped over his bare chest as he snored with a sound like rolling thunder.

Dion shook his old friend's shoulders. 'Wake up, old man.'

Cob gave a sharp snort and then his eyes opened blearily. Seeing an empty wineskin on the sand nearby, Dion shook his head as Cob licked his lips and yawned. The old man scowled at Dion and then closed his eyes again. 'Another time, lad.'

'Get up. I need your help.'

Running a hand over his bald scalp and then over his face, Cob eventually sat up, glaring at Dion. 'With what?'

Dion explained Jax's proposition. Initially skeptical, Cob caught Dion's excitement and climbed to his feet. 'A crew? How many?'

'We'll need at least sixty, one for every second oar.'

'Plus a helmsman—'

'—you,' Dion said with a grin.

'—as well as a master of oars, a sailmaster, and sailors to control the rigging.' Cob nodded. 'I'm up to the task if you are. Where to next?'

'Finn,' Dion said.

Trudging back along the beach, they passed the sailors repairing the galley, who were now painting over a crack in the hull with black pitch. Dion and Cob scanned the area but couldn't see Finn anywhere. Cob said he knew where to look next, and they climbed the trail that led up the hillside, finding Finn sitting on the porch of one of the houses, puffing on a pipe and blowing perfect smoke rings.

'Sounds fun,' Finn said in response to Dion's request. 'But I'm no sailor.'

A gruff voice called from within the house. 'Who's that, love?'

'Duty calls,' Finn said with a grin, setting down his pipe and ducking into the interior, giving the pair a final wave.

Exchanging glances, Dion and Cob walked a little away from the house. 'Where next?' Cob asked.

'This way,' Dion said. 'Follow me.'

Climbing the sloping path between houses, Dion arrived at the wooden shed where the pirates kept their stores. The door was open and rummaging sounds came from within. Peering inside, Dion saw Gideon standing next to an open barrel as he trickled grain through the fingers of his big hand.

'Weevils,' he said in his baritone, shaking his head as if the weight of the world was on his shoulders.

'Gideon,' Dion said. 'I have a proposition for you.' He repeated Jax's offer and was surprised to see Gideon's eyes light up.

'I want to be master of oars,' the ebony-skinned quartermaster said. 'I know how to do it without killing the men.'

He locked the shed behind him and Dion led his first two recruits back down to the beach. He set a direct path for the temple, climbing the steps and pulling open the rickety wooden door. 'Wait here,' he instructed his companions as he entered alone.

The priest, Paolus, looked over guiltily. He was sitting on a solitary stool, where he'd been staring up at the depiction of Silex as if seeking answers to deep questions. He had a cup in his hand and a wineskin sat on the floor by his feet.

'It's early,' the red-nosed priest grumbled. 'Services aren't 'til sunset.'

'It's midmorning. Sunset will be too late,' Dion said.

'What do you want?'

'I want you to give a sermon.'

The priest frowned. 'What sermon?'

Dion told the priest what he wanted him to say. Paolus's round face screwed up as he considered. 'If I agree, what will you give me?'

Dion glanced down at the wine skin on the floor. 'How's the wine?'

Paolus sighed. 'This rabble doesn't know the good from the bad. It's all the same to them, but if I see one more lout drinking good Sarsican red straight from the skin I'll . . .' His voice faded away as he tried to think of a threat he could actually deliver on.

'I know the marks of the best Sarsican wine sellers,' Dion said. His father and brother were both heavy drinkers. 'I'll tell you what. Any wine that crosses my path, I'll set aside the finest for you.'

Paolus lifted his head. 'You'd do that?'

'If it's within my power, I give you my word.'

'All right,' the priest said. 'I'll be here. Just let me know when you're ready.'

Pleased, Dion left the temple and gave Cob and Gideon some further instructions, pointing at the workmen painting the ship's hull with pitch. He then set off alone to accomplish the next part of his plan.

Glancing up at the sun as he once more ascended the hillside path, he felt the time passing far too swiftly for his liking. Climbing with long strides, he passed the house where he'd last seen Finn – apparently still inside – and then left behind the storage shed where he'd found Gideon. Panting and wheezing, he reached the house he'd woken up in, located high on the hill. When he couldn't see Morgana he rapped quietly on the doorframe, fearful of disturbing her if she was busy.

But the curly-haired, olive-skinned woman came to the door and smiled, fluttering her lashes theatrically. 'Returned with the silver, Andion?' She parted her yellow chiton to reveal a tantalizing glimpse of thigh. 'Your business is finished?'

'I wish it were,' Dion said, smiling. 'I came to ask for your help.'

He explained what he wanted her to do. It wasn't a difficult task, and she was obviously perplexed, but she agreed easily enough.

Then Dion returned once more to the temple and asked the priest to summon the Free Men.

36

It was after midday as word spread throughout the settlement that the priest was going to give an important discourse, a tale of Silex and the sea. Despite their status as vagabonds and thieves, most of the inhabitants of Fort Liberty were devout and prayed regularly to the god of fortune and the sea to bless their voyages with safety and prosperity. If there was one thing that would draw them in numbers, this was it.

Reece protested that there was work to be done but Jax sensed a plan in motion and freed the pirates from their duties. Soon well over a hundred men and at least a dozen women stood in front of the stone-walled temple. The brown-robed, red-nosed priest stood grandly on the threshold as he waited for them to assemble on the sand in front of him.

Cob stood beside Gideon; the two men had completed the task Dion had set them but they were as perplexed as Jax himself, who stood a little apart from the crowd, an expression of open curiosity on his face. Reece didn't attend, scowling at the people rushing to see what novel event was about to transpire as he decided he had things to do elsewhere. Finn called out for the group of stirring and murmuring sailors to be quiet when the priest raised his arms. Dion was conspicuously absent.

'Momentous times are upon us,' the priest called, sweeping his gaze across the crowd, his arms spread wide to encompass them all. 'Our fleet grows in size, and our proud home, Fort Liberty, grows in size. Our elected king'—he rested his eyes on Jax—'grows in strength and wisdom. New members join our group, adding skills and knowledge to that which we already possess.'

He lowered his arms and clenched his hands into fists.

'Today I will tell you the tale of the hero Zarkos, who vowed to sail to the edge of the world in order to prove himself to Silex the god of fortune and the sea, whom we here in Fort Liberty hold close to our hearts. Zarkos bade farewell to his beautiful wife and his five sons and five daughters, casting his eyes one last time over his palace on the slope of the black mountain as he embarked with his valiant crew to fulfill his quest. The mountain vanished behind him as he sailed west . . .'

The crowd watched rapt as Paolus told the tale of the five challenges Zarkos faced on his voyage. He described the lure of the lustful mermaids on the island of Parnos, making the onlookers shake their heads, for many among them had seen mermaids with their own eyes, and the fragile beauty of the wildren could make a captivated sailor want to leap into the sea, even if he couldn't swim.

Paolus spoke of Zarkos's capture by the twin giants Strom and Grom, and the hero's cunning when he tricked the pair into fighting over which of them would get to eat his heart. Only Zarkos's skill and experience at the helm of his renowned ship enabled him to survive the Chasm that led to the Aleuthean Sea. As he approached the edge of the world Zarkos then had to face the mighty dragon Haroth, losing half his crew to the savage monster before he was able to pierce its heart with his very last javelin.

Finally, in waters so clear that the ship's dauntless crew could see all the way to the bottom, they saw that rather than sand, the ocean floor was made of gold dust, impossibly deep, but displaying a wealth of riches tantalizingly in view. Zarkos now knew that the edge of the world was near, and it was proven true to him when he saw that the ocean simply plummeted away in a vertical precipice, as if he were sailing at the top of a waterfall so wide that he couldn't see the sides.

At the last, the crew tried to convince Zarkos to turn back, but he was undeterred, determined to prove himself to Silex, holding himself to his vow. He faced them down even as the precipice at the end of the world neared.

Suddenly, the sea fell away from beneath the ship's hull.

The ship plummeted down, down, tumbling through the void, until the hero thought he was going to fall forever. The men of the crew screamed but eventually their voices ran hoarse, and then they could scream no more.

Paolus smacked his hands together, causing the onlookers to jump. 'And then with a mighty crash, the ship struck water. The blow would have crushed the hull of any other vessel, but this was a vessel like no other.' He lowered his voice as he said the ship's name for the first time. 'This was the *Dauntless*.'

He spread his hands. 'But to Zarkos's surprise, when he sailed on this new sea, past the edge of the world, he saw something strange. He saw an island, and a black mountain, and a palace. He saw his beautiful wife and ten children standing on the shore, smiling and waving, calling him home.'

Paolus slowed, speaking more like a priest than a storyteller as he reached the tale's conclusion.

'The moral is that the gods honor our accomplishments, but they also praise duty to our loved ones, to each other. No matter how far we go, at the end of every journey is a return.' He opened his arms in the same manner he had begun the story and smiled. 'And there isn't a man here who wouldn't travel to the edge of the world with Zarkos, even if it meant arriving back at the same place again.'

The crowd assembled in front of the temple roared, raising their hands and shouting their approbation. Jax smiled, clapping and cheering with them, but his face was still curious.

Timing her arrival perfectly, at that moment Morgana ran up, calling to the crowd. Breathless and beautiful, wearing a sheer yellow chiton that barely concealed her figure, every eye was on her in an instant.

'Quick,' she panted. 'Come. Down at the shore.'

With the day growing more exciting with every passing moment, the crowd – now swelled even larger – followed the dark-haired woman to the edge of the cove where the bireme lay beached on the sand, just where Reece had left it. Morgana pointed, and with growing wonder people thronged around the ship.

Dion stood with legs apart as he waited alongside the vessel.

Dion saw Cob grinning and shaking his head, while even Gideon looked impressed. Jax threw his head back as he laughed out loud.

The warship had changed. Where, raised up on the shore, the long bowsprit jutted out, curving back into itself before spiking out in the bronze ram, the two glaring eyes on either side were now narrowed and angry, an effect given by the black paint Dion had asked Gideon and Cob to apply. Rather than the almond, long-lashed eyes of a woman, these were now the sharp eyes of a predator. The vessel's name had been scrubbed out and a new name, also in black paint, now announced itself to the onlookers.

Dauntless.

'My name is Andion,' Dion called out. 'And I am looking for a crew. Jax, our elected king, has given me a challenge.' He lifted his chin and swept his gaze over the crowd. 'A challenge that I dare you to accept. Any man – or woman – who helps me sail the *Dauntless* around this island and return before sunset will get his name carved on the bench that he rows today.'

Dion paused to let his words sink in.

'Now!' He pointed at the proud warship, stranded on the sand, out of its natural element. 'Who can I count on?'

Even Dion was surprised by the response. They began to clamor around the vessel, each desperate to find a bench to claim as his or her own. At this point Cob and Gideon took charge, making them line up on both sides of the ship.

'You can't climb on until she's in the water!' Cob growled from the starboard side. 'Line up!'

Gideon strode along the other side, nudging crewmen into place. 'I'm your new master of oars,' he bellowed. 'You'll move when I say!'

Standing back, Dion was amazed to see that almost every oar would find hands to row it. He smiled his thanks at Morgana, who appeared to have enjoyed her role, and farther away he saw the priest holding up a wine cup and mouthing something as he tapped the side. As always, Jax looked on, watching and considering.

'Helmsman!' Dion called. 'Ready to get this ship moving?'

'Aye, captain!'

'Master of oars?'

'Aye!'

Dion nodded, feeling a thrill course through him. 'On my mark,' he called. 'We need to pull together, in one motion, then pause for a single breath and go again. Once we start'—he opened his lungs to bellow—'we don't stop!'

'Aye!' the crew roared back.

'Ready? Heave!' They pulled together and the warship slid two feet. 'Heave!' Dion glanced up at the sun as he continued to call out. 'Heave!' It was at least a couple of hours after midday. The ship inched down the slope of the beach with every bellow. 'Again! Heave!'

Finally, with every crew member red-faced and panting, the ship's stern entered the sea, adding buoyancy, relieving them of some of its mass. The *Dauntless* slid swiftly now; soon half of the warship was in the shallows, with the men farthest out up to their waists in water.

Dion gave new orders.

'Oarsmen: everyone in! Through the sides! Pick a bench and get your oars out!' He then waved at his officers. 'Cob, Gideon. After me!'

Dion ran to the rope hanging from the top deck, climbing it hand over hand, feet finding purchase in the vessel's open sides. He grinned as he made it to the top, knowing he'd need to employ the gangway next time or he'd never hear the end of it from Cob.

Now half in the water, the bireme began to roll and sway with the motion of the waves. The situation was completely disorderly but Dion had confidence that his crew would become experienced with time. As first Gideon and then a wheezing Cob climbed up to the top deck Dion waved at them to join him by the sail.

'Master of oars,' Dion said, nodding at the hatch in the center of the deck. 'Head below and get the men into order. Find someone to sound the drum and have the oarsmen back away. Cob, turn us around as soon as we're in open water.'

The lumbering warship left the shore entirely as the rowers pulled. Slowly it turned, and soon it was facing the open sea. A pounding rhythm filled the vessel as the drum gave them unity. Wincing, Dion ran to the hatch. 'A little slower, master of oars. Half that speed.'

'Aye, captain,' Gideon called up.

Then Dion busied himself raising the sail, hauling the horizontal crosspiece until it climbed the mast and the white material snapped in the wind.

As the sun fell slowly behind the horizon and purple shades filled the sky, a weary crew and triumphant captain brought the *Dauntless* back into shore. This time when they approached the shore they worked in unity, and when they poured out of the sides to beach the vessel each man knew his place. Under Dion's command they had the warship above the tide line in half the time it had taken them to launch it, despite the fact they were now heaving it against the sandy slope.

Dion formed his crew up in front of the ship and walked up and down the line. He finally stopped in the center and raised his clenched fist to a resounding cheer. He made sure they heard him when he asked Gideon to have every man's name written in his place. Thanking them for their efforts, he crossed the beach to where Jax stood watching and waiting with Reece by his side.

Jax grinned. 'I have to say I didn't think you'd do it. All right, Andion. You can have the ship. But I'll be watching.' He turned to his second-in-command. 'Reece, transfer my possessions from the *Gull* to the *Dauntless*.' He nodded at the bireme as Reece's scowl deepened. 'I'm interested to see how she sails with someone who knows what he's doing.'

37

Chloe stood naked in the villa's bathing chamber and upended a bucket of heated water over her head to remove the oil she'd lathered into foam. Feeling clean and fresh, she heard a gurgle as the water drained away through the hole in the corner of the sloping stone floor. She wondered, not for the first time, who had built this villa, out in tribal lands, far from any city. There were enough bedchambers for dozens of people to live together and even the baths were opulent, with an entire room devoted to heating water over braziers filled with coals.

Three days after their rescue, she and Liana were finally rested and recovered. Vikram often disappeared during the daytime and the villa was comfortable. There was plenty of food, brought back from the village of Pao when the magus returned in the evenings. She hadn't yet learned anything about Vikram's story, but now, given they would depart in the morning, she decided to ask him tonight.

Pulling the curtain to the side and exiting the bathing chamber, she reached for the woolen towel and wrapped it around herself before leaving the room behind. Entering the adjoining chamber where she'd left her chiton to air on a rack next to one of the braziers, for a moment she stood and frowned.

Her clothing was gone.

She'd left her chiton and necklace draped on the wooden rack. She remembered undressing and setting the items down before bathing, but the rack was bare.

Scanning the room, her eye caught a stand against the wall. She remembered it being empty, but there was now a bundle on the stand's upper shelf. A moment later Chloe held up a thick woman's chiton in a strange style, with a trim of doubled blue stripes and draping folds along the hem like the shell of an oyster. It didn't appear to be silk but it shone with the same shimmer in the light.

Perplexed, Chloe donned the new chiton and left the room.

She went immediately to the villa's main chamber to find Vikram sitting on a high-backed chair near the hearth. Despite the fact that it wasn't yet dark he was staring into a blazing fire. He glanced up as she approached. With his pug nose, scraggly hair, and deep-set eyes, the garish light of the flames made his round face appear sinister.

'Chloe.' He gave her a warm smile. 'You look beautiful.' Seeing her expression, he nodded at the hearth. 'Your clothing is ruined,' he said. 'I've already given it to the fire. I've explained this to your maid. Your necklaces I am forced to trade with the villagers for food.' His expression softened. 'You both eat as much as growing boys. You understand, don't you?'

Chloe opened her mouth but he continued without waiting for her reply.

'In case you're wondering, your maid is gathering wood in the forest. She will be back soon enough. Please, sit.'

When she remained standing he sighed and met her eyes. 'I would have thought you'd be interested to hear what I have to say. You worship the goddess of music. Did you know there is magic in music? Please, Chloe. Sit.'

Chloe suddenly felt foolish. Despite the manner in which he'd done it, she couldn't expect to exhaust his stocks of food, and her chiton had been tattered to say the least. Nonetheless, her necklace was important to her, and the thought that he'd taken it from her without even asking rankled.

'Good,' he said when she took a seat opposite. 'Did I tell you my beloved wife was a skilled magus? I've seen you looking at my staff. Would you like to know what I did to those men who were chasing you?'

She bit her lip, intrigued despite herself.

'Magic,' Vikram continued, nodding at his ever-present staff with its hand-sized metal fork at the top, leaning up against the stone wall near the hearth. 'Copper magic. The magic of harmony. The magic of sound.'

Chloe stared at the device on top of the staff. She knew she wouldn't be leaving until the morning, and wondered if he would let her see it up close. 'In all my time at the temple, I haven't heard of copper magic.'

'Ah, but you have no doubt witnessed its effects time and again. Do you play an instrument?'

'The flute.'

'And have you ever captivated someone with your spell? Have you ever felt that rather than play the music directly, some greater power was being channeled through you, that you were playing without conscious thought?'

Chloe cast her mind back to when she'd played for Dion, when he'd visited her father's villa after the great earthquake, and the look of awe on his face. She remembered playing for Solon when he'd tested her.

'I think so. Yes.'

'And tell me – for I'm sure your instrument was made of copper – have you ever experienced the same effect playing a wooden flute?

Have you ever been captivated by the pounding of a drum?' Vikram asked earnestly.

Chloe shook her head. 'I don't . . . I don't think so.' She frowned and looked up at him. 'What of Edra, goddess of fertility? Her followers also wear copper.'

'They do, don't they?' Vikram grinned. 'They wear copper earrings and bands around their wrists. Have you ever seen a love priestess without her jewelry? I'm sure you've seen for yourself what effect those women have on men. Many of them play instruments too, isn't that right?'

Chloe's brow knitted. She'd never thought of magic as something that was everywhere, even in daily life.

'Copper, when worn close to the skin, and especially when directed into music, provides the power to captivate,' he said. 'It is the materia of art and beauty, and, more apt than any other word, harmony. Healing is restoring harmony, is it not? Music – surely there is harmony in music. Pleasing aesthetics are visual harmony.'

She glanced at the staff. 'But that isn't what you did to the tribesmen.'

Vikram chuckled. 'No, it is not. Each of the four materia – gold, silver, copper, and iron – can be used in battle. The eldren have their magic and we have ours. How else do you think the Aleutheans came to dominate the world? If you were to stay here longer, I could teach you.'

He met her eyes directly. But Chloe immediately thought about her father and shook her head. 'Under different circumstances, perhaps. But Liana and I . . . We have to leave.'

Vikram shrugged. 'Then there isn't much purpose in telling you more.'

Chloe hesitated. 'You said your wife was skilled. Did she also use copper?'

'She used gold.' He smiled at her eagerness. 'Gold is the materia of charisma and leadership. The display of gold makes other men feel awe and worship and the desire to follow. But it comes with a price, for more than any other metal gold inspires feelings of greed, of powerful lust for the precious ore.'

Chloe thought of the sun king and his golden pyramid.

'Watch,' Vikram said.

He rose from his seat and went to a shelf at the far end of the room. Returning a moment later, he showed her a hoop of solid gold, a bracelet, the circumference of a woman's wrist. Small symbols were etched around the circumference, strange shapes that reminded Chloe of the Ark of Revelation's exterior.

'This was my wife's.' Vikram sat down again, groaning as he maneuvered his bulk, and laid the bracelet on his open palm. He closed his eyes and his breathing slowed. A look of intense concentration appeared on his face. He made a sudden sharp sound, like a woodcutter striking a tree with a powerful blow.

The magus opened his eyes and drew in a long, slow breath.

The circle of gold began to glow.

Chloe watched with amazement as the gold grew brighter, shining with inner fire until it was casting dazzling light on Vikram's round face.

Vikram's brow furrowed despite her reaction. 'This is the extent of my ability with gold. Not my materia of expertise, I'm afraid. Nonetheless, it will continue to glow for as long as it touches my skin. A skilled magus can employ the power from a distance.' His voice lowered. 'A truly powerful sorcerer can make the light so bright it can blind.'

He handed the bracelet to Chloe, and as soon as the gold left his hand the glow faded. Examining the circle, Chloe couldn't believe that it was just metal.

'Gold is the only materia that does not tarnish, which makes it exceptionally valuable to a magus. When we draw on an object's power, the metal begins to corrode, and the more powerful the spell, the more it corrodes. Only gold can be used time and time again.' He glanced at the copper fork on top of his staff. 'I will need to sand and polish my resonator. As it wastes away, eventually it will no longer function.'

'Resonator?'

'The fork on top of the pole. The weapon itself is called a resonance staff.'

Chloe looked at the green tarnish on the copper tines and then back at Vikram. 'And silver?' she pressed. 'What can silver do?'

'Silver is the materia of the winds of fortune. Contact with the skin makes the gods smile on a man, luck shines on him more than most.'

'And in battle?'

Vikram snorted. 'I can see where your interest lies. Some magi focus on one materia only, but I am skilled with silver, nearly as strong as I am with copper. With talent and training, strong winds can be summoned, although the more powerful they are, the more difficult they can be to control.'

Chloe swallowed, thinking about what it would be like to be able to control the wind, or to defeat enemies by projecting piercing, ear-shattering sound. 'And iron?'

'The final of the four materia, and some would say the most dangerous. Touching iron makes a man feel brave . . . powerful and indomitable. But he also feels hatred and the desire to act with violence against others, which can have terrible consequences, as you may have learned for yourself.'

There was only one god whose worshippers wore iron, Chloe reflected. He was a god worshipped above all in Xanthos, where he had a lofty temple with a statue of a hoplite outside.

Balal, the god of war.

'When a warrior thrusts his spear in battle, he feels powerful, and the iron grows hot in his hand. Steel is no different – unlike bronze, which is heavily alloyed with tin, iron is only slightly tempered to make steel. When a sorcerer lifts his staff, he can project balls of fire.'

Chloe's mouth dropped open. 'But . . . surely all that power must come with a price.'

Vikram nodded. 'You have a quick mind. The magic is difficult to control, and the price for failure can be dear. Gold can blind enemies, but if the magus cannot control his power, it is he who becomes blind. The sound I project with my staff can stun a dozen strong warriors, but if I lose focus it is I who will go deaf, or bleed from the ears until I die. Iron's price is simpler. Rather than projecting from the iron in a ball of fire, the heat can transfer from the staff to the sorcerer, and it is he who bursts into flame.'

'And silver?' She noticed that he'd left it for last.

'Silver requires the most clarity of thought. One must empty one's mind of all distraction, creating a void within. If the magus fails . . .' Vikram's round face became sad. 'He becomes insane.' He faltered and then met Chloe's eyes. 'A user of silver must fear for his mind.'

Chloe let out a breath. But there was one final question she needed an answer to. 'How do you know the things you know?'

'I know because long ago, an ancestor of mine fled the fall of Aleuthea,' Vikram said. 'A group of survivors made it to these lands and built this villa. The chiton you wear is hundreds of years old. I don't know what material it is made of but the ancient Aleutheans were advanced, even beyond peoples today.' He leaned forward. 'I learned my skills from my father, but when I die, there will be no one left to carry the knowledge. Please, Chloe, will you stay? You've seen that I have no children. I have no one.'

'I need to leave . . . But one day I could come back . . .'

He shook his head. 'You would never return.' He cleared his throat and wiped his eyes. Taking a deep breath, he gave her a small smile. 'At least let me test you.' He chuckled at her reaction. 'There is no danger in it. My wife was talented. I suspect you might be even greater than she was. Surely you want to know if you are at least capable of magic?'

38

Looking at the old magus, Chloe thought about how alone he was. He was obviously enjoying showing her his skill. It was all he had left.

'Here. Put out your hand. Open it so that the palm is flat.'

She hesitantly followed his instructions. Vikram again took the bracelet but this time he placed the circle of gold in her open palm. He then laid his own palm over hers, so that their hands completely enclosed the metal.

'Now,' he said. 'Follow my words and don't falter. You will experience many new sensations. No matter what happens, once you start, you cannot stop. Are you ready?'

She nodded, suddenly afraid.

'Close your eyes and picture the sun.' She closed her eyes as he continued. 'Imagine the brightest sun you can possibly comprehend. Think of how small you are in comparison. You are floating in a void, with nothing but you and the sun in the entire universe.'

His low voice guided her as she imagined herself in complete darkness, with nothing but a distant golden orb to break up the sense of utter emptiness. Her breathing slowed as she drew on her training at the temple to bring on a calm, meditative state.

'The sun comes closer; you are being drawn to it. It fills your vision. Remind yourself of how powerful and noble the sun is, and how the light can banish all darkness before it. Let the sun in your mind become so bright that you almost cannot bear to look upon it.'

He paused for a time.

'Now change the sun into the bud of a flower. Keep it just as bright, but picture yourself growing. The bud stays as strong and as powerful as the sun, but it is you who are now even larger. Reach out with a mighty hand until you are holding the bud in the palm of your hand.'

Chloe was extremely conscious of the contact between the gold bracelet and her skin, despite not being able to see it. She was sure that the bracelet was becoming warm, even hot.

'Keep the image of a golden flower bud in your mind. Continue holding it in your mind's powerful hand. Tell yourself that the bud in your mind is one and the same with the item you are holding.'

She almost cried out in surprise. Something was happening inside her as he spoke. The feeling was warm and pleasant, a communion with some force that was greater than herself.

'Now, with your eyes still closed, remember this room as you last saw it. The sun is setting, but its light reaches us even in here. It is reflected from the walls, the floor and the ceiling. Turn your attention to the fire and the glow from the hearth. Imagine your flower slowly opening, gathering whatever light is around, from all sources. Imagine it being soaked up into your golden bud. Then when you feel ready, let the flower's petals completely unfold.'

The strange force she was touching was now probing at her mind, seeking entrance. She felt a query. It was asking her permission to enter.

It told her that her answer was important.

She assented, letting it come in. The power filled her from head to toe as she imagined the flower in her mind completely opening.

'Draw your power from within. Bring it to the surface. Focus every sense on your palm. Let it burst like a flame.' Chloe felt like she must be glowing herself. The sensation was more than pleasant. She felt glorious.

'Now open your eyes. Look at your hand.'

Chloe opened her eyes, looking down as Vikram took his palm off hers, and her eyes widened. Even though she was the only one touching it, the bracelet was glowing as fiercely as it had before, filling the room with something close to daylight. After a few moments it faded and Chloe felt suddenly weary, as if she'd been woken from a deep sleep. Flickers of golden light sparked at the edges of her vision.

Vikram grinned.

'You have a natural affinity for the materia,' he said. 'And I could feel the intensity of your concentration.' His expression was serious. 'You have it within you to become a powerful magus.'

Chloe handed him the bracelet as she shook her head. She still felt dazzled. 'I need to find Liana.' She realized that he was staring into her face intently. 'What is it?'

'How do you feel?'

'I feel fine. A little tired, but—'

Fire suddenly raged in her bones, shivering through her body until her face felt searing hot. The flickering light in her vision became stronger until she could barely see through a golden haze. Molten lava was building up inside her head, fiery magma that needed an outlet. Her mind was a volcano about to burst.

She screamed in pain as she tumbled off her stool and fell onto the floor. Gasping for breath, she tried to find an outlet for the burning power but couldn't.

The tiny part of her that could still think realized that Vikram was leaning over her. 'Chloe,' he said. 'You are a clever woman. You know that power always comes with a price, and the power of magic most of all. Otherwise everyone would be a sorcerer, rather than a warrior or weaver, fisherman or farmer.'

'What have you done to me?' Chloe whispered, fighting the terrible pain.

'I merely guided you. It is you who awakened the power within you. These first sensations will soon pass, but you now have the fire inside you. And with your strength, if you do not learn to control it'—he sounded strangely pleased with himself—'you will die.'

———

Chloe found Liana just inside the nearby forest.

Liana sat with her legs crossed. Her head was tilted back and she was staring up into the sky, at the patches of blue between the broad boughs of a huge oak. She was watching birds flitting from branch to branch.

She turned when she heard Chloe call her name and climbed to her feet.

'I see he took your clothes too,' Liana said, shaking her head as Chloe approached. 'I was trying to change my shape. If I could, I might be able to fly us—' Liana's voice changed to concern when she saw Chloe's expression. 'What's wrong?'

'Something's happened to me.' Chloe was dazed. She was struggling to find her voice. 'I can feel it now. Like fire inside my mind. If I don't let it free . . .'

She explained what had happened with Vikram. She'd willingly allowed him to bring out some change inside her. Even now she could feel the inner fire, threatening to burst if she couldn't tame it.

As she spoke, Liana's expression steadily shifted.

The eldran's eyes darkened and her brow furrowed. She finally set her jaw and lifted her chin. 'I'm going to go and talk to him. Right now.'

'No.' Chloe grabbed her friend. 'You can't.'

'Why not?' Liana scowled. 'He's insane. You realize that, don't you?'

'He says that if I can't learn how to control it, it will kill me.' She met Liana's eyes. 'If I don't let him teach me I will die.'

'And you believe him?' Liana's eyes widened a moment later. 'You do,' she breathed.

'I don't know. Perhaps it's all a lie?' Chloe's voice was hopeful, but even as she spoke, she knew that the change inside her was real.

Liana glared in the direction of the villa. 'Let me talk to him.'

'Listen to me. He said that he wants us both to stay.' Chloe drew in a deep breath. 'But you should go, while you can. He uses metal in his magic. If you don't get away from here he'll discover what you really are.'

'I'm not going.' Liana shook her head. 'I can't leave you here alone with him.'

'You have to. At least you'll be away from here. And if I can learn to control whatever this thing is, I can make my own escape before he realizes.'

Liana clenched and unclenched her fists. She was silent for a long time. 'I think we need help,' she finally said.

Chloe was holding Liana's arm, but she now released her. 'We do. You said you had your own reasons for finding my father—'

'But what if I can't find him? How do I know you'll be safe here?'

'I'll be fine.' Chloe forced a smile. 'Of course I will. He's strange, but in the end he's just been alone for too long.'

Chloe realized she was soon going to be alone, as she saw Liana come to the only decision she could.

'I'll leave as soon as I can,' Liana said. 'If I can make myself change, I can be back before you know.' She took Chloe's hand and gave her a look of fierce determination. 'You stayed with me when I had nowhere else to go. Even when I slowed you down you still didn't leave me behind. No matter what, I'll come back for you.'

Liana met her eyes.

'I promise.'

⌣

That night, Chloe couldn't sleep. She tossed and turned, her mind full of magic and metal; she couldn't stop wondering if she was doing the right thing.

Feeling the need for air, she rolled out of bed and quickly dressed, before walking out of her chamber and following the hallway until she came to the villa's main reception. The embers in the hearth had died down, leaving the room filled with a soft, red glow.

She came to a sudden halt.

Vikram stood in the middle of the room, his back to her. He wore a thin nightshirt over his bulk and was shaking his head from side to side. He was shuddering and mumbling, though his voice was too faint for Chloe to hear him.

'Vikram?' Chloe asked uncertainly.

His muttering rose and fell, so she could almost make out the words, but he didn't seem to hear her, and he didn't turn around.

Slowly Chloe approached, repeating his name as she drew near. Although she couldn't see his face she could now hear what he was mumbling; he was saying the same words over and over, shivering and shifting his head left and right.

'The wind . . .' Vikram was saying. 'The wind.'

Suddenly the old magus lifted his arms. He began to hit the sides of his head with both hands, as if trying to drive a demon out of his skull. He began striking himself so hard that Chloe winced, and racing forward she grabbed his arms from behind, dragging them down.

She turned him to face her.

His eyes were wide open and entirely black, with no whites at all, sending a shiver of fear along Chloe's spine. But she held fast, anxious to prevent him from hurting himself.

'Vikram. Vikram!'

Chloe shook him, trying to jolt him out of whatever strange state he was in. His mumbling slowed and then he stopped speaking completely. He blinked and his eyes cleared; in an instant they were the same as they'd always been.

His shoulders slumped and his breathing slowed. His eyes closed and as his chest rose and fell, making his nose rasp every time he breathed in and whistle with every exhalation, she realized that, although he was standing, he was now fast asleep.

Chloe led an unresisting Vikram to his bedchamber, helping him back into bed. She waited for a time and watched him sleep, before returning to her own bed.

As she once more stared at the ceiling, she thought about the fact that he was a skilled magus, and even he was struggling to control his power.

She had to follow his instructions, and do whatever he asked of her.

She had to learn before it killed her.

39

Dion called out, issuing an order to Cob at the helm, bringing the *Dauntless* alongside the *Gull*. Cob kept a careful distance between the bireme and the smaller war galley, mindful of the oars as Dion dashed across the deck and bellowed into the hatchway, passing an order to Gideon. The oars came in, enabling the gap between the two ships to narrow so that Jax could call out to his second-in-command.

Reece leaned over the *Gull*'s gunwale while Jax and Dion bent over the *Dauntless*'s rail, close enough that Dion could see Reece's dark eyes and the thinning hair blowing around his crown.

'We're gaining on them,' Jax cried over the wind. 'But we need to make better time in case they get support from the mainland. How are your men?'

'Tired, but by Silex, they can handle it,' Reece called back.

'Think we can circle round and cut them off?' Dion asked Jax. 'They're heading directly for Koulis. There's a growing risk they'll find support.'

Jax scratched his small moustache. 'It'll mean sailing against the wind.' He put his hands on both sides of his mouth to call out again to the *Gull*. 'Dion thinks we can cut 'em off! You'll need to work hard to get ahead though. Up to it?'

'Course we are!'

'We'll get out in front, take the southern reach, give you the better tack. Pass the word to the other captains. Tell 'em to keep their course.'

'Aye aye!'

'Over to you, captain,' Jax said to Dion. He spoke calmly, but his eyes were sparkling.

Dion ordered the drum tempo to double and gave Cob the new instructions. With more than twice as many oarsmen, the *Dauntless* swiftly left Reece's ship behind.

The rolling waves struck the hull with force, sending spray scattering on both sides of the bow. Ahead, the three merchant vessels they were pursuing became more than distant specks, but Dion's ship was angled to the south, and it would appear to them that he was leaving them behind, heading somewhere else altogether. The wind now came from directly ahead and he ordered two men nearby to drop the fluttering sail; a heartbeat later the crossbeam clattered to the deck.

'They're newly built,' Dion pointed out to Jax. 'Sleek and fast.'

'As fast as we are?' Jax grinned.

'No.' Dion mirrored his companion's grin.

The *Dauntless* was now at the closest approach it would make before it began to draw away from the trio of merchant ships. Each cargo vessel was fifty feet long, with rakish masts at the bow and center giving them a triangular headsail and mainsail. Long flags with red diamonds in the center of a white field snapped in the breeze.

Jax whistled. 'Mercilles of Koulis. Easy pickings yet again. The sun king's death was the best thing to happen to the Free Men. Few Ilean ships in the Maltherean these days.'

'Look,' Dion pointed, shielding his eyes. A distant landmass rose from the horizon. 'Land.'

'Wherever they were going, they're now making all speed for Koulis.' Jax nodded. The *Dauntless* soon left the merchant ships behind. 'Time to cut 'em off?'

'A little longer,' Dion said, shaking his head. 'We need to give Reece time to make it to the other side. At the speed he'll be able to make, even with the better approach, he won't be ready quite yet.'

Both men were silent as the Salesian continent grew larger in view. It was a mostly flat land of desert and barren earth, which meant that it was closer than it appeared. Soon they could make out low hills surrounding the wide curve of a harbor, and then buildings.

'Soon?' Jax gave Dion a worried look.

Dion paced the deck, feeling the moments trickle past, knowing that when the merchant ships saw them coming they would wheel away and he needed Reece to be there to greet them. But he also knew that they needed to avoid any naval patrols protecting the city's waters. Whatever was happening in the lands Solon had united into an empire, he couldn't count on Koulis neglecting its seas altogether.

Finally a sensation deep in Dion's gut told him it was time.

'Cob, turn us about!' Dion cried. He ran to the hatch and saw Gideon's dark face looking up at him. 'Slow the tempo, half speed!' The crew was still too fresh for Dion to attempt the sharp turns Roxana could execute, particularly with the wind coming dead on. 'Port side, back away. Starboard side forward.'

'Aye, captain,' Gideon called up.

The warship lurched as it wheeled and the deck tilted at a sharp angle. Jax looked at Dion with alarm but Dion knew his vessel, and he knew it could handle far greater pressures.

'Sail up! All the way!' Dion ordered.

The turn complete, the bireme now took a new heading: a direct path for the merchant ships recently left behind.

'Double time!'

The drum picked up pace. The oars moved in perfect synchronization, blades lifting out of the water, oarsmen leaning forward, dipping in and pulling hard, churning the sea into foam. Jax gripped the rail with white knuckles, excited as a boy taking his first ride on a horse. Dion glanced at Cob at the stern, fighting the shuddering helm. Cob gave him a tight grin.

The trio of ships that were their prey came on fast. Seeing the speeding warship that dwarfed them in size, the captains behaved as expected and executed a series of sharp tacks, still heading toward Koulis but angled slightly to the north, taking on a better reach, desperate to get away. Dion called out to Cob and pointed, and the helmsman headed higher to cut them off from the coast.

With an escape route still in sight, the merchant ships tacked yet again, now heading directly north. The bireme was swifter but at this pace the men would tire before they caught the fast sailing ships.

Then the *Gull* came into view.

Jax whooped; Reece was exactly where they wanted him to be. With the *Dauntless* blocking access to the coast in the east and the *Gull* heading down from the north, the merchant ships had no choice but to tack again, heading west, back out to the open sea.

Dion shouted at Cob to turn again. He ran to the hatch. 'Rowers, give me your best! We almost have them!' His words brought forth a ragged roar from the oarsmen.

He rejoined Jax as the last two ships in the pirate fleet appeared in the west. Slower but filled with fighting men, they were lying in wait for the merchantmen.

Dion knew that whoever was in command would be panicked as they saw the tridents on the silver flags raised on every mast of the encircling ships. Suddenly two of the merchant ships raised white flags and at the same time lowered their sails; in an instant they were dead in the water.

But the third ship spun on its heel like a cavalryman wheeling his mount. Heading for a gap between the *Dauntless* and the pair of ships in the rear, the captain made one final dash for freedom. As the merchantman neared, Dion saw a catapult on the deck and at least half a dozen archers readying their bows. He prayed to Silex that they weren't employing fire arrows, or more deadly still, naphtha.

This captain needed to be cowed.

'Ramming speed!' Dion bellowed.

Putting everything they could into one final burst of effort, the oarsmen doubled their efforts to match the galloping rhythm of the drum. If the *Dauntless* was traveling swiftly before, it was now racing over the waves, heading directly for the exposed side of its quarry.

'Are you sure—?' Jax said, speaking so that only Dion could hear him.

'They'll see the danger,' Dion said, hoping his voice sounded more confident than he felt.

The distance between the two vessels narrowed to a hundred paces, and then halved again. Just as they came within striking range of the enemy archers a white flag sped to the top of the mast and the merchant ship heeled over, heading into the wind to bleed speed.

'Back with oars! Slow us down!' Dion cried.

The gap shrank to thirty paces and then ten. With a gentle nudge the ram touched the sailing ship under the waterline, grazing against it but no more. Jax let out a pent-up breath of relief as his shoulders slumped. His face broke out in his characteristic broad smile as he shook his head from side to side.

While the oars came in and the two ships made fast, Dion crossed the deck to peer at the rest of the fleet, seeing that they had the other merchant vessels in hand. The top deck of the *Dauntless* was already filling as men climbed up from the rowing decks. Jax drew the sword he wore at his waist, raising it into the air, forming the crew into a boarding party.

'Free the slaves and seize the plunder!' Jax roared.

The pirates cheered and followed their leader as Dion checked over his ship one last time and then joined them, leaping from one ship to the next in a single bound. The merchantman had two decks, an open deck for the passengers and crew and a cargo hold accessed through a sunken hatch near the mainmast. Dozens of barrels were tied together in the bow, and a pair of bare-chested sailors manned the headsail with a further four standing by the mast.

'Remain in your places!' Gideon leveled a curved sword at the vessel's occupants as he took charge of the ship, glaring at everyone he encountered until every set of eyes was downcast. 'Take their weapons,' he instructed a pair of boarders, who disarmed the archers bunched near the gunwale.

He then bellowed to the ship in general.

'You are in the presence of the Free Men! Forget what you may have learned about us, we are tough but fair. We work to liberate the oppressed and to end persecution. This takes money! We will seize your goods where they will be used to help our cause. Your ship'—Gideon glanced back at Jax, who shook his head—'will sail you home when we are done. Any man or woman who wishes to join us may do so, and any slave who provides proof of being beaten will have justice meted out to the scoundrel who did it. Stay calm, stay quiet, and this will all be over soon.'

Meanwhile Jax ran his eyes over the occupants, taking in the skinny sailors – obviously slaves – and muttering under his breath. He crossed to a well-dressed officer, a short bearded man in a blue tunic. 'Where is your captain?'

The bearded officer lifted a shaking hand to indicate the ship's stern, the direction Gideon was already heading in. As Jax looked up, Dion saw Gideon stop in his tracks and then call back in his deep voice.

'Jax, Andion. You should see this.'

Exchanging glances, the pair left their captives under the watchful eyes of the boarding party as they headed to the far end of the ship, where a large square of white cloth placed for shade blocked their view.

Dion and Jax reached the vessel's stern, joining Gideon, and immediately stopped and stared.

A statuesque middle-aged woman with henna-dyed hair streaked with gray sat on a carpet, resting against a pile of embroidered cushions. She was olive-skinned and wore a white silk chiton belted with braided leather woven with gold, and there was even gold thread in the sandals she wore on her feet. She wore more jewels than any woman Dion had ever encountered: half a dozen earrings on each ear, a heavy necklace, and gaudy rings on every finger.

Two slaves, emaciated youths both of them, fanned her with woven palm fronds, moving ceaselessly, despite the situation. Even as they stared with terrified eyes at the three pirates, the boys still didn't pause; the thin scars on their bare shoulders told of their training.

But it wasn't the sight of the woman's wealth or even the slaves that caused the three pirates to take pause. It was the body of the well-dressed man sprawled on the deck three feet from the carpet's edge, dead eyes staring, limbs akimbo, throat displaying a wide gash. The woman still held the hilt of the bloody dagger in her hand that she'd used to do the deed. She looked down at the blade and then up to meet Jax's eyes. She smiled.

Jax glanced at the boys. 'Stop. Now,' he ordered.

It said something of the dark-eyed woman's power over her slaves that they glanced at her before she finally nodded.

'The captain?' Jax raised an eyebrow.

'He was,' she answered scornfully.

'Do you know who you are speaking with?' Gideon growled. 'This is Jax, king of the Free Men.'

'I know who you are.' The woman glared up at Jax, who was toying with his moustache as he regarded her. 'It is too late for apologies, he will take your head. But perhaps, just perhaps, if you let me go, I can persuade him that you don't need to die in agony.'

Jax simply continued to tweak the hair on his upper lip.

'Who will?' Dion looked from Jax to the dark-eyed woman.

'My husband.'

'Your husband?' Gideon asked.

'Mercilles, highest lord of Koulis,' she said haughtily, glaring up at Gideon. 'The most powerful man in the world.'

'Not powerful enough it seems,' Jax said with a smile. 'Tell me, lady, how long have the two of you been married? You know who I am, but I'm afraid to say that I don't even know your name . . . ?'

When she didn't answer, Gideon walked over to one of the slave boys and bent down. His lips parted to display even, white teeth – the first time Dion had seen him smile – and he spoke in a surprisingly kind voice. 'My young friend. What is her name?'

'Lady . . . Lady Fatima.'

'Thank you,' Gideon said. 'You don't need to fear us. Rest assured. Your life is about to get much better.'

'Lady Fatima,' Jax said, now brisk and businesslike. 'Where were you heading? What is your cargo?'

'Gold,' she said shortly.

'We have Mercilles' gold?' Jax asked her.

'No!' she spat. '*My* gold.'

Jax glanced at Dion, who shrugged. 'Best never to try to understand another man's marriage.'

'You have the right of it there,' Jax said, shaking his head as he came to a decision. 'She's coming with us.' He gave her a curt order. 'Lady, fetch whatever belongings you will need from your vessel.'

Lifting her nose, she left her cushions and Gideon escorted her back to the middle of the ship. Dion passed the boys over to the

Dauntless and saw Gideon with Fatima as she imperiously pointed at the hatch leading to the cargo hold. 'I need to go in there,' she said.

'Arman,' Gideon instructed a young sailor with his first growth of beard. 'Go with her. Don't let her out of your sight.'

Dion began to organize the passage of cargo from ship to ship as the sullen woman and her escort disappeared into the lower hold. Gideon moved from one barrel to the next, opening lids and sniffing.

'Fragrant oil,' Gideon told Jax. 'The kind the priests burn in the temples. Expensive.'

'You hear that men?' Jax called. 'Gold and oil. Good spoils!'

Word passed around and soon everyone was grinning, taking over the cargo to store in the hold of the *Dauntless*. Dion joined in, carrying a barrel and handing it up to the arms reaching over the gap. He saw Fatima exit the hatchway to the hold and approach him with a bundle in her arms and her head held high.

'I am ready,' she stated.

Dion ordered the crewmen to pull the ships close with the boarding ropes, and soon a dozen red-faced men were holding the two vessels tightly together until Mercilles' wife had made it across. Finally she was over and they were able to release, leaving the gap to increase again.

But as she glanced back from the *Dauntless*, leaving Jax, Gideon, Dion, and the boarding party still on the merchant vessel, Dion saw a calculating look on her face. It was a strange expression she wore, an evil glint of triumph.

'Wait,' Dion said. He waved at Gideon. 'Where's Arman?'

Gideon's eyes widened. Jax, standing close to Dion with a barrel in his arms, let it fall to the deck.

'*My* gold,' Fatima cried from the deck of the *Dauntless*.

Dion suddenly smelled an overpowering odor. It was so sweet it was almost rancid, an oily blend of rose, lavender, and rosemary, all mixed into a sickening melange. Another, sharper smell grew stronger: the unmistakable stench of smoke.

'Abandon ship!' Dion roared. 'Into the water! Now!'

Not waiting a moment longer, he charged into Jax, the closest man to him, and encircled his waist with his arms. Carrying them both off the ship's gunwale, high above the sea, for a moment they were out in the void before they crashed into the water with a mighty splash. Immediately both Dion and Jax sank under the surface.

Fire engulfed the merchant ship, detonations shattering the vessel in ever-increasing explosions. Every time the fire reached a quantity of oil it burst to twice the size. When the sails caught they added to the blaze, and the gusting wind that skimmed across the sea fanned the flames higher than the top of the mast.

Eyes shut tightly, Jax tried to head for the surface but Dion was a strong swimmer, and looking up, he saw that directly above their head the ship was already a raging inferno. He pulled the tall man along under the water, arms paddling and legs kicking to swim them both clear, and now Jax was swimming with him, wide eyes staring above as he realized what was happening.

Finally they were clear and Dion and Jax both shot to the surface, bursting to the top and sucking in air. Tossed around by the big waves of the open sea, they could nonetheless see what was happening.

The broken merchantman was half submerged, but the strong wind had already carried the flames from one vessel to the next. Dion watched in horror as the *Dauntless* burned and men threw themselves off the deck.

⁓

It took a long time for the fleet to pick up the survivors.

Dion and Jax were among the last men to be rescued. Cob had

dived clear, and all the men on the bireme who could swim had plunged into the water and escaped the inferno. In the confusion, their captive, Lady Fatima, the wife of Mercilles of Koulis, almost swam free of pursuit, but they picked her up last of all. She freely admitted to poking Arman's eyes out with her thumbs and then starting the fire in a hold full of oil. She smiled as she reminded them that her husband would torture them slowly.

Jax ordered her to be placed in chains.

Every face was grim as the fleet then set a course for Fort Liberty. Scores of the Free Men had drowned or burned, and among them was Gideon.

40

Ten days after fleeing Tanus, Aristocles and Amos were in the trade city of Koulis, waiting at the entrance to the grove of trees that the Council of Five called a lyceum. They were travel worn and dusty, having entered the city gates with the rising sun on their backs. They no longer had gold for gifts, and the prices at the guest houses were eye-watering. Once again Aristocles would be asking for help.

Waiting anxiously, glancing at Amos, Aristocles told himself that this time the gods would smile on them. After all, they'd made it across the Waste. The dryness of the place and the nearby presence of Cinder Fen made the crossing perilous, but they finally had some luck. The walled fort above the valley was deserted; the eldren gone.

The two travelers had explored the strange stockade on its hill, isolated deep in the Waste, but neither had wanted to spend the night. After filling their skins at the trickling river they'd swiftly mounted up and moved on. Aristocles was surprised: he'd only been familiar with the eldren who lived in the Village in the Wilds, and hadn't known them to build permanent structures. He and Amos had exchanged theories as to its purpose – and Triton's present whereabouts – but they left the fort bemused.

At any rate, Aristocles had more pressing issues on his mind. His temporary exile was beginning to feel permanent. His only hopes lay with the coming audience, but he knew the Council of Five had accepted his request more out of curiosity than anything else. They knew of Phalesia, of course: there had once been close ties between the two cities.

But Phalesia was far away. In this region Ilea was dominant.

As he waited for the guards to call them forward, Aristocles contrasted this lyceum with the huge rectangular structure in Phalesia where he'd led the Assembly of Consuls. He felt homesick more than at any other time of his life.

'You can go through now, lord.' The nearest soldier finally beckoned. 'Your man can wait here.'

Amos scowled but Aristocles placed a hand on his arm. 'It's fine. This won't be like Tanus. They just want to know why I'm here.'

The guards parted to allow him through, and Aristocles gathered the folds of his consul's dusty tunic, lifting his chin and straightening his back. The tall trees around him swayed on both sides, shading the path from the sun. The inner pair of guards also nodded for him to pass.

Aristocles took a deep breath and approached the circular stone structure, slowly climbing the steps. Reaching the summit, he approached five men in white tunics, seated at five high-backed chairs in a row, with the centermost chair slightly taller than the others.

'Aristocles, first consul of Phalesia,' the shrunken lord sitting on the taller chair said. 'Do I have that right?'

Aristocles had never met Lothar, the ruling seat in the Council of Five. He was ancient, at least seventy years old, with gray hair and skin like a wrinkled prune, but the look in his narrowed eyes was far from the rheumy gaze of a befuddled old man. The heavy silver medallion at his throat displaying two fish entwined told Aristocles that this was a man who valued commerce over power for its own sake. He stored the knowledge away for future reference.

'You do,' Aristocles said. 'And . . . how do I address you?'

'Lord? By name?' Lothar shrugged. 'I really don't care.' He rapped his claw-like fingers on the arm of his chair. 'Now, we know about your Assembly of Consuls, and you tell us you are the first among your fellows, but why not send word of your visit? Or if time did not permit, where is your retinue?'

Aristocles cleared his throat. 'You arrive straight at the purpose of my visit, lord. I've come because I have been usurped as first consul of Phalesia. I still have the support of the people, and of the Assembly of Consuls, but my homeland has fallen under the dominance of the king of Xanthos.'

'Nikolas, is that right?' the high-browed lord on Lothar's left said.

'Yes, that is correct.'

The same man frowned. 'But is he not the same Nikolas who saved your city from the sun king's forces?'

Aristocles' lips thinned. 'His late arrival enabled us to throw back the Ilean forces, it is true, but it was the soldiers of Phalesia who held off the brunt of the assault. As a result we lost more than we would have if our ally had come to our timely aid.' He turned to Lothar once more. 'I once thought to strengthen the ties between us . . . Nikolas tarried because he was burying his wife and son, and at the end, he did come. I even pledged my beloved daughter Chloe to become his wife.'

Aristocles stopped speaking for a moment, wondering if his daughters were safe.

'I now know better,' he finally continued. 'When matters came to a head, and Nikolas saw that the Assembly would vote against his own desire, he instituted a change by force of arms. In the night he killed many of my colleagues – murdered them. I've been lucky to escape with my life.'

'And what do you want from us?' a plump lord at Lothar's right asked.

'I seek your support in restoring independence to Phalesia. A few ships and a small force would allow me to return to my home, where I can forestall any plans Nikolas has of becoming king of Phalesia. I want to resume my rightful place.'

Aristocles didn't mention the events at Tanus. Queen Zanthe had chosen her side, and with the size of Nikolas's army increased, Nikolas might even now be on his way to Koulis to give Lothar the same choice he'd given her.

'We will discuss it,' Lothar said. When Aristocles still didn't move, he raised an eyebrow. 'Anything else?'

Aristocles bowed. 'I need lodgings and food. I am a nobleman, exiled from my country. When I have my position restored, I will repay any kindness with interest.'

'You shall have your needs met while we deliberate,' Lothar said. 'But remember, Aristocles, Phalesia is far away, and we have our own problems with Ilea. If you have another course of action, I suggest you pursue it.'

'I thank you all,' Aristocles said, nodding to each member of the Council of Five. Gathering the folds of his white tunic, he descended the steps and walked along the tree-lined pathway that would take him out of the lyceum.

Halfway along the path, his eyes went wide and his mouth dropped open as he saw the last person he'd expected to see walking down the path, toward the structure in the middle of the grove.

Kargan of Ilea swept past. The last time Aristocles had seen the barrel-chested naval commander he'd been leading an assault on his homeland. Long before that, he and Kargan had hosted each other at banquets, but the overlord of the sun king's navy had used his opportunity to steal away Aristocles' daughter.

Paying him no attention, Kargan headed directly for the circular structure buried within the grove. Aristocles thought furiously, casting his eyes at the pathway's far end, where Amos waited outside. The two guards had their backs to him. Foliage obscured the pair closer to the structure.

Making a sudden decision, as soon as Kargan and his companion had passed, Aristocles shrank into the trees. He buried himself in the thick shrubbery, trying to still the beating of his heart and slow his breathing as he listened.

'. . . hand over the gold in exchange for Lord Mercilles' beloved wife,' Lothar's ancient but incisive voice was clearly audible. 'This is a delicate task, and above all else you must ensure Lady Fatima's safety.'

Kargan's rumbling voice replied. '. . . pirates are not to be trusted . . .' Frowning, Aristocles moved closer until the Ilean's voice became clear. '. . . dangerous men. How do we ensure a safe exchange?'

'That is for you to decide,' Lothar said.

'Lord Mercilles?' Kargan asked. 'Do you want to be present?'

'No,' a new voice said. This man, Mercilles, spoke in a weary manner, full of sorrow. 'My wife is so close to my heart that I fear my presence would only add emotion to the situation. I trust you, Lord Kargan, and my prayers go with you.'

'I'll make my preparations then,' Kargan said. 'By your leave.'

Suddenly Kargan was on the pathway again, heading away from the structure. Aristocles froze, but Kargan was walking briskly, and soon he was past again. Hiding in the trees, Aristocles decided to wait a few moments.

'Lord Mercilles?' Lothar spoke up. 'Are you sure this is what you want?'

When Mercilles spoke now, his tone was bitter. 'I must answer the insult – no one must think that Mercilles of Koulis cannot protect his own wife – but the woman was stealing from me. She deserves her fate. This way I rid myself of the Free Men, and you rid yourself of the Ileans.'

'It is a dangerous plan.'

'The risks can be managed.'

'But if she dies?'

Mercilles snorted. 'The gods don't allow divorce. I'm counting on it. Now, I must be on my way . . .'

Moving swiftly, Aristocles left the trees, deep in thought as he headed back along the path to join Amos outside. He knew he had a valuable piece of information.

It only remained to see how he could use it.

41

Chloe stood a few hundred paces from Vikram's villa, where the cliff dropped away and she had an unparalleled view of the village of Pao and the plains beyond. With the precipice near her feet, she held the resonance staff high in the sky, clutching it near the top so that her skin was in contact with the copper. She closed her eyes.

She drove out all negative thoughts. The magic of copper was about healing and harmony, music and beauty. She remembered Vikram's teachings. She had to think of a single, pure note, to imagine humming the note soundlessly, containing it within her mind, holding it for a length of time that would be impossible using her voice because she would have to take a breath.

The note could never waver, and she couldn't allow anything but peace and tranquility to fill her mind. It couldn't just be a low sound; the tone had to be beautiful, sweet and bright, the pitch matching what she could produce with her voice or an instrument.

Taking slow, deep breaths, her eyes closed, Chloe imagined playing her copper flute. She pictured another version of herself, mouthpiece pressed to her lips. The note commenced in her mind and she held it, letting it neither rise nor fall, but simply sustaining itself.

She could feel the cold metal of the copper touching the skin of her clenched fist. Sweat broke out on her brow. If she couldn't take control of her power, it would gain the upper hand, and would be released in a torrent rather than a focused stream.

She opened her eyes. She prepared to release the fire that was constantly pent up inside her, raging to be free.

In a single swift movement she brought the base of the staff crashing down to the stone. She released, channeling the energy to her hand. The metal fork began to hum.

The sound was far from the high-pitched warbling that Vikram had projected from the staff to stun the tribesmen, but it continued to grow in volume. Feeling triumph, Chloe stared at the tip of the staff and raised it into the air again.

A dull ache began to grow between her ears. The note in her mind began to falter. It shifted pitch, becoming flat.

The growing headache throbbed in her temples as the resonator suddenly emitted an ear-splitting shriek. Frowning, she tried to restore her concentration but it became ever more difficult as the pain increased in intensity.

She realized she was gasping, drawing in breath in great heaves. Fire sparkled in her vision; red lights darted like shooting stars, replacing the sight of the sweeping plain with a million searing pinpricks joined by a matching number of needles poking into her skull. The terrible agony was impossible to control. The crystal note shattered.

Chloe cried out and her white-knuckled fingers released their grip as she nearly dropped the staff, sending it tumbling off the cliff, only grabbing it again at the last instant. Panting as if she'd been sprinting, she struggled to take in gulps of air. With the end of the contact between the metal and her skin, the quavering metal fork stilled. She put a hand to her ear, surprised that she couldn't feel any blood.

'That is enough for today,' a voice said behind her.

Whirling, she saw Vikram standing behind her, picking at his pug nose as he watched. With her ears ringing, it sounded like he was in another room.

'You've forgotten every warning I gave you,' the old man in the dirty robe said, shaking his head. With his greasy, thinning hair, deep-set eyes, and scraggly beard, he looked like the most unlikely magus Chloe had ever seen. 'Do you want to become deaf? Or kill yourself?'

'No.' She shook her head. Even her own voice sounded far away.

'Give it to me,' he said, holding out his hand so that Chloe could pass him the staff. He then lifted it and examined the copper, frowning at the green on the twin tines of the fork.

Chloe knew she'd been pushing herself too hard. But there were moments when the fire in her mind was so strong that she felt the only way to ease the pain was to release it. 'Perhaps another try with gold . . .'

'No,' Vikram said abruptly. 'There is something I need to speak with you about. Come.' He waited impatiently until she fell in beside him and then began leading her toward the villa. 'I have a gift for you,' he said as they walked. He reached into a pocket of his robe and pulled out a long necklace with a finger-sized tube of copper dangling from the center. 'I know you are without your necklace, and so I searched the villa and found this. Please.' He stopped and faced her. 'Let me put it on.'

She wrinkled her nose as he came in close to clasp the necklace around her neck; his body reeked of sweat. In the entire time she'd been at the villa, she'd never known him to bathe.

'There,' he said.

Chloe straightened, relieved when he backed away, and she looked down at the tube of copper, now dangling between her breasts. 'What does it signify?'

'It's just a necklace.' He flashed his yellowed teeth. 'But it looks good on you.'

'Thank you,' Chloe said, examining the copper cylinder as they resumed walking.

The area just outside the villa was paved with square stones, surrounded by rows of flowering shrubs: rosemary, lavender, and rose bushes. Chloe saw that near the central stone basin was a large sack, resting on its side on the ground. As she neared, she saw that it was filled with a large motionless lump. On one side the cloth was red and wet.

Seeing Chloe's attention, Vikram waved a hand. 'I traded the villagers for a doe. Come.'

He continued to escort her to the villa, staff in hand. Despite his age he now held her with a strong grip around her waist, herding her up the steps and through the broad entrance. Chloe wondered why he was taking her inside, and what it was he wanted to say. She decided that if he asked her about Liana's whereabouts she would tell the truth, and admit to the fact that Liana had gone but would return. She was worried, though. His behavior was sometimes unpredictable.

'I have something to ask you,' he said, glancing at her as he walked, 'and I would like you to tell me the truth. Did you tell Liana that she too must stay? I thought I was quite clear.'

'I told her that I needed to remain here, but that she did not.'

'So you told her she could leave.'

'I did.'

Vikram shook his head. 'You should not have done that.'

He paused near the hearth and leaned his staff against the wall. He then glanced at the fire, burning red and hot.

'Why?' Chloe frowned. 'People need to know where I am.'

Turning back to her, Vikram stared grimly into her eyes. 'Isn't it clear?' His nostrils flared. 'If I allowed her to go she would tell others you are here. They would come looking for you.'

'They'll come looking for me regardless—'

'No,' he interrupted. 'They will not.'

He spoke matter-of-factly but his next words filled her with horror.

'Soon after you arrived I found a couple of village girls who match your descriptions. I killed them and marked their faces. I then dressed them in your clothing and put your necklaces on them. Finally I left their bodies on the Phalesian Way.' He smiled and reached forward to brush a lock of dark hair away from Chloe's face. 'You're dead. And you are not leaving here. Not ever.'

Chloe felt the blood drain from her face as she glanced outside, to the place where she'd seen the sack on the ground. 'Liana. Where is she?'

Vikram's next words made her feel sick. 'You've guessed for yourself.'

Heart pounding in her chest, Chloe prepared to take action. He was more crazed than she'd realized. She was going to have to fight. Her eyes flickered to his staff. She wondered if he'd be able to reach for it before she could disable him.

He was a powerful sorcerer. She would have only one chance.

'I enlisted the help of some hunters, skilled trackers from one of the more fierce tribes,' he said. 'She didn't make it far. Your friend is not dead, but she soon will be.'

With a surge of strength, Chloe moved.

She clasped the old man's wrist and squeezed in the spot that she knew would cause his hand to go limp. As Vikram winced, she levered his hand to push his wrist in to meet his forearm. His eyes went wide and he gasped.

But before she could punch him in the throat, Vikram's free hand reached out and he gripped the copper tube that hung from the chain around her neck. His brow furrowed in concentration.

Sharp pain burst inside Chloe's head.

A terrible roar filled her ears, stunning her senses. She could hear only a constant thunder, a sound so overwhelming it threatened to burst her eardrums. Her knees went limp; her hand dropped away from its grip on Vikram's wrist. The magus cradled her as she fell, and when he spoke his voice was distant, like she was hearing him underwater.

'You betrayed my trust, Chloe.' He sounded like he was far away, although his face was close to hers as he supported her body. 'I thought we understood each other. I was going to give you knowledge, and you would live here with me. Your life would have been a good one. Now? My eyes will be on you always. You'll have no maid.' He glanced at the hearth. 'And I am going to brand you to make sure you've learned your lesson.'

Stricken with agony, disabled by the sound in her head, Chloe tried to will her legs to move but couldn't even manage a feeble kick. Her arms hung weakly. She fought to scream but struggled to gasp in breath. Vikram still held the copper tube, and she now saw the same sparkles across her vision that she'd seen when she'd been practicing on the cliff, but there were now so many she could barely see. Not even when she'd been in Solon's power had she felt so defenseless.

She tried to blink her vision clear as the old magus continued to scowl down at her.

Then, even over the thunder inside her head, she heard a growl.

Catching movement in the corner of her vision, fighting the specks of fire that dazzled her sight, Chloe saw something terrifying.

The villa was high-ceilinged, but the giant's shoulders were hunched, her head grazing the ceiling. Twelve feet tall with muscled limbs and a woman's shape, she had skin like leather and a strangely familiar heart-shaped face. But her jaw was enlarged and her eyes were menacing. Fists bunched at her sides, she roared, parting her mouth to show sharpened teeth.

Vikram whirled to face the threat, so stunned he could only gape. He dropped Chloe to the ground and when his hand left the copper tube the paralyzing hum faded away. The giant's gaze landed upon them both, breath rumbling, immediately taking in the scene. The creature came forward and gripped the old magus around the neck.

As easily as a child plucking a flower, the giant picked the old magus up and lifted him into the air. Taking another stride, the giant bent to one knee to dash the old man's head against the wall.

Vikram's skull splintered on the first strike, but still the giant roared and continued to pound the remains of his head into the stone. Bright pulp smeared the wall but the giant continued to smash, crying out with every blow.

'Liana!' Chloe cried, finally regaining her breath and climbing to her feet.

In moments the giant didn't have anything to hold onto and the old man's ruined body dropped to the ground. Clasping her two immense hands together, Liana now raised her arms over her head and brought them down onto Vikram's crumpled corpse.

'Liana!'

The giant pounded until the corpse was unrecognizable as once being human. As Chloe cried out the creature suddenly whirled, eyes filled with rage. Chloe lifted a warding arm as the creature raised a clenched fist. Chest heaving, the giant opened the fist, crimson liquid dripping from her fingers.

'Liana! Your name is Liana! It's me, Chloe!'

The hand hovered in front of her, wavering for what felt like an eternity. The giant's breath heaved as Chloe continued to say the eldran's name, praying for her friend to return.

Finally the giant slumped, looking down at the ground. Chloe sighed with relief as gray mist surrounded the creature from head to toe.

Chloe stood again on the cliff, gazing out at the surrounding plain as the sun set on one of the strangest days of her life. A reddened sky matched the color of blood. Streaked and smeared, it reminded her of the wall inside the villa.

Sensing movement, she turned and saw Liana, now a young eldran with a heart-shaped face, soft green eyes, and wild auburn hair. Her face and body was bruised and battered but if there was one thing Chloe knew it was that her friend was stronger than she looked. Liana joined her at the cliff, and it was some time before a voice broke the stillness.

'I buried his body,' Liana said.

Chloe turned to regard the eldran, whose face was inscrutable. 'You didn't have to do that,' she said softly.

Liana shrugged. 'I killed him.'

'I'm sorry you had to. But . . . Liana . . .' Chloe's mouth worked soundlessly. What should she say to the woman who had saved her? 'Thank you.'

'I beat him to a pulp,' Liana said, suddenly looking at Chloe with shimmering eyes. 'I became a monster.'

'No, you didn't. You fought in the only way you could. You saved my life. It was only when you began to turn wild that something else showed itself.'

'I hope you're right,' Liana said, taking a deep breath as she gazed out at the land below.

Another silence ensued. Watching the vivid sunset, Chloe once again remembered why she had asked Tomarys to teach her to fight. She'd made a promise to herself never to feel helpless, but she'd failed.

'So I suppose we're leaving now,' Liana said.

'No,' Chloe said. She faced the eldran and saw Liana looking up at her in surprise. 'I'm not leaving. I won't ask you to stay with me'—she smiled as she reached out to squeeze her friend's shoulder—'even though I hope you will.'

'You're staying? But why?'

'Vikram has books here, and he has items of magic. I'm not ready to leave just yet.' Chloe's voice firmed. 'I have something within me that I need to control. Before we go, I'm going to learn what I can.'

42

'A heavy purse then,' Dion said to Cob.

'As soon as the oil is sold in Myana, without a doubt.'

'Was it worth it?'

Dion shielded his eyes. He and Cob were sailing the *Calypso*, the old man at the tiller and Dion manning the sail, although the vessel could just as easily be managed by Cob alone. But Dion had missed the polished timbers of her interior, and the way she danced in front of the wind.

And after the loss of the *Dauntless*, with the *Gull* once again Jax's flagship under Reece's command, it was better for everyone that he sail the smaller vessel.

'Dion . . . It wasn't your fault.'

'Reece certainly thinks it was.'

'Reece is a fool. No one was expecting that crazed woman to start a fire on her own ship. You saved Jax's life, he said so himself. Reece is just upset about Gideon, we all are. But unfortunately for you, he's decided that you're to blame.'

'We'd better get a good ransom,' Dion muttered.

'We will. Mercilles is giving us six talents of gold. Six! And better yet, he's going to have to live with Fatima for the rest of his life. I can't think of a better revenge than returning her to her husband.'

Dion scowled up at the sky. He'd lost his ship, which was worth far more than six talents of gold. He'd done his best, yet here he was, a one-time captain without ship or crew.

'Lad,' Cob said softly. 'The men will remember the fire, but they'll also remember the way you captained the *Dauntless*.' Glancing back, Dion saw the old man shaking his head. 'You handled her like you'd been sailing her for a lifetime. The men will pass their tales on to the others. Like Zarkos's crew, they'd sail with you to the edge of the world, given the chance.'

Dion nodded, still discouraged after the loss of the ship and the death of Gideon, who cared more for slaves than he did for cargo. He glanced at the two ships nearby, both single-decked war galleys: the *Gull* and the *Sea Witch*. His role was to sail to port, upwind of the fleet, and use the *Calypso*'s agility to pass down any messages from the outlying scout vessels still farther out.

It was Dion who'd pushed for caution. They would soon be meeting with the representative of Mercilles of Koulis to exchange Lady Fatima for the gold talents. They could take no chances.

Now looking for the scouts, Dion frowned. 'Cob.'

The tone of his voice made the old sailor look up sharply. 'What, lad?'

'Is that smoke?'

Cob peered for a time and then shook his head. 'Can't tell from here.' His face became worried. 'You think they've run into trouble?'

'Perhaps.' Dion scratched the stubble on his chin. 'It could just be cloud.'

'What do you want to do? Think I should investigate?'

Dion thought for a moment and then made a decision. 'Do it. I'm going to tell Jax to be on the alert. You all right to manage the *Calypso* on your own?'

Cob snorted. 'With my hands tied behind my back, pulling on the sheets with my teeth.' His eyebrows rose when he saw Dion stand up and stare into the water, gripping the mast with one hand. 'You're not serious . . .'

'Take care, old man.'

Without another word, Dion gazed down into the rough waves of the open sea, and dived in head first.

⁂

The swim was arduous but Dion was a strong swimmer and the wind was with him, relentless waves pushing him toward the *Gull* as he angled his approach to reach the war galley from the side. Soon a sailor threw a hemp rope off the ship's side and Dion swam over to the trailing line, gripping it tightly and pulling himself forward through the water. He reached the ship and grunted, arms on fire as he hauled his way up hand over hand, assisted by a pair of strong men. Taking the offered hand, he climbed over the gunwale and stood drenched on the deck.

'What is it?' Reece was the first man to reach him, his face curled into a scowl. 'Why not sail over?' He pointed out to sea. 'And why is Cob breaking formation?'

Dion stood panting on the deck, chest heaving as he regained his breath. He coughed and tasted bitter sea water in the back of his throat.

'Andion,' Jax called as he approached. The leader of the Free Men wore his angled cap, and his white tunic was belted with a yellow cord. 'What is it?'

'Smoke,' Dion wheezed, one hand on his hip as he pointed in the direction of the *Calpyso* as Cob sailed the vessel away.

Reece peered for a moment and then shook his head. 'That's not smoke. It's cloud.'

'It does look like cloud to me,' Jax admitted.

Dion shook his head. He drew in a deep breath. 'Cloud doesn't rise like that. And we've lost contact with the scouts.'

'The starboard scouts are still there—' Reece began.

'Well the port scouts aren't!'

'Andion . . .' Jax soothed. 'It's fine. You want to be careful, I understand. Cob's investigating?'

'He is.' Dion looked out at the horizon, seeing the gray mist that had first occupied his attention. He had to admit that it now looked like nothing more than cloud.

Jax pondered for a moment, tugging at his neat moustache before nodding. 'Reece,' he ordered, 'raise the flag to tighten formation. Bring the starboard scouts in close. Tell the men to be on high alert.'

With a black look at Dion, Reece nodded and stalked away, bawling out orders to his crew.

'Don't mind Reece, he sees only the same things in you that I do.' Jax's expression was earnest as he met Dion's eyes. 'It takes years before a man gets the confidence to stand tall in front of others. That is, unless you've led before, and not fishermen or boy sailors, like the old man said.'

Dion glanced at Reece, striding to the bow and gazing at the horizon as he waited for sign of Mercilles' agent.

'He's been with me since the beginning,' Jax said, following the stocky man with his eyes. 'And he's dependable, good at keeping the men in line. But you saved my life. I'm not about to betray your trust, and certainly not to Reece. You'd be surprised how accepting I can be.'

'But all the talk of equality . . .'

'There's no talk of equality,' Jax said. 'We simply say that every man should be judged on his skills and merits, rather than his blood. It doesn't mean nobles aren't welcome among our number.'

He stared out to sea. 'I'm also well aware that at some point we're going to have to make an accord with society. We can't always live in fear.'

'But where would everyone go?'

'My plan is to one day have enough gold to buy land, perhaps in Sarsica. We can build real homes, and everyone can start anew, connected to the greater world but also apart. Our values we will keep, and yes, even nobles will be welcome.' He grinned, his eyes twinkling. 'After all, even I was raised in the household of a certain lord, the richest trader on the Maltherean Sea.'

Dion's eyes widened. He remembered Fatima's reaction when she'd met Jax. 'I thought you left your father's farm when you were twelve?'

'Well, it was more of an estate, but the part about my age is true. I was born Mercilles' fifth son, and for some reason we instantly hated each other. He always beat his slaves, but with me he preferred to use a club.' Jax shrugged. 'I spent my youth explaining to healers why I kept climbing trees and breaking limbs when I fell. My mother tried to protect me but she died when I was nine. After that things got worse. I made my escape and never looked back.'

Jax's usually jovial face was grim.

'His lust for gold is insatiable but, more than that, he's lost sight of what it means to be human. He once caught me playing a clapping game with my favorite nursemaid, a slave of course. I told her I loved her and then he walked in and said he'd been listening. Know what he did? Cut off her hands and sealed them with pitch, no more clapping for her.' He grimaced. 'Her wounds mortified and she died. I was ten years old. She meant everything to me after I lost my mother.'

'But why do such a thing?'

'He told me love is weakness. I used to think that he couldn't stand to see anyone else happy, even his own children, but I now think he truly believed that he needed to stamp out any sign of feeling.' Jax glanced up. 'Trust me, my friend. I know the value of freedom.'

'Warships ahead! Biremes! I count four!'

'Let's hope this woman and my father make each other miserable,' Jax said, bringing forth a smile. 'She's costing him six talents of gold.' The twinkling in his eyes returned. 'The knowledge will kill him.'

'Jax,' Dion said. He gripped the king of the Free Men's shoulder, suddenly wanting to tell his secret. 'I'm . . . My name is Dion. I'm the second son of Markos of Xanthos. Nikolas is my brother.'

Jax stopped short, stunned into silence as his mouth worked. Finally he spoke. 'That's some title. What are you doing here?'

'I came to be free.'

'And you are,' Jax said simply and clapped him on the back. He raised his voice as he left Dion behind, striding across the deck to join Reece at the bow. 'We are all of us free, isn't that right, men!'

The Free Men roared, arms raised in the air.

43

The bireme dwarfed the *Gull*, coming alongside while the crews of the two vessels glared at each other. The towering warship's name was the *Dalix*, and although it flew the striped yellow and white flag of Koulis, the swarthy crewmen wore loose trousers that reminded Dion of his time in Lamara. Even the marines had orange suns on their triangular shields.

The two ships approached until they were well within bowshot of each other while the *Sea Witch* drew apart, ready to be called on if needed. The other three biremes in the opposing fleet waited half a mile away.

'Who's in command?' Jax called up to the bireme's top deck.

'I am,' a gravelly voice boomed.

A barrel-chested man with a mop of dark hair and a curled beard came to the rail. He cast his eyes over the deck of the smaller vessel. 'My name is Kargan, and I'm negotiating the handover.' Dion realized he was looking at the same Ilean commander who'd abducted Chloe, although he'd never seen him up close.

'Let's get this over with,' Kargan said. 'Lady Fatima – where is she?'

Jax nodded at Reece, who came forward with a struggling Lady Fatima in hand. The statuesque woman's wrists were bound behind her back but her legs were free and she was making every possible difficulty for Reece as she kicked and writhed.

'Right here.' Jax jerked his chin.

'Bring her across.'

'No. You bring the gold over here.'

Kargan scowled, turning to speak with a tall warrior at his side, a huge man with thick lips and wiry dark hair tied back behind his head. Kargan leaned back over the rail a moment later. 'My man comes with me. We'll bring half the gold over to you, then you bring Lady Fatima over here and collect the other half. No one carries a weapon, agreed?'

'Agreed!'

Sailors flung ropes from both ships and soon they were hauling them tightly together. A rope ladder descended from the bireme as the tall warrior descended first. Dion saw that he wore a vest, open at his hairy chest, and brown trousers. Despite his size, the warrior's movements were graceful as he landed lightly on the rising and falling deck of the *Gull*, spurning a sailor's offer of help. Kargan was the next down, obviously accustomed to the movement of ships, and soon the two newcomers were facing Jax and Dion, while a grim-faced Reece was half a dozen paces away, standing behind Fatima with an arm around her neck.

'Jax, I take it,' Kargan said.

'The gold?' Jax raised an eyebrow.

Fatima decided in that moment to stamp down on Reece's foot. Crying out in pain, his rat-like face turned bright red. Cursing at his captive, Reece fumbled at his waist and a moment later lifted a dagger, pressing the blade against the woman's throat. Suddenly Fatima was wide-eyed and perfectly still. Dion saw a vein throbbing in Reece's forehead.

'I said no weapons,' Kargan said with a dark glare. 'Your gold's on its way.' He glanced up at his ship and waved an arm. 'Send it down!'

A wooden chest dangled from a rope, slowly descending from the bireme. A pair of the *Gull*'s sailors caught the heavy container, grunting with effort as they took its weight and helped settle it to the deck.

'Is that it? Half?' Jax asked Kargan.

Kargan nodded, opening his mouth to reply but then suddenly closing it again. He was looking to the north, with the fresh wind blowing directly into his face. He frowned. 'Why can I see smoke?'

Jax glanced at Dion. Everyone turned to look at the horizon.

The cloud of smoke was now unmistakable, rising in a steady stream to disperse in the upper air. Shielding his eyes, Dion realized with a start that there were several plumes in a line; the haze wasn't localized to one particular place in the distant sea.

'I could ask you the same thing,' Jax said, eyes narrowed at Kargan.

'If you've betrayed us, she dies,' Reece growled, pressing his blade hard against his captive's throat.

'If she dies,' Kargan called up to his ship, his booming voice easily reaching his men. He pointed at Jax. 'He dies.'

Dion heard a familiar creaking sound. Up on the bireme's top deck, three archers lifted their weapons, strings drawn, arrows aimed squarely at Jax's chest. Glancing at the huge warrior, whose face was impassive, Dion knew that he also posed a threat despite his lack of weapon.

'Everyone, calm down,' Jax called, glancing back at the smoke before facing Kargan once more. He looked directly into Kargan's eyes. 'We had a couple of ships out there, scouts. Something must have happened to them. Know anything about it?'

'Nothing,' Kargan said, meeting Jax's stare. 'I came here to do the handover. That's all.'

'We've come this far,' Dion said. Turning back to the horizon, he saw that whatever it was that was burning, the wind was blowing it nearer. 'Let's just do this quickly and leave.'

'Listen to your friend,' Kargan said to Jax. 'He speaks sense.'

'Open the chest!' Jax called to the pair of sailors.

'It's locked.'

'Then break it open!'

Kargan folded his arms and stood with legs astride as jangling and crashing sounds came from the pair of sailors, crouched on the heaving deck as they worked at the chest.

'Why is it locked?' Dion asked Kargan.

'That's how it was given to me.'

'So the second chest is locked also?' Jax lifted his chin. 'You should have said.'

'I didn't know until now.' Kargan's eyes narrowed. 'I'm not in the business of counting a man's gold when he's trying to get back his wife. I give you the chests, you give me the woman, that's the deal.'

The tension grew as the sailors bashed at the chest with the hilt of a dagger. The huge warrior watched Jax, never taking his eyes off him. Dion glanced up at the three tensed archers, knowing they couldn't hold their arrows drawn forever. Hearing a cry, he glanced at Reece to see how he was faring.

Fatima until now had been quiet, but she started to writhe in Reece's grip. 'You're hurting me. Take that thing away from my neck!'

'Settle down, lady,' Jax called out to her.

'Jax,' Dion finally said.

'What is it?' Jax asked, his eyes on Kargan and his bodyguard.

'Perhaps an axe?'

'Good idea.'

Dion called out to a nearby sailor, telling him to fetch an axe. The heavier weapon made short work of the chest, and finally they all heard a crash and a cry of satisfaction as the pair of sailors got the lid open. But rather than shout out confirmation, the two men exchanged glances. A sailor took something in his hand and crossed the deck, handing it to Jax.

'What's this?' Jax said softly. He stared down at the iron ingot in his hand and then looked up at Kargan. 'Tell me, what, in the name of Silex, is this?'

Kargan's eyes widened. 'I had no idea—'

Jax threw the ingot to the deck. 'What am I supposed to do with iron?'

'Jax!' A sailor cried, pointing out to sea.

The *Calypso* was racing with the wind, the triangular sail growing larger with every passing moment: Cob was getting every bit of speed from the vessel that he could. Dion saw the old man standing and waving his arms, calling out, his bellows finally becoming clear as he neared.

'Fire ships! Get out . . . here!'

Dion realized what he was seeing in the distance.

On the horizon were multiple plumes of smoke, all in a row, dozens and dozens of them. Dark floating specks each bore a snaking gray cloud, the small boats carried forward by the current and the wind. Dion saw in an instant that there were enough fire ships to envelop both fleets. The attack was indiscriminate; placed to destroy everything in its path. The Ilean ships were in as much danger as the Free Men.

'Listen,' Kargan said, glancing up at his warship. 'We need to get out of here. I swear I had nothing to do with—'

Taking advantage of the confusion, knowing that there was no gold and hence no chance of freedom, Fatima bit down hard on Reece's hand.

Reece screamed, eyes boggling as he lifted a bloody palm. Fatima squirmed as she tried to escape but he reached out and snatched her arm with his free hand. But when he grabbed her, pulling her close to his chest once more, his dagger was leveled between them.

Fatima gasped. Reece's eyes went wide. He released her and she staggered backward, taking two steps and then a third. She stared down at the blood spreading outward from the center of her chest, drenching her white silk chiton with red, and then the wife of Mercilles toppled backward over the gunwale, tumbling through the space between the two vessels, plummeting into the sea.

The huge warrior beside Kargan reacted swiftly. A blur of motion, in a flash he'd drawn a slender knife from the inside of his vest, holding it high. Dion lunged forward, moving faster than he'd ever moved before. He grabbed hold of the man's thick wrist.

'No,' Dion grunted. Knowing he couldn't keep his grip for long, he directed his words to Kargan. 'We've been betrayed. This is an attack on all of us. You have to save your ships and we have to save ours.'

'Javid!' Kargan barked.

Dion breathed a sigh of relief when the bodyguard nodded and he was able to release the man's wrist. Kargan whirled and began to climb the rope ladder back to his ship, moving with speed now, frantic to save his fleet.

Looking up at the bireme's top deck and seeing that one of the three archers was standing open-mouthed with his bowstring still quivering, Dion turned to Jax. He suddenly felt his whole world crashing down around him.

Jax was looking down at the center of his chest. He appeared more surprised than anything to see blood welling on his tunic, forming a crimson patch around the sunken arrow shaft, a bloom of red that grew larger as he watched.

Dion lunged, and as the king of the Free Men crumpled, he caught him and lowered him to the deck, until Jax was lying on his back, staring up at the clear blue sky.

'Save the men.' Jax coughed, and blood spattered from his lips. 'I know I can count on you.'

Dion shook his head. He opened his mouth to say something, although he didn't know what, but then he stopped before he'd even started speaking.

Jax's breath rattled in his chest. His eyes were wide open, but they were unseeing. He was dead.

Dion straightened and glanced at Reece, who was standing dazed, looking at the bloody dagger in his hand. Knowing that swift action was needed to save the fleet, Dion took command.

'Detach the ropes!' he bellowed. 'Push us off!' A moment later the two ships began drifting apart. 'Raise the sail!' he cried. 'Oarsmen to your benches! Get us moving!'

The sail snapped in the wind and the oars slid out, plunging in but pulling haphazardly until Dion got the men into order.

'Reece,' Dion said. 'Reece!' The stocky sailor finally looked up. 'Take the helm.'

When Reece simply met his command with a numb expression, Dion cursed and ordered another sailor to do it. He then ran to the rail and called out to Cob.

'Sail to the *Sea Witch* and tell them to follow. Find us a path through the fire ships!'

Dion then lifted his gaze to the heavens, praying to Silex that with the nimbler *Calypso* picking a weaving path through the fire ships, they would be able to make it out alive.

———

A scout ship blazed, sinking in front of their eyes, and with fiery boats all around Dion couldn't even turn the *Gull* back for the crew. The *Sea Witch* bumped up against a flaming vessel but the captain was ready with long poles and buckets of water, suffering only a blackened hull.

As the *Calypso* found a safe route, the three vessels behind – the *Gull*, the *Sea Witch*, and the sole surviving scout – finally escaped the fire ships and turned back for Fort Liberty. Cob had saved them twice over, for in addition to his skillful sailing, without his warning they would have been enveloped and both the Ilean ships and the pirate fleet would have been destroyed.

But then, as the fleet of three vessels approached Fort Liberty, Dion felt cold fear clutch hold of his stomach.

This plume was unlike the thin streams rising from the fire ships.

This smoke was as black as night and billowed like a thunderstorm. Miles from the island the setting sun became darkened by the immense trail rising from the home of the Free Men.

44

Only when Lothar's soldiers threw Kargan, Javid, and the surviving members of his crew into prison did Kargan realize that the Council of Five and Mercilles were united in the betrayal. As night set on a day that he'd lost a ship and over a hundred men to the flames and the sea, he paced his small cell for hour after hour, his rage and frustration making him unable to sit still.

There were too many prisoners for the normal jail, so the Council of Five had employed a compound that was once a training ground, located just outside the city walls. Every tiny sleeping chamber had been stripped of furnishing and converted into a cell, locked by means of a sliding bolt on the outside, with the entire compound sealed off while Lothar decided what to do with them.

Spinning on his heel, Kargan glared at Javid. 'What manner of man doesn't care about the life of his own wife?'

'An angry man,' Javid said with a shrug. 'Either that, or a cold-hearted man of logic. Perhaps both.'

'Eh?' Kargan frowned.

'Both your actions and the actions of the Free Men were based on an assumption that proved to be wrong: that Mercilles cared about his wife. We may never know the nature of their relationship, but we know one thing. He saw an opportunity to rid himself of the pirates, for he would know exactly where they were.'

'That trap wasn't just intended for the Free Men. They wanted us all dead.'

'You and your men are an inconvenience. They don't trust you.'

'Lothar could have just sent us back to Ilea.'

'It is better to sacrifice you fighting pirates.'

'I know, I know,' Kargan said, pounding a clenched fist into his palm as he reached the end of the room and turned around again. 'Now what's to become of us?' He scowled at his bodyguard. 'Don't you even care?'

'I care,' Javid said. 'I simply don't see the purpose in what you're doing now.' The big man yawned and stretched, squeezing himself onto his bed pallet. 'Now, if you don't mind, it's late.'

'What's that?' Kargan held up a hand. He looked at the door; he could distinctly hear voices. 'You hear it?'

Javid sat up.

Together with the men the Council of Five had kept as a bond there was a multitude of sailors and marines in the prison. It now sounded like they were all speaking at once. Footsteps clattered out in the corridor, growing louder.

Staring at the door, Kargan stood back as he heard someone sliding the bolt. Exchanging glances with his bodyguard, he wondered what was about to happen. Had Lothar decided to execute them all in the night? Were they being rounded up in batches and taken out to the training ground to be killed, their bodies thrown into a ditch?

The door swung open.

Kargan saw a craggy face he thought looked familiar. The man had dark curly hair cut close to his scalp and the athletic frame of a warrior, and it was clear from his leather armor and short protective skirt that he was a soldier, most likely Galean. He carried a sword in his hand as he scanned the cell and its occupants before calling back over his shoulder.

'I found him.' He waved to Kargan and Javid. 'Come. Quickly.'

Bemused but not about to give up the potential for escape, Kargan followed the warrior and saw his Ilean crewmen thronging the corridor, emptying out of their cells and streaming toward the exit.

'Help your fellows! Open every cell! Assemble outside!' the Galean called. 'You too,' he said to Kargan.

'What—?'

'Outside.' The Galean glared. 'Now.'

The craggy-faced soldier disappeared further down the corridor and suddenly Kargan was surrounded by his men, all clapping him on the back and grinning as they rushed for freedom. Finding himself swept along with them, Kargan passed unconscious guards lying prone on the ground. Soon he was outside in the practice arena, breathing in dry, fresh air and watching as his men milled around.

'Lord Kargan.' He heard his name and, turning in surprise, he saw a face that stunned him speechless.

The older man walking toward him had a high forehead, with white hair at the sides leaving his bald crown bare. He wore a thick white tunic and his expression was rueful as he approached.

Kargan's rescuer was none other than Aristocles, first consul of Phalesia.

'What in the name of Helios—?'

'Form your men up,' Aristocles instructed. He then looked past his shoulder as the craggy-faced warrior approached. 'Amos, is that all of them?'

'Every last one. Quite a number.' Seeing Javid standing nearby, the Galean soldier, Amos, sized him up, each man almost nodding as they recognized a brother warrior. 'Who are you?' Amos asked.

'My name is Javid. I am Lord Kargan's personal guard.'

'You're about to have your work cut out for you,' Amos said. He glanced at Aristocles. 'We can't stay long.'

'Understood.' Aristocles turned back to Kargan. 'Well? Form them up.'

'I suggest we do as he says,' Javid said.

Kargan nodded, still utterly bemused. He raised his arm and called out an order, singling out his officers, getting his men into order, lining them up into a wide formation. He then glanced at Aristocles.

'Good,' Aristocles said, coming close and speaking for Kargan's ears alone. 'Now tell them that you planned this. The Council of Five was going to have them killed, and you wouldn't let that happen. Thank them for their loyalty.'

Kargan addressed the formed-up crewmen and marines, repeating what Aristocles had said.

His men cheered, shouting out his name as they raised their arms into the air. Kargan raised an eyebrow at Aristocles when he'd finished.

'Now tell them that they'll all be well rewarded for their efforts, that each man here has a claim that you will personally deliver on.'

'Personally—?'

'Say it.' Aristocles met Kargan's gaze.

When Kargan had finished, Aristocles continued.

'Let them know that any man who wishes to choose his own path may, with your blessing and gratitude. But any who wants to reclaim Ilea from the tyrant will be first among his fellows.'

Kargan spluttered. 'Reclaim—?'

Aristocles folded his arms over his chest and tapped his foot. Kargan sighed. He took a deep breath and bellowed to his men, stunned when they met his words with a combined roar that made him worried they would hear the shouting back in the city.

'Good.' Aristocles nodded. 'Now let's talk.'

He led Kargan away until they were standing near the training ground's main entrance where another pair of guards lay unconscious. Kargan gained respect for Amos; he'd single-handedly defeated every one of them.

'What's this all about? I would've thought I'd be the last man you'd help.'

'You remember Nikolas of Xanthos? A big man with a black beard . . . He threw you back when you assaulted my city.'

'I remember.'

'Well, he's become powerful. Too powerful. I've been forced to flee Phalesia. My fellow consuls are afraid of him; he's already had many killed.'

'And what does this have to do with me?'

'Politics makes strange bedfellows. I want to make a bargain. I want your help bringing peace to the Maltherean. Nikolas's power lies in the fear the common people have of Ilea. His power will wane if peace is declared.'

Kargan frowned, pondering for a time. 'Listen,' he finally said. 'I hear what you're saying, but Mydas can think of nothing but Ilea's humiliation. He's set on sending the navy back to your homeland and razing your city to the ground. You'll never get him to agree to peace.'

'Yes, but you're a popular commander, Kargan. And Mydas is an unpopular ruler.'

'What does popularity have to do with anything?'

Aristocles smiled.

45

Dion found Finn sitting on one of the highest cliffs on the lopsided island, shoulders slumped as he gazed out to sea. He settled himself down beside the slender man and sat in silence, letting his companion decide whether he wanted to speak.

'So that's it, then,' Finn finally said. He turned and Dion saw that his eyes were reddened, with tears on his cheeks that he didn't bother to wipe away. 'It's all over.'

'It doesn't have to be.'

Finn shook his head. 'First Gideon dead, now Jax. We have no home. No king. No future.'

'There are still many of us left,' Dion said. 'If we go, most of the Free Men have a future only as slaves.'

'Do you . . .' Finn cleared his throat, 'do you know how I escaped? I hid in the forest, climbed a tree. I watched the few men brave enough to fight the raiders die. I smelled the smoke as they burned down our homes. I heard them laugh.'

'You're not to blame,' Dion said softly.

'Then who is?'

'Mercilles. Did you know he was Jax's father?' Dion shook his head. 'When someone hates when they should love, it's the worst hate of all.'

'I knew,' Finn said. 'I'm one of the few who did.' He lifted his head as he met Dion's eyes. 'I'm glad he told you. It means he liked you . . . trusted you.'

'He was a good man.'

'The very best.' There was silence for a time and then Finn spoke in a stronger voice. 'So you think we still have a future? What will we do for homes? It took us a long time to build this place. And we might still have ships, but there aren't enough to start raiding again. Everyone's scared. The people left behind would be defenseless.'

Dion had been thinking on this very topic. 'I have an idea . . .'

'So you'll be standing then?' Finn's lips suddenly parted in a smile. 'Please tell me you will be. If I have to take Reece's orders I'll throw myself off this cliff.'

'Standing?'

'To become the leader of the Free Men. Marmat's content as captain of the *Sea Witch*, and he's too old to lead anyway.' He snorted. 'They'd never follow me.'

Dion opened his mouth to reply when he heard a rough voice call out his name. He and Finn both turned and saw Cob approaching.

'Come on,' the old man said. 'It's time to bid Jax farewell.'

———

Every one of the Free Men stood on the beach, arrayed in an arc around an old boat stacked high with wood. Hundreds of former slaves, retired soldiers, dispossessed farmers, petty criminals, and common people looking for a better life stood sober-faced and red-eyed. The smell of char still hung in the air. The final fire would soon be lit.

Jax lay composed on top of the pyre, facing the sky, rakish cap clutched to his breast. His handsome face, framed by the long scar stretching from his forehead to his chin, appeared peaceful. Dion remembered his last conversation with the pirate king, wishing he'd told him more. The Free Men had pledged to take in any man or woman despite their differences. Something told him Jax wouldn't have cared even if he'd revealed his eldran heritage.

The priest, Paolus, had survived by hiding with his wine in the cellar beneath the temple, which, although blackened, was one of the few structures still standing. He said some words about Jax's dedication to their cause, and his veneration for the articles of agreement carved into the wall of the temple. He asked Silex to look after their leader's soul, and then he took a flaming torch from Cob and walked down to the boat. Lighting the tinder, he gave the boat a push.

They'd chosen the moment so that the tide would drag the vessel out to sea. As the flames caught and red spears flickered between the bigger logs, the boat drifted until smoke was pouring from the pyre, rising in a steady stream to cloud the sky. Passing the twin arms enfolding the small cove in their embrace, the boat continued to travel into the region of deep blue water. Finally it rounded a headland and was gone from sight.

Dion glanced at Reece, surprised when he saw the stocky sailor already staring at him with a dark gaze. Tearing his eyes away, Dion scanned the assembled men and women and saw many of them returning his look.

When the priest walked away, leaving a void in the middle of the arc of people, Reece stepped forward.

'As Jax's second-in-command, I am now leader,' Reece said, folding his arms over his chest as he stood with legs apart and glared at every face in the crowd. 'You all know me. I've been part of this group since the beginning. I'm here to tell you that there are going to be some changes in our organization.'

He scowled as he lifted his chin.

'Having to vote on every small decision made us weak. We'll still divide booty according to the articles, but we've been too preoccupied with freeing slaves and leaving the weaker traders alone. The reason Jax lies dead now is his feud with Mercilles of Koulis. But the feud was foolish. Attacking the strongest merchants, biting the hide of a bigger beast, makes us exposed to retribution.' His face became grim. 'As you've all seen for yourselves.'

Without thinking about what he was doing, Dion was suddenly moving. He walked forward until he stood a stone's throw from Reece and turned to face the group. He felt the pressure of their eyes on him as he spoke.

'Jax believed in the articles – all of them – with his heart and soul,' Dion said, speaking loudly and clearly. 'He believed in liberty and equality, with every man and woman having a place according to his or her skills and merits. It's not my place to say who is chosen as Jax's successor, but I made my mark on that wall'—he pointed at the temple—'just like all of you. You think we're powerless to repay Mercilles for what he did here? I disagree. You think it's wrong to put out the call of liberty, to be a refuge for anyone persecuted in his homeland, for any slave who wants to be free? I disagree. If we want to grow and be strong, we have to stay true to the articles. If we want our numbers to increase, we must continue to be a beacon of hope. And more than anything . . .' He raised his voice. 'We need revenge!'

A roar of approval came from the crowd.

'You think he can lead us?' Reece spat on the ground. He raised his arm and pointed at Dion. 'Listen to his speech. He can read and write. He's a nobleman! He probably grew up with slaves at his beck and call. He no doubt lost his inheritance and decided he could find a new people to rule.'

'Jax was a nobleman.' Finn spoke up from the crowd. Instantly every set of eyes was on him. 'But he kept to the articles . . . He wrote them, for Silex's sake.'

'So,' Reece growled. 'You show your true colors.'

Finn shrugged. 'I just don't think you're the best man to lead us.'

As the clamor of voices threatened to break into chaos, Dion raised his arms and called out. 'I'm not saying I should rule. I'm saying there should be a vote. And I, for one, nominate Cob.' He nodded at the bald old man, standing at the edge of the circle.

Cob smiled and shook his head. 'Thank you, lad. But no.' He raised his voice. 'It should be Andion. He's the best captain in our number. And . . .'

The rest of Cob's speech was drowned out by the cheer that met his words. Looking to the red-nosed priest, Dion saw Paolus give him a nod.

But then Reece's stentorian voice overwhelmed even the crowd. 'I invoke article seven of the charter!' he cried. 'When there's a dispute that can't be resolved any other way.' He drew the dagger at his waist, the same blade that had killed Fatima, and leveled it at Dion. 'It must be resolved by combat.'

A mighty roar came from the Free Men and they immediately shifted as those at the back tried to get a better view. The arc became a wide circle with Dion and Reece at the center as Reece tore off his shirt and threw it to the ground, revealing a thick torso covered in scars.

Dion looked wildly around for a weapon. He felt dread sink into his stomach. He was a skilled archer but he'd never been able to master the art of melee combat. He'd taken lessons, and he knew the moves, but aside from the sole occasion that he'd carried a spear at the Battle of Phalesia, he'd never killed a man with a physical blow.

And he'd never fought like this.

Reece now faced him and weaved in a fighting stance on the sand as he waited for Dion to take a weapon. Dozens of men in the circle called out to offer swords and daggers, iron clubs, and even harpoons. Dion shook his head, knowing that he couldn't fight with metal. He faced Reece but stepped back, keeping distance between them, feeling his heart hammer in his chest as he knew he was going to die.

Then Cob came through for him.

The old man weaved his way through the crowd until he came to someone he knew, a dark-skinned pirate with a strip of cloth tied around his forehead and an axe held high above his head. The pirate readily gave Cob his weapon and the old man called out.

'Dion!'

Cob tossed the weapon and it fell down in the sand at Dion's feet. He saw that it was an obsidian axe, with a wooden haft as long as his arm and as thick as his wrist. The head was as glossy as the ocean at night, a heavy quarter-circle slotted tightly into a carved depression, bound solidly to the wood with gut. The volcanic stone it was made from was rare and could cut more sharply than steel. There was no metal in the weapon at all.

As soon as Dion lifted it, Reece attacked.

The stocky man came in, weaving and dodging, presenting a difficult target to follow. He held the long dagger out at the level of his waist as he thrust toward Dion's chest.

Dion lunged to the side and Reece's blow met empty air. The crowd roared. Dion then hefted the axe and turned to face the bigger man, who snarled at him as his feet shifted on the sand.

The next time Reece attacked, he slashed at Dion's face. Dion leaned back as the sharp steel whistled in front of his nose. Holding the axe with both hands, he then lifted the haft to smash into his opponent's arm from below. Reece winced but managed to keep hold of his weapon. Dion then swung at Reece's head, but the experienced fighter easily evaded the blow.

Panting, the two men circled each other as the onlookers bayed for blood. Reece's eyes glared murderously. He cut the air with his dagger and smiled.

Reece's next lunge barely missed as Dion dodged to the side, the dagger skewering the air where he'd been only a moment before. As he moved Dion brought his axe to bear, swinging it down, but his position was awkward and he only pushed the dagger away with the obsidian head's blunt edge. With watching men all around, Dion and Reece again faced off. The stocky man shuffled his feet from side to side, looking for an opportunity. Dion held his axe with two hands, one high and one low.

Around them the onlookers howled, but Dion forced himself to ignore them and instead concentrated on the fight for his life. The words of his older brother long ago told him that combat was about keeping pressure on an opponent. Dion was the slighter man, but his weapon had longer reach.

As he wondered what move he should attempt, it was Reece who attacked first.

Reece brought his weapon down from overhead as he came forward, slashing in a sweeping diagonal motion. Dion jumped back, nearly tripping over a depression in the sand. Reece grew confident, but when he came in again, this time Dion stepped forward.

He removed his right hand from the top of the axe and held it by the base alone. He then used the axe to block the dagger and had an advantage, for the haft of the axe was thick while the dagger was light and he barely registered the connection. As Dion punched with his right fist at full extension, his shoulders twisted as he put force into the blow.

He struck Reece squarely in the jaw, but the stocky man was tough. He grunted and shook his head from side to side. Dion was overextended, with his weapon in the air and his right arm outstretched. Reece pushed forward, using his superior mass to put Dion onto his back foot. The dagger inched forward as he shoved, despite Dion's attempts to hold him back. Dion felt a sharp pain in his side as the dagger made contact. He gasped with pain and the onlookers cried out at the first sight of blood. But then Dion punched Reece in the face again, feeling his fist crunch against his opponent's nose. Reece howled and pulled away.

Finally the two men ended up facing each other once again, both breathing heavily. The onlookers were screaming and roaring.

Reece spat a tooth on the ground, spattering blood just near Dion's feet. 'You're weak. They'll never follow a man who can't fight.'

Dion now held his axe in his right hand, halfway up, where he could grab the bottom of the haft with his left if he needed to. He realized that the watching men had gone silent, waiting to hear what he had to say. Dion pointed with his weapon.

'I can fight,' he said. He smiled. 'You don't know the half of it.'

As Dion said the last words he shot forward. Reece's dagger came at him but Dion spun around the thrust and somehow he knew exactly where to be. He took the axe in both hands and struck hard, in a savage but swift blow.

Dion felt contact as the blade of the axe hit his opponent's lower abdomen. Reece screamed in pain as he struck. Blood shot out in a spray.

Dion completed his turn and saw Reece crumple to the ground. Gathering himself, Dion gasped and realized how much energy the fight was taking out of him.

'Are we finished?' Dion said.

Reece was on one knee, but when he looked up, all Dion could see was hate and rage. Reece would rather die than lose in front of the men.

The onlookers bayed like wolves howling for blood as Reece slowly rose to his feet, standing shirtless, with the blood on his body dripping down, tainting his trousers.

Then Dion looked down at himself.

In the heat of battle he'd forgotten the wound in his side, but now saw a growing stream of bright blood. He put his hand to the wound, relieved to find that it was shallow, but the pain was steadily growing.

Reece came in with a roar, dagger raised above his head. Dion prepared to lift his weapon but his opponent changed his attack at the last moment, cutting low. With Dion's stomach sucked in, the blow missed narrowly, but he suddenly felt Reece's free hand grip hold of the axe handle and the stocky man grunted as he yanked hard.

Dion tried to keep hold of his weapon but the axe fell out of his hands and he tripped backward onto the sand. The ground came up to meet him as he struck hard. Now unarmed, Dion was suddenly helpless and on his back.

Reece loomed over him, axe held in one hand and dagger in the other.

Dion's heart pounded in his chest as he saw the axe raised above his enemy's head in the blow that would end his life. Sweat trickled down Reece's brow, coating his face, which was curled into a snarl. Blood reddened his lips.

Unarmed and on his back, Dion's chest heaved, his eyes wild and staring as his breath ran ragged. The onlookers roared at him. He heard voices cry out for him to do something.

Then something inside him snapped.

Dion roared like he'd never roared before as he climbed to his feet, and suddenly Reece's head was far below him, staring up at him with an expression of utter horror. Straightening, Dion glared down at the man whose weapons now appeared puny, incapable of harming him no matter what he did.

Filled with sudden strength, he formed his right hand into a fist, feeling the might in his arms, matching the wild sensation of primal rage that banished all other thoughts from his mind. Reece lifted his weapons but Dion swatted them aside, brushing them away like irritating thorns. His fist struck his enemy squarely in the head, and then a second blow crushed his face into pulp. Dion's mouth opened and he roared in triumph as Reece crumpled, dead before he hit the ground.

What is happening to me?

Dion shook his head from side to side. He whirled to face the crowd of onlookers, stunned into silence. A short old man was calling out a name. It was his name.

Forcibly taking hold of himself, looking at the tiny pummeled corpse on the ground far below, he felt an odd sense of falling, accompanied by a strange . . . changing.

Suddenly Dion was lying on the sand. He realized that he had his eyes closed and opened them, slowly sitting up. He looked at his hands, seeing fingers, normal, human fingers.

He climbed unsteadily to his feet and looked around him.

He was standing in a circle of people. Every gaze was on him, every face looking at him in awe. Reece's broken body was nearby, crushed by the giant with the force of mountains in his arms.

Moving into a stumbling run, Dion pushed his way free of the circle as the crowd made way for him. He didn't look back.

⁓

'Dion.'

He heard a gravelly voice and turned to see both Cob and Finn approaching.

'What is it?' Dion said, standing at the end of the beach and staring at the curling waves. Nearby was the crippled bireme, far enough from the settlement to escape the burning. Dion sighed and didn't look up to meet the old man's eyes.

'The vote is in. You're the new king of the Free Men.'

Dion glanced up. 'What did you just say?'

'It's you. You're our new leader.'

'But they saw . . .'

'Yes, they did.' Cob grinned. 'And now they'll follow you farther than the edge of the world. By Silex, you were terrifying.'

'Shouldn't you have silver hair?' Finn asked, his face curious more than anything else. He turned to Cob. 'That's right, isn't it? Eldren have silver hair?'

'He's only half eldran,' Cob said.

'The half-eldran king of the Free Men,' Finn said, his eyes lighting up with inner fire. 'What a tale! We'll be famous throughout the Maltherean and beyond!'

'You speak the truth?' Dion asked Cob.

'Aye, lad. They're afraid, all of them,' he clapped Dion on the shoulder, 'but with you to lead them . . . They don't have to be.'

'You'll do it?' Finn asked.

Dion was pensive for a time. He needed to prove both to himself and to Nikolas that people would accept him for who he was. As the leader of the Free Men, he would have his chance.

He lifted his chin. 'I will.'

Finn whooped. 'We have a new king!' he cried.

Leaving Dion and Cob behind, he shouted as he ran back toward the crowd on the beach.

'We have a new king! Andion, the king of the Silver Road!'

46

Chloe concentrated. *No fear.* She focused on the single thought. *No fear.*

'Chloe!' Liana's voice called from inside the villa. 'I have the fire going. You're not still there, are you?'

Chloe sat on a stone bench that framed the gardens, near the wide basin filled with water. It was close to dark and she'd been sitting in the same position all afternoon, staring at the heavy iron pot in her hands, half filled with water. Her brow was furrowed.

She had needed to have a break from practicing with copper after the buzzing in her ears became too loud to bear. She'd also had no luck with the golden bracelet; try as she might she couldn't get it to glow a second time. The old magus had said that different sorcerers had affinities with different materia but she hadn't been able to find any silver. Nonetheless, the power still raged inside her, pushing at her will like a dam threatening to burst. She summoned her courage and decided to try iron.

There was a codex in the villa's small library devoted entirely to the mastery of iron. Most of the text was incomprehensible, but there were a few exercises she could try and this was one of them. Control of iron was completely unlike copper. Rather than thoughts of beauty and harmony, and concentration on a sweet, pure note, Chloe instead tried to put herself into the mindset of a warrior.

She thought of enemies she'd faced in the past: Solon, who had tortured and impaled her loyal bodyguard Tomarys, and the tattooed tribesmen who had hunted her and Liana in the plains. She remembered Triton's sneering look as he'd prepared to kill her at the Temple of Aldus, and the savage wildren she'd encountered at Cinder Fen. She knew she was scowling down at the iron pot as she summoned hatred beyond what she normally allowed herself to bear. But it wasn't the desire for violence that would make the iron respond; she also needed feelings of strength and courage. She needed to think of warlike images: swords and spears, and helmeted soldiers like the men of Nikolas's king's guard who had murdered her father's allies among the consuls. Above all else, she couldn't feel any fear.

The iron pot began to grow warm.

No fear, she told herself. *Be brave. Be strong.*

The heat increased, but it was projected out of her hands, and provided she controlled her power she would be unharmed. Steam began to rise from the water as she concentrated still harder.

As she maintained contact between her skin and the iron, the warmth in her hands grew and the first bubble appeared in the water. Her apprehension rose with the knowledge that with nothing more than her hands she was causing the water to grow hot enough to boil. Her hands suddenly felt burning hot until she stamped down on the fear.

No fear. She repeated the mantra. *No fear.*

Chloe felt sudden weariness descend on her, threatening to break her concentration. The crushing fatigue seemed to grow no matter which metal she was working with. She now had to combat both her own trepidation and the fatigue that dragged at her eyelids and made her shoulders slump.

But at the same time she felt intense relief as the power within her was released through the palms of her hands.

The water began to hiss and then bubble.

'What are you doing?' Liana gasped. 'That looks dangerous.'

Distracted by the eldran, Chloe saw Liana keeping her distance, wide eyes on the iron pot. Liana put her hand to her chest and grimaced as if in pain. She took three steps back.

Chloe forced herself to concentrate again on the iron pot, even as she felt her own fear rise, mirroring her friend's. The heat in her hands grew rapidly, increasing her fear still further. The pain fueled the panic, and as her courage failed her the fire in her palms became agonizing.

The iron suddenly grew blisteringly hot.

Chloe's palms sizzled against the pot's surface and she cried out in pain. She recoiled and threw the vessel forward, splashing hot water everywhere as the heavy metal clattered to the ground.

Her eyes closed and she crumpled.

———

What you are doing is more dangerous than you realize.

The voice was soft and sibilant, undoubtedly female.

Stop before you kill yourself. For now you must live with the fire inside you.

Have patience.

The woman's hiss was vaguely familiar.

I will send for you.

———

Chloe opened her eyes. The voice was still in her ears; her dreams had been strange. She was lying on her bed and staring at the ceiling.

She felt pain in her palms and lifted her hands to examine them, seeing that the skin was bright red but fortunately wouldn't blister.

Leaving the bedchamber, she found Liana sitting on one of the high-backed chairs close to the hearth. The eldran had her satchel on her lap and was looking at something inside. As soon as she saw Chloe, Liana swiftly closed the satchel and bundled it in her lap.

'Are you all right?' Liana's face was worried.

'I'm fine.' Chloe hesitated, and then put a hand on her friend's shoulder. 'Thank you.'

'I know you said the power causes you pain, but surely there is another way.'

'I'm trying to learn.'

'If you don't control it, you say you could die. But from what I can see, even using it can still kill you.'

Chloe wished she didn't agree with her. 'The iron pot. Where is it?'

'Where you left it.'

Leaving Liana behind, Chloe exited the villa. She found the iron pot lying upended near a damp patch in the stone. Crouching and picking it up, she turned it over in her hands. Her eyes widened.

The bottom was rusted through, even to the point of flaking away under her touch. A chunk broke off when she pulled at it.

She shook her head. Vikram was dead. There was no one else who could teach her.

She went back inside to study further.

47

High on a hill overlooking the wide harbor of Koulis, a manse of three levels stood proud and lofty. Gardens of thorny plants and palm trees surrounded it on all sides, giving it a wide buffer of privacy from any of the smaller villas nearby. A tall stone wall surrounded the grounds, crowned at regular intervals with sharpened wooden spikes. It was the dead of night and the manse was dark, still, and silent.

Only a keen eye would have seen the men in black clothing creeping up to the exterior of the wall and tossing a looped rope over a handful of the spikes. After fastening the other end around the broad trunk of a tree, the most slender of them, his face darkened with soot, now climbed up the tightened rope, moving like a trained acrobat. He carried a thick carpet with him.

Reaching the wall's summit, he struggled with the heavy material as he draped the carpet over a section of the spikes. Watched by his companions at the wall's base, he finally finished his covering and nodded to the men below. He then climbed over, falling gracefully to the ground on the wall's other side.

One after another, the men in black climbed up the rope and over the wall, with those already over bracing the falls of the next to come.

Everything was done in silence.

Soon over thirty pirates had made it across, and they now looked to a man in the center for orders. His face was blackened and his flaxen hair was dyed with soot. He wore a loose black tunic and like all of them his feet were bare. He was the only man among them carrying a bow.

'Wait here,' the leader said.

He took an arrow from the quiver on his shoulder and fitted it to the string. He left on his own while the rest of the group stood tense, waiting for a cry to split the night. Time passed, the tension growing before the bowman returned, and then he nodded to his men.

'That's all of them. I've cleared the grounds but there will be more guards inside. Ready your weapons.'

As soon as Dion finished speaking, sliding steel and jangling metal filled the air until every man in the group soon stood with eyes gleaming, brandishing axes and swords, clubs and daggers. There was no way to quiet the noise. A dog started barking somewhere and as he glanced at the manse's second level, Dion saw movement at a window.

'We need to surround the place,' he said. 'We can't let him flee.' He tapped men on the shoulders. 'Head off any escape. The rest of you, follow me!'

Dion almost groaned aloud when the pirates cheered, unable to help themselves. Scanning the area and seeing a path winding through the gardens, leading to a doorway in the manse's lowest level, he waved for his men to follow.

Two of the biggest pirates pushed past him as they charged the heavy wooden doors with their shoulders. The crash as the two men burst into the interior was the loudest noise so far; suddenly more than one dog was barking and loud voices called inside.

A uniformed guard ran forward and shoved his sword into the foremost pirate's chest, withdrawing his weapon as the man crumpled and then hacking at the next intruder. Dion's arrow took him through the throat. Another guard popped out of an interior doorway and behind him still more kept coming. Reaching for another arrow Dion cursed as he saw that too many of his men were now running into the manse for him to fire.

But these were the Free Men, and if there was one thing they were good at, it was fighting.

He saw Cob crack the head of his steel axe into a guard's jaw and another pirate thrust his sword into a soldier's abdomen. The clang of steel against steel was so loud it made Dion wince. Cries of pain and grunts of released energy accompanied each blow as over twenty men poured into the manse's interior.

Dion looked for Finn and saw him in the distance, back in the gardens, tossing a coiled rope to an upper balcony. The rope went around a support and the end fell down from the other side. Finn saw him and waved, eyes shining with excitement as he began to fasten the rope to form a climbing line to the second storey.

'I thought you said you were no pirate,' Dion said as he joined him, helping him tie the rope around the trunk of a gnarled olive tree.

'I said I was no sailor,' Finn said with a smile and a final tug on the rope. 'This is exactly my kind of caper. Want to go up first?'

'After you.'

Finn nodded and pulled himself up, shimmying along the angled rope with ankles crossed. Dion swallowed when he saw how high he was getting and hoped his courage wouldn't fail him when he made his own climb. Soon Finn was clambering over the balcony rail and drawing his stiletto as he gestured for Dion to follow.

But without waiting further, Finn then pulled the curtains apart and entered.

Cursing, Dion wrapped his fingers around the rope as high as he could and took a deep breath. Before he could think about what he was doing, he pulled and shuffled his arms still higher as his ankles wrapped around the rope lower down. Grunting and panting, moving with a series of pulls, kicks, and gasps, he kept his eyes on his destination and tried not to think too hard about the drop. When he reached the rail and awkwardly pulled himself up and over, he heard voices.

Knowing Finn might need him, Dion pulled aside the thick curtain of glossy silk to enter an opulent bedchamber.

He found himself in a room so large that it occupied the manse's entire top level. Carpet after thick carpet lined the floor, the patterns barely distinguishable in the low light. The center was kept bare but items of furniture lined both sides: shelves filled with decorative baubles; stands displaying golden plates and vases; two silver mirrors; and bowls on benches, with each bowl containing ripe fruit. An immense bed draped in white cloth dominated the far end.

A gaping stairwell of marble steps led down to the lower levels, and it was there that Dion saw Finn.

Ignoring the shouts and clashes of arms downstairs, Dion walked forward to join him. Finn was crouched by the prone form of a grimacing man in a silk sleeping robe, holding his face pressed down against the floor. Finn had tripped him just as he'd been about to dash down the stairs.

'Look who we have here,' Finn said. 'It appears our friend was about to make his escape.' He grinned as he pushed down harder on his captive's head. 'Or at least try. I'm sure one of our men would have caught him.'

Dion examined the man's features in the low light. He had a hooked nose and a gold ring in his flaring nostril. Jax's nose had been sharper, more angular, but the hair and eye color were the same; the resemblance was unmistakable.

'Lord Mercilles, I presume?' Dion asked as he crouched.

'You want gold?' Mercilles glared back at him. 'You won't have it, not unless you want to raid every moneylender in the city.'

'We don't want gold,' Dion said. He glanced at Finn as his companion put the point of his stiletto under Mercilles' chin. 'What we plan on taking is far more valuable.' He smiled. 'We're going to seize your ships. No, not your merchant vessels, your warships. At this very moment my men are at your docks, seizing your four biremes and waiting for our arrival.'

'Then what do you want with me?' Mercilles snarled. 'My son is dead. Killing me won't bring him back.'

'We want vengeance,' Finn said.

Dion straightened and scanned the room. On a nearby table, he saw a wineskin and recognized the sigil of Stavros, the best winemaker in Sarsica. He strode over and picked up the skin, shrugging when Finn raised an eyebrow.

'For the priest,' Dion said. He nodded at the stairwell. 'Should we get going?'

'I'll join you in a moment,' Finn said. His face was grim as he glanced up. 'Did Jax tell you how he got that scar on his face?'

Dion shook his head.

'Leave me here for a bit. I want to take my time sending Lord Mercilles on his way to hell.'

48

Not far from the great city of Lamara, on the banks of the wide brown river, a secret gathering took place. The sun was low in the sky, casting a crimson glow over the yellow terrain as close to a thousand people milled near a natural rise where a platform had been hastily erected.

In the week since Aristocles had freed Kargan and they'd made the swift journey to Ilean lands, they'd been busy, and every member of the gathering had been carefully selected. The sailors, marines, and laborers who were Kargan's first followers had entered the city and spoken with representatives from the army and the navy, as well as leading craftsmen and even the priests that they knew were friends. These key figures were taking a risk by attending, but for this first assembly Mydas was unaware of Kargan's plans. That would soon change.

'If Mydas was after my head before, he's now going to want me tortured for a year,' Kargan said. He scowled at Aristocles. 'In the name of Helios, why are you so concerned with my appearance?'

Aristocles stood back and looked at him from head to toe before nodding. 'That will do.'

Kargan glanced down at himself. He wore one of the bright orange robes he was known for, tied around his thick waist with a yellow cord. 'The colors of Ilea I can understand, but should I not look more kingly?'

Aristocles smiled and shook his head. 'You have to trust me. At this gathering you want to contrast yourself with Mydas. I know what I am doing. This is how you become king of kings, and rule the Ilean Empire.'

'Then you and I bring about peace between Ilea and Phalesia. I remember.'

'Just give the speech exactly as I've told you.' Aristocles' gaze turned to the milling crowd, waiting uncertainly for Kargan to climb to the podium. 'It's time.'

Kargan took a steadying breath as he scanned their worried faces; he'd addressed entire armies but now he was suddenly nervous. They all had grievances: the empire was crumbling around them; Mydas had melted the gold from Solon's pyramid but rather than constructing improvements or equipping more soldiers he was using it to decorate his palace; and the weakened Ilean fleet was being readied for another assault far across the sea. In many ways these were the same complaints the middle ranks had always had; problems that were ignored by the king of kings, suppressed by force if necessary. But Aristocles had said that listening to their demands and promising change would give Kargan power. He already had the support of the navy, and likely the army as well; now it just remained to win over the common people.

'They'll carry stories to their friends and colleagues,' Aristocles said. 'Make this count.'

Kargan strode up to the platform and climbed on with Amos's help, the weathered Phalesian trying to hide his aversion to helping a man who'd so recently been his enemy. Ignoring him, Kargan raised his clenched fist as he strode to the center of the podium and a ragged cheer went through the crowd, while most of them continued to look worried.

Suddenly Kargan's anxiety melted away. He was a leader of men. He was committed. He was destined to become the king of kings. And he knew he could do it better than Solon's gold-loving brother.

He gave the speech that Aristocles had prepared for him, his parade-ground voice booming over the members of the gathering. He reminded them that he'd helped Solon form the Ilean Empire, and been pivotal to conquering the cities of Efu, Verai, and Malakai. He told the tale of his naval blockade of the Shadrian passage, holding out against sortie after sortie from Shadria's allies as they tried to come to their neighbor's aid. He disclaimed responsibility for the defeat at Phalesia, explaining that the sun king wouldn't listen to his advice, and the nods of the sailors and soldiers among them told the civilians that his words were true.

He spoke of Mydas's sacrilege in removing the gold from the pyramid that Helios had decreed, and his greed in using the gold to fill his fat belly and decorate his bedchamber. He said that Solon's three sons had been kind-hearted, generous men, and that anyone with friends among the palace guards could find out for himself that Mydas had murdered the three heirs who stood in his way while they slept in their beds – and were under Mydas's protection.

With passion he scorned Mydas's failure to hold the empire together, evidenced by the unchallenged secession of Koulis and the open rebellion in Shadria.

'Ilea needs change,' Kargan said. 'Not just a change in govern-ance, but a change in the system of governance. Every man should have a say, and vote on matters of importance. We should elect consuls who are accountable for their actions, and the king should be accountable to his consuls.' He knew Javid would be loving every word of this foolishness, but he kept his voice sincere. 'I don't want to be a king. I only want what is fair for Ilea. I am no noble. I am a military man, a man of action.' He had balked at this: he was, in fact, a minor noble, but Aristocles had insisted on the wording. 'I only want what is best for all of you. To institute the change we need, I have a *plan*'—Kargan emphasized the word—'and you have a part to play—'

He broke off.

At the very moment that he'd mentioned a plan, a huge warrior wrapped from head to toe in white cloth with a wicked curved sword in his hand appeared from where he'd been hiding in the crowd. Shoving aside laborers, priests, craftsmen, and swarthy soldiers, waving his sword above his head, he ran directly for the platform and threw himself up without pausing.

Kargan stood frozen with shock. He was unarmed, wearing civilian clothing. But then his brow furrowed. As the swordsman swung clumsily at his head he ducked under the blow and struck his assailant in the chest with a clenched fist, followed by a powerful uppercut to his intended assassin's jaw.

The huge man's eyes rolled back into his head and he fell to one knee. The stunned people in the crowd looked on in shock as Amos then climbed up to the platform and ran the assassin through. They exchanged glances as voices began to fill the air with muttering.

Kargan stood tall and glared out into the crowd. 'Anyone else?' He pounded onto his broad chest. 'Is that the best you can do, Mydas?'

The sailors from Koulis scattered through the crowd began to chant his name. The murmur became a rumble, and then a roar. Kargan raised his arms above his head as he left the platform.

⌣

'Well?' Kargan asked Aristocles, striding over after everyone in the crowd who wanted to speak with him had finally departed. 'How did it go?'

'Perfect,' Aristocles said with a smile. The Phalesian was in his element. 'Couldn't have gone better.'

Kargan scowled as he looked over at Javid, now stripped of his white cloth. 'Are all these theatrics truly necessary?'

'Trust me. Stories are more powerful if they end in a fight. To them, it will be as if Mydas himself confronted you and you knocked him down. The poets and singers will tell your tale in Lamara.'

'What about when Mydas actually does hear about what we're doing?'

'He will react. For now it's best that we keep our ears to the ground and keep moving. For a time, we'll let the people do your work for you. Even Mydas has a part to play, unwittingly perhaps, but important nonetheless.'

'Eh?'

'You will see, Lord Kargan. You will see.'

49

With festivity and fanfare, the city of Koulis welcomed King Nikolas of Xanthos, who had crossed the Waste leading three armies and a great number of mercenaries.

The citizens scattered flowers in front of him as he entered the gates at the head of his Xanthian king's guard. They saw a burly black-haired warrior wearing a shining steel breastplate and leather skirt, with a helmet over his head that displayed a tall crest of crimson-dyed horsehair, matching the color of the billowing cloak on his back. At his waist was a broad-bladed sword with an iron hilt. A nose guard covered his face but couldn't hide his thick black beard and the intensity of his dark eyes.

Nikolas ignored the women calling out his name from the crowd lining both sides of the broad avenue that was the city's main thoroughfare. Men cheered and pointed him out to their sons as they lifted them high in their arms. He hadn't come for adulation; he was here for war.

'The lyceum is in the middle of our agora,' the lanky man in the yellow toga at his side said, skipping to keep up with his long strides. 'The four other representatives await your arrival. Lord Lothar is anxious to meet you.'

Nikolas glanced at his escort and saw a weak man with soft hands and jewels on his fingers. He was a member of the Council of Five, but Nikolas couldn't remember whether he represented trade, defense, agriculture, or water supply. The man reminded him of the consuls in Phalesia, someone who spent his time talking rather than taking necessary action, who expected others to fight his battles for him. He gave the orders, but he would never risk his own life on the field.

The lord licked his lips when Nikolas remained stone-faced. 'Tonight there will be a feast. We will host you in—'

'I didn't come for feasts,' Nikolas said shortly. He saw that they were approaching the harbor, where tall surrounding hills sloped down to the water, dotted with the villas of the wealthy. The buildings on both sides opened up in an agora, nearly as large as the Phalesian agora but unpaved, with market stalls framing the edges and a grove of trees in the center.

'Of course,' the lord said. 'Please, King Nikolas, this way.'

Formed up behind Nikolas, the helmeted soldiers of the king's guard marched in unison, their heavy steps resounding through the city. There were only fifty of them but they were Xanthos's best, which made them the finest warriors on the Maltherean. He'd left four thousand men outside the city but the Council of Five already knew the number he commanded. He wanted them to see for themselves that the men of Xanthos, followers of the war god Balal, formed the core of his army and were men who would never break.

Nikolas saw a file of Koulisian guards standing motionless with spears erect outside the grove's entrance and quickened his pace without realizing, cursing under his breath at the lord from Koulis as he was forced to slow – it wouldn't be right to enter the lyceum with just four of the five members seated.

When he was a stone's throw from the file of guards, Nikolas barked an order. 'Halt!'

Showing fearsome discipline, the Xanthian king's guard took one more step and then came to a complete standstill. Nikolas raised an eyebrow at the lord.

'Er, yes,' the lanky man in the yellow toga said. 'Please, follow me.'

Confidently leaving his retinue behind, Nikolas entered side by side with the lord. As soon as he passed the first guard, the man's spear went up as he held the point high, followed by the next in line, their movements keeping abreast with his long strides.

He shook his head, wondering if this was supposed to impress him. Their movements were sloppy; even the boys at the training ground in Xanthos could manage better precision. He even saw rust on the head of a spear and almost stopped to berate the guard who held it before remembering where he was.

'King?'

Nikolas realized he was scowling and smoothed his expression as he passed the guards and came to a tree-lined pathway. Ahead he could see a circular structure made of stone, raised like a dais and covered in a peaked roof.

'Please, enter first, King Nikolas. I will follow behind.' The lord bowed.

Nikolas gave a short nod and climbed the steps. He approached a row of five high-backed chairs and saw a sixth chair placed in the center of the structure to face the others. His escort scurried up the steps and took his place as Nikolas glanced at the chair, evidently for himself, and then looked at the skeletal silver-haired old man with the white tunic and heavy medallion dedicated to the god of fortune around his neck. Nikolas didn't bother examining the other lords; they were unimportant.

'King Nikolas of Xanthos, the Council of Five bids you welcome. Please.' Lothar indicated the seat. Nikolas noted that his and Lothar's chairs were of equal size and height.

'I am a warrior,' Nikolas said, his words contrasting him with the wizened lord in front of him. 'I prefer to stand.'

'As you wish,' Lothar said.

Nikolas stood with legs apart and his fingers tucked into his belt. 'I hear you are a plainspoken man, Lord Lothar. So I will arrive straight at my purpose. I come to reform the Galean League. Recent events have pitted Ilea against Galea, and—'

'Yes,' Lothar interrupted, his curled fingers tapping on the arm of his chair. 'You have my sympathy for the loss of your family. A great tragedy.'

Nikolas frowned. 'I hear you have your own troubles,' he said. 'We all have our disputes with Ilea, and as brother Galeans it is time for us to band together, as we did long ago when we fought the barbarians of the north.'

'At that time, Koulis was little more than a trading outpost,' Lothar said with a slight smile.

'A Galean outpost.'

'But we are close to Ilea.'

'Geographically, yes. But culturally you are closer to us. Or'— Nikolas lowered his voice—'is that not the case?'

Lothar continued to rap his fingertips against the arm of his chair, silent for a time. 'War is bad for business,' he finally said.

Nikolas barked a laugh. 'You can't have it both ways.' His gaze swept the five lords in their entirety. 'None of you can. People value losses more than gains, and according to the rulers of Ilea, your city was a part of their empire and will be so again.'

He paused to let his words sink in.

'You want me to leave you be, while we go and fight Ilea on your behalf? You think you can sit back and ally yourself with the victor when it's all done? It is not going to happen. You have to make a choice. Either join with me and throw off the Ilean yoke'—he lifted his chin— 'or I will consider you an enemy and raze your city to the ground.'

He heard someone gasp, but kept his eyes on Lothar.

'Please, King Nikolas, your threats are not required. Let us negotiate.' Lothar spread his hands.

'No,' Nikolas said. 'I am no merchant. I seek no bargain. We go now to fight Mydas of Ilea, brother of Solon, and in the name of the Galean League, I ask that you join your forces with ours. Mydas makes no secret of his desire to punish us for his defeat at Phalesia and the death of his brother.' He smiled grimly. 'Just as I make no secret of the pleasure I felt at seeing Solon's body burn as his soul went to hell. This conflict won't end until I have Mydas's head.'

Lothar continued to tap the arm of his chair. Nikolas scowled; the sound was growing irritating. 'Let us say for a moment that we are able to capture Lamara – and I'm sure you are aware that Mydas can field an army far larger than yours – what then is your plan?'

Surprised by the question, Nikolas hesitated. 'We declare the Ilean Empire no more,' he said. 'We sign a peace. We appoint a new ruler in Lamara.'

One of the other lords spoke. 'It's clear to me that we need some time to plan—'

'No!' Nikolas glared at him. 'I am weak at sea. The more time that passes, the greater the danger at home.' He clenched his jaw tightly as he gazed directly into Lothar's eyes. 'We march to war. I await your response.'

Whirling, Nikolas stalked out.

50

The mob filled Lamara's largest square from wall to wall, surging back and forth, swelling in numbers as city folk poured in from every quarter. Impassioned men stood on crates and gave speeches to anyone who would listen. Women held hands and sang songs. Children crawled between legs and snatched purses from belts. Traffic everywhere came to a complete standstill.

A circular space in the center remained empty.

Soldiers with spears and triangular shields stood facing the crowd, ignoring the heckles as they pushed back anyone who tried to break through, indiscriminately breaking bones and bruising flesh in the process. Within the circle a raised platform was visible to all, and on the platform two trimmed logs had been crossed at angles and lashed together to form an 'X'.

'Stay hidden,' Aristocles murmured. 'Your face is known.'

Kargan glared at him. 'You think I'm stupid?'

It wasn't the first of these events to take place since Kargan's speech by the banks of the river, but it was the first he'd come to see for himself. He and Aristocles were somewhere in the middle of the mob, watching as Mydas's soldiers carried a lean man in rags up to the cross. His back was cut with red whip lines, bleeding and raw, but he was moving feebly. The soldiers handed him up to their companions on the platform. As he was dragged toward the cross, the lean man's wide eyes stared back at the faces looking up at him.

The crowd surged again but Amos and Javid worked together to give Aristocles and Kargan a buffer, and there were few who would challenge the two warriors. The city folk cried out with one voice as they watched the soldiers at their grisly work.

'Look at him,' Kargan said. 'I'm surprised he's still moving.'

'He's a believer, dying for a cause,' Aristocles said. 'Mydas is acting just as I knew he would. Our histories say that the tyrant responded the same way in Phalesia.'

The soldiers proceeded to turn their captive upside down. With a pair of them at each limb, they held him to the cross as a burly bare-chested companion came forward with a mallet and a clutch of iron nails. The prisoner screamed as a nail pressed into his left ankle and the burly man began to efficiently pound the nail through bone and flesh to fasten it to the wood. The ragged captive's other ankle followed immediately after, and then his wrists, until he was stretched out on the cross with his head only a couple of feet above the platform. Facing the crowd, the prisoner screamed until his voice was hoarse, and then his face began to turn bright red.

Kargan glanced at Aristocles, gaining new respect for the Phalesian when he saw that he wasn't turning away: the consul wasn't squeamish. The soldiers descended the platform when they were done, and now the mob had nothing to look at but their compatriot being crucified.

Hanging upside down, the bleeding man's pain-filled gaze roved over the crowd. Kargan was surprised when the man opened his lungs and bellowed with surprising strength.

'Freedom for all!' His breath rasped as he drew in a second lungful of air. 'Leadership by the people!'

The mob roared out again. Women wailed and tore at their hair. Priests called out for Helios to take the brave man's soul into his embrace.

'These punishments will scare people away from our cause,' Kargan said.

Aristocles shook his head. 'Quite the opposite. His courage will inspire others.'

'Inspire? Who would want this fate?'

'We're managing to convince people that our cause is worth more than their own lives. That it is worth dying for. The idea will spread. Every time Mydas reacts in this way, it strengthens us.'

'Death to Mydas!' a youth nearby cried, his words met with a cheer.

Kargan faced Aristocles, deliberately turning away from watching the crucifixion. He reminded himself that the man's death wasn't his fault; he'd made his choice to give his life for the promise of democracy. 'What next?'

'Next we wait for a crisis. A crisis we can exploit.'

'More waiting? I want to do something,' Kargan said vehemently, pounding his fist into his palm. 'My supporters in the army and navy are ready.'

'In time, Lord Kargan. In time.'

'How do you know a crisis will come?'

Aristocles' lips parted in a smile. 'They always do.'

51

Eiric stirred the coals with a stick as the aroma of roasting rabbit filled the cave. He kept his ears open, his vision occasionally flicking to the cave's gaping mouth and the darkness of night beyond. In Cinder Fen there was always the chance that wildren would come to investigate the light or the smell. He needed to be wary.

But rather than rumbling ogres or the flutter of fury wings outside the entrance, he heard a groan from the deepest section of the cave. Straightening and stretching, he walked unhurriedly to the low-ceilinged rear, stepping lightly on the dirt floor.

Eiric crouched as he looked down at Jonas. 'Did you say something, traitor?'

Slumped on the ground, Jonas was embracing a stake, wrists and ankles bound with deer gut tied around the thick pole embedded in the dirt. The older eldran's face when he slowly raised his head was harrowed, with dark shadows around his gray eyes and lips dry as bone.

At first Eiric had needed to watch his prisoner constantly, worried that when Jonas recovered from his head wound he would change his shape. But in the time that had passed Eiric had given him no food or water, and when his enemy finally woke, he continued to watch, scratching at his sharp chin, and finally Eiric knew that Jonas no longer had the strength to alter his form. For the first time in an eternity Eiric was able to leave the cave, and when he returned, Jonas was still tied just where he'd left him.

Eiric now watched grimly as Jonas panted with short gasps, lean chest rising and falling. His parched lips moved, showing a swollen tongue as he met Eiric's eyes. He'd swallowed just one sip of water in the last two days. The smell of the rabbit grilling over the coals would torment him beyond belief.

Yet even so, when Jonas whispered something and Eiric leaned in close to hear what he was saying, he couldn't believe what he was hearing.

'You call this torture.'

'I don't have the stomach for more,' Eiric said. 'Just tell me where I can find Triton.'

'Water . . .' Jonas coughed. 'Water.'

Eiric glanced at the bulging water skin he'd left on the ground nearby. 'Answer my question.'

'Water . . .'

Shaking his head, Eiric straightened and left his captive behind, returning to the embers of the fire. He examined the rabbit, deciding that it was done. With deft movements he took the skewer that had both ends resting on upright rocks and lifted it away, setting it down on a flat stone. Leaning down to blow on the crispy meat, he slid out the skewer and juggled it in his hands as he returned to the back of the cave.

'My mother became wild and is now dead,' Eiric said, seating himself as he tore his first mouthful. 'My father, after killing her, vanished. You led Triton to our village. You turned your back on us and destroyed our homes. We trusted you. Why did you betray us?'

Jonas's eyelids fluttered. 'Lost my wife. My son . . .'

Setting down the half-eaten carcass, Eiric lifted the water skin at his feet, trickling liquid down his throat as he swallowed. 'And now you've visited your pain on me. What did Triton promise you? That the horn of Marrix would be able to bring your family back?'

'That's what . . . stories.'

'No. The stories say that when we fought the Aleutheans the horn would summon our people directly after battle, before they passed the point of no return.'

'Triton . . .'

'Triton lied to you.'

'Zachary lied . . .'

'And you took Triton's word for it?'

Jonas's eyelids closed.

'Tell me where I can find him and I will give you water and food. I'll loosen your bonds and do what I can for your wounds.'

Jonas's head slowly shook from side to side.

'Listen.' Eiric glanced at the half-eaten rabbit, telling himself that he couldn't yet give it to his prisoner. 'I take no pleasure in your pain. Please . . . Jonas, just tell me where I can find Triton.'

Jonas's eyes were closed, but his chest was still moving, and Eiric persisted.

'When I found you, you were returning from the west. What were you doing?'

'Spying . . . Questioned humans.'

'Why?'

'The horn . . . missing . . .'

Eiric's eyes widened. 'The horn is missing? Who has it?'

'We tortured humans . . . don't know . . .'

Feeling disgust at the things Jonas had done, Eiric leaned forward. 'Jonas. Who has the horn?'

Jonas shook his head slightly as his eyelids slowly opened. His gaze met Eiric's. 'Gone.'

'Where is Triton?' When there was no reply, Eiric lifted the skin but Jonas barely had the strength to swallow when he leaned over to trickle water over his dry lips. 'Where is he?'

'Plans . . . destroy wellspring.' Jonas slumped. 'Eldren with him . . . Afraid . . .'

'Where?'

'In the heart,' Jonas whispered.

'What is the heart?' Eiric's fists clenched in frustration.

'Center of Cinder Fen . . . pool . . . the wellspring. Source of power. Triton . . .' Jonas licked his lips. 'Strong . . . blood of Marrix . . . you won't . . . defeat him.'

'The war between eldren has to end,' Eiric said. 'Jonas?' He straightened as he lifted the skin once more. 'I'll give you more water now. Jonas? Lift your head.'

Jonas couldn't hear him. His breath no longer whispered; his chest no longer moved. He was dead.

52

Aristocles walked through the encampment, weaving around men sitting by fires and tents of all shapes and sizes. He saw soldiers sharpening swords and bowyers fashioning arrows. Cooks stirred huge iron pots and horses whinnied, tethered in long rows. An aura of readiness permeated the air.

'This is now a military camp,' Amos said beside him. 'We won't be able to keep moving as easily as we once did.'

'We'll have plenty of warning,' Aristocles said confidently. 'Our people in the city will send word long before anyone comes.'

The pair finally reached Kargan's tent, larger and grander than any other, crowning a hill apart from the others. Aristocles walked inside without announcing himself as Amos trailed behind him.

'So as soon as I give the word—' Kargan ceased speaking, looking up when the two men entered. He was seated on a stool, facing an olive-skinned officer in full uniform. 'We'll speak more on this later,' he instructed. 'Just be ready.'

'Lord Kargan,' the officer acknowledged as he bowed, glancing at Aristocles and Amos before departing through the tent's wide opening.

Armor hung from a stand and carpets and cushions covered the floor. Javid stood motionless against the wall, fingers in his belt, silent and watchful as ever.

'Who was that?' Aristocles demanded.

Kargan slowly stood, straightening until he was towering over him. 'It's none of your concern. Why are you here, Aristocles?'

'You've heard the news?'

'Of course. The Galean nations have united behind Nikolas and he's on his way to Ilea.'

Aristocles nodded, ignoring Kargan's glare as he rubbed his hands together. 'This is it.' He started to pace. 'The crisis we've been waiting for. We—'

'I know,' Kargan said, interrupting him. 'We're seizing the palace in two days.'

'Two days?' Aristocles stopped in his tracks. 'No.' He cut the air with his hand decisively. 'I need more time.'

'We're ready,' Kargan said. 'I'm tired of waiting.'

'You need to listen to me—'

'No.' Kargan set his jaw. 'I don't.' He sighed. 'Now is as good a time as any. The fact is, Aristocles, soon I will be the ruler of the Ilean Empire. I don't have to listen to a thing you say.'

Aristocles' eyes narrowed. 'You promised me ships and men . . .'

'I have bigger things on my mind than worrying about your fate. You don't appear to realize that Phalesia means nothing to me. I have to rescue the empire before it all falls apart. Also'—he frowned—'I don't want my men asking any more questions about the foreigner who dogs my footsteps.'

Kargan waited a moment for his words to sink in as he waved Javid forward. 'I could order you killed, and no one would stop me, but you've helped me and so I'm sending you home. You may not have the men you wanted but you have your peace treaty, and you have your life. Consider this a show of my gratitude.'

Aristocles stood transfixed; for a time he was speechless. But then he lifted his chin and his high forehead furrowed in a scowl. 'This isn't right.' He turned to his captain. 'Amos.'

Amos put his hand on his sword. At the same moment Javid reached into his vest, saying nothing, but causing the Phalesian warrior to freeze mid-movement.

'I wouldn't go up against Javid,' Kargan said. 'No matter how good your man is. Face it, Aristocles. You're going back to your homeland.'

'What about our peace treaty?' Aristocles was undeterred. 'Mydas still rules. How will I know you've succeeded?'

'You have my guarantee of success,' Kargan said, crossing his arms in front of his broad chest. 'There.'

'I have to—'

'Enough!' Kargan raised his voice. 'Your ship is waiting. You sail from Lamara first thing tomorrow morning. Javid will escort you both.'

'But—'

Kargan's voice cut through Aristocles' protestations.

'Listen, you fool. You may think you're informed, but there's something you're obviously not aware of. Mydas is leading the army against Nikolas and he's confident of victory. But more importantly for you, despite my efforts I'm too late, and he's also sent the fleet to attack Phalesia and Xanthos. Your ship travels alone . . . you can probably outrun them.' He emphasized his point by prodding Aristocles in the chest. 'Probably. If you're fortunate you can still be a savior to your people. I have my crisis. You have yours.'

Kargan jerked his chin at the tent's entrance.

'Now get out. I've got work to do, and you'd best be quick if you're going to get home in time. Watch out for pirates, the Maltherean is a dangerous place these days.'

53

Nilus was at his villa, discussing the state of Phalesia's silver mines with the two overseers seated across from him. They had to speak above the tapping of hammers and rough voices of workmen; Nilus was making improvements to his residence.

'First Consul,' the older of the two overseers said. 'I can see what you're getting at, and of course we all want increased production, but to meet your demands we'll need to employ slaves as well as convicts in the diggings. As you know there is a shortage of slaves . . .'

Nilus nodded as the overseer continued. He enjoyed hearing his title on other men's lips. His role was only temporary, unfortunately, for he'd stepped in to fill the void that Aristocles had left behind and there would be a vote in coming weeks. But he'd already started enlisting support among his fellow consuls in the Assembly and soon he would have the votes he needed. He'd played a delicate game between the nationalist faction and the consuls who feared Nikolas, but he thought he'd accomplished quite a feat. As long as Nikolas remained king of Xanthos, Nilus could count on his support. He was also proud of himself for the aid he'd given Aristocles. His friend was better off alive in exile than dead in a Phalesian crypt.

'. . . it's this Andion plaguing the slave markets across the sea,' the younger overseer was saying. 'Slaves and the lower classes are flocking to join the Free Men.'

Nilus frowned. 'Can't we do something about him?'

The older overseer snorted. 'His fleet is bigger than ours, nearly as large as the fleet of Xanthos. It is we who have to look to our defenses. He's taken to raiding settlements, so I hear.'

'The Xanthian fleet makes regular patrols,' Nilus said. 'I'm sure we're safe.'

'I can't believe Nikolas has a woman in charge. And she's a foreigner, a Salesian no less!'

'I think she might even be Ilean.'

'No,' Nilus said. 'She's from Efu.' When the two men gave him a bemused look he sighed. 'In Haria. On the Ilean Sea.'

'Well, wherever she's from . . .'

Nilus's eyes drifted to the doorway when he caught movement; a small figure in a white chiton peered hesitantly inside.

His mouth dropped open in astonishment.

'My friends,' he said softly. 'My apologies, but I'm going to have to ask you to leave. We'll resume this conversation another time.'

Caught mid-sentence, the older of the two overseers harrumphed but he nodded to his companion and they both rose from their seats. 'First Consul,' each man said with a stiff bow.

The girl in the doorway backed away as they departed, and Nilus prayed she wouldn't flee, but she stood fast until they were gone. Nilus approached until he stood in front of her, but remained several paces away.

'Sophia?' he whispered.

She was twelve, he remembered. Dark-haired and pretty, with a wide mouth, pert nose, and dimples on her cheeks, she was old enough that he didn't know whether to crouch. He settled on placing his hands on his knees as he gave her a warm smile.

'Sophia . . . We've been so worried about you. Where have you been?'

'I've . . . I've been living with a family.' She nodded in the vague direction of the lower city. 'My father. Has he returned?'

'No, I'm afraid not,' Nilus said, shaking his head sadly. 'Who has been taking care of you?'

'They're poor,' Sophia said. 'I want to go back to being a princess.'

'Of course you do,' Nilus said. 'This family. Who'—he started to say *hid* but changed his mind—'settled you with them?'

'My sister . . . Chloe . . . Is she here?'

'Listen, Sophia. Of course you can go back to being a princess. You're special to all of us.'

Sophia frowned. She showed surprising strength as she came forward and glared up at Nilus. 'Where is my sister?' she demanded. 'I want to go back to the way things were. When is my father coming home?'

'Your father has been missing for a very long time. And . . .' Nilus licked his lips; he didn't know how she would react to what he was about to say, but she had to know. 'I have some news. I'm very sorry to tell you this, but Sophia, your sister is gone. Some bad men robbed her and . . . did bad things to her. They killed her.'

Sophia's chin jerked up. She became completely and utterly still. Her blue eyes went wide, moisture shimmering on their surface, brimming until tears dripped from first one and then the other, trickling down her cheeks.

It was a long time before she spoke, but when she did, she whispered so softly that Nilus almost couldn't hear her.

'When?'

Nilus wrung his hands. He wished he wasn't the one delivering this news. 'They found her body, along with that of another girl, on the road to Tanus a week ago.'

'How could I not know?' Sophia began to cry, great sobs racking her body. 'Why didn't somebody tell me?'

'The ceremony was small. We decided to keep it quiet. She was well liked. I'm truly sorry, child. We've been looking for you everywhere.'

Sophia suddenly collapsed, falling to her knees, her body rocking back and forward as she grieved, staring down at the hard stone floor. Nilus tried to console her, enclosing her in his arms.

She'd lost everything, and there was nothing he could say.

By the next morning, Sophia was dressed once more as a Phalesian princess, wearing a pale blue chiton of flowing silk, bunched at the waist with a cord of plaited wool dyed with indigo. She had sandals on her feet and a copper chain graced her neck with a heavy medallion displaying the symbol of the goddess Aeris. Her long dark hair was fashioned in a complicated twist.

Standing with her on the white pebbled shore of Phalesia's harbor, Nilus thought she now looked far older than her tender years. Despite her age, she was beautiful, he realized with a flash of envy. Nilus's own wife was even plumper than he was.

'Is that it?' Sophia asked, looking up at the merchant ship drawn up on the beach. Sailors scurried on the decks, readying the vessel for departure, and more crewmen carried over barrels and sacks, handing them up to their fellows.

As she glanced at Nilus, Sophia's brow was creased with determination. She had a satchel on her shoulder that she clutched as if it were a lifeline to carry her through dangerous waters.

'It is,' Nilus said. 'I've spoken with the captain. He's experienced, and assures me you'll get there safely.' He hesitated. 'But . . . Sophia . . . Are you sure you want to do this?'

'I am.' She nodded firmly. 'My sister fled her fate and died for it. I won't let that happen to me.' She looked up at Nilus. 'Will he be pleased to see me?'

Nikolas would be more than pleased, Nilus knew. Kings needed wives, and even more crucially, heirs. As a warrior king Nikolas's advisers would be pressing him constantly to take a noble wife, but his task of dealing with the Ilean threat had always taken priority. Aristocles had been first consul for as long as anyone could remember, and marrying a daughter of his would bond the two nations together, as well as giving their future child a claim on both nations. With no children of his own, and no plans to sire any, Nilus was content to help the king of Xanthos. It would be a long time before Nikolas and Sophia had a child old enough to wield real power, and Nikolas would be indebted to him for the rest of his life.

'He will be very happy to see you,' Nilus said. He wouldn't be surprised if, after hearing of Chloe's death, Nikolas married Sophia on the spot. A wedding would bolster the morale of the men and the sooner Nikolas produced an heir, the better.

'Good,' Sophia said. 'I don't want him to turn me away.'

Nilus's eyebrows went up. Sophia was nothing if not precocious. 'You've made yourself clear,' he said. 'And you do look lovely.' He glanced at the satchel she was holding so tightly. 'What do you have in there? Everything you need is on the ship.'

'Supplies from the apothecary. I am a priestess,' Sophia said. 'Where I am going, there might be wounded who need my help.'

'Of course,' Nilus said. 'Please be careful.'

'Once we're married the trouble will stop,' Sophia said firmly. 'Father will come home. And I will be queen.'

'That's right,' Nilus said. 'You will be queen.' Hearing voices, he looked up and saw a crewman waving. 'I think it's time for you to go. Don't forget to tell him what I said.'

'You brought us together.' Sophia nodded. 'I will make sure he knows.'

Nilus reflected that Nikolas was fortunate to have a chance at marrying the younger of the two girls. Chloe had a kind nature, but she was also obstinate and strong-willed; she would have made a difficult wife. Sophia was only twelve but she would grow up to be an attractive woman. She had a sweet nature and was eager to become queen of Xanthos.

'May the gods go with you, Princess Sophia,' Nilus said.

54

Under their new leader, the Free Men finally felt the benevolent smile of the god of fortune. Their daring raid had paid off: the slaves they liberated from the slave market at Koulis swelled their numbers, hope returned after the death of Mercilles, and powerful warships now sailed with every sortie.

Though he still needed to find his men proper homes, Dion focused instead on building up their strength. Using the knowledge he'd gained from Roxana at Lamara's shipyards he repaired the crippled bireme on the shore of Fort Liberty, and together with the four biremes stolen from Mercilles they suddenly had more ships than crew to man them.

Dion ordered the slower merchant vessels to Myana to get supplies and equipped a new, swifter fleet, with only warships in its number. After the raid on the slave market at Koulis he led a daylight assault on the Ilean city of Abbas, where there was a thriving slave trade, pirates pouring into the main square while the wretches were still being paraded on the block. Leading a trio of biremes at full complement, he visited the isles of Ibris and Tarlana, places he'd traveled to with Roxana. With small Ilean garrisons that were powerless to stop him, he was able to stay for a full day in each while he put out the call for anyone who wanted to join the Free Men.

He kept the two sleek war galleys, the *Gull* and the *Sea Witch*, smaller than the biremes but powerful nonetheless, in constant patrol in the waters around the isle of Fort Liberty; they wouldn't be taken by surprise again. He quizzed every man and woman as he watched them make their mark in the temple near the scorch mark that had once been a picture of Silex, asking them about their skills. When he found an Ilean carpenter from Abbas who once worked for Mydas, and asked him if he thought he could turn his talents toward building catapults to protect the island, the man pondered and then gave a short, sharp nod.

The population of Fort Liberty swelled, and with the settlement still in ruins, there was nowhere to house so many people. Fortunately it was late summer, and at night they slept side by side on the beach, staring up at the stars and the constellations depicting frozen battles between heroes and gods. But summer would end, and at the back of his mind, Dion knew he would need to find a more permanent solution.

To rebuild Fort Liberty would require a great deal of timber, cloth, iron nails, tools, candles, and ceramics. He needed to restore the forge, masonry, and lumberyard. He needed more silver than seemed possible.

Wondering if he'd taken on too much, he scoured the seas for prey. His searching took him closer and closer to the Salesian continent; with Xanthos and Phalesia at war with Ilea, he knew that by focusing on Ilean ships, he was helping his people from afar.

Riding the motion of the high seas, Dion now stood close to the bow of his new flagship, the largest of his five biremes and tried to think of a solution for feeding, clothing, and housing so many people.

Aristocles clutched the merchant galley's rail with both hands, looking down at his white knuckles and then up at the surging sea. The pounding of his heart sounded louder in his ears than the booming drum as it spurred the slaves on to greater efforts. Sweat trickled down his high forehead. He couldn't believe this was happening. Rather than gaining on the Ilean fleet that was already ahead of him in the race for Phalesia, he was about to be murdered by pirates.

The two immense warships dwarfed the rowing galley, bearing down on the smaller vessel from both port and starboard. The blades of their countless oars plunged into the water, hauling on the sea and then lifting up again, moving in perfect synchronization. They'd chosen their approach with care, for the galley needed both oars and sail to achieve any speed and if the captain wanted to turn about they would lose the wind.

Aristocles glanced at Amos but his steadfast companion had never had a strong head for sea travel, and was curled up on the floor of the boat, his face tinged a sickly green. Amos knew what was happening, but he couldn't even lift a limb to do anything about it.

Frozen with fear, Aristocles looked again at the pair of looming biremes. The warships flew across the water, despite traveling against the wind, and were now close enough that he could make out individual figures on the decks. Long silver flags with black tridents fluttered in the wind, crowning each vessel's mast.

'It's the Free Men! The pirates are on us!' the master of oars cried.

Aristocles' eyes darted to the white-faced Ilean, seeing him lower the whip in his hand as he looked back to the mainland and then again at the pirates. Despite the fact that they were at least five miles from land, he appeared to reach a decision, throwing down the coiled leather and ripping the tunic off his back.

Without another word, the Ilean raced to the back of the galley and dived into the water. Immediately he started swimming for shore with a strong, overarm stroke.

His fear was contagious, and suddenly most of the officers were leaping off the sides while the one crewman who couldn't swim, a young sailor barely into his teens, pleaded with his fellows not to leave him alone with the pirates and their own chained-up slaves.

'Flee if you want. You're on your own,' the captain called to Aristocles as he made his own departure, taking his chances as he dived off the side.

With the master of oars gone, the drum was now silent as the oarsmen slowed and then stopped. There was no one forcing them to row, but they were chained to their benches and unable to leave their posts.

'Hey. You up there. Man in white. Yes, you!'

Aristocles tore his grip from the ship's gunwale and turned to see a sunburned slave calling out to him.

'Get down the sail if you want to live. Else they'll think we're running and spear us with their ram.'

Aristocles looked up at the sail. He knew next to nothing about boats and couldn't decide what to do. Then he heard a cry and saw another slave pointing and staring toward shore. A triangular fin pierced the water and then lowered again, traveling in a direct path for the swimming crew.

His decision made for him, Aristocles crossed the deck, running over to the young Ilean sailor who'd been left behind, taking his shoulders and shaking him.

'The sail,' Aristocles barked. 'How do we get it down?'

He glanced up and saw the two warships hadn't slowed; they were now close enough that he could see that the decks swarmed with weapons-wielding pirates and hear the tempo of the drum that matched his racing heart.

The terrified youth nodded, running over to a cleat and unraveling the line, fingers fumbling in his haste. With the galley slowed after the oarsmen stopped rowing, it now coasted as the sail became loose and fluttered in the warm breeze.

'Go to the helm,' the youth said, jerking his chin toward the stern as he gripped the sailcloth and tried to tug it down. 'Bring us round so we're facing the wind.'

Aristocles nodded and sped across the boat under the watchful eyes of the slaves. He levered the tiller hard across and the galley immediately listed so sharply that he wondered if they were going to tip over. But then it settled again, and the vessel sat bobbing in the water, sliding around on the waves, as the lead bireme drew close enough for Aristocles to read its name: the *Black Dragon*.

Waiting in the helmsman's seat, he pressed fingertips into the palms of his hands, wide-eyed and fearful as the pirates threw out a line for a slave to hold as they pulled the galley close. He muttered a prayer when ruffians in a variety of costumes dropped to the deck and inspected the galley's interior. He watched as one after another the slaves were freed and led clambering from one ship to the other, stumbling and staggering as they disentangled themselves from their chains; during the chase they'd been worked so hard that their legs had now cramped, and the scars of the whip were plain to see.

Aristocles' eyes followed Amos as he was carried up, and then more pirates leaped down to the galley and began to search the vessel. He glanced at the bireme's top deck, overhearing the captain call out to each slave in turn, his voice carried on the wind. When he asked them if they wanted to join the Free Men, and be free to live as they chose, with a share in plunder and their liberty granted immediately, not one of them said no.

Aristocles remained seated near the helm as he wondered what his fate would be. He supposed that Nilus might be able to help him if the Free Men demanded a ransom. But he knew his situation was hopeless: if the Ilean fleet was successful in its aim of razing Phalesia and Xanthos to the ground, there would be no one left alive to help him.

He thought about his daughters, praying they were safe. Xanthos had a new but untested fleet under the woman Roxana; it was possible she could hold off the attack.

He heard a rough voice as someone called down to the young Ilean sailor nearby, asking him if he wanted to join. The youth stammered a negative and they told him to stay with his ship; he would have to manage it on his own if he wanted to sail home.

Aristocles then saw men approaching and felt strong hands pick him up under the armpits and march him across the small galley. As instructed he lifted his arms and sailors on the warship hoisted him up, eventually planting him down on the deck of the mighty bireme.

'Andion!' someone called.

Aristocles gazed away from the pirates, staring out to sea, in the direction of Phalesia. But accepting the inevitable, he sensed a man approach him, and turned to see bare feet and simple but well-stitched sailor's trousers, an athletic frame filling a tunic fastened with a leather belt at the waist, and a neck devoid of any chain or medallion. Continuing to look up, he met the brown eyes of a young man in his early twenties, his square jaw clean-shaven, with tanned skin and flaxen hair.

'By Aldus and all the gods!' Aristocles gasped.

55

A stunning sunset filled the sky with pale pink and midnight blue, the golden orb's reflection tapering in a line that shimmered on the waves of the silver road. A bonfire burned at the midpoint of the crescent strip of sand, lighting up the faces of the hundreds of men and women standing on one side of the flames. Those who'd been with the Free Men the longest stood in front, while to the rear and on the wings were ragged former slaves, those freed most recently.

On the other side of the bonfire, Dion stood with Aristocles. They both faced the stirring crowd, which became silent as Dion lifted his arms.

'My people,' he began.

Aristocles looked at Dion in amazement. Where was the uncertain youth? Bold, yes, he'd always been bold, he had to have been to sail across the Maltherean and rescue Chloe from the sun king, but Aristocles had never before seen him like this. The young prince had grown into a leader.

'I've always promised you that we would vote on the most important decisions, those that affect us all. Tonight we will be faced with our most important decision yet. The man standing beside me,' he said, gesturing, 'is Aristocles, first consul of Phalesia. He brings news that is grave to me, and that the other Galeans among you will also find dire.'

Dion paused to let his words sink in.

'Mydas, king of Ilea, has sent a raiding fleet to Phalesia and Xanthos. This time the Ileans don't seek gold, slaves, or dominion. They intend to punish these two nations for what they see as their humiliation in the last conflict. Despite the fact that it was the Ileans who initiated the war, Mydas believes he won't be seen as a strong king unless he finishes what his late brother started. If he succeeds'—Dion glanced at Aristocles—'the first consul's homeland will be destroyed.' He leveled his gaze on the Free Men. 'As will mine.'

'What does this have to do with us?' a tall pirate with a shaved head called out.

'Fort Liberty is our home!' said another.

'Yes,' Dion said, nodding along with them. 'Fort Liberty has always been the home of the Free Men. But we have more silver than food, and more men than places to sleep. We have a decisive force here, and we have the skill and the experience to make a difference, should we choose to come to the first consul's aid. As for why . . .'

Dion trailed off, looking down at the ground, and the crowd stirred uncertainly. But then he lifted his chin, and his expression was firm.

'Jax once told me his dream for the Free Men. He said that if he could gather enough money, he would buy land in Galea, and build a new settlement where every man and woman could enjoy the same liberties we do here, but build real lives . . . where we could watch our children grow without living in fear that one day an enemy fleet would appear on the horizon and destroy this place forever. We all lost friends when the raiders came. Eventually'—his voice was grave—'it will happen again.'

Many among them looked to the ruins of the town on the hillside, thinking about the coming winter, worrying about the future.

'The first consul's proposal is thus. If we set sail immediately, and row harder than we've ever rowed before, we may be able to catch the Ilean fleet. If we come to the aid of Phalesia and neighboring Xanthos, he promises to find new homes in Phalesia for anyone who chooses. The Free Men will still be free, and Fort Liberty will remain in our possession, but we will be legitimized.'

'What about slavery?' Finn called.

'Phalesia has few slaves, but those there are will be liberated, and earn pay for their efforts.' Aristocles' eyes widened and he opened his mouth, but Dion simply smiled and continued. 'Our values and ideals we will bring with us. Those in fear of persecution will have their comrades close by, but I can assure you that Phalesia is a place where liberty is valued. The system of governance by voting we use here – it originated there. In a way, we will be returning to our home.'

'Will you live there with us, Andion?'

Dion hesitated; he'd been thinking of the future of the Free Men, and hadn't given thought to himself.

'Yes, he will,' Aristocles answered for him. 'And he will be most welcome.'

Voices rose in the crowd as small groups began discussing the proposal with each other.

'I have one other question.' A gravelly voice rose above the din, silencing the murmurs. Dion was surprised to see Cob, standing at the front of the group, his face lit up by flickering firelight. 'Tell us why you think we can trust the first consul.'

Cob crossed his arms over his chest, lowering his head as he stared at Dion intently.

Dion frowned and then the creases in his brow relaxed. He slowly nodded.

'We can trust Aristocles because he and I know each other. We have a past.' Suddenly every set of eyes was on him; every man or woman was waiting on his words. 'I rescued his daughter from Lamara when she was held captive by the sun king. I fought at the Battle of Phalesia. My true name is Dion, and Nikolas, king of Xanthos, is my older brother.'

When a cacophony of startled voices met his pronouncement, Dion raised his hands and called out.

'Like all of you, I came here to be free. My brother cast me out of my home, and I lived with the eldren in the Wilds. But I didn't belong there either, and fortune led me to the Free Men. None of us can escape our heritage, but we get to choose how we live with it. I will no longer let myself be judged as different, for no other reason than that my father loved my mother. I am who I am, and I will never again let anyone tell me otherwise.'

Dion held his head high as the Free Men gave a resounding cheer, and then he glanced at Aristocles, surprised when the first consul gripped his shoulder.

'Time is of the essence,' Aristocles said. 'You have someone you trust to leave in charge here?'

'Yes.' Dion thought of Finn. 'But we still need to vote.'

'I know votes, and this one is a foregone conclusion.'

'You're sure you can handle the Assembly?'

'It all depends on whether I can be a returning hero.'

Dion looked out to sea. 'Then let's go and make you one.'

56

The muscular dragon clad in scales of shining silver flew high over Cinder Fen, well within the confines of the surrounding peaks. The wedge-shaped head craned as wings the size of a ship's sails beat down at the air. Almond eyes roved over the land below.

Eiric was searching for what Jonas had called *the heart*.

He had said something about a wellspring, a pool, in the middle of Cinder Fen. As Eiric searched he saw a region of swamps with charred trees leaning at odd angles; there were pools in multitudes, the water as black as tar, dirty and viscous. Long trailing weeds lined the rocky edges of the fens. Gnarled trees clustered in forests and groves. Wildren roamed: packs of ogres with lank silver hair and the occasional giant standing head and shoulders above the rest. Distant furies congregated on fleeing prey, plummeting from the sky and swarming on a rabbit or goat, fighting each other for food.

Cinder Fen was immense. It was early morning and he'd been looking since dawn, the long shadows making it easier for him to read the terrain, but it would take him time to search it all and he couldn't stay in this form forever. He was now approaching the very center, equidistant between the encircling mountains.

He decided that the last place he investigated would be a winding, steep-walled canyon.

Flying overhead, he caught a glimpse of a thin black river at the canyon's base, fed by the swamps that seeped trickling water through the ground. Following the gully with his eyes, he couldn't see a pool.

He put on a burst of speed, wind whistling so loud that it filled his senses. His powerful limbs clawed at the air; his wings stretched out at both sides as he soared over the canyon. He suddenly wondered what he was doing. He felt the urge to fly higher, to leave this place behind and search for food.

Eiric forced himself to focus on his task. Knowing he couldn't remain changed any longer, he slowed his progress, wings fluttering as he reached the end of the canyon and hovered. Braking his speed, he descended to a wide boulder. His clawed limbs settled to the rock.

He felt the familiar sensation of shifting, changing size and shape. A moment later he was himself again, a broad-shouldered eldran in deerskin leggings, with golden eyes and skin so pale it was nearly translucent, high cheekbones, a hawk-like nose, and close-cropped silver hair.

Scanning the area but seeing he was alone, Eiric descended to the base of the canyon, picking a path over the loose scree. He climbed down until walls rose up on both sides, pausing for a moment to listen, peering into the depths ahead.

Trickling water was the only sound other than his heavy breathing.

The thin stream here at the canyon's terminus was little more than a rivulet, but he could see that further in, as the walls became higher, the watercourse was a little broader. He would only find out if he was in the right place by pressing on.

As Eiric moved slowly into the canyon, he stopped at regular intervals and pricked his ears. He wrinkled his nose; the air smelled of mold and damp. Black water slithered down a steep slope at his left, filling the sluggish stream that he followed as it weaved through the twisting chasm.

The walls became still steeper, closing in so that he was cast in perpetual shade as he explored, peering around each corner, his heart rate speeding up the further he progressed. He glanced overhead and saw that the two opposing sides of the canyon were starting to meet high above. The passage he followed was beginning to become a tunnel.

He followed the black river around three more bends. The limestone walls were now steep and jagged; the graveled path at the stream's side led ever onward. He felt confined between the walls of rock and the flowing water, which was wide now, and so dark that he couldn't hazard a guess at how deep it was. Surprisingly the chasm's sides gradually became lower, now only twice his height. The summits began to draw apart once more, like a flower opening its petals.

At the next sharp bend, Eiric came to a sudden halt. He could hear voices.

His pulse racing, he crouched low to the ground. Creeping slowly forward, he craned his head around the rock to peer ahead.

He saw an immense circular basin, too wide to throw a stone from one edge to the other, well lit, for it was open to the morning sky. He would have seen it from the air but for the gnarled trees framing the rim, growing thick enough to tell him there was a forest on the higher ground. In some places the limestone walls of the great bowl looked melted, in others the sides were splintered and broken.

An expanse of black earth and muddy banks surrounded a pool of oily water, fed by the stream he'd been following. The pool dominated the area, occupying at least half of the basin. Its surface glistened, perfectly flat, without a ripple.

The gray sky overhead matched the smoky hue of the trees, and the pool was as black as the ground around it. There was little color to break up the dark monotony.

Eiric saw scores of eldren scattered about, walking, standing and talking, doing normal things. A pair of hunters skinned a deer's carcass; several men carried firewood, nodding to a silver-haired man who sat by a fire, speaking with an older woman working with mortar and pestle. More eldren mended clothing, scolded younglings, and pounded root vegetables into powder. They were no different from the eldren Eiric had grown up with in the Village in the Wilds.

He frowned as he watched them, wondering where Triton was.

'I could sense you a mile away,' a low voice whispered in his ear.

Eiric whirled and saw a face right next to his: a bald eldran with a cruel brow and the sharp ridges of his skull clearly visible. One of Triton's eyes was a wrinkled pit, the other as dark as the swamps of Cinder Fen.

Eiric started to imagine himself as a giant, but he'd spent too long in dragon form and couldn't shake the impression of wings that would shatter against the walls of the narrow passage. Triton thrust out his hand and gripped Eiric's throat, squeezing his breath away. When strong fingers clutched under his jaw, Eiric tried to use his wild fear to bring on his ability to shift form.

But his opponent growled and gripped his neck still harder, making him gasp. Even unchanged, Triton's frame was the most powerful he'd ever seen on one of his kind. Lifting Eiric in the air, Triton hauled him forward, taking long strides. He carried him from his hiding place directly to the pool of black liquid and then Triton threw him forward. Eiric sucked in a breath of air before he plunged into the water with a mighty splash.

Eiric felt chill send a thousand poking needles into his flesh. Darkness filled his vision so that he couldn't tell up from down. His legs kicked at the water, trying to find purchase below, but the pool was impossibly deep and, even as he struggled, he couldn't bring his head to the surface.

Flailing frantically, his arms pulled at the black liquid, vainly trying to bring his body closer to the surface. His toe finally kicked into hard rock, sending a burst of pain through his body that made him gnash his teeth. His head came out of the water near the edge of the pool and he opened his mouth to breathe in a lungful of air.

More immense than any creature he'd ever seen before, a monstrous giant stood waiting for him on the bank.

Triton smiled as he pushed down on Eiric's head, drowning him in the black liquid.

Eiric fought back, but his legs once more found nothing but an open void beneath them. His struggles became feeble.

Darkness closed in.

———

Eiric shuddered when something clicked around his neck, making his skin crawl with a painful prickling sensation. He sucked in a ragged breath as he writhed and struggled, and then started to choke. Ejecting a stream of water, he wheezed and coughed before he was finally able to think.

He was upright, tied to a thick stake embedded in the black earth with his wrists bound behind his back and his ankles fastened to the stake's base. A middle-aged human woman, her face bruised beyond belief, eyes nearly swollen shut, hovered nearby and looked fearfully at Triton, who stood watching nearby.

'Well done,' Triton said to the human woman. 'Now go.'

Eiric wondered at the sickening feeling and then glanced down, seeing black links connected one to the other. The human woman had fastened an iron chain around his neck. The contact with his skin was more than uncomfortable, it made him shudder; he desperately wanted it gone.

As long as his neck was confined, he wouldn't be able to change.

'Did you really think I would not sense you? I can sense all eldren, known to me or not.' Triton's lips parted in a malicious smile. 'I am far more powerful than any other. I am your king.'

Triton backed away, and Eiric could now see that the other eldren had stopped what they were doing and gathered. They stood in a somber crowd, arrayed around the stake, watching impassively.

'Behold,' Triton called to them. 'Eiric, the spawn of Zachary.' He suddenly came in close, jutting his head forward so that his face was inches from Eiric's. 'I would ask you to bow, but a nod will suffice.'

Eiric lifted his chin. 'You are no king of mine.'

'I have the blood of Marrix,' he hissed.

'My father always said there are many who can make that claim.'

'Ah.' Triton lifted a finger. 'But here I am, in the heart of our homeland, doing what no other has had the courage to do since my ancestor, Marrix, first created his horn. The result will be a permanent change to the way our magic functions.'

The broad-shouldered eldran turned to face the pool, speaking loud enough that the crowd of over a hundred onlookers could hear.

'Our power stems from this land, and its ultimate source is deep within the wellspring. The horn was stolen from us, and we may never get it back, but it no longer matters.'

Triton walked over to stand beside the pool, peering into it, his voice filling the area. 'I have been communing with the wellspring, and I believe I can find the great gemstone in the depths – the last fragile remnant of this land's once-great power.'

His voice became triumphant as he lifted his gaze to look at Eiric. 'I will then destroy it. Sindara will be gone forever, but we will be free. Free to change our shape for as long as we wish to. There will no longer be any risk of losing who we were. We will roam as far and wide as we please, and with such power at our disposal, no human will be able to stop us.'

'It's a lie!' Eiric called to the onlookers. 'The one thing binding us all, whether from the Wilds or the Waste, has always been that no eldran can call himself king until he reclaims Sindara. How do you know that if he destroys the source of our power we all won't die—'

Triton strode forward, crossing the distance in moments, and smashed his fist into Eiric's face. The blow rocked his senses, the pain so strong he almost sank into unconsciousness.

An ancient eldran, with wrinkled skin like parchment, so old his hair was almost white, spoke up. 'What do you intend to do with him? He is no threat to anyone.' He shook his head sadly. 'Eldren should not be fighting eldren. The attack on his village was wrong—'

'Silence!' Triton rounded on the old man, who furrowed his brow as he closed his mouth but continued to shake his head. Triton then turned back to Eiric. 'I beg to differ. He has power, this one. And he hates me.' His one eye narrowed. 'Don't you?' He tilted his head as a new thought occurred to him. 'Tell me, Eiric son of Zachary, where is Jonas?'

'Dead.'

'You fought him and won. I see it in your eyes. And where is your father. Where is Zachary?'

'Gone,' Eiric whispered.

Triton's gaze suddenly left his captive as he scanned the area. Walking to a fire, he picked up a piece of flaming wood, bright red and smoking. Returning to Eiric, his dark eye flickered to the crimson glow at the end of his brand as he smiled.

'What are you doing?' the old eldran cried.

'I believe you do know where Zachary is,' Triton said softly.

Triton brought the smoking brand toward Eiric's bare chest, gradually approaching his stomach. As the end came close to his pale skin, Eiric couldn't take his eyes off it.

'Where is he? I will ask you only once.'

'It's the truth,' Eiric panted, staring down at his abdomen. 'He may be wild or he may be dead. I came to Cinder Fen to find him.'

Triton paused.

'With Zachary dead, and you here, there is no one left to lead the eldren from the Wilds,' Triton said, more to himself than anyone else. 'But I need to be sure.'

Eiric's flesh sizzled as he screamed.

57

Halfway between Lamara and Koulis, on a wide featureless expanse of yellow dirt and rock, two armies faced each other across the plain.

Though it was just after dawn the air was already dry and hot, baking the soldiers in their armor, sending sweat trickling down the backs of necks and making palms slippery as anxious men clutched spears tightly. Flies buzzed constantly, sucking at the corners of eyes and alighting on parched lips. Horses whinnied, sensing the growing tension.

Astride a tall ebony-hued stallion, the man the Ileans were calling Nikolas the Black rode in front of the columns of lined-up soldiers, dark eyes shifting between his troops and the distant pennants of the opposing army. He passed the Xanthian cavalry on the flank and straightened in his stirrups but couldn't see his archers and javelin throwers behind. Coming abreast of the tattooed mercenaries from the north, he continued his inspection as he cantered, taking in the next column of lightly armored infantry from Koulis, formed up alongside the leather-clad contingent from Tanus. He wheeled in close to the Xanthian hoplites, armed with shield and spear, wide-bladed swords in scabbards at their waists, with his elite king's guard in front. Crimson cloaks billowed in the hot breeze, the horsehair crests marking out the officers. The stallion reared as Nikolas drew up.

He glanced down at the Xanthian captain, standing in front of the army with the trumpeter at his side. 'Report,' Nikolas ordered.

'You were right, sire. They don't know the range of our bows. As soon as their left flank advances they'll meet a hail of death.'

'The plan remains unchanged,' Nikolas said, gazing out at the six thousand men under his command, noting the blue cloaks of the Phalesians on the far side of the Xanthian hoplites and beyond them the sling throwers he'd merged into a single force. 'I will personally lead our center. We'll draw Mydas by rushing in and then retreating. As our center withdraws, he will give chase.'

He shifted in his armor; the heat was taking a toll even on him.

'Men will always pursue a fleeing opponent,' Nikolas continued, 'like a wolf chasing a sheep. But this wolf will soon realize he is facing a bear, and that he is alone, and far too close to the claws. As they rush forward the Ilean line will thin. We will envelop the enemy as our cavalry outflanks them and charges from the rear. That is when we reach the river and hold our ground.'

'Sire . . .' The captain hesitated. 'You know my thoughts on this. It's a dangerous plan. When we reach the river, with water at our backs, there's no escape. We have close to twenty thousand Ileans standing against us. And we should have listened to Lord Lothar – we're too heavily armored and this heat is worse than anything on our side of the Maltherean. It will sap our men's strength, and your plan calls for much running as well as fighting . . .'

'For our strategy to work, there can be no escape,' Nikolas said grimly. 'A false rout can too easily become a real one. We've left a thousand men at the river to bolster our numbers when we turn and fight. And don't forget'—the restive stallion reared again before Nikolas got his mount under control—'I will be there to lead.'

'Yes, sire.' The captain nodded.

'We'd best not wait any longer,' Nikolas said. He grimaced; the sun's rays were reflecting from his steel breastplate; the metal was hot enough to cook meat. 'Order the advance.' He drew his sword and raised his arm into the air. 'We attack!'

58

Liana stood on the tall cliff and felt a cold fist squeezing her heart. She tensed, every thought screaming at her to flee, but continued watching to make certain.

A mob of tribesmen had left the village of Pao, already heading directly for the steep path that would take them through the forest and up to the villa. Hundreds of men and women held spears and fiery torches. The journey wasn't long, and even as she watched they swarmed into the trees.

It was morning. They didn't need torches to see.

Liana turned and fled, sprinting for the villa, calling out Chloe's name. She found her friend standing at the stone basin near the gardens, splashing cool water on her face; despite the early hour, the day was already scorching hot.

Hearing her urgent tone, Chloe glanced up and saw her running.

'The villagers,' Liana panted. 'They're coming this way.' She pointed in the direction of the forest that spread over the hills surrounding the villa. 'They'll be here in moments!'

'Villagers? How many?'

'Too many! We have to go! Right now!'

Chloe's jaw clenched tightly. Thoughts visibly crossed her face and then she gave a sharp nod. 'I have to get some things.'

'They'll cut off our escape. There's no time!'

Liana's words were in vain; Chloe had already turned, running past the gardens and climbing the short set of stone steps that led into the villa. Liana moved away from the villa and shielded her eyes as she scanned the direction of the forest, silently urging her friend to hurry.

She saw the villagers in moments. The men appeared first: tattooed tribesmen wearing skins, holding spears and heavy clubs. At least a dozen warriors led from the front, marching toward the villa, every element of their posture angry as a bearded bald man waved an iron-tipped spear, hectoring them forward. Liana saw still more villagers behind them, running to catch up to the warriors, holding anything they could find to use as weapons: sticks, slings, and dozens of fiery torches.

They'd already seen her and began to fan out, surrounding the villa and its environs to prevent any escape. Liana wrung her hands as she glanced from the tribesmen back to the villa's entrance and then at the villagers again.

'Chloe . . .' she muttered. 'Where are you?'

Voices reached her; the closest warriors were shouting, and then she could make out individual faces. Most of them looked fearful but aggressive, men who'd been summoning their courage over a long period and were terrified at the outcome of violence, but found themselves faced with no other choice. They urged each other on with brutal cries as they approached, stalking with long strides, spears jabbing the air.

Liana caught motion out of the corner of her eye and saw Chloe racing away from the villa, but she was too late, and now they were surrounded.

The bearded leader came to a halt twenty paces from Liana. He had a thorn pierced through one ear and soot rubbed under each eye. He warily cast his eyes over the area before raising his spear and opening his mouth to call out.

'The holy man,' he cried. 'He has not been seen in many days. Tell him we want to see him.' The dozen warriors around him gave guttural cries, bellowing until their leader waved them to silence.

Chloe joined Liana's side. They exchanged glances as more villagers arrayed themselves behind the bearded leader, their voices raised in an unintelligible cacophony as everyone tried to cry out at the same time. The men rattled their spears and some held up slings, showing them to Liana and Chloe. The shrieks of the women were loudest of all. The air smelled like smoke, carried on the breeze from their burning torches.

The leader again waved his arms for his people to quiet as he scowled and waited for an answer.

'The holy man . . .' Chloe swallowed. 'He is not here.'

'Where is he?'

'He is . . . on an important quest,' Liana said. 'He won't return for many days.'

The voices rose again. The leader lifted his spear high and gave a barking yelp, bringing silence once more.

'Two of our girls have disappeared. They have not returned. The holy man has also disappeared. Where has he taken them?'

'Search the house!' a woman's voice cried from the crowd.

More voices joined the din. 'Search the house!'

Liana knew with a terrible sinking feeling which girls the village leader was referring to. Chloe had told her what Vikram had done. A sudden realization occurred to her. She felt the blood drain from her face. 'Chloe,' she hissed. 'My satchel.'

'I have it,' Chloe murmured.

413

Glancing across at her, Liana saw that Chloe also held the tall staff with its strange copper fork at the end. As she watched, Chloe's lips thinned and she put on a fierce expression.

She took three steps toward the villagers and raised the staff, her fingers gripping tightly, clutching it high with her skin in contact with the metal. Eyes on the weapon, the villagers all fled back several paces, huddling in fear.

But nothing happened.

The moments trickled past. Chloe continued to hold the staff high but her face was now panicked. She cast a horrified look in Liana's direction.

The bearded leader was crouched with his hand over his head as if to shield himself from a blow, but he slowly straightened and recovered his courage as he took heart from the people around him.

'We will take the two of you,' he cried. 'We will keep you until he returns.'

Liana's chest heaved as she watched the villagers advance. The bearded leader leveled his spear at the height of Chloe's chest and strode warily forward.

Chloe stood stock still, frozen in place.

At that moment something strange happened.

Liana felt a contact, a fleeting recognition that came with a voice and a face. It passed as quickly as it came, but then she felt it again. She sensed the presence of someone she knew. Trying to take hold of the sensation before it fled, she knew she was brushing her mind against another eldran. She focused on the brief contact, feeling it begin to slip away, but using long-forgotten memories to bring it near.

Once more she was in the Wilds, standing under the trees not far from the village that would soon be destroyed forever, staring up at him.

'We all worry for the ones we care about,' Eiric said with a smile. He opened his palm. 'Here, I made this for you. I thought you might like to wear it at the next feast.'

He gave her a leather thong with a circle of polished amber. The gift made her smile.

Eiric?

⌣

Eiric's eyelids fluttered. His body had been burned time and again, his face and chest bruised by pounding fists, but with nothing more to tell Triton than the truth about his father, the self-proclaimed king of the eldren had eventually given up and gone to the pool's edge to contemplate the depths.

The old eldran with the whitened hair, seeing Triton occupied, came over and looked sadly at Eiric. 'We only intended to destroy your dwellings. Triton . . . He said you were living as humans, even using metal, but that wasn't what I saw. I saw beautiful houses made from trees. By then it was too late.'

The old eldran turned as he heard a loud voice.

'I can feel it!' Triton clenched his fists as he stared into the depths. 'The wellspring is weak. This day'—he looked up at the open sky—'this very day, I will swim down and reach the bottom. I will clutch the jewel in my fist and squeeze. Sindara will be no more, but a new age of glory will be ours.'

'You can challenge him,' the old eldran said softly.

'How?' Eiric whispered.

'Your mother was Aella?'

Eiric nodded weakly. 'Yes.'

'My name is Dalton. I knew your mother'—he gave a faint smile—'long, long ago. I also know this. The blood of Marrix did not flow in your father's veins.' His next words made Eiric look up.

'But it did in your mother's.' He saw Eiric's reaction and nodded. 'Your father knew, but he did not want you to be forced into confrontation with Triton, as you are now. Zachary could never be king.' Dalton's voice firmed. 'But you can.'

'No,' Eiric murmured when he felt dry fingers fumbling at the bonds at his wrists. He hissed. 'No!' He drew in a breath. 'There's no purpose in it. You will only get yourself killed. Go from me. Go!'

Dalton hesitated, taking three steps back. Looking toward the pool, Eiric saw Triton suddenly turn and see them standing together, close but not touching.

'Get away from him,' Triton ordered. He strode over, his one eye glaring, cruel brow furrowed, standing near Eiric and waiting as the old eldran rejoined the group. 'Something you told me, Dalton. Every eldran alive lends energy to the wellspring, just as every wildran drains it. I want the source to be weak.'

Triton made sure every set of eyes was on him, as he finally turned and pointed at Eiric. 'This one has to die.'

Lunging forward, Triton's long fingers again clutched hold of Eiric's throat, but this time he was squeezing hard enough to crush his neck. Stars sparkled in Eiric's vision. He choked and felt his face turning red.

As he realized that his life would soon be over, Eiric thought about the people closest to his heart. He relived his pain at the death of his mother. He wondered weakly whether Dion had ever found his place in the world. More than anything, he wished he had found his father, alive and well, smiling at him and saying wise words.

Then another mind brushed across his own. He sensed a familiar presence, a soft, gentle, feminine mind. He felt her surprise and shock as he tried to strengthen the contact, even as it waxed and waned, along with his last stirrings of consciousness.

Liana . . . Please . . .

'Chloe!' Liana screamed. 'We have to go. Eiric is at Cinder Fen. He needs our help!'

Fearful of turning around, Chloe backed away from the approaching tribesmen, still holding the staff high, retreating toward Liana. She kept her eyes fixed firmly on the spear-wielding warriors. Once more she lifted the staff and tried to focus on a single, pure note.

As soon as she lifted the staff, despite the fact that nothing had happened, the warriors stopped.

Suddenly it was the tribesmen who were backing away, their faces filled with more terror than Chloe had thought the staff could inspire even if she'd managed to make it function. To a man, they brandished their spears and torches, and then she realized they weren't looking at her, they were looking past her shoulder.

She whirled.

The beautiful soft-eyed dragon quivered with impatience as she dipped a wing, and it was obvious what Liana wanted her to do. The dragon's breath rumbled. Powerful forelegs scratched at the ground. The broad, veined wings stretched out and then drew in again.

Taking a deep breath, Chloe clambered up a bent foreleg, grabbing hold of the ridges behind the angular head. She was barely on before the wings stretched out, fluttering and then pounding at the air. Her stomach lurched as the ground dropped away in an instant.

The dragon lowered a wing and turned on the tip, leaning to the side and then straightening back to the horizontal as they headed south. The sensation of flying high in the sky was both exhilarating and terrifying. Fearful of falling, Chloe was forced to face straight ahead, blinking tears out of her eyes as the wind howled past her ears.

It was some time before she felt able to swing her body around to look at Vikram's villa one last time. Smoke was already rising from it in a billowing cloud as the villagers took their fear and rage out on the structure, setting it aflame.

Chloe had Vikram's resonance staff.

But her heart sank; every last book of magic would soon be ash.

59

The brave sailor took a running start, grabbing hold of a rope trailing from the top of the bireme's mast. One moment he was sprinting on the deck and the next his body was over the water as he swung across to the adjacent flagship. The waiting arms of the *Black Dragon*'s crew caught him, breathless and panting.

'What news?' Dion strode over.

'The battle has already started.' The sailor spoke the words in a rush. 'Some ships are on fire.'

Dion squinted and now that he knew to look for it, he could make out thin gray streams of smoke snaking into the sky on the distant horizon.

The smoke was in the north. Orius was behind them and the triangular peak of Mount Oden, on the island of Deos, was ahead. The naval battle was taking place out in the open ocean. With the secret route through the Shards now common knowledge, Roxana and the Xanthian fleet had challenged the Ilean fleet before it could divert to either Xanthos or Phalesia. But if Roxana was defeated, both cities would soon be in flames.

'Signal the advance!' Dion bellowed. 'Double speed!'

The drum gained tempo and the oarsmen hauled at the water, blades dipping in and out with swift repetition. Dion watched the four other biremes form into a row, with the two war galleys on the flanks. Now arrayed side by side, Dion's fleet of seven warships gained momentum as he prayed to Silex that he wouldn't be too late.

Cob stumped up to join him. 'Out here in the open sea, the sound of the battle will draw them. Cinder Fen is not far.'

Dion had only half his attention on the old sailor. 'Draw what?'

'Creatures hungry for blood,' he said in his gravelly voice. His eyes opened wide and he pointed. 'Wildren.'

At first Dion thought they were whales, but they were long and sinuous, with frills behind their heads and long crests behind their backs. Each was as wide as a bireme and longer: these were true leviathans, with glossy silver scales and jaws that could snap a sailing boat in two with a single bite. They were carving the waters directly ahead of the fleet, ignoring the approach of the comparatively soundless warships, instead consumed with the havoc of the battle as they plunged in and out of the surging sea.

Dion's heart sank. 'How many?' he raised his voice to call.

'I count three, cap'n!' a sailor cried.

Dion cursed. The wildren were approaching from the same direction as his fleet, and would prevent him making a surprise attack.

They were also dangerous beyond imagining.

This was the last thing he needed.

60

'I said let him go.' Dalton stood with the other eldren from the Waste arrayed around him. 'You have gone too far, Triton. Yes, in the battle at Phalesia we fought those from the Wilds when the horn was within our grasp, for reclaiming Sindara was always our goal, just as humans were always our enemies. But we were fighting for a cause, we had an objective. We never sought to destroy Zachary or those with him because we never thought of them as enemies. Now we keep captives and burn the homes of our kin. You have changed, and we have followed you into darkness. Your desire for power has perverted your spirit.'

Triton released his grip around Eiric's neck and wheeled on the old man. Eiric's throat opened and he gasped. Everything around him was taking place in a haze; he was only dimly aware of the confrontation between Triton and Dalton.

Eiric watched as Triton strode over to the smaller man, and when he saw the expression on Triton's face he knew that Dalton was going to die. Filled with desperation, he sucked in another lungful of air. He had to do something to save the old eldran's life.

'Let me speak,' he croaked.

Triton spun again. 'And now you have something to say.'

Fighting the pain, Eiric forced himself to speak loud enough for them all to hear, directing his words at the eldren from the Waste.

'Dalton is right. Eldren should not be fighting eldren.' He drew in another labored breath. 'But nor should we be fighting humans. Our ancient enemy was the king of Aleuthea, and Marrix had his revenge. The Aleutheans are all gone.' He saw their eyes on him and summoned the last of his strength to continue. 'My father always wanted peace. He wanted—'

'Enough!' Triton bellowed. 'There will never be peace between the races.'

As swift as the eye could follow, a plummeting silver dragon dived from above, legs outstretched, jaws parted as it roared. It flew directly past the circle of trees and descended on the basin.

Triton whirled. His eyes widened with sudden fear.

The dragon struck him head on.

61

Roxana ordered her fleet to close ranks, forming the Xanthian warships once more into a row, with each ram facing forward like a volley of javelins thrown by the sea god. She would now make a second pass at the enemy. Perhaps this time she would be able to split their line and fragment them into two smaller forces, which would give her the advantage she needed. She left the sinking wreckage of two of her biremes behind.

'We're making another pass!' she bellowed. 'Set the helm for the center of their line. When we're within hailing distance we'll bear to starboard and then change our approach and veer to port. We need to outsteer them. Lads, you'd best be ready!'

She peered out to sea as the drum below decks pounded along with the waves smashing against the hull of her flagship, the *Anoraxis*. The ships of her fleet began to wheel like a flock of birds turning as one. Dead ahead, the Ilean fleet came on, each ship flying a yellow flag with an orange sun.

Roxana strode across the deck and hectored the Xanthian archers. 'You've got the better range, so I want every shot to count as we come in! You'll have a chance for two, maybe three shots, then I want those shields *up*. They're using fire arrows so you'd better stop them or we'll be fighting flames on the deck. Understood?'

'Aye!'

'Raise that sail!'

'Captain.' A swarthy hook-nosed man approached. Hasha was originally from Ilea but he'd also been captured after the Battle of Phalesia and was now her second-in-command. 'With the sail up there's twice the chance we'll catch fire. All it takes is a single arrow—'

'We need the extra speed. Get it down before we're in range. Make that your priority.' Roxana lifted a finger. 'But not until you have to.'

'There's . . .' Hasha looked out at the enemy biremes, counting the yellow flags, 'There's a dozen ships, to our six . . .'

'Thirteen, you mean.'

'Thirteen.' He shook his head, lowering his voice so only she could hear him. 'There's too many of them. It's not too late to ask for parley. I can run the white flag . . .'

Roxana whirled him off to the side, gripping him by the shoulder. 'So we ask for parley. Then what happens?'

'Well.' He licked his lips. 'We come to terms.'

'What terms?' she barked.

'Our surrender.'

'And then?'

'Then . . .' He hesitated. 'They'll ask the Ileans among us to join them.'

'Demand, more like it. And then . . . ?'

'Well . . .'

'They're not going to return to Lamara empty-handed. They'll kill the Galeans in our crew and then force the rest to join them in sacking Phalesia and Xanthos. This is a mission of vengeance, so we're talking about more than simple conquest. You have friends among the Galeans. How do you feel about witnessing their homes burned to the ground? I promised Nikolas I'd defend his kingdom and I'm not going to go back on my word.'

'I understand,' Hasha said. 'I do. But this is suicide.'

Legs astride, first glancing around to see that the *Anoraxis* was ready for combat, Roxana crossed her arms over her stocky chest. 'Were you ever a child, Hasha?'

'I . . .' He frowned. 'Of course, Captain.'

'Were you ever attacked by a bully?'

'I suppose—'

'When we fight back, and win, the bully withdraws. But he always returns, because to keep his status he must repay the humiliation. The new king of Ilea is the bully. But the people of Xanthos and Phalesia? They're only defending themselves.'

'But the Ileans . . . They're going to win.'

Roxana's broad face split into a grin. 'Have you so little faith? Yes, we're outnumbered. And yes, our enemies have more experience than the Xanthians fighting at sea. But you're forgetting something.'

'What?'

Her smile became fierce. 'Commanding ships is what I was put on this earth to do.'

62

A heartbeat before the collision Chloe jumped off the dragon's back, rolling and tumbling onto the ground. Leaping to her feet, she saw dozens of eldren staring at her with wide eyes, indecisive, so stunned they were frozen into inaction.

She was in a wide circular basin with low rocky walls, encircled by gnarled trees on the high ground, with a bottomless pool of black water filling half the space and the rest made up of a carpet of burned flakes like the remnants of an old fire. Hammocks made of skins slung from stakes lined the back wall. Campfires dotted the area with butchered carcasses ready to cook nearby. The thick air stank of ash and mold.

She barely had time to take the scene in before she finally spotted Eiric and started running. He was bound to a wooden pole, hanging limp and wretched but with eyes alert. Staff in hand, encumbered by her and Liana's possessions, it felt like an eternity before she reached him. Eiric's golden eyes barely registered her approach; he was watching in horror as Liana grappled with Triton. Behind her, the snarls and roars spurred Chloe on.

'Eiric . . .' Chloe panted.

Throwing staff and satchels to the ground, Chloe hardly recognized Zachary's son. His face was swollen and his chest was bare, displaying savage burn marks. An iron chain was fastened around his neck and the breath rattled in his chest. His shoulders were slumped and his knees were bent, his weight entirely supported by the stake behind his back.

'Liana,' he whispered.

Chloe glanced over her shoulder and her breath caught when she saw Liana, still a wiry silver dragon, now battling the biggest giant Chloe had ever seen. The one-eyed giant bellowed, ropy arms batting the dragon's attacks aside like a man swatting a fly. The dragon's jaws snapped at empty air as the giant wrapped a hand around her long neck. A clenched fist the size of a barrel smashed into the wedge-shaped head once, twice, three times. The dragon's almond eyes fluttered, one wing over the water becoming submerged as she rolled to the side, limbs closing in to protect her body from the blows.

'Liana!' Eiric cried.

Chloe furiously tugged at the bonds behind his ankles but couldn't free the tough deer gut.

'Here!' a reedy voice called. Chloe turned and saw an eldran with silver-white hair and wrinkled skin. He threw something and she saw a piece of dark stone fall to the ground nearby: an obsidian knife.

Knowing she was running out of time, Chloe grabbed the knife and returned to Eiric's side as he screamed Liana's name. She cut the bonds at his ankles and then wrists; immediately Eiric fell to the ground.

Looking to the struggle between the two eldren, Chloe gasped in horror as she saw the fight had gone out of Liana: the giant had put a knee on the dragon's back. His one eye glaring, mouth parted, teeth bared, he now leaned down on her.

Triton was going to break Liana's spine.

'You have to change!' Chloe begged Eiric. On his hands and knees, she saw that he was struggling to stand, let alone change.

Then she realized the purpose of the iron chain around his neck: his power was confined; as an eldran he could never touch it.

Her fingers fumbled at the chain's clasp. The dragon roared with pain. The roar became a scream. Finally the chain fell to the ground. Chloe straightened, fists clenched at her sides as she waited for Eiric to change.

He looked at her in desperation and shook his head.

Chloe's eyes went to the staff lying on the ground. Rushing over, she picked it up and faced the pool's edge, where the giant had the dragon's back half bent, body twisted in a contorted position. At any instant Chloe would hear a spine-shattering crack.

She took two steps forward. Gripping the staff tightly, her encircling fingers touching the copper, she lifted it high.

Chloe again touched the fire that raged inside her, yearning to be unleashed. Her power sensed the copper and she felt it being drawn to the metal, but then it pulled back, losing focus, becoming a torrent rather than a directed stream. Filled with urgency, she knew she had to concentrate harder than she ever had before. She had to drive out the fear and the desire for violent action; she was working with copper. She needed to bring her thoughts into harmony.

Never before had Chloe realized how difficult it would be in the heat of battle. Trying to think of something that would bring her thoughts into focus, she thrust her mind back to the time she'd played her copper flute for Solon, with the great pyramid looming over her, its shining surface clad in gold. But his dark eyes had been on her; she hadn't been as calm as she needed to be.

Chloe cast back still further, to a time when she'd been in a place where she felt safe, in the company of the people she loved. Seated at her father's table, her flute was pressed to her lips as she sat directly across from a young man with flaxen hair, a square jaw, and tanned skin. Her father sat at her side, gazing at her fondly. Dion was watching her face as if interpreting a beautiful painting, trying to memorize what he was seeing, attempting to uncover hidden secrets.

Chloe closed her eyes. She found her moment of harmony.

As she'd learned from Vikram, she imagined a pure, crystal clear note, banishing the roars of the giant and anguished moans of the dragon, and then let it grow in intensity. Once she had the sound perfected, conceiving it, holding on to it, she opened her eyes.

She now had to throw it.

She tilted the staff so that the two pointed tines of the copper fork faced the giant's monstrous head, which was so high above her that she was pointing up at the sky.

Chloe cried out.

She released her power.

The copper fork flared, glowing brightly. A warbling shriek filled the air, the sound of a million birds crying out with one voice. The entire staff, from base to tip, shook like a branch in a storm. The resonator hummed and quivered as she projected her power in the direction she was pointing.

The giant released the dragon and rose to his immense height. He emitted a terrible groaning scream. His huge hands clapped over his ears.

As soon as he released her, the dragon clouded with gray mist that wavered for a moment before vanishing, leaving Liana in its place, sprawled out on the black earth with limbs akimbo, half her body in the black water, eyes tightly closed so that Chloe didn't know if her friend was alive or dead.

The other eldren all fell to the ground, grimacing, hands pressed tightly against the sides of their heads.

Chloe held the staff pointed directly at the giant's head as he stumbled and lurched. He nearly tumbled into the pool but then staggered in the opposite direction. He kicked a fire but didn't appear to notice, scattering red embers across the ground. Finally, when he fell to one knee, she began to feel triumphant. Walking forward, she kept her weapon pointed at her enemy and glanced at the copper fork.

Horror sank into her chest.

The metal was tarnishing even as she watched. Green discoloration crept up from the base, spreading to the apex of the fork, traveling along both tines at the same time. Suddenly the copper was entirely green, and then the metal began to flake away, falling to the ground.

The sound stopped as suddenly as it started. Chloe felt exhaustion descend, like a crushing weight on her shoulders. A headache pounded at her temples, along with a painful buzzing in her ears. She was now holding a wooden staff with nothing at the end at all.

The giant shuddered. He glared at her as he climbed back to his feet. With long, ground-shaking strides, he began to walk toward her.

But then Chloe heard a soft, female voice. She glanced at the pool's edge and saw Liana lift her head and look past Chloe's shoulder.

'Do it,' Liana said.

Liana had her eyes on Eiric. Chloe whirled, expecting to see Eiric changed into some powerful shape, but he was still on his hands and knees. He had his eyes on something on the ground, something that had spilled out of Liana's satchel and was now just a short distance from his hand.

Eiric set his jaw in determination. He reached out and grabbed the object, just as Chloe realized what it was.

It was a horn.

Every set of eyes was now on the tall eldran with the golden eyes who climbed to his feet, panting as he looked at the glowing conch shell in his hand. Despite the fact that the shell was white, it scattered bright rays of all colors over the area, a rainbow of light that was both captivating and terrible.

Chloe turned back to Triton, seeing that he was once again a one-eyed eldran. His fists were clenched at his sides, his face displaying more fury than she had ever seen on an eldran's visage.

'Do it!' Liana cried.

Eiric met Chloe's eyes, and then Liana's. He put the horn to his lips.

For a moment nothing happened, and then a powerful rumble came from the horn, making Chloe's teeth slam together so that she nearly bit her lip. She felt the noise with a shattering pain inside her skull, but now it was the eldren who were unperturbed as they watched Eiric with mouths open.

Sudden thunder pealed. A glowing circle with the horn at the epicenter rolled out, a ripple of multicolored light that started at Eiric and reached the edge of the basin in an instant and continued, both into the sky and out into the surrounding land. Gazing up, Chloe could see the concussive wave projected onwards and upwards. She knew that at the rate it was moving it would be striking the range of mountains encircling Cinder Fen in minutes.

Chloe had no idea what would happen next.

Eiric, son of Zachary and Aella, had sounded the horn of Marrix.

63

Dion ordered his fleet to increase to ramming speed. Beneath him, the *Black Dragon* leaped forward like a horse stung in the flank.

'Dion!' Cob growled, grabbing hold of his arm. 'You can't do this.'

Dion urged his warships on, feeling the precious seconds trickle away with every passing moment. 'We have to reach the battle. They're about to close in again. Roxana's going to be crushed!'

'Can't you see the danger right in front of you?' Cob cried.

The three immense serpents ahead leaped out of the water and plunged back in, paddle-like tails visible for a heartbeat as they thrashed at the sea. With the increase in speed the fleet of the Free Men narrowed the distance between their line of warships and the wildren. Three hundred paces became two hundred paces, and then one.

'You can't attack them!'

'I know that,' Dion muttered.

Unlike the men he'd fought with alongside Roxana, his crew had no experience fighting wildren, and even Roxana would never take on more than one. For the time being the leviathans were consumed with the smoking wreckage and drowning men ahead, but if they turned . . .

Dion saw Aristocles standing at the bow, his hands gripping the rail as he watched the unfolding confrontation a mile away, urging the fleet of the Free Men to come to the aid of the Xanthian fleet before it was too late. The naval battle ahead was a scene of confusion as archers released volleys of arrows, rams tore gaping holes in vessels' sides, and sails caught fire, becoming vertical sheets of flame. Ships flying yellow flags crashed alongside biremes flying crimson pennants. Splintering wood flew into the air.

Then the worst happened.

It was impossible to silence the shouts of Dion's sailors and the clang of wood against wood made by the oarsmen. The pounding of the drums and smacking of the hulls on the crests of the waves were louder still.

First one serpent and then the other peeled away to the sides, and then their tails kicked and they whirled. All three wildren turned baleful eyes on the *Black Dragon*, the lead warship of the fleet, and converged.

Dion was under attack, and he knew his ship would never survive the concerted assault of three leviathans.

'They'll be busy with us,' Dion said grimly. 'Order the fleet on!'

White-faced sailors raced to the rails and cried out at the ships on both sides, bellowing so that the other captains would hear. The rest of the fleet of the Free Men drew apart from the *Black Dragon*, creating distance at both sides.

The central leviathan, flanked by two nearly as large, headed in a direct line for the bireme where Dion, Cob, and Aristocles, along with the crew, watched in horror. A wave of water crested in front of the monster as it charged. Even if the ram struck the lead wildran, the other two would pummel the vessel from the sides. The three serpents were each as wide as the *Black Dragon* itself, their length greater still.

'I suppose this is it,' Cob said.

'The rest of the fleet will reach the battle.'

'While I get eaten alive. For the second time.'

'Sorry,' Dion said with a smile. 'There's still a chance—'

Cob never heard Dion's next words as the heavens rumbled, the air becoming filled with the sound of a sonorous horn. The low boom grew louder until it was pealing like a roar of thunder. Dion and Cob exchanged glances as both men looked toward the hazy triangle of Mount Oden, but there was no smoke trickling from the peak of the volcano.

But there was another land on the other side of the island: Cinder Fen.

Dion gasped.

A wave of shimmering light, colored like a rainbow, sped out from the direction of Cinder Fen, rolling like an explosive detonation. When the light reached the *Black Dragon* the lead leviathan was just forty paces from the ship's bow.

The serpent shivered as if it had been struck by lightning.

Dion realized he was holding his breath and let it out in a whoosh as all three leviathans shuddered. The wildren thrashed their tails at the water and turned, their eyes fixed hypnotically in the direction of Cinder Fen. The three serpents now sped in the direction of their homeland, leaving frothing wakes behind them.

In the time it took Dion to draw in another breath, they were gone.

He tried not to think about what must have happened. An eldran had sounded the horn of Marrix. The wildren were being drawn home.

'Ramming speed!' Dion cried out.

He could distinctly make out each ship of the Ilean fleet now, embroiled with the warships of Xanthos. Eyes darting, he separated the biremes into friend and foe by the flags flying from each vessel's mast: crimson or yellow. Fire arrows left bright trails as they sizzled from ship to ship. Timbers shattered as a Xanthian ship raked an enemy.

He pointed at the Ilean flagship, a vessel with a red pennant flying above the yellow. 'Helmsman, angle us into their side! We're going to strike!'

64

Wildren traveled toward the heart of Cinder Fen.

They ran from caves and plummeted from the sky. Ogres and giants lumbered, furies and dragons flew, and merfolk and serpents sped through the sea. Many, though, were deep beneath the sea or a great distance away. It would take more than one blast of the horn of Marrix to summon them all, and the serpents would cling to shore like half-drowned humans, but in time the holder of the horn would summon them all.

'He has the blood of Marrix!' Dalton cried.

The old eldran sank to one knee, and the eldren arrayed behind him followed suit. All eyes were on Eiric as he took the horn from his lips. A moment later he looked at the magical conch in his hand, his expression as stunned as the rest of them.

Chloe looked up as fluttering shadows suddenly clouded the sky. She gasped.

She couldn't see the slightest patch of blue. Dragons and man-like furies hovered above the wide basin, wings sweeping back and forth, staring down as if awaiting instruction. Pushing through the gnarled trees, multitudes of giants and ogres encircled the perimeter, all gazing down at Eiric. Chloe had never imagined so many wildren could exist. Seeing so many congregated in one place was terrifying.

She looked to Liana lying on the ground near the pool's edge, head raised, her wide eyes on Eiric. The only people standing were Chloe, Eiric, and Triton, for the other eldren were all on their knees, heads bowed.

For the first time, Chloe saw Triton's shoulders slump. The once dauntless king of the eldren stared at the ground and then looked up at the wildren clouding the sky.

'Command the wildren,' Triton said wearily. 'Order them to kill me.'

Eiric shook his head. 'No,' he said. He glanced at the conch in his hand. 'It . . . It speaks to me. You, Triton, even you never knew the truth.' He swept his gaze over all the eldren. 'The horn doesn't allow us to control them, only to summon them. My father always told me that when we change we draw on the power of our homeland, and that as more and more became trapped in their form, the magic of this place drained away until it is as you see it now. It became this way not because of the humans, but because the magic of Sindara has been spent.'

Triton's fist clenched and his body tensed. Seeing Eiric's attention on the kneeling eldren, Chloe started to issue a warning when Eiric lifted the horn into the air.

'I now know what the horn was made to do. Its main purpose is to bring our changed brethren home so they can be reminded who they are. But if they are too far gone . . .' He called out in a voice that filled the heavens: 'You who were once eldren, but are not any more'—and his next words were the last Chloe expected him to say—'I put you all to rest!'

Another concussive blast of energy left the horn, the circle growing larger as it rippled out from the magical conch. This time the light was green, the color of fresh growth. It struck the nearest of the wildren and continued onto the next. Flying or standing, each creature shivered as the light passed over it, and for an instant it was as if the wild eyes cleared, and they were once more as they had been, intelligent eldren in changed form.

Even Triton looked awestruck.

Dragons and furies dropped out of the sky as if they'd been turned into stone. Giants and ogres fell forward or crumpled where they stood, tumbling to the ground one after the other like toppling statues. Bodies of all shapes and sizes crashed into the pool and sank immediately, one after the other. An ogre tumbled to the bottom of the limestone wall near Chloe. She saw an expression that was surprisingly peaceful on the creature's broad face.

As she continued to stare at the ogre's body, it began to change. Gray mist elongated and thickened, and then the ogre shimmered like a haze of hot air rising from the ground on a summer's day. But when the mist cleared, rather than a new form in its place, the ogre was gone, faded away to nothing.

Turning back to the pool, Chloe realized that all the wildren she'd seen just a moment ago had also vanished, returned to their homeland, becoming part of Sindara once more.

Chloe saw Eiric put the horn to his lips again. He blew a thunderous blast and then lifted the horn into the sky. The rainbow circle rippled out again. More wildren came to Cinder Fen's heart. Once again dragons clouded the sky and ogres and giants peered down from the basin's perimeter. Like the others, Eiric put them all to rest.

Cinder Fen began to change.

Chloe gasped when a blade of grass sprouted from the charred earth beside the pool. It was followed by a second, and then a dozen more. Tiny patches of plant life appeared, here and there on the blackened ground, and each patch grew until they were brushing up against each other. Tangling vines climbed the limestone walls, reaching up to the gnarled trees that encircled the wide basin.

The trees above straightened as fresh growth sprouted from their branches. Waxy leaves appeared a moment later. Suddenly emerald colors were everywhere, with plants sprouting underfoot and the green grass growing thicker than any carpet, becoming inches high and finally taller than Chloe's ankle. She stepped to the side as a sprout appeared directly underneath her, jumping further away as it grew to become a willow with a trunk as thick as her wrist. The eldren gazed around them in awe.

'Kneel!' the old eldran called to Triton.

'No.' Triton shook his head. 'I won't do it.'

A glowing light the color of jade now shone from the depths of the black pool. The radiance below the surface became stronger until the light poured from the pool to shine on the faces of everyone present. The wellspring returned to life, restoring the energy to Sindara that had been contained in the wildren for so long.

Still more dragons and furies traveled to Cinder Fen's heart, responding to each call of the horn. Ever more ogres and giants approached the basin's rim. One after the other, they faded away.

The air fairly hummed with life and new growth. The fresh scent of plants and sweet floral odors became overwhelming. Flowers sprouted from the vines.

Stunned by what she was seeing, Chloe looked at Eiric. Her eyes were on him when tears suddenly welled in his eyes, spilling down his cheeks. He was staring up at the sky.

Wondering how he could feel such sadness in a moment of triumph, she followed his gaze.

Chloe put a hand to her mouth.

An ancient dragon with mottled silver scales and a crescent scar on the side of its face hovered above the very center of the basin, wings fluttering. Some of the scales were torn away, displaying dried blood around angry gashes. Sad brown eyes flecked with golden sparks looked at Eiric.

The dragon then looked at Chloe.

'Zachary . . .' Chloe realized she was crying. She'd known him since she was a child. He'd saved her sister's life. Eiric had blown the horn, and like all the other wildren, he had come.

'Eiric!' Liana suddenly cried.

Whirling, Chloe saw Triton picking something up off the ground. When he straightened, she saw that it was an obsidian knife. Triton snarled and the muscles in his arms bunched. His one eye was fixed on Eiric.

But Eiric was consumed with what was happening above.

The dragon roared, plummeting from the sky, descending with claws outstretched. Each forelimb gripped hold of Triton's shoulders as jaws closed around his head. Powerful wings beat at the ground, lifting the one-eyed eldran into the air. With a sickening crunch the yellowed teeth tore at Triton's neck, blood erupting in a fountain. The dragon then released, and Triton's body fell through the air, crashing into the glowing pool and immediately sinking.

The dragon's movements became weak and for the first time Chloe realized the creature was wounded, struggling to finally alight on the ground in front of Eiric. The wings folded in; hoarse breath wheezed and rumbled.

Chloe remembered the first time she'd visited the Village in the Wilds as a child, when Zachary had crouched and opened his hand to reveal a shiny green frog, taking away her initial fear and making her smile. She felt a terrible sadness grip her heart as Eiric came forward to stroke the angular ridges on the dragon's head.

'Father,' Eiric said. His eyes shimmered.

The dragon's head sank to the ground. Mist started to well around the ancient creature.

But when the mist cleared, Chloe felt a surge of joy.

Zachary could barely stand. Leaner than his son, looking like every one of his years was weighing on his shoulders, he was gaunt, the crescent scar on his cheek pale and angry, his shoulder-length hair now streaked with white. He stumbled, and his son caught him as he fell forward to clasp Eiric's shoulder.

'I never wanted this for you, but I was wrong,' Zachary said. Taking strength from Eiric's support he lifted his gaze. 'I have now lived to see it, the return of our homeland, and our new king.'

'Father . . .'

'No.' Zachary shook off his son. 'I want to be the first.' Zachary's gold-flecked eyes met Chloe's and he smiled. 'Will you help me, Chloe? I want to see Sindara.'

65

Nikolas scowled as the surgeon examined the wound in his upper thigh, his mind on something else altogether. He stared at the canvas wall of his tent and reflected on the battle.

It had gone badly.

His plan had been partly successful, and he'd lured Mydas into chase, attacking and then retreating. As his center withdrew, he'd left his cavalry to close in around the main host of the Ilean army. With their greater range his bowmen had decimated the enemy as they charged, and his cavalry had wiped out the Ileans archers to a man.

Then it started to go wrong.

They'd reached the river, too wide to cross, and Nikolas had reformed his infantry. He'd evened the numbers: the Ileans still had far more men, but the slower units were miles away while only the chariots and elite Lamaran infantry faced a greater number of Galeans.

As he bellowed orders and called on his men to prepare the counterattack he'd been surprised to see the chariots at the front of the horde. A line of four or five hundred wheeled vehicles drawn by racing thoroughbreds led a host of yellow-cloaked Ileans, sprinting to keep up with the horses.

He'd ordered his men to charge. He'd led them from the front, on foot now, for his stallion had taken an arrow to the flank.

Men who'd run all day forced unwilling limbs into action, marching forward in the blazing heat. On Nikolas's command they charged. The two forces collided.

And then Nikolas learned about the chariots.

Each wheel had a pole jutting out from the center of the spokes. It was a steel blade, sharpened like a razor, whirling over and over with every turn of the wheels. Lothar had mentioned them but Nikolas had never seen them in action.

He'd trained his men to attack cavalry from the flanks, spearing the mounts and stabbing up to strike the riders. But as his king's guard crashed into the chariots they were too encumbered to dance around the scything blades. They were too hot, and too wearied from the previous chase. A lesser force would have fallen under the Xanthian hoplites' spears and sharp swords, but the Ilean chariot drivers were skilled and knew their business.

He lost his entire king's guard, most of them when their legs were cut out from under them. Their short skirts of leather strips did little to prevent their knees slicing cleanly away. It was a sight Nikolas never wanted to see again.

Nonetheless, with a strong position and the skill of his remaining hoplites and archers, he'd managed to destroy the chariots before slamming against the Lamaran infantry. The forces of Koulis and Tanus fought valiantly, and finally the Galeans prevailed. With Nikolas's cavalry pressing against their flanks and his archers harassing them, the Ileans fled.

But his army had suffered devastating losses, and Mydas was far from defeated.

Still wearing his armor, Nikolas now sat with his legs wide apart and his left foot on a stool. The old surgeon was seated on the ground, needle and thread in his lap as he took a bloody cloth from the wound in Nikolas's inner thigh and glanced up.

'Another inch . . .' The surgeon shook his head, frowning. 'Half an inch . . . The blow would have opened your artery. You wouldn't be sitting here now. You'd be dead.'

'Finish your work,' Nikolas said.

'You shouldn't be walking . . . You need to be in bed. And as for fighting again in battle . . .' The surgeon continued to shake his head, undeterred by Nikolas's glare. 'The slightest tear could still cause you to bleed out. Even walking increases the chance of mortification.'

The surgeon began to stitch, causing Nikolas to wince inwardly, but he didn't allow any sign of pain to cross his face. The sound of raised voices came from outside the tent, and he frowned as he saw Lothar of Koulis push past the guard stationed outside, ignoring the soldier's protestations.

'Nikolas,' Lothar said as he stormed in. The old lord glanced at the surgeon and shuddered at what he was doing but pressed on. 'We've received word from the enemy. They request parley.'

'Parley,' Nikolas snorted. 'This is no time for talk. We have them on the run.'

'On the run?' Lothar's eyes narrowed. 'We lost a third of our men!'

'A quarter,' Nikolas growled. 'We'll have them tomorrow.'

Lothar was old but he was strong-willed. A silver circlet held back his long gray hair and he wore a leather skirt and breastplate, despite playing no role in the fighting.

'I've spoken with Zanthe of Tanus and we both agree that it can't hurt to hear what Mydas has to say.' Lothar lifted his chin. 'I will return and report.'

Nikolas frowned. He felt the needle stabbing the soft skin of his thigh and remembered the Ilean spear that had almost killed him. He'd barely felt it at the time.

'Are you done?' He demanded as he looked down at the surgeon.

'Hold on,' the surgeon said. 'And be still.'

Nikolas waited impatiently as the surgeon finished stitching and wrapped his thigh in a tight bandage. He finally stood, testing his body. He felt satisfied that he could walk.

'Fine,' he said to Lothar. 'We'll go and see Mydas up close. I can tell him what I did to his brother's corpse, and what I plan to do to his.'

———————

Nikolas told himself that he was walking slowly for the benefit of the older rulers, but in truth he was struggling to hide the pain he felt at every step. He grimaced as Lothar of Koulis and Zanthe of Tanus, flanking him on both sides, reduced their speed to the pace he could manage. Nikolas saw their anxious looks, but he was more concerned about appearing weak in front of the dozen crimson-cloaked soldiers behind them.

They had traveled on horseback to the center of the plain, between the two distant army encampments, but as agreed they'd then left the horses behind. The expanse was flat and featureless, broken only by the cloth tent they were walking toward. It was the only thing to look at, and it was clear at a glance that there was no chance of betrayal, for no more than twelve Ilean soldiers stood waiting a stone's throw from the central pavilion.

When he reached a similar distance, Nikolas turned and instructed his soldiers to stay behind. He and the other two rulers then approached the peaked tent, open at the sides. He could make out the figures of two men within, one seated and the other standing.

Suddenly he was forced to slow as the wound in his thigh sent a stabbing pain throughout his body, becoming far more than a dull ache. The surgeon was right, he realized, he was in no fit state for combat. He caught Lothar and Zanthe exchanging glances.

'I'm fine,' he muttered. 'It's a shallow wound.'

Taking a deep breath and pushing on, he immediately felt relief from the scorching heat as he entered the pavilion, where four square carpets had been laid over the ground. His jaw was tight as he looked at the man in the high-backed wooden chair.

Then Nikolas saw who was sitting in the chair.

He paused in stunned surprise before swiftly masking his expression and continuing until he stopped in front. Glancing back, he saw that Lothar was as shocked as he was.

The seated man wasn't Mydas, but an Ilean commander Nikolas recognized from the Battle of Phalesia. He was barrel-chested and swarthy, with a curled beard and a thick mop of black hair. The scars on his hands confirmed the Ilean's identity: he was a warrior; this was no courtier.

Beside the chair stood the biggest man Nikolas had ever seen, a tall warrior with thick lips and wiry hair tied behind his head with a leather thong. Contrasting with the Ilean in the chair, who was clad in a bright orange robe, the warrior wore a leather vest open at his chest and tight trousers.

'King Nikolas,' the barrel-chested Ilean said without preamble. 'My name is Kargan.' He nodded his head in Lothar's direction. 'He knows who I am,' he said with a brief smile.

'Kargan—?' Lothar began incredulously.

'Silence,' Kargan said softly, turning his dark eyes on the silver-haired lord. 'You've had your fun, Lothar. How about you wait outside and let the important men talk?'

Lothar spluttered but Nikolas turned and squeezed the old man's thin shoulder. He glanced at Queen Zanthe, who nodded and led Lothar back outside the pavilion.

'It's just you and me,' Nikolas said grimly. 'And I have one question for you. Why am I speaking with you rather than Mydas? Where is he? You asked for parley and I came. But I'll have you know that I intend to destroy your army—'

As Nikolas spoke Kargan nodded at the warrior at his side, who crouched and lifted up a wooden box. He stepped forward and passed the box over as Nikolas fell silent.

'Open it,' Kargan said. 'It's my gift to you.'

Holding the box with both hands, casting a bemused glance at Kargan, Nikolas set it down on the ground. He lifted the lid and then frowned.

Inside was a human head.

It was the head of a heavyset man, with long, greasy dark hair in ringlets and eyes wide open in a blank stare. Golden earrings enclosed both his earlobes. His head was arranged so that he was staring out at Nikolas, which meant that Nikolas could see the jagged wound made by the sword or axe that had killed him. Nikolas was an experienced warrior; he could see at a glance that the man had died only recently.

'Mydas, one-time king of Ilea,' Kargan said. 'Not far from here, he and I had a recent conversation that ended with his death. Take it with you. Show it to anyone you wish.'

Nikolas was momentarily speechless. He looked down at the head and then up at Kargan. 'Why?'

'Enough of my men have died, and I'll wager enough of yours too. I have an empire to rebuild, and I have no interest in your lands across the sea. The Salesian continent is enough for one man. Now'—Kargan's eyes narrowed, and Nikolas recognized a will that matched his own—'you are a fighting king, a soldier, and I risked speaking with you on the basis that you understand a certain concept.'

'What concept?'

'The idea of following another man's orders. I took no part in killing your family, and the last of Solon's line is dead.' He inclined his head at the huge warrior. 'My friend Javid here killed all three of Solon's sons, and now you have the head of his brother. Solon ordered that I attack Phalesia and I did, but I have no wish to fight with Galea any longer. Nikolas, king of Xanthos, you and your people have suffered enough. Can we make peace?'

Nikolas glanced outside at Lothar and Zanthe. 'I'll have to confer . . .'

'Nonsense,' Kargan growled. 'The Galean League is yours to command. You've shown you have teeth. I have no interest in your lands, and I'd like you to leave mine. Koulis can stay independent, or continue as part of your league. But the rest of Salesia . . .' His voice lowered. 'Now that is my domain.'

Nikolas thought about his wife, Helena, and son, Lukas. He sighed, and was surprised to find tears welling behind his eyes. He'd more than had his vengeance. Enough blood had been shed.

'I agree to it,' he said. 'Let us have peace.'

66

Roxana whooped as, on the other side of the enemy fleet, a bireme's bronze ram tore open the hull of an Ilean ship. Water poured in the side of the vessel and it immediately listed, sinking in moments. Seeing the danger, the enemy warships tried to turn their vessels to face the new threat, which only exposed them to more of the sharp rams. Two warships flying yellow pennants were sinking and then three. Around Roxana the Xanthian archers ducking under their shields began to warily raise their heads.

She scanned across her fleet, seeing that she'd lost another ship to the fire arrows, but she still had five intact warships, and this new force was striking the Ileans from the rear, sinking them in numbers. She didn't know who they were but she wasn't about to draw alongside and shout questions during a pitched naval battle.

'Archers! Fire!' she bellowed.

The Xanthian fleet and the newcomers met in the middle, dividing the Ilean fleet neatly. It was what she'd wanted all along, but she'd never have been able to accomplish it alone. Their commander was canny, she decided. Rather than thin his line he'd sought to combine his strength with hers, at the same time splintering the enemy into two smaller forces. She was looking forward to finding out who he was.

Four Ilean biremes now turned sharply, heading directly away from the merging force of the allied fleets. On the other side five surviving warships, one burning fiercely, headed in the opposite direction.

Glancing at the newcomers, Roxana saw that they were turning to give chase to the larger Ilean force. She frowned as she saw that each vessel flied a silver flag with a black trident; it was nothing she was familiar with.

'They're forming a line!' Hasha cried. 'What orders?'

'Join up with them, of course,' Roxana barked. 'Pursue!'

The two fleets now became one, charging like a line of cavalry at the smaller force of five Ilean warships, which fled in front of them but must have seen the looming cliffs of the isle of Coros. As if on cue, the five Ilean biremes turned, but the line of pursuing ships was too long for them to outdistance.

'Now the hunters become prey,' Roxana muttered.

With shattering force the allied fleet struck the Ileans. Two lean war galleys flying silver flags assaulted the smoking ship from both sides, making short work of the larger bireme. Their nearby flagship tore into two Ilean warships in quick succession. Roxana's archers peppered the crew of the fourth before one of her warships struck the enemy vessel with a blow that made her wince. The final Ilean ship burst free of the envelopment, sail raised to give it extra speed, but then flaming arrows rained from the Xanthian archers and the sail caught fire, the inferno spreading as crewmen leaped off the sides and into the waters of the open sea.

Roxana allowed the *Anoraxis* to slow, within sight of the Galean mainland; the last burst of speed would have been hell on the oarsmen. They would never catch the four Ilean warships fleeing for home.

The battle was over.

Dion made a dramatic approach, swinging on a rope to cross from the *Black Dragon* to the deck of the *Anoraxis*. He landed lightly, poised like a dancer before straightening.

The crew saw him and cheered. He smiled but then the cheers became louder and louder, stunning him with the sound, and then he realized why they were roaring so stridently. He glanced at the sailors and archers, the helmsman and the young boys securing loose lines.

They were almost entirely men of Xanthos.

These people knew his face. Many were the sailors and fishermen he'd grown up with under Cob's tutelage. And they'd just seen his arrival save them from certain death.

He gazed around in amazement as someone cried his name, and then in unison they were shouting the single word. He turned slowly, looking at the multitude of men, all cheering as loudly as they could. A powerful mixture of emotions threatened to overwhelm him, ranging from exhilaration to relief, and he felt a catch at the back of his throat as tears welled behind his eyes. Transfixed, he was surprised by the stocky woman with short sun-bleached hair who strode across the deck and without pausing wrapped her arms around him.

'Dion of No-land,' she said into his ear. She thrust his shoulders back to look into his face. 'Why am I not surprised?'

'Dion of Xanthos,' he said.

'I know,' she said. 'I know.' She shook her head, grinning broadly. 'We have a lot to catch up on.'

———

Now working as one, the fleet would travel to Phalesia before continuing on to Xanthos. Dion and Aristocles stood together at the *Black Dragon*'s bow, watching as the mainland grew larger in their vision.

For the first time in what felt like eons, Dion saw the marble temples clustered around the Phalesian agora and the huge horseshoe structure that was the lyceum. He saw the beautiful city spread its arms to embrace the white-pebbled beach and the tall cliff leading up to the Temple of Aldus, near the sloped embankment leaning above the shore. Bright midday sun shone from the glistening buildings, reflecting from the statue of the god Aldus standing outside the lyceum.

Dion watched in silence, the city now filling his vision as the *Black Dragon* peeled away from the surrounding vessels to disembark Aristocles and Amos at Phalesia's small harbor. The *Black Dragon* would then rejoin the fleet, for Roxana had insisted that she escort the Free Men to Xanthos, where she'd built shipyards and a sailor's mess. As their leader, he would travel with them, but the thought of returning to his home made him more anxious than he cared to admit.

'Dion.' He heard his name and saw Amos approaching, his face tinged green and his steps a little unsteady. The veteran warrior gripped his hand. 'This is where we part ways. But not for long, I hope.' He gave Dion an inscrutable look. 'Your home is here. In Galea. You realize that, don't you?'

'We'll see each other soon,' Dion said with a smile.

Amos nodded and left Aristocles and Dion to talk as the warship's oars barely slapped at the water, angling them in to a bare patch of shore with the lightest of touches.

'He is right, you know,' Aristocles said, turning to Dion. He hesitated. 'And there is something else I want you to hear. My daughter . . . I realized too late that she had feelings for you. She thought she was keeping me happy by not saying anything, and by accepting my foolish idea of wedding her to your brother.'

Aristocles sighed, reflecting.

'It may not be too late,' he continued. 'It's possible Nikolas did not make her his wife before leading his army to Tanus and then across the

Waste. When I see her . . . If she is unmarried I will tell her she should follow her heart. And I will pray that the gods lead her to you.'

Dion shook his head. 'My brother . . .'

'He has nothing on his mind but vengeance. What will he be like when he has to worry about the fate of his subjects? You have it within you to become a wise ruler.'

'That's treason.'

'It is truth.' Aristocles smiled.

'You'll send me word when you're ready to find homes for the Free Men?'

'If that is what you want.'

When Dion frowned, Aristocles gripped his shoulder. 'My daughter said you always wanted Xanthos to have a navy. Now you have your wish. I'm not about to take your men away. In Phalesia we consuls must pretend to perfection, and we seize on any difference as weakness. In Xanthos matters are different. Men follow a strong leader, which is what you have become. Find them homes in Xanthos.'

Dion's brow furrowed as he thought about his responsibility to the Free Men, but he slowly nodded. 'I will try.' He looked up at the city of Phalesia. 'How do you know that you'll be safe here?'

'I am a returning hero,' Aristocles said with a smile. 'Trust me. I know how to use that to my advantage.' He glanced at the craggy-faced soldier, waiting nearby. 'I also have the men you're leaving with me and, most importantly of all, I have Amos.' He surprised Dion by embracing him. 'Don't worry about me, Prince Dion of Xanthos. I have nothing to fear.'

———

A full moon rose, exchanging places with the setting sun as it climbed above the blue horizon. The silver shimmer of its reflection glistened on the sea like a rippling pathway. A multitude of oars dipped in and out of the water slowly, the sound unsynchronized but pleasant, for the men had fought beyond all endurance and now rowed at their ease, with even the drum allowed to fall silent.

Dusk became early evening and stars twinkled above the city of Xanthos. Dion felt strange as he saw the familiar sights: the grassy bank above the curve of the harbor; the cleft in the shore forming a small ravine and dividing the shoreline into two halves; the three-storied Royal Palace dominating the vista, larger even than the temple of Balal with its bronze statue of a spear-carrying hoplite.

There were some new houses on the residential side, but with the city on a war footing the area was close to deserted. A defensive palisade of sharp wooden spikes jutted out from the shoreline and a thin line of soldiers stood behind. But already word was spreading and more people appeared in ones and twos, coming out of hiding when they realized that Xanthos wasn't under imminent attack.

The soldiers rushed to pull aside barriers of thorn bushes and uproot the spikes to create space for so many ships. Seeing the defenses, Dion felt proud of his older brother. He'd had the wisdom to recruit Roxana, and he'd realized that naval power would determine the future. Nikolas had been too bold in leading his army to Ilea: without the intervention of the Free Men, Phalesia and Xanthos would likely be in ruins, with more blood spilled than Dion cared to imagine. But now, not only Salesia but also Galea had a chance to shape the future, to ride the ever-shifting tides, to trade and prosper on the silver road.

Dion felt torn by mixed emotions as each vessel waited its turn and then slipped in to lie side by side with a fellow, slotting into its place as if the two fleets had always worked together as one. Finally the *Black Dragon*'s gangway went out and he disembarked, soon standing with Roxana and Cob on the soft sand of his homeland.

He glanced up at the bank as he saw a rangy man in a thick white tunic approaching.

'Dion?' he said in wonder. 'Is that you?'

Dion smiled as he recognized the tall man with the neat beard and close-cropped gray hair. 'It's good to see you, Uncle Glaukos.'

'But . . . how are you here?'

'We were all but lost,' Roxana said. She grinned and nodded at Dion. 'Until Prince Dion here arrived with a fleet as big as ours. It was a decisive victory.'

The two men embraced, and then Glaukos held Dion back to get a good look at him. 'Lad, I have to know. Is it true, what your brother says?'

Dion glanced at Roxana and Cob before looking back to his uncle and nodding. 'It is.'

'Bah,' Glaukos said. 'You look the same as you always did, if a little taller, and a little stronger.' He glanced up at the palace. 'This isn't my home, it's yours. Come. We can sit on the Orange Terrace and talk.'

Dion shook his head. 'I must . . .'

Cob squeezed his shoulder. 'I can take care of everything here. Go to your home, lad.'

'Don't think you can do this better than I can,' Roxana said with a broad smile.

He swallowed and then nodded. 'Thank you,' he said. 'Both of you.'

Dion followed his uncle to the stairway leading up to the Orange Terrace and the two men ascended together. As he climbed he caught the scent of citrus wafting on the breeze and felt sadness overwhelm any other emotion. He missed his mother, and even now he kept expecting her to appear to fuss over him.

'Nikolas has me overseeing the kingdom while he's away,' Glaukos said. 'There are a thousand matters requiring my attention. I could sorely use your help.'

'I'll help in any way I can.'

They reached the terrace and followed the path that led through the orange trees, heavy with bright fruit. Coming to a halt not far from the stone table and its benches, laid out to face the harbor and the sea, Glaukos called for a steward to bring wine, and a moment later he handed Dion a goblet filled with crimson liquid. Dion's uncle then instructed the steward to ready Dion's chambers.

Dion almost pinched his arm. It felt strange and unreal to think that he would be sleeping in his own bed.

Glaukos then led Dion back to the terrace's stone rail and for a time they watched the activity at the harbor.

'I'm sure you wish to rest, but there are matters we should speak about first. You know your brother is somewhere in Ilea?'

'I know.'

'There will be news soon enough.' He glanced at Dion. 'The kingdom is vulnerable, more vulnerable than at any other time in my memory. It would be wrong for you to leave again, you understand that? Nikolas has no wife, no heir, which makes you next in line for the throne. You have responsibilities, Dion.'

'I have responsibilities to others also. The men down there . . . I've promised them homes. They fought for us.'

'Homes? Here in Xanthos?' Glaukos frowned. 'Who are they?'

'They are the Free Men.'

Glaukos spluttered into his cup, breaking into a fit of coughing. 'The pirates? We have to feed and house hundreds of pirates?'

'We do.'

Glaukos's lips thinned. 'I will need to speak with their leader.'

'You are.' Dion smiled. He took a sip from his wine as his uncle stood speechless, his mouth gaping.

'You . . . You're Andion, the king of the Free Men?'

'That's what they call me. But I was elected by vote, and one day another may take my place.'

Glaukos was speechless, only able to shake his head.

'We . . .' Dion wondered how to explain. 'We also have a new territory to administer, an island in the Maltherean, roughly between Orius, Parnos, and Athos. Its name is Fort Liberty. I've promised help and protection, but also a degree of autonomy. Stationing ships there will give us an invaluable port, strategically advantageous for both war and trade.'

'I can see we have a lot to talk about.' Glaukos turned away from the harbor and faced Dion. 'Now it just remains to bring two brothers back together. You can help me find a wife for Nikolas. He doesn't realize it, but he needs you. Now that Chloe, daughter of Aristocles, is dead . . .'

The wine cup fell out of Dion's hand, clattering to the stone. The shock was like a punch in the stomach, robbing him of breath.

'You didn't know?' Glaukos was saying, but his voice was distant, as if he were in another room.

Dion shook his head. He turned away from his uncle and left him behind, walking numbly past the orange trees and entering the palace's interior.

He collapsed onto the raised stone platform, sitting on a step by the high-backed wooden throne.

67

Surrounded by Dion's pirates, Aristocles waited on the white pebbled beach while Amos scouted the city. Pacing anxiously, he breathed a sigh of relief when he saw his loyal captain standing up on the embankment and waving, with a dozen strong Phalesian soldiers surrounding him.

Aristocles climbed up the diagonal steps and then he was looking around him, taking in the agora, breathing in the scents both sweet and foul, feeling pleasure at being in a place where so many people lived together, side by side. He took a moment to breathe a prayer of thanks to the gods. He was home.

Hearing a commotion on the agora's far side, he smiled when he saw that city folk wearing bright Galean clothing draped over their bodies were dancing and cheering, wine skins pouring into wooden mugs and flute players trilling festive music. Aristocles had brought help to his city in its time of need. Already word of the victory of the Xanthian fleet would be spreading through both the upper and lower quarters.

He allowed himself a moment to watch his people. The blood of consuls had been spilled, but soon he would have Phalesia back to the way it was. Time had passed. Nikolas was far away. Soon he would be reunited with his two beautiful daughters.

'It's safe,' Amos said, approaching. 'Nikolas took his king's guard with him. Not a single soldier of Xanthos is here. Come, First Consul.' He gave a rare smile. 'Let me take you back to your villa.'

Soon Amos and the escort of Phalesian soldiers were leading Aristocles through the familiar streets. Casting his mind forward to the coming days, as he walked, already Aristocles was making plans.

'Tonight I will rest, but I'll start seeing the consuls tomorrow, starting with Nilus. I must maximize the impact of our victory against the Ilean fleet. Then, when Kargan overthrows Mydas, I'll reveal my peace agreement with Ilea. Finally, with the support of the entire city behind me, I'll call an election.'

'But you are already first consul.'

'Amos, you are brave and loyal, but you need to understand how the Assembly functions. I need to be seen as a strong leader at all times. I need a mandate from the people.'

'Whatever you say.' Amos smiled, evidently pleased to see Aristocles' excitement.

Then they were climbing up to the villa, and as his anticipation grew, Aristocles' feet quickened on the steps.

'Wait here,' Aristocles ordered when they reached the terrace. He dashed inside, calling out. 'Chloe? Sophia?' He exited again a moment later. 'Where are my daughters?' he anxiously asked Amos.

'I assumed they would be here . . .' Amos cast an inquiring glance at the soldiers.

'Your daughters are missing,' a soldier with a squashed nose said.

'Missing?' Aristocles felt a stab of fear.

'Lord Nilus may have more information,' the soldier answered.

Amos sighed. 'I'm sorry, First Consul. Don't worry, wherever they are, we will find them.'

'Would you . . . Would you go now? Find out more?' Aristocles asked anxiously.

'Of course I will. This very instant.'

Amos dashed down the steps without another word, leaving Aristocles standing on the terrace with the dozen soldiers of his escort. Muttering, shaking his head, Aristocles descended to the servant's quarters on the villa's lower level, but even Aglea and old Hermon were gone; the place was completely deserted. Then, as he climbed back up, he saw a newcomer waiting for him outside the villa's main entrance.

The slim young man with the embroidered yellow tunic bowed. 'First Consul. I bring a message from Lord Nilus. He wishes to speak with you at the lyceum.'

'Lead the way,' Aristocles said with a sharp nod. He waved at a pair of the soldiers. 'Come with me, please.'

Filled with worry for his daughters, Aristocles followed the messenger back down to the city, passing through the cobbled streets and crossing the agora. Climbing the broad marble steps to the horseshoe-shaped structure with the peaked triangular roof, he glanced up at the statue of Aldus as he passed under the god's stern gaze.

'I will leave you now.' The messenger bowed.

'Thank you,' Aristocles said absently.

As he entered the lyceum he saw it was exactly the way he remembered it, open at the sides but with a central floor accessed by a descent of steps that also doubled as seats when the Assembly of Consuls was in session. Flaming torches ensconced at the columns scattered light throughout the structure's interior, but there were no columns in the center, so it grew dimmer as he approached the floor. Aristocles saw a group of four consuls in white tunics standing below, waiting for his arrival.

Recognizing Nilus's round face, Aristocles descended swiftly, leaving the pair of soldiers at the top of the steps.

'Welcome home, Aristocles,' Nilus said as he reached the floor.

'Consul Nilus,' Aristocles said. He would have greeted his friend warmly, but he was far too consumed with concern for his daughters. He nodded at each of the other three consuls in turn. He was surprised to see Nilus with men whom he'd long considered opponents. 'Consul Harod. Consul Leon. Consul Anneas.'

They were all acting wary, but Aristocles supposed some strangeness could be expected.

'The fleet that allied with the Xanthians. That was your doing?' Consul Anneas asked.

'It was,' Aristocles said.

'What other news do you bring?' Nilus asked.

Aristocles' intuition told him that although he'd initially thought to save the revelation, now was the time to show strength. 'Mydas is going to fall,' he said. 'There may already be a new king in Ilea. I bring his assurance of peace.'

'You have this written?' gray-bearded Harod asked.

'I do,' Aristocles said proudly.

'We'll see what the future brings.' Anneas glanced at Harod. 'Let us be clear though. The present danger is past?' he pressed.

'It is.' Aristocles turned to face Nilus, ignoring the other three men. 'Nilus, where are my daughters?'

'Sophia has gone to Koulis, where she will marry King Nikolas of Xanthos.'

Aristocles rounded on Nilus; he couldn't believe what he was hearing. 'What . . . ?' he stammered. 'But . . . Chloe?'

'Our alliance with Xanthos will be strong,' Nilus said. 'Nikolas and I have an understanding. He will be grateful that I found her and sent her to him.'

'Nilus . . .'

'Be at peace, Aristocles,' Nilus said, clasping Aristocles' shoulder. 'I have other news.' He met his friend's eyes, and something passed between them, a fleeting look of regret. 'Chloe is dead.'

Nilus pulled him close and pain flared in Aristocles' chest. Aristocles looked down and saw that Nilus's hand was around the hilt of a knife. The weapon fell out of Nilus's fingers, remaining in Aristocles' torso as Nilus stepped back, staring at what he'd done.

Aristocles watched crimson blood bloom around the blade in his chest. He felt as if he'd been kicked in the guts. He was surprised to find that the pain didn't feel sharp at all. His breath shuddered as he gazed up at the two watching soldiers. They looked on impassively. Neither man stepped forward.

'You'll be seeing her shortly,' Nilus said. His voice was shaking, but he managed to nod at the other three consuls as he took another step back. 'We all have to do it.'

Each man suddenly brandished a blade. Harod was the first to strike, stabbing Aristocles in his side. Anneas pierced the area just below his heart. Leon came in low, thrusting into his abdomen.

Aristocles sank to his knees. He saw blood pooling around him. So much blood . . .

'Why did you have to return?' Nilus pleaded softly. Aristocles looked up at him, clutching at his arm, until Nilus fended him off.

Consul Harod lifted a finger at the pair of watching soldiers. 'Not a word about this. Not ever. The city must be united behind the first consul.'

Aristocles tried to stand but fell backward, sprawling out in the pool of his own blood. He found himself lying on his back, staring up at the ceiling of Phalesia's lyceum. This was where he gave speeches. It was in this room that he became first consul. This was where he stood fast with the eldren.

Chloe was dead.

His eyelids fluttered and then his eyes closed. He hoped he would see her soon.

68

After a day of talking and deal making, with agreement after agreement being reached and then renegotiated at the last moment, Nikolas was exhausted.

His army was now encamped a good distance from the walls of Koulis, and it was dark when he finally rode in and immediately dismounted, handing his horse to a waiting groom and heading directly for his tent.

He limped as he walked; the wound in his thigh was paining him more than he cared to admit. The surgeons were worried. Infection had taken root, and they'd told him that if it didn't clear soon, he could be in danger of his life.

Lothar had said that negotiations could go on without him, but Nikolas knew that if he didn't attend the wily old man would try to foist some ploy on the new treaties and trade deals between Ilea and the four Galean nations. Cursing Lothar, Zanthe, and the spear that sliced him, he thrust the tent flap aside and entered the dimly lit interior.

A solitary oil lamp glowed on the table, but Nikolas found the darkness soothing. Wincing, he went directly to the flask lying beside his scabbarded sword. Searching the table, he finally spied the golden goblet lying on its side under his rumpled cloak, and with a sigh of relief he immediately lifted the flask to pour the cup full of sweet Sarsican wine. Setting the container down, he lifted the goblet and drained it to the bottom. He was about to refill his cup when he heard a voice.

'Sire.'

He frowned when he heard the young, female voice. He turned in surprise and saw a girl sitting on a pile of cushions in the corner. She had long dark hair and dimples on her cheeks. Her blue eyes regarded him intently.

'Sophia?' Nikolas wondered if his eyes were deceiving him. 'What in Balal's name are you doing here?'

She remained seated, her gaze meeting his directly. 'Lord Nilus sent me but, in truth, I came of my own accord. I've taken a long journey to be here.'

'By all the gods, why?' Nikolas still couldn't believe she was here. 'The crossing is dangerous.'

'I know. But I wanted to see you. I told Nilus that I want to become your wife.'

Nikolas drew back, nonplussed. His head was still full of border lines and trade guarantees. 'My wife?' He scowled at her. 'I have a wife, girl.'

'My sister is dead.'

Nikolas's eyes widened. 'Chloe is dead?'

He poured himself another goblet of wine as he thought furiously. Tossing a gulp of the tart liquid back, he kept his back to her. Chloe was dead . . . She was always going to be a difficult wife . . .   .

Realization slowly dawned.

There would soon be peace throughout the Maltherean Sea. He needed a wife and an heir.

'Yes, lord. Ask the men who brought me here. She is dead.'

Nikolas turned to face her. 'You are a woman? You have had your season?'

'Yes, lord.'

Her piercing blue eyes were staring at him with fierce determination. He felt a thrill course through him. She was pretty, and would grow into a beautiful woman. She was a child, but certainly wouldn't remain one.

'Remind me how old you are,' he mused, appraising her.

'Twelve, sire.'

'You're quite bold for your age. Nilus said you disappeared. Where were you?'

'With a man in the city and his family. An apothecary.'

'Your sister . . . How did she die?'

'She was murdered on the road to Tanus.' Sophia swallowed, but when she spoke, her voice was clear as she looked up at him. 'You forced her to marry you,' she said. Her eyes lingered on the goblet in his hand. '*You* killed her.'

Nikolas's mouth gaped; he couldn't believe what he was hearing. He had to resist the urge to strike her; she was only twelve. But no one spoke to him in this way. The words shocked him, spoken so flagrantly. It was some time before he replied.

'I did not kill your sister.'

'It's your fault that she's dead.'

He lifted a clenched fist. 'Shut your mouth!'

Sophia climbed slowly to her feet, staring at him defiantly. 'I came a long way to be here. I'll say what I like.'

Nikolas moved to strike her.

Suddenly his legs collapsed from under him and he found himself on the ground.

It happened so quickly that he couldn't understand why his body had failed him. The wine goblet clattered to the floor beside him, spilling crimson liquid over the thick carpet. His vision blurred and he blinked but couldn't clear the haze. He tried to pull himself back to his feet, clawing at the table, but instead he pulled it down on top of himself. The oil lamp tumbled before righting itself just a foot from his head, filling his eyes with bright yellow light.

'Wha—?' Nikolas tried to speak but his tongue felt swollen. His mouth was dry and he felt thirsty, more thirsty than he'd ever felt in his life. 'What . . . ?'

He looked up to see Sophia standing over him. She glanced down at him sadly. Her eyes flickered to the wine goblet and then back at him.

'Goodbye, sire,' Sophia murmured.

Nikolas felt darkness encroaching. He tried to fight it but barely managed to twitch his fingers. His blurred vision was now filled with black shadow. He tried to speak but all that came out was a gurgle, and then he heard his own breath rattle in his chest.

It was the last sound he heard.

69

Kargan couldn't banish the slight smile on his face as he strode through the corridors of the grand palace in Lamara. From here he would rule an empire. It was all his.

Six of his most loyal soldiers, recently promoted to palace guards, followed him as he reached the audience chamber and approached the throne, an immense high-backed chair of ebony with engraved lion's claws at the arms, raised on a high dais. He climbed up to the throne and sat down, wriggling in his seat.

'How do I look?' he grinned at one of his men.

'Imperial, king of kings,' the soldier said, bowing low.

'Perhaps not yet, but I will have new clothing to suit the part, and a crown of solid gold.'

Uncertain what response was expected, the soldier hesitated and then bowed again.

Barking a laugh but becoming restless, Kargan slipped off the throne and left the audience chamber to head out to the nearby terrace. It was night and the lights of Lamara, greatest city in the world, filled his vision. He clasped his hands on the rail and gazed out at the city below and then lifted his vision to the harbor, watching the dark shadows of the ferry boats coming and going, fighting the current to make their way across the wide brown river.

He had a difficult task ahead of him to reform the Ilean Empire and bring it to greater heights than even Solon had dreamed of, but for now, he was enjoying his moment.

Kargan heard a voice clear behind him and turned.

'You summoned me?' Javid asked, frowning.

'Yes, Javid,' Kargan said. He glanced past the tall warrior at the guards standing behind him, and then nodded to himself. 'I want to inform you that for the stability of the realm, it might be some time before we have our first vote. In fact,' he scratched at his beard and then smiled, 'there might not be any voting for a very, very long time.'

He waited to see what reaction his words would have.

Javid's frown deepened. He crossed his arms in front of his broad chest and now he was truly scowling. 'I will speak plainly. When we made our bargain, you said you would always be truthful. You gave me your word.'

Kargan shrugged. 'Words come easily.'

'The Phalesian, Aristocles . . . He helped put you where you are now. You promised him help in turn, but you sent him home.'

'I gave him his treaty. I spoke the truth. I have no interest in Phalesia.'

'Then why not give him what he needed?'

'I was busy with other matters. I had bigger things on my mind than an accord with a weak foreigner.'

'You know how I feel. Now why am I here?' Javid asked bluntly.

Kargan sighed. He stepped toward his bodyguard and gazed up at him. 'Your problem, Javid, is that you're a dangerous man. You're here because I need to know where you and I stand. The only person you can hold to your own ideals is you, and if you want to know what I value, it's loyalty. I'll be loyal to you, and I'll even put up with all your talk of justice and truth. But if I have to worry about my safety then we won't be friends anymore. Which is it to be?'

Javid opened his mouth and then closed it. He frowned. 'The god Helios says—'

Kargan cut him off sharply. 'Throw him in a cell,' he ordered.

He turned away as he heard the grunts of his guards; Javid was strong, but there were enough of them to see the job done. He didn't look back as he went once more to the rail and tried to turn his mind again to the changes he would make.

Javid called out his name.

Kargan told himself to ignore him. He had an empire to worry about now.

But before he knew it he was turning around and calling. 'Well? What is it?'

'I value truth,' Javid said. 'And I will always tell you what is in my heart.' He glanced at the guards who held him. 'Can you say the same for the other people around you?'

Kargan strode up to his friend and looked into his eyes. 'No.'

'Then let me advise you. Give me a position as more than just your guard.'

Kargan pondered for a time. 'Friends should be loyal to one another. Agreed?'

'Agreed.'

'And kings need friends.'

Javid gave a grim smile. 'King Kargan, ruler of the Ilean Empire . . . This time, you certainly speak the truth.'

70

Nightfall found Chloe and Zachary exploring an unbroken forest of ash, elm, cedar, and willow, crossing bubbling streams and listening to chirping birdsong and humming insects, brushing fingers against drooping flowers, smelling the fresh scent of plant life.

'I wish Aella could have seen this,' Zachary murmured.

'So do I,' Chloe said.

She'd initially been concerned about his health, but there seemed to be some property of the land that gave him strength, and the farther they'd wandered, the more his back had straightened and stride had lengthened.

They stopped at a clearing, the green grass thicker and softer than any Chloe had seen before, as tall as her calves. Coming to a halt, Zachary turned to face Chloe. He reached out to take her hand.

'Thank you for keeping me company, dear one,' he said. 'It is always a pleasure to have you near, but I think I need to be alone for a time. I have decided that this is the night to put my wife's memory to rest.'

Chloe suddenly grimaced.

Zachary looked at her in concern. 'Are you well?'

'I'm fine,' she said. The headache had returned, and along with it she could again hear a painful buzzing in her ears, like she was trying to swim too deep in the water. 'Please, Zachary. You should go.'

He gave her a soft smile. 'I will see you again at the heart.'

It was only when Zachary vanished into the trees, soundless as ever, that Chloe realized how alone she was, and how foreign this place was to her. She put her hands to her temples and felt intense relief when the headache began to fade. Finally able to take stock of where she was, she realized she was lost.

The thought didn't fill her with panic; she was in the homeland of the eldren and she knew she could trust one of her friends to find her. She headed for higher ground, deciding to make her way to a mighty oak tree crowning a hill.

She now gazed up at the spreading branches as she climbed. Pausing halfway up the slope, she turned to look back behind her at the surrounding landscape.

The moon had risen and cast a warm glow on a scene of complete renewal. Where before Cinder Fen had been a region of swamp and ash it was now an immense, green valley: Sindara. Forests filled the expanse, along with blue lakes and broad rivers. Pine trees covered the mountain heights; winged creatures soared in the sky but these weren't dragons or furies, they were birds. Rather than the stench of char and decay, the summer breeze carried the scent of moss and flowers. Eiric would put the serpents and merfolk to rest and the growth would continue.

It was a beautiful land, but all Chloe could think about was home.

She turned away and continued to climb the hill, knowing that when she reached the top she would be able to get her bearings. She thought about her future. Nikolas had led his army to Tanus and beyond; it was safe for her to return to Phalesia. She might see

Dion. Perhaps her father would have returned; she was desperate to see his face.

As Chloe thought about her father, reaching the oak tree at the top of the hill, she stopped and put her hands to her temples.

She suddenly gasped. The pain struck her with renewed force.

The fire inside her head raged with so much intensity that she fell to her knees and cried out. Thunder roared in her ears, stunning her senses so that she could barely think. Her skin crawled and she realized she was shivering uncontrollably.

She was dimly aware of men walking toward her.

There were four of them, so skinny that they were emaciated, with white robes clinging to their thin frames. They approached Chloe from the direction of the oak tree and surrounded her.

She realized that all four men were identical in every way, with shaved heads and features of extreme sharpness, all bones and tightly drawn skin. One crouched at her side while the other three watched impassively. Groaning in agony, Chloe looked at the man beside her and saw the sunken cheeks and deep-set eyes.

She knew this face. She'd seen it before.

'The Oracle warned you,' the magus said. 'You are fortunate we found you in time.'

One of the men standing spoke. 'You are coming with us.'

Chloe shook her head, though it was a struggle. 'My father . . .' she mumbled.

'Your father is dead.' The magus beside her spoke again. 'His heart stopped beating as you climbed this hill.'

'No . . .'

'There is nothing you can do,' said another. 'He is already gone from this world.'

Even as she fought the pain in her head, tears shimmered in Chloe's vision and then spilled down her cheeks. Every memory of her father flashed through her eyes; every fond look and overprotective warning, every word of praise and smile . . . It all crashed around her. The villa she'd grown up in would never be home again. She no longer had a home to return to.

'I have to see him. My sister . . .'

'As you are, I doubt you could even stand. We have come a long way . . .'

As the magus from Athos spoke, Chloe heard his words more and more distantly. Her vision shrank into a pinprick before fading away altogether.

She toppled forward, falling into darkness.

71

Far out in the open ocean, far from the Ilean, the Maltherean, and even the Aleuthean Seas, a black galleon wandered aimlessly.

The stomachs of the men in the rigging were shrunken; the once-proud warriors of Necropolis had been humbled by hunger and despair. Even the sorcerers barely left their quarters below decks, resting to conserve their energy, and the king didn't need to maintain discipline, for no one had the energy to fight.

The *Solaris* was lost.

Over a tenth of their number had succumbed to starvation, seventeen men, yet even with fewer mouths to feed rations had been cut in half, and then in half again, until each person received a hand-sized piece of dried fish and a cup of water a day. Storms had torn the sails and ripped spars from the masts; not only were the present-day Aleutheans lacking in navigational skill, they were also inexperienced with their ancestors' vessel. Blazing heat forced them to hide away from the sun, for thirst was ever present, and its dehydrating effect was worse than torture for men who had been born on the ice. Worms had eaten the hull, forcing them to man the pumps night and day.

Kyphos the hunchback found his king at the stern, gazing out at the vessel's wake, lost in thought. Palemon's broad-shouldered frame had become skinny along with the rest of them, his height now making him more rangy than broad. Like the others, he'd doffed his heavy furs, but he still wore his bleached leather vest, black woolen trousers, and high boots. The braids in his gray beard were loose, beginning to untwist, which made Kyphos truly alarmed. His king always maintained iron control of himself. Just the small sign told the hunchbacked warrior that even his ruler was losing his fortitude.

'We're going to have to halve rations again,' Kyphos said. 'Buys us another week, but then that's it.' He shook his head. 'A man fell from the side of the ship yesterday . . . He just . . . fell. Didn't even bother to swim. Sire, this can't go on any longer.'

King Palemon tore his eyes away from the sea and straightened, bringing himself to his full height as he met Kyphos's eyes. 'So it is time then, for desperate measures.'

'Sire, if you have any plan, now is the time to hear it.'

The king nodded. 'Find Zara. Bring her to my cabin.'

Kyphos knocked on the door to the cabin that had once housed his liege's ancestor, the ancient King Palemon who fought the eldren long ago. He glanced at the sorceress beside him. In her figure-hugging midnight blue dress, Zara was as haughtily beautiful as ever, but even her high cheekbones were now so sharp they jutted above her sunken cheeks. Her lips, always blue, were thin and dry. She was beginning to look skeletal.

'Enter,' Palemon called.

Kyphos opened the door and allowed Zara to enter first before following the sorceress in. Palemon didn't look up as the door swung closed. He was seated at the desk, and in front of him was a bizarre object.

475

It was a cone, the size of a big man's hand, fashioned of twisting metal that curled in a spiral. At its base was a small circle where a staff could be fitted. The metal was paler than steel, the color of the moon reflecting from the sea.

Kyphos knew at a glance that the metal was silver, but other than that, he was completely perplexed.

He glanced at Zara, surprised when he saw her draw in a sharp intake of breath. 'How is it that you have this?' The sorceress went immediately to the desk, ignoring her king, and placed a dainty finger against the metal. She closed her eyes as if communing with the materia.

'It was in the ship. It's been here since the beginning. I personally polished it with oil every time I visited. Is it . . . functional?'

'Oh yes,' Zara said, almost purring as she opened her eyes and removed her finger. But then she narrowed her eyes at the king. 'Why have you kept it secret? I am the foremost of the magi. It belongs with—'

'When we reach the Realm of the Three Seas, we will need to subdue the people we find there as we did long ago. We are a race of strong warriors, but it is our magic that built us an empire, and our magic that will enable us to get the fleet we need and return for the rest of our people. I chose to keep this, the last of our silver, secret because I wanted to save it for the coming struggle, I didn't want us to turn to it every time the wind didn't do what we wanted. The temptation would have been too great. But now . . .'

'You think I can summon the wind to take us out of this plight?' Zara frowned.

'I am counting on it,' Palemon said. He glanced at Kyphos. 'We all are. Sorceress, our fate is in your hands.'

'Sire . . .' Zara shook her head. 'The magnitude of wind you are talking about is far more dangerous than you realize. Focused, in battle, yes, I can control it, and believe me when I tell you that there is none other with my skill. But to propel a ship of this size . . . You know what happened at the fall of Aleuthea. The fleet was scattered by a storm so powerful it became lost.'

'We have no other choice,' Kyphos said. He glanced at his king. 'I'll call everyone to the deck.'

'No,' Zara countermanded. 'Tell everyone to fasten down everything that can move, and if that isn't possible, to throw it over the side. Order them into their cabins, for what I am about to do is going to be like nothing anyone has ever seen before.'

———

Despite Zara's words of warning, both Kyphos and Palemon stood with the sorceress on the stern castle as she prepared to summon her magic.

'Which way?' Kyphos called to his king from the helm.

The king pondered. 'East,' he finally replied, his eyes grave. 'Take us east.'

Kyphos set the course, waiting until the ship's bowsprit came around to point directly away from the setting sun. He lashed the helm into place and then looked up. Every sail was set, but the decks and the rigging were devoid of activity. The sky was filled with elongated clouds that traveled slowly in the breeze. They were casting their fates to fortune.

Nearby, the slender sorceress also glanced up as she held a tall staff in her right hand, with her clenched fingers touching the spiral silver cone at the end. She drew in an interminable breath.

Kyphos looked at his king but Palemon was grim-faced, facing forward with legs astride. The hunchback hurriedly scanned the area and then lurched across the listing deck to grip hold of a nearby rail.

'Sire,' Kyphos said. 'You should hold o—'

The sorceress lifted the staff and slammed it back down onto the deck. Kyphos glanced up again and saw the clouds suddenly change direction, speeding toward the east, with more and more of them gathering pace as they suddenly filled the sky. A gusting wind caused the masts of the *Solaris* to creak. Glancing at Zara, Kyphos saw that she had her eyes closed, an expression of supreme concentration on her face, but then her eyes shot open.

The irises were entirely black.

The sorceress lifted the staff high into the air and cried out. The gust became a gale, yet she didn't hold on to anything at all as her dress flattened against her body. Even the king, his jaw set, stumbled to a rail, clutching hold of the wood with a white-knuckled grip.

The heavens turned as dark as night, filled with racing shadows from one horizon to the other. Faster than any bird the clouds sped across the sky, all heading east. Zara's cry became a scream, eerie and high-pitched, audible even over the groans of the wooden vessel and the shrieking wind.

Then Kyphos realized that this had only been the beginning.

The wind struck the ship.

———

'Kyphos. Kyphos!' The warrior ran down to the beach, ignoring the ruinous hulk that had once been the *Solaris* and coming to a halt in front of him, panting.

Seated by the campfire, Kyphos swallowed another chunk of fried fish and glanced up. 'What is it?'

'There are strangers approaching.'

Kyphos wiped his hands on his flanks as he climbed to his feet. With local water, fresh fish, and barrels of salvaged supplies, they'd all been gorging ever since reaching land, and strength had returned to the warriors of Necropolis.

'Inform the king. Then get Zara. We might be able to find out where we are.'

'The sorceress . . . Are you sure?'

'Just do it!'

Kyphos climbed the windswept dune and waited alone as he saw a pair of tall men wrapped in white cloth walking toward him. Even their faces were swaddled in material, evidently to protect their skin from the burning sun. They both carried wooden spears that were nearly as tall as they were.

'Kyphos . . .'

He turned and saw the king nearing, leading the sorceress by the left hand. Zara's right hand was clutched around a wooden staff crowned with a hoop of gold; she was using it to aid her stumbling walk over the uneven ground. Kyphos looked at Zara's face, sculpted like marble, feeling hope stir, but then his heart sank when he saw that her eyes were still entirely black, and she was muttering under her breath.

'The wind . . .'

The two strangers were now close enough that Kyphos could see that one was older than the other, with creases around his dark eyes. They came to a halt and faced him, slowly appraising the hunchback with outsized arms and a shining steel axe at his belt, the tall king with the gray braided beard, and the slim blue-lipped woman with the strange eyes.

The older of the two strangers spoke. 'Have you come from across the sea?'

'Yes,' Kyphos said.

'Where are we?' the king demanded.

The younger man looked at the older, who hesitated and then answered. 'Imakale.'

'Imakale,' Kyphos said.

He glanced at his king. Palemon closed his eyes and inhaled, releasing a long, pent up sigh. He then opened his eyes and smiled at Kyphos. 'We made it.'

Zara shuddered. She closed her eyes and opened them, and Kyphos felt a surge of joy when he saw that her eyes were a clear blue, as they had been before. She spoke, making sense for the first time since they'd arrived. 'We made it?'

'We did, sorceress.' Kyphos grinned at her.

'It has taken us three hundred years,' the king said. 'But we are finally home.'

The two strangers exchanged glances. 'Our headman has a message for you,' the older man said. 'You must come with us.'

'No.' Palemon shook his head. His eyes narrowed. 'You give him a message from me.'

The king reached over his shoulder and slowly drew his broadsword. The whisper of steel sliding in the scabbard filled the air as he freed it and gripped it in two hands, the only symbol of his kingship that he'd ever needed.

Leveling the point at the older of the cloth-swaddled men, Palemon spoke in a low intonation. 'Go to your leader, your king, whoever he is. Tell him this.' As he spoke the long blade held between his body and the stranger's began to glow red, the strange light welling from within the metal becoming fiercer with every word. 'Tell him we were raised in the city of the dead. We are cold bloods. We have no warmth in our hearts. We are as strong as iron, as hard as ice.'

The blade flared up, suddenly so bright and hot that Kyphos could feel the heat washing off it even from where he was standing. The older stranger's material caught fire and he screamed, tearing off his cloth to reveal a skinny chest, a wrinkled, bearded face, and eyes filled with terror.

The two strangers looked at each other.

In unison they turned and fled, with the king's words following after them.

'Tell him that King Palemon has come to reclaim his dominion.'

ACKNOWLEDGMENTS

My sincere gratitude to the team at 47North for inspiring dedication at all stages of the publishing process, with particular thanks to my editor, Emilie, for giving more support than any author could hope for or expect.

Thanks go to Ian, for editorial strength and persistence, and to my readers Amanda Blanche, Harley Boyer, Jessi Burland, Amanda Collins, Marc Forbes, Annaleigh Goudreau, Priscilla Mante, Amy Nedrow, Tebo Ndlovu, and Hannah Slane, for invaluable insight and feedback.

Thanks to all of you who have reached out to me and taken the time to post reviews of my books.

Finally, thanks must inevitably go to my wife, Alicia. With your love and encouragement the steepest mountain becomes a gentle climb.

ABOUT THE AUTHOR

James Maxwell grew up in the scenic Bay of Islands, New Zealand, and was educated in Australia. Devouring fantasy and science-fiction classics from an early age, his love for books translated to a passion for writing, which he began at the age of eleven.

Inspired by the natural beauty around him but also by a strong interest in history, he decided in his twenties to see the world. He relocated to London and then to Thailand, Mexico, Austria, and Malta, developing a lifelong obsession with travel. It was while living in Thailand that he seriously took up writing again, producing his first full-length novel, *Enchantress*, the first of four titles in his internationally bestselling Evermen Saga.

Following on from *Golden Age*, *Silver Road* is the second novel in his latest series, The Shifting Tides.

When he isn't writing or traveling, James enjoys sailing, snowboarding, classical guitar, and French cooking.